KAY JENNINGS

A PORT STIRLING MYSTERY:BOOK 5

COLD ROCK ISLAND

Author's Note

I have no idea whether or not there is an island as I have portrayed in this story off the coast of Oregon. Therefore, any specific settings, owners, or residents are purely the product of my imagination and are not intended to resemble any that may exist in reality.

Cold Rock Island/Kay Jennings — 1st ed.

ISBN (Hardcover edition): 979-8-98555-44-9-6
ISBN (Paperback edition): 979-8-98555-44-8-9

Publisher's Note: *Cold Rock Island* is a work of fiction. As of this publication date, the events and circumstances that occur within are a product of the author's imagination. While certain locales may draw on real life, they are used fictitiously to add authenticity to the story. The cast of characters are fictitious and are not based on real people, businesses, or organizations.

Cover design and Port Stirling Map: Claire Brown
Interior design: Steve Kuhn/Kuhn Design Group

Printed and bound in the USA
First printing 2024
Published by Paris Communications
Portland, Oregon, USA

www.kayjenningsauthor.com

Other books by Kay Jennings:

Shallow Waters

Midnight Beach

Code: Tsunami

Dark Sand

Phantom Cove

Mourning Bay

For Sharon, with deep affection

COLD ROCK ISLAND

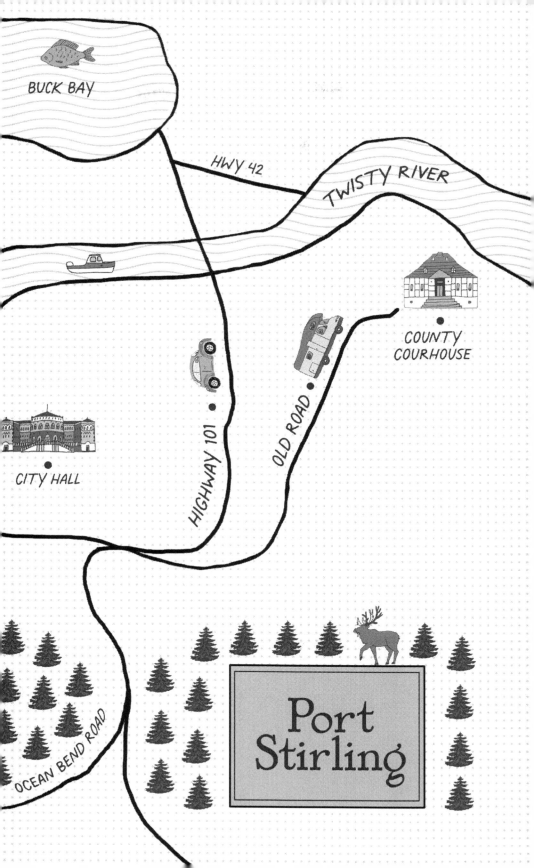

CHAPTER 1

Saturday, February 24, 2024 — Buck Bay, Oregon

Unusually for her, U.S. State Department Special Agent Fern Byrne awoke with an uneasy feeling, which intensified as she pulled up in the parking lot of the Coast Guard headquarters in Buck Bay, Oregon. Expecting only her boss, Joe Phelps, the head of covert operations, to be waiting for her, she was surprised to see her good friend, Dr. Bernice Ryder, parking her snazzy BMW hardtop convertible.

Fern patted the dashboard of her beloved VW bug. *I still love you the best*, she told her powder blue car as she exited. *Try not to look at Bernice's car.*

"Bernice, hi, why are you here?" Fern asked, hugging her friend. "I'm meeting Joe Phelps and Captain Adams."

"Ditto," said Bernice, who for the past decade served as the Medical Examiner for Chinook County. "Apparently, we're going to look at a dead body."

"Joe told me we're going for a boat ride, and he would explain this morning," Fern said. She frowned. "What the heck is going on?"

"I got a phone call at 5:00 a.m. from his D.C. office. All they told me was that Joe wanted me here, and I'm to accompany you with my bag of forensic tricks." She yanked a mid-sized wheelie suitcase out of the trunk of the BMW.

"Wonder why all the mystery?"

"Guess we're about to find out," Bernice said. She looked up at the blue sky, kissed by a few fluffy white, harmless clouds. "Nice morning for a boat ride. You look terrific, by the way."

"So do you," Fern said. She was dressed in black pants, her best white tee shirt, and a zip-front raspberry leather jacket. "It was tough deciding what to wear this morning. I wanted to look professional for my boss, but a boat ride?"

Bernice laughed. "Same here. I don't give a rip what Joe thinks of me, but I do represent our beloved Chinook County, and it felt like a jacket-required day." Hers was a nicely fitted lightweight black wool, which she'd paired with tan skinny pants and a black and tan leopard-print top. "Plus, I can't possibly compete with tall, gorgeous you, but I can strive for put-together."

"I have never seen you not pulled together. Well, maybe the night you saved my husband's life," Fern amended. She put her arm around Bernice's shoulders as they both thought of that horrible night. "Shall we go in?" Fern whispered.

"Let's. Before we both chicken out."

The two buddies strode off together toward the Coast Guard building.

• • •

Fern and Bernice were greeted by the commander of the regional Coast Guard, Captain Bob Adams.

"Oh, my," Fern said, reaching out her hand to shake the Captain's. "I've never seen you in your full-dress white uniform."

"That's because I rarely wear it," Adams said, returning Fern's handshake and turning to Bernice. "Wasn't even sure where it was," he smiled. "But today is important. Got to look the part."

"Well, from where I stand," said Fern, "you should wear it more often. You look like Richard Gere in An Officer and a Gentleman."

"I second that," Bernice said.

"Guess I nailed the image part, then. Hope I can live up to the service part."

"You look nervous, Bob," Fern said. "Enough chit-chat. Why are we here? And where's Joe?"

"He just called from Buck Bay Airport, and he's on his way. Should arrive any minute. The Secretary of State is with him."

Fern's eyebrows shot up. "What? My boss's boss? Fred Leufeld?"

"The same. The Secretary of State is about to set foot in my headquarters. So, yes ma'am, I'm a little nervous."

"Does anyone else know they're coming?" Bernice asked. "Thank God we wore jackets," she said to Fern. "A heads-up would have been nice."

Captain Adams said, "I didn't know until late last night when Joe phoned me. He said their trip was covert, and I wasn't to breathe a word of it."

"Do you know where we're going?" Fern asked, all senses alert now.

"Yes, we're going to an island in the Pacific, about four nautical miles due west of Port Stirling. Should take us about thirty minutes."

"What island?" Fern asked. "I don't know of any."

"I'll let Joe explain further." He glanced at both women. "But there's a reason you're going with us, Bernice."

"Somebody is dead, right?" Bernice said. "Otherwise, I'd be home watching golf on TV."

The three waited quietly, alone with their thoughts. Fern and Bernice sat in club chairs in the captain's roomy HQ office, which looked out through large windows across Buck Bay to the magnificent bridge. The bay, at high tide, sparkled in this morning's sunshine. Adams stood, not wanting to wrinkle his dress pants before their visitors arrived.

A knock at Adams' door startled all three.

Joe Phelps and two young men entered Adams' office. Tall, lanky Joe Phelps, with his protruding ears and black straight hair, still reminding Fern of Ichabod Crane from The Legend of Sleepy Hollow, came in first.

But the two men accompanying him quickly moved past Joe and surveyed the room, carefully eyeing the three people present. Each man was wearing a black suit with white shirt and black tie, and each had a wired security earpiece, the wire looped around the back of their ear. The younger of the two smiled engagingly at red-haired Fern, but the older by a few years was grim-faced. He now said, "All clear," and the universe must have picked it up because through the door came Secretary of State Fred Leufeld, followed closely by two more young men dressed identically to their colleagues in the U.S. State Department's protective detail.

The Secretary approached Captain Adams, and the two shook hands. "That's a lot of jewelry," Secretary Leufeld said, his deep voice flowing out of him like mellow molasses. He pointed at the ribbons and medals pinned to both sides of the captain's tunic jacket and grinned.

"Yes, sir, I've had a good career," Adams said. He returned Leufeld's grin, and immediately relaxed for the first time today.

"Hope it continues," Leufeld said, his smile disappearing. "Joe says we've got a real mess on our hands, Captain. Of course, he's always a negative nanny." The Secretary cast a sly glance at Joe.

"Thank you for that, Mr. Secretary," Joe said wryly. "I'd like you to meet Fern Byrne, our west coast liaison."

Fern stepped forward.

"You're the lucky woman who replaced our guy who got his head chopped off, right?" the Secretary said.

"That's me, sir," Fern answered simply. For once in her life, she couldn't think of a snappy reply.

"But you love your job, right? Love working with Phelps here?"

"I do, sir."

"That either makes you really smart or really dumb, Ms. Byrne. I've heard it's really smart." He grinned again. "Welcome to the U.S. Department of State, Fern. So far, we're thrilled to have you. You handled that British cock-up in exemplary fashion. Captain Adams here should give you one of his ribbons." Again with the grin. "Kidding, Captain. I'm a kidder."

"I understand that, sir," smiled Adams, his hands clasped behind his back.

"If you all keep calling me sir, it's going to be a very long day. My name is Fred. And you are Bob, Fern, Joe, and…?" He approached Bernice.

"Dr. Bernice Ryder, ME for the county you're standing in. And if I'm here, it means it will be a very long day for sure." She shook hands with Secretary Leufeld. "It's an honor, Fred." Like the two were old friends.

"My pleasure," he replied.

"Now, who's dead?" asked Bernice.

CHAPTER 2

December 9, 2023 — Honolulu, Hawaii

Surrounded by plumeria and yellow hibiscus, retired Admiral Hiroshi Matsuda took his coffee on the terrace of his sprawling Diamond Head home. It was shortly before 7:00 a.m. The sun-kissed view from his elevation over Honolulu was spectacular by any measurement.

Hiroshi was dressed in tennis whites and would soon meet his son at the gated community's courts for their weekly match. His gray, close-cropped hair belied his youthful energy and outlook. The 63-year-old Hiroshi could still keep up with his 33-year-old son because he worked hard on his tennis game, while his son, Shuji, was obsessed with his business, and worked more than he played. Intelligent and well-educated like his father, but not as adventurous, Shuji had chosen a career in banking, and was a senior VP at a young age.

Hiroshi rose at 5:30 a.m. every day, a habit left over from his military days. Even though he and his son would put in a vigorous, competitive hour of tennis later, he still did a tough 30-minute workout on the Tonal equipment in his home gym. Through his sweating and grunting, he managed to laugh along with his pre-selected personal coach for the day.

By the time Hiroshi finished his workout, Naomi, his wife, was usually up and ready for her day. If she had risen, Hiroshi made their bed, another discipline from his career. This morning, Naomi had left her pale green silken negligee at the foot of their bed, and Hiroshi raised it to his face to inhale his wife's beautiful fragrance. He folded it neatly and placed it on her pristine white pillow.

"Would you like some more coffee?" she asked now, joining him on the terrace.

"I would," he answered, smiling. He held his cup up to her.

"If I pour you another cup, will you let Shuji beat you today?" Naomi grinned, knowing the answer to her question, but asking it anyway.

"I most certainly will not," Hiroshi replied vehemently, but his eyes twinkled. "He is perfectly capable of beating me, even when I play my best. Do you want him to get soft? He has a cushy job, and he needs to move more."

Naomi, the Hawaiian-born daughter of a Japanese father and an American mother, knew her husband was right, but she adored her first-born son, and wanted him to succeed at everything he did. Being the son of a man of Hiroshi's life accomplishments wasn't easy and was the main reason they'd moved to Honolulu—Naomi's birthplace—from Yokosuka City after Hiroshi retired from service. It had been the correct move for both of their children.

"He will not get soft," she said, shaking her head. "Shuji takes care of both his body and his mind. It just might be good for his self-respect to occasionally win one off his old man."

"Oh, now I'm the old man, am I?" he laughed. "What about my self-respect?"

"Your ego needs no boosting," Naomi said dryly. She kissed him on top of his head, refilled his cup, and set the pot on the terrace's breakfast table.

"What are you doing this morning?" Hiroshi asked her.

"I thought I would go shopping at the farmers' market, unless you want to go with me this afternoon?"

He shook his head.

"Do you remember that the Anakonis are coming over for dinner tonight? I thought I'd get some fresh Ono and sear it with the honey soy glaze. How does that sound?"

"One of my favorites." He smiled. "What time are they coming?"

"Well, sunset is at 6:19 tonight, so I told them to be here just before 6:00, and we'll have our cocktails and an appetizer out here and watch the sunset."

"Perfect. I'm a lucky man, aren't I?"

"Darn right," Naomi agreed. She turned to go back inside the house. Over her shoulder, she said, "Let him win."

• • •

As it turned out, Shuji did win in a close match, 7-5, 6-4. Hiroshi played well, but his son was a maniac on the court this morning. Once he won his serve at 5-5 in the first set, Shuji knew he had his father. The 'old man' had battled brilliantly, but he didn't have quite enough to overcome Shuji's determination.

"That's nice playing, son," Hiroshi said, meeting his son at the net for a handshake. "I played well, and you just took it to me."

"You did play well, but I played better on a couple of key points," Shuji said. "You didn't slack off on those, did you, dad?"

Hiroshi toweled the dripping sweat off his face. "Nope. I tried my damnedest on every point. You were a crazy man today. Maybe I'm just washed up."

"Ha. That'll be the day," Shuji laughed. "It's only one win, but I may have a plaque made for my office: 'On December 9, 2023, Shuji Matsuda defeated Hiroshi Matsuda in a tennis match'," he said. "Since, you know, it will probably never happen again."

"Well, I love you, son, but I hope that's true. Let's go get a cool drink—do you have time? Loser buys."

"Sounds good," Shuji said. "Something happened at work yesterday I want to run by you."

"Oh?"

"Yeah."

"I need advice, and it's kinda in your wheelhouse."

Father and son left the court and strolled alongside the Hawaiian Sunset yellow hedge until they reached the steps up to the outdoor café overlooking the courts. At 5'11", Shuji was about two inches taller than his father, and almost as lean. His black hair, trimmed short but spiked ever-so-slightly on top, gave the impression of a professional young man on his way up. Clean-shaven with well-groomed eyebrows and perfect white teeth behind an easy smile, he was—as his mother liked to say—pleasant to look at.

He chose a table off to the side of the patio with a large shade umbrella.

"I'll have a mango lemonade," Hiroshi told their waiter, after Shuji waved at his father to go first.

"Make that two," he said.

When the waiter was some distance away, Hiroshi asked, "What's going on with your business? Do I still have money in your bank?" He smiled.

Shuji laughed. "Yeah, dad, your money's safe. It's not that." He hesitated, as if choosing his words carefully. "Do you remember last month when they added supervision of the IT department to my duties?"

"Yes," Hiroshi answered. "And it's an ideal fit for your skills."

"I do like it. I'm in charge of maintaining all our regional bank locations' hardware and software systems…applications, security, devices, servers, databases, and training." Shuji took a sip of his drink and leaned back in his chair. "I have good people working under me in every area, and it's a well-run department."

"So, what's the problem?"

"This past week, my security chief was out—his wife is having a baby—and I've been covering for him. This has been an area of big concern for me since I took it over because many of our execs, my colleagues, have preferred a cut and paste approach to cybersecurity," Shuji explained.

"What do you mean?"

"They chose to double-down with the systems we already have in place and do piecemeal adjustments as needed. Fine-tuning the existing software has worked so far, but I think something might be going on and we're at risk."

"What makes you think that?" Hiroshi asked. "And keep it simple because this is above my pay grade knowledge."

"The first thing that caught my attention was on Thursday when four of our managers from different regional locations got some weird notifications on their email. They didn't make much sense, and no two were identical, but they came to me because each of the managers thought the messages were somewhat threatening. They all felt uncomfortable."

"Which of your banks were involved?"

"Two in Honolulu, one in Seattle, and one in Sendai in Japan. Which is also what makes it weird in my view."

"What did the messages say?" Hiroshi asked.

"One of the Honolulu ones said something like 'You're sitting there all smug in your suit and tie, not paying attention'…words to that effect. The three others had some similar themes, like 'you don't know what you're doing', 'you don't really care about your customers', stuff like that. I tried to trace them but ran into a digital brick wall."

"But your servers weren't overwhelmed, or customers locked out of their accounts? Anything like that?"

"No," Shuji said. "Our digital defenses hadn't been breached on any front that I could find. All mobile and online banking channels were working properly, no denial of service—nothing that would indicate deep trouble. What do you think, dad?"

"I think you've been warned," Hiroshi said, his tone serious. "You need to take a hard look at your cyber-defenses. Push it with your old-school colleagues who might be living in the past. This stuff is real, as you well know."

"I know, and it scares the shit out of me," Shuji said. "If we're vulnerable, a ransomware attack could cost us millions, not to mention the lack of productivity that would be involved in a situation like that. It would be a nightmare."

"Does your company have good insurance against an attack like this?"

Shuji nodded. "We do, and of course the governments of Japan and the U.S. insure customers' deposits, albeit only to a certain level. But what worries me almost more than the financial damage is the damage to our brand and reputation. What kind of bank would we be if we left ourselves vulnerable to the possibility of attack? Things could go south in a hurry."

"What will you do?"

"What you suggested; I will go to the CEO and take my chief information officer with me and make a plea to investigate new cybersecurity providers. We have a false sense of security I fear, and we need to pull our head out before it's too late."

"Please don't tell your CEO to pull his head out," Hiroshi suggested with a sly smirk.

Shuji laughed. "Yeah, I'll probably leave that one between you and me." He pushed his chair back and stood up. "Thanks for the match, dad, and the lemonade. I'm going to shower up and pop into my office for a few hours."

"Keep me posted, OK? I'll read up on this issue."

"That would be great. Something is telling me I might need your help."

"You don't need me," Hiroshi said to his son, patting him on the back. "But I'll pitch in if I can."

CHAPTER 3

Saturday, February 24, 2024 — Cold Rock Island, the Pacific Ocean

U.S. Coast Guard cutter Resolve was moored at the end of the dock at the Port of Buck Bay. She was a fine-looking ship, a Sentinel-class fast-response cutter. Gleaming white with a wide red off-center stripe that ran from the first deck down to the water, her 154-foot length was imposing.

Fern tried not to notice the chain-gun autocannon and four large machine guns mounted at the front of the ship, as she and Bernice were ushered aboard by Captain Adams.

Bernice noted them, too. She said to Fern, "Do you know how to fire those? Just in case?"

Fern laughed nervously. "No. I've had lots of firearms training, but not on those puppies. They're probably just for show."

"Right," said Bernice, her mouth in a tight line as she nodded.

Captain Adams led the two up an interior staircase that opened to the bridge, a tight room loaded with equipment, with windows on three sides, and two open-air decks leading off it. The three people squeezed into an aisle in the middle, surrounded by all sorts of monitors and control panels, most of them at waist height, although one smaller bank of monitors overhead required ducking on one side.

Secretary of State Leufeld, Joe Phelps, and the security detail had stayed on the main deck.

"Do either of you get seasick?" Adams asked Fern and Bernice.

"Not since I was seven years old, and went deep-sea fishing with my dad," Fern answered. She looked around, fascinated by the blinking monitors. "I ate tuna fish sandwiches as we crossed the bar on the way out and puked the entire trip. I learned from that experience and have been fine ever since."

"I grew up going out with my parents, too," Bernice said. "But it's never bothered me. We'll be fine, Bob. Do you want us to stay in here, or can we go out on the deck?"

"Your call," Adams replied. "We've got about a thirty-minute ride with nothing much to see, but it's a pleasant day and you might enjoy the space on the decks instead of this cramped room. The forward one has the best view, but the aft deck is more protected from the wind."

"When is someone going to tell us where, precisely, we're going and what's going on?" Fern asked.

Captain Adams rubbed his chin. "I'm only authorized to tell you about the location. Leufeld and Phelps want to fill you in on the particulars once we arrive."

"OK," said Fern. "They're the boss and…the boss."

Adams said, "We're headed to an island that served as a joint U.S. and Japanese secret military base for about thirty years. It's now owned by a west-coast billionaire, Rohn Reid, who bought it from the government when it was decommissioned in 1995."

Fern and Bernice exchanged a look.

Bernice said, with characteristic bluntness, "We know Rohn Reid. He's done a lot of amazing things for Oregon and the west coast, as well as around the world. But he's a little weird, right?"

"I think eccentric might be a better word than weird," Adams said with the trace of a smile.

"Will he be there when we get there?" Fern asked.

"I really can't say anything further," Bob told them, gesturing in frustration with his palms up and a shrug. "I'm sorry. Why don't you go out on the forward deck and get some fresh air. I'll let you know when we're getting close."

Fern and Bernice did as they were told. The sea air was bracing, but beautifully fresh as the Captain said. Both women held tightly to the white railing, as the steady ship rose and fell gently with the ocean's waves. The sun sparkled off the dark blue water, telling them the ocean here was deep. Seagulls dipped and swerved among the bright whitecaps, curious about the ship.

They seemed to be headed southwest, more west than south, according to Fern's excellent sense of direction. She had laughed at her husband Matt on their honeymoon when he couldn't make a move without the car's GPS; she always knew which direction to go. Matt would drive right into the Pacific Ocean if his GPS told him to.

"Did you know about this island?" Bernice asked her.

"Nope. Did you?"

"No, also. Big secret. But I guess you must be getting used to big secrets in your job."

Fern laughed. "Let's just say that nothing Joe Phelps says or does surprises me anymore."

"You won't get bored," Bernice noted.

"That's the truth. No time. There's always something happening."

"But don't you wonder why we—who've lived in Chinook County all of our lives—didn't know about this island?"

"It is strange," agreed Fern. "I can't wait to talk to my dad tonight to see if he knows about it. He's fished out here since he was a kid. Not as far out as it sounds like we're going, but still."

"Yeah, you would think the old-timers would have heard about it," Bernice said.

"And, why wasn't it news when Rohn Reid bought it?" Fern asked. "Everything that guy does is tracked and newsworthy. Remember when he and his wife divorced, and he got custody of their small children? I was young then, but I remember my mom going nuts about it. I don't get it." She shook her head.

"Yeah, it seems odd that we wouldn't have heard about the island, although he's turned reclusive. Maybe he made the government promise to keep the buyer a secret. I wonder if he's the dead body?" Bernice speculated. "You know that I wouldn't have been invited if there wasn't a crime scene of some sort. And this top-secret stuff likely means someone important is involved."

"I hope it's not Rohn Reid," Fern said, biting her lower lip. "He's done some wonderful, life-changing things with his money. Very generous man, even if he is…eccentric."

"I only hope it's not too gruesome a scene. But I'm starting to get a bad feeling about this," Bernice said. "Prepare yourself." She took some deep gulps of the sea air.

• • •

Captain Adams came out to the deck about twenty minutes later and told them they would be approaching the island soon. They hadn't seen the Secretary of State or Joe since they boarded the Resolve.

"You will want to stay on this deck to get a good look at the island," Adams said. "Leufeld and Phelps are coming out soon to join you." He turned sharply and went back to the bridge.

"Our handsome captain is stressed," noted Bernice.

"Got a knot in my stomach, too," agreed Fern. "I'm not loving this." The two women moved to the most forward part of the bow and gripped the rail tightly. "What the heck are we doing in the Pacific Ocean with the Secretary of State?" she mused.

"You're here because we're going to need your help back on land, Fern," said Joe Phelps quietly, coming up behind the women. Fred Leufeld was trailing a step behind Joe and followed him as he joined Fern and Bernice at the railing. The Secretary's protective detail filled the remainder of the bow's deck space.

"Spill it, Joe," Fern said toughly. She'd had enough of this secrecy and drama. "What's going on?"

"Rohn Reid called Fred yesterday," Joe began.

"Rohn and I go way back," Fred interrupted. "College." He nodded at Joe to continue.

"I talked to him right before I called you out of your police department retreat. Reid is on his island, and yesterday afternoon he discovered a body hanging from the rafters of one of the island's buildings. The victim is deceased." Joe delivered the obvious line is his usual flat monotone.

"Why did he call you, Mr. Secretary?" Fern asked. "Why not call the local police, or the Coast Guard?"

Fred frowned. "Because he's afraid he knows who the dead man is, and he knew I would want to know first."

"Who is it?" asked Fern.

"Rohn thinks it might be a retired admiral in the Japanese Navy. Hiroshi Matsuda." The Secretary of State looked down at his shoes, sadness emanating from him. "A finer man you'd never meet."

"And you know this man well?" Fern asked.

"I do," Fred answered. "Almost forty years ago, Hiroshi and I were both stationed here on Cold Rock. We were young and our respective navies threw us together on this hateful island. The U.S. and Japan had come together after WW2 when it became apparent that China was becoming the real enemy. We operated Cold Rock jointly in secrecy as a military base to keep our eyes on the Pacific theater. I left in 1992 when politics beckoned, but Hiroshi stayed on until the bitter end in 1994. He was the presiding officer when the base was shut down for good."

"Why would he have been back here now?" she asked. She stared at the ominous land mass ahead of her, as the cutter drew near. A stray cloud blocked out the sun momentarily.

"That's the question," Fred said quietly. "I hope and pray it's not him."

"The other news is that Admiral Matsuda's wife reported him missing yesterday," Joe told the women. "They live in Honolulu, and he left their home on Wednesday and didn't return yesterday as expected. She called the Honolulu police last night."

"Where did she think her husband went?" Fern asked.

"I'll share the police report with you," Joe said, "but Mrs. Matsuda said he was vague about his destination. Said it was a favor for their son, and he'd be back Friday afternoon. He never showed. She said Hiroshi didn't seem worried about anything, so she didn't worry either until he didn't arrive, and his phone kept going to voicemail."

"Why does Rohn Reid believe it's him?" asked Bernice. "Does he know the admiral?"

"Yes," said Fred. "He met him during the negotiations when he purchased the island. But he told me that he's not positive it's him, and that it was twenty-nine years ago. He also said that the victim is wearing a military uniform."

For the second time today, Fern had no comeback.

The four stood shoulder to shoulder as Cold Rock Island came into closer view. There was something forbidding about the island rising up higher from the crashing waves than Fern expected. The land mass was, in fact, monstrous in size compared to some of the rock islands closer to Port Stirling, and from their distance, looked to be about a mile long and wide.

A rock jetty curving around a substantial man-made harbor tamed the raging surf, and Fern could feel the engine slowing as the ship nosed in carefully. Ahead of them, about ten anonymous buildings loomed large up a steep roadway leading from the ship's docking station. There was a non-descript single-story white building at the end of the dock, and beyond that a fortified wall appeared to encircle at least this side of the island. The paved road rose behind the white building and wound its way up the ter-raced land mass. The terrain was mostly rocky with some wild green shrubs and weeds poking out occasionally.

Near the top of the island on the end closest to where they were docking, Fern spotted what looked like an immense airplane runway. She was unable to clearly see the end of it. On the island's opposite end was a substantial water tower, along with a shiny white lighthouse perched on the furthest tip of land. Most of the ten buildings had few, if any, windows, and looked to be on average three stories high. But one building—low-slung and hugging its rocky perch—was a grace-ful residence, surrounded by a manicured garden, and looked as if it didn't belong on this island.

Three men stood on the dock to greet them, surrounded by a flock of squawking, swooping seagulls who seemed happy to have additional com-pany. Two of the men looked young-ish to Fern, maybe late twenties, and were clearly brothers. The handsome young men were dressed somewhat differently; one in well-worn jeans and a black hoodie, and the other more pulled together in newer jeans and a navy cashmere crewneck sweater.

The third, older man she recognized as famous philanthropist and weirdo billionaire Rohn Reid. He appeared to have tried to make an effort to greet their prominent guest appropriately. He was attired in khakis, but as they drew nearer, Fern could see they were wrinkled and dirty around the bottom. A tie was escaping sloppily from its knot, and the black bomber jacket had seen better days…like thirty years ago. Not known for his sartorial splendor, his sandy-streaked-with-grey hair seemed to be searching for a comb. Black-framed glasses kept slipping down his nose, and Reid pushed them up with his index finger twice since Fern had been eyeing him.

Fern, Bernice, Joe, and Fred waited at the top of the portable staircase that had been lowered to the dock as Fred's protective detail went down first and addressed the three men. Fern and Bernice's eyes widened as the three were given a brisk frisking by the secret service. The senior man turned and nodded to his colleague who stood behind the Secretary, and the four started down the staircase, Joe in front with Fred's guy sandwiching the two women and Fred in between them.

"Mr. Secretary, welcome to my island," said Rohn Reid, stretching out his hand to Fred. His face was pasty and slack around a bulbous nose, and his body reminded Fern of dumplings. She couldn't help but notice the dandruff on his shoulders.

Fred grasped Reid's hand and pulled him in close for a hug. He whispered something into Reid's ear that Fern couldn't make out. *None of my business anyway*, she said to herself.

Pulling away from their embrace, Fred said, "It's good to see you again, Rohn. Not so good to be on this ground again, however." His eyes swept the island from end to end, sunlight beaming down on it, with a few stray clouds tracking across at a fast pace and leaving their shadows at intervals.

"Didn't think you'd be eager to return here," said Rohn. "But I really appreciate you coming under these circumstances. I couldn't think of anyone else to call."

Fern noted that Rohn Reid wiped his hands on his pants and recalled that he was a renowned germaphobe. But she thought he also appeared nervous.

"You did the right thing," Fred said to him. "I hope I can't identify the body, but if it's who you think, it will be an international story and State needs to get out in front of it." He turned and looked at his colleagues standing mutely behind him. "I'd like to introduce you to Joe Phelps; he works with me in the State Department."

As head of Covert Operations, Fern thought. *Guess it's not a title they want thrown around.*

"This is Fern Byrne," continued Fred. "Fern also works with me as our west coast liaison."

She stepped forward and shook hands with Rohn Reid. "It's nice to meet you, Mr. Reid. Thank you for all you do."

Reid acknowledged Fern's remark with an awkward nod and averted his eyes. No smile, no comment.

"And this is Dr. Bernice Ryder," Fred said. "Dr. Ryder is the medical examiner for Chinook County." Bernice shook hands with Reid, too, but she didn't say anything. Reid was looking past her and said to Captain Adams, "Is this your ship, sir?"

Adams said, "Yes. Captain Bob Adams, U.S. Coast Guard out of Buck Bay, Oregon." He stepped forward.

Reid looked longingly at the cutter. "It's a nice boat, Captain."

"I hear you've got a nice one, too, Mr. Reid," Adams said with a smile.

That got a twinkle from Reid, and a snort from the young man standing beside him in the navy cashmere sweater. "I do, Captain, but I don't have any cannons on mine." He swiveled his head to the men on his right.

"These two chaps are my brilliant and smart-ass sons, Rick and Randy." Rohn beamed as his two boys waved at their guests.

"You brothers look a lot alike," Fred said.

"There's a reason for that," said Rick, standing next to his father.

"We're twins," said Randy, grinning.

"Ah, no wonder. I knew Rohn had kids, but I didn't know he had the pair of you," Fred said. "Where'd you get your height?" He looked over at their five-foot-eight-ish father.

"Mom is six feet tall," one of the twins answered.

"We passed her when we were about twenty," the other one added. They stole a glance at each other and laughed at their private joke.

"Well," said Fred. "We might as well get this over with." He looked at Rohn.

The Reids had three golf carts on the dock to transport their guests up the hill. They all piled in and took off.

CHAPTER 4

The golf carts came to a stop in front of one of the anonymous buildings with a gaping hangar door that was being opened as they arrived.

"This isn't pretty," Rohn Reid warned. "Ladies, you should…"

"We've likely seen worse in our work, Mr. Reid," Fern interrupted. "Please, let's proceed." She and Bernice took off toward the opening, as the men hustled to keep up. Bernice whispered in Fern's ear, "You just interrupted the eleventh richest man in the world."

Fern whispered back, "He was about to say something stupid."

"It's this way," said a young man in jeans and a red hoodie sweatshirt, pointing to a dark corner of the immense building. His face was pale, and his hands were shaking as he pointed across the open space. Fern, Bernice, and their entourage followed him.

There were no interior walls in the structure, and the only furniture was a sleek Gulfstream G400 private jet parked in the center of the hangar.

In spite of her tough girl admonition to Rohn Reid, Fern's hand ran to cover her mouth, and she let out a half-moan, half-gasp as she saw the victim hanging from a crossbeam in the darkened corner of the hangar. The building's roof looked to be about forty feet high, and the beam about fifteen feet lower in this corner. A long fiberglass extension ladder sprawled under the body.

"Oh, doggone it," Fred blurted out, coming up behind her. "It's him. It's Hiroshi Matsuda." Pure anguish in his voice. The Secretary of State started toward the body, but Bernice reached out her hand and grabbed him by the arm. "Please don't approach the scene, sir. Let me establish a perimeter around him first."

"Yes, right," Fred said, stopping in his tracks. "Of course. Sorry, doc. Can we cut him down?" His eyes were full of pain, and he visibly trembled.

"I will handle that as soon as we can protect the scene," Bernice said, as softly as she could manage. "Has anyone approached the victim?" she asked, eyes scanning the gathered men.

Rohn Reid stepped toward Bernice and said, "No. I was notified when Tyson here"—he pointed toward the man in the red hoodie—"found him, and I instructed everyone to stay clear until we could get some help. What do you need, Dr. Ryder?"

"Good," Bernice answered, while starting to pull her protective gear out of her case. "Do you know if anyone touched the ladder?"

Rohn looked at Tyson. "I didn't touch it," Rohn said. "Did you?"

Tyson shook his head. "No, sir."

To Fred, Bernice said, "Are you absolutely sure of the identity of the victim?"

"I'm sure. I worked with this lovely man for years." His eyes strayed back to the dead man. "You didn't deserve this end, my friend."

Rohn approached his long-time pal and awkwardly put his arm around Fred's shoulders. "I'm so sorry."

"Who could've done such an awful thing?" Fred asked the universe.

The others stood silently as Bernice and Fern slipped into crime scene paper protective suits and face masks. They covered their hair with netted caps and pulled on latex gloves. When they finished their investigator outfitting, Bernice handed Fern one end of the crime-scene tape she always carried with her, and the two women began to tape off a large square area under Mr. Matsuda's body and around the ladder.

When they finished, Bernice spoke into the small recorder she retrieved from her bag. "As the medical officer on scene representing Chinook County, Oregon, and the United States government, I am pronouncing that the life of Mr. Hiroshi Matsuda is extinct. The victim has been identified by U.S. Secretary of State Fred Leufeld on Saturday, February 24, 2024, at 11:52

a.m." She hit 'pause' and looked up at the body for a few moments. "Mr. Matsuda appears to be of Japanese descent and is wearing a military uniform of some sort. His age, cause of death, and time of death are to be determined. Death by hanging, either by his own hand or persons unknown, is probable, as the body is high enough off the ground for that result. The scene has been cordoned off, and a forensic sweep will be done, followed by an autopsy of the victim at a later time. Recorded by Dr. Bernice Ryder of Buck Bay, Oregon." Bernice clicked off her recorder and tossed it in her bag.

She said, "Gentlemen, Fern and I will be here for a while. When we've finished gathering any forensic evidence, we'll need some help retrieving Mr. Matsuda's body. I suggest you retreat to somewhere more pleasant while we do our initial work. Mr. Secretary, I'm really sorry for your loss." She took the liberty of patting him gently on his back.

"Thank you, doc. Hiroshi was a terrific man and a great friend to me. Please do your best on this bad deal, OK?"

Uncharacteristically choked up, Bernice simply nodded.

Rohn Reid spoke. "Let's adjourn to my house. There is nourishment if anyone wants anything. And bourbon."

"I'll wait here," Joe Phelps said, as he watched Bernice crouch down with a fine brush and eye a spot on the floor that was visible to only her trained eye. "Carefully out of the way of these two."

Fern smiled behind her face mask and then set about her grim work.

• • •

After they'd completed a sweep of the area with the tools Bernice had with her, and she properly stored everything in her medical examiner's bag, she turned to Joe.

"I'm going to do a thorough fingerprint powdering of the ladder next, and then we'll need you to help us position the ladder under the victim. Do you think the three of us can get it set up?" she asked him.

"Yes, I'm good with ladders," Joe said. "Much to my wife's dismay sometimes."

Bernice smiled a tight smile. "Good. You two can hold it, and I'll climb up and do the beam and the rope. Then, can you round up a couple of those strong young men to help us cut him down?"

"Sure," said Joe. Working together, they set up the ladder, and Fern and Joe held it tightly, stabilizing it for Bernice as she slowly climbed to the top until she could reach the beam, while clutching her field fingerprint kit. She spread her legs as wide as the step would allow, and balanced herself, placing the kit cautiously on the ladder shelf that she unfolded in front of her.

Fern and Joe held on for dear life, not saying a word while Bernice did her thing. Not for the first time — and probably not for the last — Fern marveled at Bernice's bravery and competence. From the night Bernice had saved her husband's life by admitting she didn't have the skills his critical condition required, Fern had nothing but complete confidence in her friend's professional capabilities. If anyone had assisted Matsuda's death, Bernice would uncover any evidence left behind.

Finally, just as Fern's arm muscles were beginning to tire, Bernice said, "That's it. I've got everything I can get. Coming down now. Fern, I'll hand my kit to you, and then go back up to snap some close-up photos."

"Got it," Fern said, and stepped up a couple of steps to meet her. "Did you get any prints?"

"Yes," Bernice said and handed off the kit to her. "Back in a minute. I'm going to hand you another bag."

She climbed back up until she was level with Matsuda's face and found her camera she'd attached to a lanyard and tucked inside her top. She moved in close to inspect his face and neck, snapping some pictures as she peered intently.

Then Bernice took a swab kit from her pocket, took out a swab, inserted it into one of Hiroshi's nostrils, and then repeated the process on his other nostril. Carefully, she placed the two swabs into a small bag, zipped it closed, and handed it down to Fern. "Please label this packet with Hiroshi's name, the date, and the time."

"Got it," replied Fern, taking hold of the bag.

At that moment, a harsh, cold wind blew through the cavernous building. Hiroshi Matsuda's body swayed with it. Fern saw Bernice shudder as she drew even with Hiroshi's face and then quickly backed away.

"Let's get this poor man down from here," Bernice said.

· · ·

Red-hoodie guy brought two of his co-workers, and a second tall ladder. Between them, Fern, Bernice, and Joe, they cut the rope and wrestled Hiroshi's body to the hangar floor. Bernice unfolded the body bag from her suitcase, and she and Joe placed him in it, zipping it up.

"Please get the captain and let's have Mr. Matsuda's body loaded onto the ship," Bernice said to Joe. "I'll have my team meet us at the dock in Buck Bay, and we'll take him to the morgue. Does that suit you?"

"Yes," said Joe. "I want you to do the autopsy. But you'll need to wait until we've notified his family. Fred wants to do that personally."

Bernice nodded her understanding. "Where does his family live?"

"Honolulu, apparently. The Secretary was there recently. He was on a State Department visit to Japan and stopped on the way back to D.C. for an overnight visit with his old friend."

"When was this?" Fern asked, standing with them.

"About six weeks ago," Joe said. "He told me that Matsuda was healthy and in good spirits. They had a great time together reliving old times." Joe's lips tightened in a straight line, and he shook his head. "Such a shame."

"So, why would he kill himself?" asked Fern.

"Maybe he came back to this island and realized how creepy and depressing it is," Joe said, dripping with sarcasm.

Bernice, always one to appreciate gallows humor among cops, appeared to smirk slightly. "There are several possibilities," she said. "On the surface, it looks like suicide. Mr. Matsuda climbed the ladder, strung himself to the beam, and then kicked the ladder out from under him."

"What's the second option?" Fern asked.

"The victim may have hung himself, and then Rohn Reid—or somebody else—moved the ladder."

"Why would he do that?" Fern asked.

"Maybe he wanted to protect Matsuda's reputation?" Joe surmised. "Didn't want his hero record soiled by suicide."

"Possible, I guess," said Bernice, sounding like she didn't really believe her own suggestion.

"Why do you say that?" Fern asked her. "You sound skeptical."

"For starters, there is no sign of manual strangulation around his neck, which would be the most likely scenario if someone killed him first, and then wanted to make it look like suicide. However, there are other possibilities."

"Like what?"

"I don't like that the victim's eyes are bloodshot, and there may be some bruising around his nose. But I'll be able to tell once I can get my forensics analyzed and do the autopsy. Unless it was murder, there would be absolutely no other reason for any prints other than Matsuda's to be on that beam." All three of them looked back up at the beam. "It's too high, and in this out-of-the-way corner. Wouldn't interfere with the plane or anything else going on in the building."

"So, your third option is murder?" Fern questioned.

"I'm not ruling it out," Bernice said quietly.

"Any guess at the time of death?" Fern asked.

Bernice looked up at Matsuda, and then cautioned, "You know I can't tell you that definitively until I complete the post-mortem, but my educated guess is that it's between thirty-six and forty-eight hours. Rigor mortis has completely disappeared, and there's no discoloration showing that decomposition is occurring yet."

Fern looked at her watch. "So, that would put it sometime after Thursday about noon."

"That's my guess," Bernice said.

"Why was he even here?" asked Fern. "On this island? Did you ask Rohn Reid?" she inquired of Joe.

"Fred did. Reid said he didn't know he was here until Tyson found him yesterday afternoon."

"Which one is Tyson?" asked Bernice.

"The guy with the red hoodie," Joe replied. "He came into the hangar Friday afternoon to check on Reid's airplane—part of his daily security rounds. That's when he saw him."

"I will want to take fingerprints from everyone currently on the island," Bernice said.

Joe nodded.

"Did Tyson do all of his rounds, including this building, on Friday?" Fern asked.

"Don't know," Joe said. "I haven't questioned anyone yet. My boss was adamant that Bernice does her thing, and then we attend to Mr. Matsuda's body. I don't even know how many people total are on this island."

"Let's take care of Mr. Matsuda, and then round up everyone," Fern said. "I have questions."

"Figured you would," Joe said with a sad smile.

● ● ●

Captain Bob Adams took charge of moving Hiroshi Matsuda's body from the hangar to his ship. He and his crew placed Matsuda in the cooler of the vessel's galley. Out of respect, and for the chain of evidence, Adams personally stayed in the galley to protect the body.

Joe showed Fern and Bernice the way to the house, where the others awaited them. All three took in big gulps of the fresh sea air as they walked, silently trying to expel the hangar's air of death.

Rohn Reid, when he first acquired the island, had attempted to remodel the building that had served as the headquarters and officers' barracks of the joint base. But it had proved futile to make it over into the comfortable, luxurious home he'd wanted. So, he'd knocked it down, hired a world-famous Brazilian architect and a renowned New York interior design firm to create the retreat. And, while not much in the way of a lush garden could grow on this wet, cold rock, a trendy English garden designer had consulted on what Reid could and could not plant to surround the house with some semblance of nature and life.

The result had stopped Fern—with her own beautiful home in Port Stirling—in her tracks as they approached the gate leading up a stone path to the house's veranda. "Wow."

"Agree. Wow," said Bernice.

"More money than brains," chipped in Joe. "And he has a lot of brains."

Sinuous rock walls wrapped gracefully around the long, rectangular house and enclosed artistically terraced gardens. Those were mostly filled with grasses blowing wildly in the wind that had picked up, interspersed with dozens of white Japanese Bottlebrush plants and the hot pink spidery flowers of Grevillea. Constructed of mostly stone and wood, the house had big windows on all four sides that looked out to the watery view.

"Try not to piss him off, Fern," Joe instructed.

Fern looked sideways at her boss. "Why would I do that? He's done a lot for Oregon, and I admire him. Why would you even say a thing like that?"

"Oh, I don't know. Perhaps your zealous quest for truth and justice?"

Bernice snorted. "If his prints are on that beam, I won't care one whit about his philanthropic deeds."

Joe gave Bernice the stare. "What possible motivation could Rohn Reid have for wanting Hiroshi Matsuda dead?" he said.

She shrugged. "Guess that's up to my girlfriend here to find out."

"Let's go," said Fern.

CHAPTER 5

Tuesday, December 12, 2023 — Honolulu

Hiroshi Matsuda drove his wife down the slope of their Diamond Head Heights home into the heart of Honolulu. It was 9:30 a.m. and she had a 10:00 a.m. appointment at her favorite spa near Waikiki Beach.

"What time should I pick you up?" Hiroshi asked.

"Two-thirty," she smiled. "Going for the full meal deal today."

"Not sure why. You couldn't be any more beautiful."

She pointed at him with a long, slim finger. "You are a keeper, handsome husband. But look at this nail." She wiggled her finger.

"I stand corrected. I can see that your nail polish is chipped. What a catastrophe."

She laughed. "See you later, alligator."

He watched her walk through the heavy bamboo doors of the spa, and then drove his British Racing Green Jaguar around the circular driveway, turning back the way he'd come toward home. His beloved car had been a gift from his wife on the day he'd retired from thirty years in the Japanese military. Hiroshi wasn't big on possessions, but he damn well loved that car.

He was tempted to just drive for a while on this glorious sunny day in paradise, but with Naomi out of the house, it was a good opportunity to poke into Shuji's bank's business. He could tell that his son was worried about the odd emails some of his managers had received, and when Shuji had been called to headquarters in Tokyo yesterday, he'd phoned his father to tell him he would be gone for a couple of days.

"Is this about the threatening emails?" Hiroshi had asked him.

"Sorta," Shuji said. "I've asked for a meeting to discuss our internal security policies, and the president agreed. My hope is that we will cover the wide breadth of security procedures."

"I'm sitting here sucking my thumb in retirement. Can I do anything to help you?"

Shuji laughed long and hard, a laugh that since he was a young boy, had always made his father laugh, too. "I was hoping you would say that. I want to share some internal login and IT info with you. I wish you would spend a little time while I'm away delving into our system and see if you notice anything suspicious."

"I'm not an IT expert — you know that, right?"

"You know more than a couple of my managers. Which unfortunately is probably part of my problem. Will you do it?"

"You might get canned if anyone discovers you gave me this company information," Hiroshi cautioned.

"Trust me, dad, no one will know. No one but me is even looking. Just don't do anything or go anywhere obvious. You know the boundaries."

"OK, then, I'm on it. Hope I can help you."

"You always have, dad. And I appreciate it. Here's what you need to get started." Shuji shared some codes and passwords with Hiroshi. "I'll be in touch when I get home."

"Safe travels, son, and don't be afraid to knock some heads together if you need to. They're paying you to keep the bank safe."

● ● ●

Hiroshi took the long way home on the Lunalilo Freeway to let his Jaguar run free for a few extra minutes. With the top down, sunglasses on, he felt like James Bond. *An old, gray James Bond*, he chuckled to himself. *Going the speed limit.*

Once home, he went to the far end of his home where his office was located. 'Office' was a generous word to describe the room. When he'd retired, he and Naomi had carved out a small space along the back wall of the large garage, enclosed it, and inserted one sad window that looked out on an unused part of their back yard. Their mutual hope was that he wouldn't need an office much, but the couple was realistic to know that Hiroshi wouldn't sit on a beach the rest of his life either.

So far, he'd toyed with the idea of writing a memoir focused on his unique career, and he had even made a brief outline and jotted down some ideas for a book. But the truth was, he'd hardly visited his room.

He switched on the desk lamp and fired up his PC, situating his chair so he could look out the window. He studied the notes Shuji had given him, and logged in. In the deep quiet of his empty house, Hiroshi, educated by the Japanese military on IT security and someone who kept up with technology, was soon engrossed in the inner workings of his son's bank.

• • •

Saturday, February 24, 2024 — Cold Rock Island

Fern took a good, hard look around the living room of Rohn Reid's house, where they were gathered with their host and the Secretary of State. Her eyes paused on Reid himself as he sat in a lived-in leather club chair at an angle to the sofa where Joe and Fred sat. She and Bernice plopped down on the facing sofa. Reid put one foot up on the corner of the coffee table nearest his chair. The only other thing on the wood and glass table was a book entitled 'Quantum Physics In Daily Life.' Fern, whose reading tastes ran more toward crime fiction, thought, *Rohn Reid and I inhabit different planets.*

The room was both gorgeous and comfortable. It smelled of money. Low-slung furniture, matching how the house itself hugged the ground, was scattered around the large room, creating more than one conversation area. Most of the seating was camel-colored, and cushy in a soft, warm fabric. Scattered about casually but neatly were several gray and camel cashmere throws, some on the back of chairs and some on the numerous ottomans. Wall-to-wall soft gray carpeting felt cozy underfoot. The only hit of color in the room was a brilliant purple and red modern painting, whose stout dimensions must have measured at least ten feet by ten feet. It hung on the long wall opposite the window wall that looked out to the terraced garden and the sea beyond. Sleek sculptures on granite pedestals filled two corners, and Fern, an art major in college, was dying to take a closer look at them. *Not now, business first.*

An older man, slim with a slight stoop to his posture, wearing nice charcoal slacks and a white dress shirt topped with a sleeveless, fully buttoned black wool vest entered the room holding a tray with a coffee service and cups for the five people gathered.

"Thanks, Leonard," said Rohn. He motioned for him to set it down on the coffee table.

"Can I get anything else for you or your guests?" Leonard asked, looking from person to person.

"The coffee is wonderful," said Fern when none of the others spoke up. "Thank you."

"It's my pleasure, ma'am," smiled Leonard. "Don't hesitate if you change your mind."

"Allow me," said Fred, reaching forward and pouring for everyone when Rohn Reid sat there like a lump. *Not big on the social graces*, thought Fern for the second time since she'd met him.

Dr. Ryder cleared her throat and said, "Mr. Matsuda's body has been moved to the Coast Guard ship, and Captain Adams is overseeing the custody of the body until I can take coroner's control and remove the victim to my morgue." Fern thought she'd never heard Bernice sound so formal and stilted, but she agreed that the circumstances demanded it. She was grateful to her friend for moving the conversation to the issue at hand.

"What happens next?" asked Rohn.

"Hiroshi's death will be investigated by the closest police jurisdiction, which is Chinook County, Oregon," said the Secretary of State. "Fern will be State's representative on the ground, and we will follow her lead on the direction and local personnel involved. It's also likely, considering the victim, that the FBI may want to take a look as well, but we'll start with the local investigation today. Do you have any questions about how this will work, Rohn?"

Reid hesitated for a split second. "Sounds like it will be intrusive. This island is my getaway from an intrusive world."

"A man is dead, Rohn," Fred said. "A decent, kind man who didn't deserve to die this way. I'm sure Fern and Bernice will be as considerate of your privacy as possible, but Hiroshi's family—and his nation—are entitled to answers."

"I understand. I'm just asking that you limit people overrunning my island and keep this story as private as possible. What will you need from me?"

"We will certainly do our best to contain this story," Fern interceded. "It's not in our best interests to have the public running amuck either. In fact, for our investigative purposes, I ask that you instruct your folks here on the island now that they are not to discuss this case with anyone off the island—at least, not until we've had a chance to interview everyone and get a feel for what might have happened to Mr. Matsuda."

Rohn nodded. "Already done. No worries there."

"Great," said Fern.

Joe added, "Fern and I will spend tonight here while Bernice accompanies Mr. Matsuda's body back to the mainland."

"That's no problem," said Reid. "We have a nice four-bedroom guest house behind us. There's a short breezeway from the kitchen to it."

"Sounds perfect," Joe said. "Fred, I assume that you will go back now with Captain Adams?"

"Yes," Fred said. "I've alerted my staff that I'm changing my schedule again. I will fly to Honolulu as soon as they can get my plane serviced and turned around instead of going home to D.C. I'll go straight to Naomi and notify her of Hiroshi's death."

"In addition to your Secret Service detail, you should take a detective or two from the Honolulu police department," Joe instructed him. "Fern and I will want to know if his wife and family have any idea why he was on this island."

"Yes," said Fern. "Also, if he had been acting unusual at all, or anything strange had happened to him or the family. The Honolulu cops will know what to ask. Please ask them to connect with me; here's my cell phone number." She scribbled on a page from her notebook, tore it out, and handed it to the Secretary of State.

Rohn Reid looked from Fern to Fred to Joe, and back to Fern. "Who are you, exactly?" he asked her.

"Good question," piped in Bernice, smiling.

"I'll take that question," said Fred. He leaned forward, placing his elbows on his knees and clasping his hands in front of him. "But the answer is not to leave this room," he said sternly. "Is that clear?"

Rohn and Bernice nodded. "Whatever you say, Mr. Secretary," said Rohn.

Fern, too, gave Fred a quick nod that silently said, 'It's OK to proceed.'

"Fern is the west coast liaison for the Department of State. It is her job to keep eyes and ears on any issues that might affect the good will and reputation of the United States at home or abroad. She is also a skilled former police officer and"… he paused, "a deep undercover agent for us."

"You're a spy?" Bernice blurted, both eyebrows shooting up.

"Sort of," Fern replied. She held up her index finger to her mouth, giving Bernice the universal shhh! sign, and then turned to Rohn Reid. "Are you up to answering a few questions from us now?" Even though she was in firm cop mode, her voice was soft and respectful.

To her surprise, Reid laughed. "Guess I'd better, or you'll spike my coffee or something."

"That's only in the movies, Mr. Reid." She gave him her friendliest smile to let him know she could take a joke, and then dug in.

CHAPTER 6

s it correct that you didn't know Hiroshi Matsuda was here on your island?" Fern started.

"Yes," answered Rohn Reid. "I don't know how or when he arrived. He didn't notify me, and I didn't see him until Tyson found him yesterday."

"Had any airplanes landed in the past week?" Joe asked.

"No. Not to my knowledge."

"How long have you been here?" Joe, again.

"We were at the Super Bowl in Las Vegas earlier this month, and we came here the day following," Reid said. "I think it was something like February 11 or 12."

"When you say 'we', who are you talking about?" asked Fern.

"My two sons, Rick and Randy, traveled with me. The three of us."

Fern knew that Rohn Reid and the boys' mother were divorced — the news had been juicy and front page for several days. It had been an amicable separation, and quite lucrative for her. There had been no rumors about any other female companions for him in the years since. That might be a question for a later time, but Fern thought now was not the proper time.

"Can you explain who else is currently on the island, and what their role is?" she asked now.

"Leonard — who you just met — is my personal assistant when I'm in residence. He lives here most of the year and runs the place while I'm elsewhere. He has a home in Seattle, too."

"Is Seattle your primary residence?"

"It used to be," Rohn said, "and I do spend time there. But now, I guess I might say that Palm Desert, California, is my primary residence. I find the older I get, the more my bones and joints don't love the Seattle rain and cold." He paused. "Tyson Anderson — who found the body — also lives here most of the time. He's our resident handyman, and takes care of general maintenance on the houses, the dock, the runway, and hangars. And when I'm here, he's in charge of security as well."

"How long has Tyson worked for you?" Fern asked.

Reid scratched his head, causing a flake or two of dandruff to fall on his shoulders. "Don't know exactly, but about four years, I'd guess. Leonard could tell you when he was hired."

"Where did he work before he came here?" Joe asked.

"He was in charge of warehouse security for Amazon in Seattle."

"Who else is here?" asked Fern.

"Well, we have a cook and housekeeper — Moira and Lynette. Lynette lives here full-time, but Moira, my cook, only comes when I'm here or we have guests staying. She lives in a wing of my desert home the rest of the time. Been with me for years. I'm a finicky eater," he smiled.

Fern thought he looked like he ate pretty much anything set in front of him.

"Then, we have Simon, the gardener and landscape guy. He comes and goes as needed, but he's here now. He likes to do a tidy up before spring. He was hired when I bought the island. Does a great job."

"Anyone else here this week?"

"Yes, Tyson has two other guys who work with him, Aaron and Noah — I don't know their last names. They do odd jobs and help with security. They trade off shifts, so one of them is on duty during the night. That's it, I think. Oh, and my two sons, of course, who you met."

Fern looked down at her notes and did a quick count. "So, two women and seven men, eight including you. Ten people total. Does that sound right?"

"Yes, that's everyone," Rohn confirmed.

"Who flew the plane here?" Fern asked. "You didn't mention a pilot."

"That's because I'm the pilot," Rohn smiled. "I've been flying for over three decades, and I love it. Rick was my co-pilot on this trip, but if the boys aren't with me, I keep a pilot on retainer in Palm Springs. Moira flies with me, and she takes care of all the food and any guests that may be onboard. This trip it was just her, the boys, and me."

"What a sense of freedom it must be to have your own plane and be able to fly it," Fern noted.

"It is," Rohn nodded. "First thing I did when my company went public, and I made some real money."

Bernice raised her hand. "I will want fingerprints of everyone currently on the island before I take off," Bernice said.

Rohn looked from Fern to Bernice and stared at her. "Why?"

"Isn't it obvious?" Bernice responded. "I never make assumptions in my business, but it's highly likely that Mr. Matsuda ended his own life, or someone on your island killed him. I take fingerprints to mostly eliminate possible suspects by comparing them to crime scene prints, but in a case like this, if it ends up being the latter, it would be remiss to not print everyone present."

Rohn fidgeted in his chair and shifted his foot from the coffee table to the floor. "I would rather not have my prints taken by the government," he finally said. "Nor those of my sons."

"It's routine, Rohn," Fred spoke up. "Nothing to worry about."

"I can appreciate that, Fred, but it's a matter of privacy to me."

Awkward silence.

Bernice swallowed. "I understand your reticence as a public figure, Mr. Reid, but I can assure you that your prints and those of your boys will be handled with every discretion possible; they are mainly for my eyes only."

"Are we suspects?" Reid asked her.

"No, of course not!" Fred interjected vehemently.

"Actually, Mr. Secretary, we have ten suspects…harking back to the count of people actually present on this island," Bernice said. She hesitated. "And, if I can't identify the fingerprints I found on the beam as belonging to Hiroshi Matsuda, I will request a judge to approve a search warrant for any additional prints I want to compare to my crime scene." She slightly emphasized 'my.' "Again, Mr. Reid, it's in your favor to be ruled out of the police investigation early on."

Reid didn't respond, and there was another silence.

Joe broke it. "Can a boat dock where we did without being seen up here?"

Reid seemed relieved to have a change of topic. "It would depend on the size of the boat. If it's a ship like the CG cutter, no, I could see it from the family areas of the house—TV room, my bedroom and bath, my office. If you're talking about a dinghy of some sort, yeah, it could probably slip in unnoticed. But Tyson keeps a pretty close watch on both the landing strip and the dock. It would be difficult to get by him or his guys, I think."

"What about at night? Are there lights at the dock?" Fern asked. "And what about the runway at night? Is it lit?"

"No on the runway. And besides, I would definitely hear a plane landing at night. It's very loud inside the house. There are lights at the dock that are kept on at night. I suppose someone could come ashore in a boat, especially if they cut their engines out to sea aways, if that's what you're getting at. But they'd have to time it right to slip in without my guys noticing, even if it was a small boat."

"Are there any other places on the island where you could land a boat besides the dock?" asked Fern.

Reid thought for a minute, and then shook his head. "It would be very difficult because the shoreline is mostly rocky. There is one tiny sandy beach on the north side of the island, but it's very remote and hidden."

"I know where you mean," whispered Fred, almost to himself. "Hiroshi and I used to go there to smoke without being seen."

• • •

Saturday, February 24, 2024—Port Stirling, Oregon

Tamryn Gesicki, detective in the Port Stirling Police Department, was walking on the beach below her rental house on this fine Saturday morning. In the days since she'd moved into her new home, 3,000 miles away from Boston, her former home, Tamryn walked on the beach every morning she could.

It was a different world among the sand, grassy dunes, and rock pools, hidden away from the stresses of her police work and life's realities. On the day that Fern had helped Tamryn move into her new home, she'd shown the newcomer the little pools that gathered around the rock crevices. Sure, they have tide pools in Boston, too, but the Pacific Ocean creatures somehow seemed happier. Tamryn especially loved them now, filled with life from the sea, and she always paused to poke around in the shallow waters warmed by the sun. Out early to discover what the high tide at 4:00 a.m. may have deposited on 'her' beach, Tamryn got distracted by some bright coral intertidal sea anemones attached to a good-sized rock about twenty feet above the now lower, noisy surf line.

She knew not to touch the tentacles, as even the small ones could give her a slight sting, but she loved to jab them with a small stick and watch them respond. This one, when agitated, showed off a lighter coral color inside than its slightly darker outside. Gorgeous. *You're a beauty*, she said. *I apologize for bothering you, and I'll leave you alone now.*

Continuing down toward the water and having taken off her shoes and socks to feel the warm sand between her toes, Tamryn breathed in deeply and marveled at how fast the weather could change around here. Yesterday, when her department had left the retreat, the wind had been a ghostly howling, and the rain came down in relentless sheets. This morning, she could feel the stirrings of spring in the soft, mild air.

The retreat had been the brainchild of her boss, Chief Matt Horning, to help her integrate better with her new colleagues. She'd ended up baring her soul—way more than she had intended to do—and had been engulfed in a room suddenly filled with love.

Escaping her bad marriage and the Boston PD had been the single best decision of her life. She had tried too hard the first few days in her new job, wanting her colleagues and Port Stirling residents to know she was a good cop and an excellent detective. It had had the opposite effect. By nature, Oregonians didn't appreciate showoffs and aggressive behavior, and Tamryn had appeared that way to them early on.

But once people understood what was driving her need to be successful in her new hometown, they opened their arms and embraced her fully, as Matt and Fern had done from day one. The past few days had changed Tamryn; she could feel the difference in her bones. She was more relaxed, a state of being that had become foreign to her in Boston. And dare she say it, *I think I might actually be happy.*

The ocean, wild just beyond the breaking waves, turned frothy and white around the giant sea stacks that broke their progress to the shore. She jammed her hands in her jacket pockets, and headed north on her beach at a brisk, cobweb-clearing pace.

• • •

Matt Horning had risen early that Saturday morning and made coffee, as he had done most of the mornings in the three years that he'd carried out his duties as the Port Stirling Chief of Police since relocating from Texas.

He did some paperwork in his home office while his wife, Fern, had slept in. He waited for her to get up to have breakfast together before she had to leave for Buck Bay to meet Joe Phelps, her boss.

When he heard her in the shower upstairs, he thinly sliced two red potatoes and cooked them in some oil and butter, just the way this Texas son liked them. In the pantry, he found some beautiful Honeycrisp apples she'd bought at the Port Stirling farmers' market a few days before and cut them into wedges on a separate plate. Four eggs and whole wheat bread for toast sat on the kitchen counter, waiting for Fern to appear.

Matt was still learning about his wife a few months into their marriage, but one thing he knew for sure was that she liked to eat a big breakfast on workdays. She always told him, "you never know when we might get to eat again, and we should start off fueled for action."

He thought that might be especially true today since Joe had not fully shared why he was flying out from D.C., and why he needed Fern. Just that they were going for a boat ride. It was a bit too mysterious for Matt's liking, but he knew it came with the territory of her new role.

She came into the kitchen, fully dressed, and looked ready to rock 'n roll, wherever the day took her. As usual, the sight of his gorgeous wife, resplendent today in a berry-colored jacket, took his breath away for a split second.

"I haven't seen you wear that before." He gave her a hug and kissed her cheek. "That's a good color on you, darlin'. How'd you sleep?"

"Straight through the night. You?"

"Yeah, I did, too. I think my brain was glad to have the department retreat behind me."

"That was a good thing you did yesterday for Tamryn," Fern said, smiling at the thought. "I'd bet she probably had her first good night of sleep, too, since she arrived in town. You're the best boss ever."

"Speaking of bosses, any more thought as to what yours is up to?"

"It's kinda crazy, isn't it? I'm trying to look professional, but all I know is we're going on a boat ride on Saturday."

"The Coast Guard is obviously involved somehow, or why would you be meeting him in Buck Bay? Don't you think?"

"Yes, I agree. Plus, Joe doesn't leave D.C. at the drop of a hat—something's going on."

"Take your gun," Matt said, giving her another hug and holding her tight. "Already packed."

• • •

After Fern left and his breakfast had settled, Matt decided to take a run on the beach. He, Jay, and Ed were going fishing this afternoon on the Twisty River at their favorite hole, which meant he'd probably drink too much beer…best to get ahead of the extra calories.

He liked the run in both directions on Port Stirling's six-mile beach, but he usually went south in the morning and north if he was running after work. The wind seemed to work more in his favor that way. He took off south at a slow, warm-up jog, before cranking it up about one-half mile into it, leaping over a couple of the small streams that streaked across the sand and fed into the Pacific Ocean.

His mind, except for a dull, nagging worry about Fern's day, was clear this morning. The resolution of Hannah Oakley's murder had been especially satisfying, plus he was happy about how yesterday's department retreat had worked out. His staff was clicking on all levels now, and maybe they would have a break in the violent crimes that had plagued the county in recent months. Happily married, job that he loved, and a fabulous house in a place he had grown to cherish beyond belief—life was good. *Now, if I can keep from getting shot at by hired hitmen, maybe Fern and I can enjoy life for a while.*

Matt ran easily along the high end of the surf line where the sand was firm, his breathing in tune with his legs. Approaching his three-mile turn-around rock, he saw a lone female figure up ahead. Tamryn. He would have to stop and talk to his new employee for a minute. He waved in greeting.

Tamryn waved back and approached him yelling, "You don't have to stop!" She grinned at her boss.

"I was just about to turn around and slow down. How are you today? Yesterday was good, no?" He returned her grin.

"Yesterday was great. I can hardly wait for Monday." She tried to control her wind-blown black curly hair, to no avail.

"Don't wish for work when you have a weekend off," he laughed. "Let Rudy and Walt take over for a couple of days. And, has no one told you that you need to wear a cap when you're walking on this beach?"

"Is it always windy?"

"Yes, ma'am, I'm sorry to tell you, but it is almost always windy. The degree just varies. What are you doing the rest of today?"

"I thought I would go down to Old Town and check out all the shops. You know, go in each one and see what's up. I need some stuff to fully settle in my new place. What are you and Fern doing today?"

He frowned. "Well, just between us, Fern's boss is flying in from D.C., and she has to work today. She just left for Buck Bay."

"What's up with that?"

"No idea. She said that Joe was guarded on the phone and told her he'd fill her in later. I don't like it."

"No, I can understand why." Tamryn looked out to sea. "Why would he come here now when things are quiet?"

"I guess I'll know when she gets home. In the meantime, I'm going fishing with the boys this afternoon. See you around."

Matt turned to head back home, but stopped and said over his shoulder,

"Tell the shops who you are, or everyone in town will go nuts trying to figure you out."

Tamryn bent over laughing, slapped her thighs, and waved him goodbye. She, too, turned around and headed south to her house, following the surf line until she spotted the big log embedded in the sand. That was her landmark that indicated the skinny path to her deck was just beyond and up through the low, shrubby vegetation that separated her house from the beach.

As she turned away from the surf, something up at her house caught her eye. Some kind of movement, or something glinting off the sliding glass doors to her deck. She put her hands up to shield her eyes from the sunshine and squinted at the house. Nothing. *Must have been the sun on the glass*, she thought.

z

CHAPTER 7

Saturday, February 24, 2024 — Cold Rock Island

Bernice went about her business, taking fingerprints from all of the island's residents. All except for Rohn Reid and his two sons, Rick and Randy, who continued to object. Bernice, unusual for her, had backed down in deference to the Secretary of State, who took her aside and said, "It's not like we can't find Rohn later if we truly need to."

She had to agree with that. A man as famous as Reid would be easy to find, and she couldn't really see why he or his family would want to call attention to their private island by killing Matsuda here and then reporting it to the U.S. State Department. So, she collected prints from the other residents, who were all cooperative. They didn't like being printed, but nobody does. Only Moira, the cook, and Aaron, the handyman, seemed to understand the potential benefit of being ruled out quickly.

After the fingerprints were carefully stored, Bernice asked Fern to help her take some samples from the island's flora.

"Why are we doing this?" Fern asked her. She bagged some seeds from a plant near the hangar, while Bernice scooped up a cup of mud from a puddle formed during last night's rain. "I think I know but I want you to tell me."

"If it's murder, and our killer is a resident of this island, we won't need these," Bernice explained. "But if your investigation goes another direction, it might help me recognize if an accused person was here at the homicide location. This island's flora might be unique."

"Gotcha," said Fern.

Later, Joe and Fern accompanied Bernice to the Coast Guard ship and made plans to talk tomorrow. The Secretary of State and his security detail were already on board, and Captain Adams prepared to launch. Bernice had alerted her team at the hospital that they were bringing a body and instructed them to meet the Resolve at Buck Bay port.

A grim-looking Fred shook hands with both Joe and Fern, and his only words addressed to the two were, "Figure out what happened here."

• • •

Back at Reid's house, Lynette showed Joe and Fern to the guest house, and both went to their respective rooms to call their spouses.

Fern was relieved when Matt answered his phone because she knew he'd gone fishing with the guys.

"Wait a sec," he answered, and Fern could hear him move to a spot out of earshot of Jay and Ed. "OK, I'm here."

"Thanks for picking up," Fern said. "Are you on the river?"

"Yes, but we're about ready to leave. Almost caught our limit. How about you? Where are you?"

"I'm on Cold Rock Island about thirty minutes by ship off the coast of Port Stirling. And I'm the guest of billionaire Rohn Reid."

"Huh?"

"Yeah, and it gets weirder. There's been a homicide, we think. Could be suicide, but I don't think so. Bernice came with us at Joe's request, and she has custody of the body and is headed home."

"I have more questions than you probably have time! Who's the victim? Can you tell me that?"

"Yes. Joe wanted me to call you. We're going to need your help. The victim is a retired Japanese military admiral who was stationed on this island when the U.S. government owned it. His name is Hiroshi Matsuda if you want to look him up after we hang up. He was identified by none other than Fred Leufeld."

"As in Secretary of State Leufeld? What the hell?"

"Told you it was weird. Fred, my new best friend, was stationed here with Matsuda decades ago, and they remained good buddies. Our resident billionaire called Fred when the body was found. He suspected it was Matsuda, and he knew the Secretary would want to know first. Are you following?"

"Think so, but this sure isn't what I thought you were going to report. How did he die?"

"Hanging. He was swinging from a beam in an airplane hangar on site."

"Good God. Are you alright?"

"I'm fine. Wish I'd brought a nightgown and a change of clothes in my suitcase instead of just my gun and official stuff, though."

"You're not telling me that you are spending the night there?"

"'Fraid so. Turns out that Fred wants Joe and I to head up the investigation. Fred is headed to Honolulu now to tell the family. Once they decide what to do, Bernice will perform the autopsy. Joe and I are to remain here and interrogate the island's residents and snoop around."

"Absolutely not," Matt said vehemently. "There's probably a killer on that island. Get on the CG ship now and come home. You can go back tomorrow in the daylight and do your job."

Fern paused. "The ship has already left for Buck Bay. Bernice is taking the body to the morgue, and the Secretary's plane is meeting him to fly to Honolulu tonight."

"You're stranded there?" Incredulous voice.

"Well, not technically. Rohn Reid has a rather substantial yacht moored, and there is a beautiful Gulfstream airplane in the hangar. But for tonight, yes, Joe and I have been instructed to do our jobs. It's the Secretary of State, Matt, I had no choice. I would've looked like a complete wimp."

Matt's turn to pause. "I get it, but I sure as hell don't like it. How secure do you feel?"

Fern checked out her surroundings. "There's a lock on my door, and the windows seem secure. I've got my gun. Joe is next door, and he's got his gun, too. If Rohn Reid doesn't poison us at dinner, I think I'm good."

"So not funny, wife. Put a chair under your doorknob. And don't drink too much at dinner." Matt knew his wife liked her Chardonnay. "When do you think you'll be home?"

"Captain Bob Adams is coming back midday tomorrow to pick up Joe and me. We'll have talked to everyone on the island by then — there's only eight men and two women. It shouldn't take long."

"Do you trust your host? He's rather eccentric, I've heard."

"He's an odd one, no doubt. But he's very private, and Bernice and I can't figure out why he'd kill Matsuda here and expose his private island getaway to public scrutiny. But I'm going to grill him, for sure. I don't care if he is one of the richest men in the world. This whole thing stinks."

"I want to say, be careful, my love," Matt said haltingly.

"Don't. You know I will be. I love you."

"I love you back."

• • •

"Was that Fern?" Jay asked Matt when he came back down to the river. "What's my favorite redhead doing today?"

"She's working."

"Can you tell us on what?" Ed asked. Both Jay and Ed knew the truth about Fern's real job, but they understood that they might not always be in the loop, even though the two cops were close friends with both Matt and Fern. At twenty-nine years old, Jay was Port Stirling PD's senior detective in rank, if not in age. He'd filled in admirably for Matt during last year's troubles and was the chief's right-hand man now that Fern had moved on to the State Department. Jay had a knack for the obscure details of a case that often led to progress.

Big Ed Sonders was the area representative for the Oregon State Police, and the lieutenant had worked this region for almost twenty-five years. Everyone in town knew gangly, home-grown Jay, and tall, barrel-chested Ed, and also knew they were lucky to have such smart professional cops on the beat. Good friends before Matt had last year's personal distress, Jay and Ed would now be his best friends forever. In fact, he now thought of them as more like his brothers — one younger, and one older — than just colleagues.

"Well, Fern did say that she and Joe were going to need our help, so I guess I can share the basics until she gets home tomorrow and fills us in. Turns out there is a secret island about thirty minutes from Port Stirling out in the Pacific. She's there now with the Coast Guard and the State Department. There's been a homicide, and apparently the victim is some military hotshot. From Japan. Found hanging."

"Do you mean Cold Rock Island?" asked Ed.

"You know it?"

"Vaguely. It's not a huge secret to some of us who have been here since the Stone Age. The government used to own it, but they sold it to some rich guy years ago."

"Rohn Reid," said Matt. "The billionaire owns it now."

"Yeah, that's the guy," Ed said.

"How come I don't know this?" Jay asked.

Ed shrugged. "No reason to, I guess. I've just stored that info up here"—pointing to his head—"with all the other mostly useless stuff I know."

"Your useless stuff may come in handy this time," laughed Matt. "What did the government do with the island?"

"Don't know," replied Ed. "The function was kept secret. We always assumed it was some sort of military base, probably to keep tabs on the Chinese and North Koreans. Some of the local fishermen told tales of scary-looking fighter jets landing and taking off regularly. I wonder what Rohn Reid does with the island now."

"Fern didn't go into much detail, but it sounds like he uses it for a private getaway. There are only a few people there now, family and caretakers."

"So how did a Japanese guy get himself hung?" Jay asked.

"It appears that's what we're going to find out," Matt said. He sounded subdued, which his mates picked up on.

"You and Fern were probably hoping for a quiet period, huh?" asked Ed. "Millie and I were, too. She wants to go on a cruise."

"I wouldn't book it just yet," Matt said wryly.

Ed shook his head. "In all honesty, can you see me on a cruise anyway?"

Matt and Jay looked at each other and laughed. "No, we cannot," they answered in unison.

• • •

Saturday, February 24, 2024 — Cold Rock Island

Lynette, Rohn Reid's young housekeeper, knocked on Fern's bedroom door. Cautiously, Fern opened the door a crack. "Yes?" she said.

Lynette smiled and said, "Mr. Reid sent me to make sure you find the closet with women's clothes you can borrow while you're here if you like. There's also every toiletry you will need in the bathroom."

"That's very thoughtful," Fern said. "Thank you. I was just thinking about how I should have planned ahead better for tomorrow. I didn't see the closet."

"No one ever does see it. I'll show you," Lynette said, coming into the room. Before Fern could say anything, she was past her and moved toward the wall on her right. Near the corner, she pressed on a small, embossed black square at waist height, and, sure enough, a door sprung open revealing two long racks of clothes and some shelving with packaged underwear, tee shirts, and neatly-folded sweaters. Boots and outerwear jackets hung at the far end.

"Oh, my, Mr. Reid has thought of everything," Fern laughed.

"He wants his guests to be comfortable," Lynette said, smiling. "Is there anything else I can get you?"

"I'm not really a guest, and you don't need to wait on me."

"Maybe not, but you're important," Lynette said. She stood looking at Fern. "Imagine a woman having your job. I think you're very impressive."

"Thank you," Fern said to the younger woman. "I do have an important job, but it doesn't make me important. All I do is work hard and try to do the right thing. No different from what you do every day, too, I would guess. Right?"

Lynette thought about that. "I do work hard and try my best, but I'd never have the courage you do. To see that poor man hanging there." She shuddered.

"You might find you are braver than you think if you ever had to be. I've surprised myself on occasions when I just did what I had to do."

"Hope I never have to be. I'm a chicken."

Fern laughed. "No, you're not. You live out here in the middle of nowhere. That takes guts. And to answer your question, no, there's nothing further I need for now. I'll be talking to you and the others as soon as I freshen up a little, OK?"

Lynette nodded. "Mr. Reid said to tell you that dinner would be served at 7:30 p.m. in the dining room."

"Great. That will give Mr. Phelps and me time to interview most of you. Where is the dining room?"

"You know the living room you were in? Go back there, and then walk away from the windows and turn right. It's the next room on your right down the hallway, also facing the ocean."

"Got it. Thanks, Lynette. See you soon."

CHAPTER 8

Tuesday, December 12, 2023 — Honolulu

S *huji has a problem*, thought Hiroshi Matsuda, closing the lid on his laptop. He sat there for a few minutes, staring out his lone office window. After spending several hours going through his son's bank's backdoor internal system, he began tracing a second email address for one of Shuji's fellow vice-presidents that he came across almost by accident.

The message he found contained some sort of code among the text, and he didn't have time right now to navigate, but, on the surface, it looked to Hiroshi that the VP might be running a separate cryptocurrency operation. While he knew there was no prohibition for banks to serve companies in the crypto space, Hiroshi thought this guy's operation seemed separate and that he was trying to hide it. *Risky business if you ask me. What if he is personally holding crypto codes for their customers' digital assets, and hiding it from his managers and the regulators?*

The VP in question had not been on the list of managers who'd received the threatening emails; Hiroshi had followed a thread between him and a female manager who had reported getting one. He had forwarded her message to himself at the different email address, which struck Hiroshi as odd. And from there, he'd gone down the rabbit hole.

He checked his watch and realized it was almost time to go pick up Naomi. He quickly reached for his phone and placed a call to Shuji. He expected to get voicemail because he knew his son would either still be on the plane or in his first meeting, but he wanted to leave him a message. *Voicemail, as expected.* "Hi, it's dad," he said. "No hurry, but please give me a call when you can. I may have found something you might want to know. And, you should delete this voicemail after you get it."

• • •

Saturday, February 24, 2024 — Cold Rock Island

"Did you get ahold of Matt?" Joe asked Fern on his cell phone.

"Yes, I told him what was going on. Just a quick overview. He's prepared to meet us in Buck Bay tomorrow when we get back."

"Did you think to ask him to attend the post-mortem with Bernice?"

"Shoot — I didn't think of that," Fern said. "I'll text him. He'll probably get in touch with her anyway."

"Please do that. I'm coming to your room if you're ready."

"I'm ready. Jotting a list of my questions to ask the residents. Come over. Let's get organized and strategize."

The two State Department employees compared their list of questions for all ten of the island's residents; they were almost identical. "Who do you want to start with?" Fern asked her boss. She rested her arm on a big, fluffy purple pillow on the ivory sofa in her room, while Joe took the purple and gray print armchair opposite her. A low cocktail table sat between them with two Diet Cokes from her room's minifridge.

"We need to respect that Rohn owns the place. We started with him, but we both have additional questions for him," Joe said, comparing their two lists.

"Agree." She scratched her nose with her pen. "I'm having trouble believing that Hiroshi somehow landed on this island without Rohn knowing it. I'd like to quiz him further on that issue."

"Me too. And we need details from Tyson about how their so-called security works. Does he make rounds? Regular times? Just the dock and runway areas or the entire island?"

"Might be a good idea to interrogate Rohn and Tyson together on this question. See if he tells his boss the same thing. If I were Rohn, I'd like to hear his answers."

"Good point. We might be able to tell by Rohn's reaction if he believes his guy or not."

"OK," Fern said. "Let's get them in the room together and pursue this line of questioning first. You should kick it off because you're the boss and I suspect that will carry more water with Rohn. Even though I'm a killer." She grinned.

Joe looked up from his list and eyed her. "Does the fact that you can laugh about it now mean you're moving on from the Phineas Stuart case?"

Fern looked pensive. "I wouldn't say I've moved on completely. But when I had Matt's hitman in my sights last year and I didn't pull the trigger, that told me that I'm not a killer at heart. I really wanted to kill him, but whatever that thing is inside us that guides us to the right decision, I know I have it. I'll always do what I have to do in my line of work, Joe, but I'm not a bloodthirsty human being."

"I know you're not. We all know you're not. And I'm glad to hear you've come to that conclusion, too. I have really good judgment when it comes to people, and I knew who you were before I hired you." He took a drink of his Coke. "And the sooner men like Rohn Reid understand that women like you will someday rule the world, the better for all of us. So, you take over the questioning from the get-go, and I'll sit there and nod like a dope."

"You're sure?"

"Positive. I run spies, Fern. I don't have the cop mentality that's a huge part of your makeup. I'll interject if I think of anything you haven't covered, but I'd be surprised if that happened. If we end up with a suspect who you believe is trying to do damage to the Japanese or U.S. governments, I'll step in where I have to."

"It might very well turn out to be an espionage case," she said. "Why else would he have been wearing a uniform? That's really bothering me. If he snuck onto the island like our host has indicated, why would he be wearing that? If you didn't want to be discovered, wouldn't you pull up to the hidden beach that Fred said Matsuda knew about in a dinghy wearing sea-worthy clothing? Or jeans?"

"The uniform bothers me, too. Sneaking on to this rock dressed like that doesn't add up. Do you think Rohn is lying about knowing he was here? And, if so, *why* would he lie about it?"

"That seems the central question to me," Fern said. "But he seemed sincere about being surprised, didn't he? Am I reading him all wrong?"

"We don't want Rohn Reid to be lying to us," Joe smiled. "It complicates matters even more than they already are. But knowing that, I still agree with you—he seemed genuine. He was forthright in his response to us, and I didn't get a hit that he was hiding anything."

"How do you feel about him not wanting to be fingerprinted?"

"To quote my teenage son, it sucks. But in these paranoia days, lots of people, especially celebrities, don't trust our government to protect their information. I don't think his reluctance necessarily makes him a murderer. But if Bernice thinks we need his prints, I'll run interference with Fred Leufeld, and we'll make it happen. Hopefully, our investigation won't come to that."

"Is there anything else bothering you that's not a question on one of our lists?" Fern asked.

"Maybe one thing," Joe said, and he leaned forward, resting his arms on his thighs and clasping his hands. "Why didn't Matsuda's wife report him missing earlier?"

Fern thought. "Well, putting myself in her shoes, being married to a man who has held positions of importance and has a demanding job, I would have assumed that he was busy with something and knew what he was doing. That he would call me as soon as he could. I probably would have been a little bit worried, but not enough to call the authorities. This was a man with a military career; she was likely used to his absence."

"Still…" Joe said.

"You should call the Secretary of State then if you feel that way. Tell Fred to ask her that question. I think I understand her reasoning, but it's a valid question. Poor woman," she said, wiping a small getaway tear from her cheek. "Let's go do this, boss."

As they moved from the guest house through the covered walkway toward the main house, Fern and Joe discussed how they wanted talks to unfold. Occasionally, their voices were drowned out by the increasingly vexed, mountainous seas as they hit the jagged rocks of Cold Rock Island, accompanied by a barking wind.

Fern smoothed her hair, and they entered the living room of the house and found Rohn Reid and his cook Moira having a cup of coffee and chatting. She stood to go the minute she saw Fern and Joe.

Fern said, "Hi, Moira. Could you find Tyson and ask him to join us? We'll talk to Mr. Reid and Tyson first. Is that OK with you?"

"Doesn't matter what I want," Moira said with an edge. "You're the lady in charge. I'll fetch Tyson."

"Thank you," Fern said. She gave Moira a smile, but the cook had already turned to leave the room.

Rohn Reid gestured to the club chairs opposite him. "Please, make yourselves comfortable," he said to Joe. "Why do you want Tyson?"

"We have questions about your island security," Fern said, moving Reid's gaze from Joe to her. "We'd like to discuss it with both of you."

"Tyson's your guy then. I leave it all to him."

"The thing we find most puzzling is why Hiroshi Matsuda was here on your island," Fern said. "Do you have any idea what might have brought him here?"

"I really don't," said Reid. "It's so strange. Someone like him would know how to reach my people and arrange a visit. There was no warning he was coming at all."

"It is strange," Fern agreed. "How do you think he landed here without being seen?"

"No ideas there either. Like I said, Tyson is the man to answer that question. He's taking this personally because we've never had a security breach before…or, obviously, anything like this happening."

"I am taking it personally," Tyson said, entering the room. He had cleaned up some. Still wearing jeans, but a nice dress shirt was tucked into them now, replacing the hoodie. His curly hair looked slightly wet on top, and Fern guessed he'd taken a shower. "You wanted to see me?" He took a seat in one of the three empty armchairs, closer to Reid than to Fern and Joe.

"Yes, thanks for coming," Fern said. "We're all puzzled over how Mr. Matsuda arrived on the island. What are your thoughts?"

"A dang puzzle is what it is," Tyson said forcefully. His muscled arms rested on the armchair, but his fists were clenched. In classic marking his territory mode, his feet were firmly planted on the floor and his knees were spread wide apart. "There have been no boats or ships of any size at the dock for over a week. We watch it carefully."

"So, you're sure of that?" Fern asked.

"Dead sure." Tyson paled slightly when he realized that probably wasn't the best thing to say under the circumstances. "I mean, yeah, I'm positive. No boats at the dock."

"And, even more obvious, I'm guessing, no planes have landed either?" Fern said, turning it into a question.

"Nope." He paused. "The only possibility is that he landed a small boat somewhere on the other side of the island."

"Could he have parachuted onto the island?" Fern asked. "You haven't found any canopies or fabric?"

Tyson shook his head. "Nope, nothing. We make rounds over there on occasion, but we don't watch that side like we do this one. There's no real road over there, it's more like a path, and I never thought someone would sneak on that way." He looked over at Rohn. "I'm sorry, Mr. Reid. I let you down."

"It is a security fail," Rohn said. His voice was flat. "But if Matsuda came here with the intention of killing himself where he'd served so many years of his distinguished career, I imagine that nothing would have stopped him."

"You believe that's why he died here?" asked Fern.

"Nothing else makes any sense, does it?" He stared at her.

"Not so far," she said, "but we're just beginning our investigation." She turned back to Tyson. "When you say you 'make rounds' as part of your security process, does that mean you have set times to check on different island locations?"

"I wouldn't say they are set times," he said hesitantly. "But, yeah, we have a kind of rotation, I guess."

"Tell me about that," Fern said.

"Well, we take the golf carts around—all three of us, me, Noah, and Aaron—and we go to the dock, the runway, the hangars, inside and outside, and then we run up and down the roads. Oh, and we also check the locks on the other buildings that aren't in use."

"Did you go to the north side of the island at all this week?" Fern asked. "Thursday or Friday? Is there much over there?"

"Not really," Tyson answered. "It's undeveloped, like I told you, with just that rough path that leads up from the one small beach. Aaron goes over there the most—he likes that beach—but I don't think he was there on Thursday or Friday. I'll ask him."

"No, that's OK," Fern said hurriedly. "We'll talk to him later. When is the last time you personally were at that beach?"

He thought. "Probably not for a couple of weeks, at least."

"So, you did not see Hiroshi Matsuda land a small craft there, and kill him?" Fern asked in a calm, cool voice.

Tyson flinched and leaned back away from her. "No, ma'am."

She expected Rohn to come to the defense of his security chief and put her in her place, but he did not. He sat silently.

"When, exactly, did you first see Mr. Matsuda on this island?" she continued.

Tyson looked nervously at Rohn. "It was yesterday afternoon about one o'clock when I went to the airplane hangar to check on Mr. Reid's plane. Like I told you," he said to Reid. "I saw him hanging there and came straight here to tell you."

"When was the last time you were in that hangar prior to yesterday at one o'clock?" asked Fern.

"It was the day before. I check on the plane every day."

"So, you were inside the hangar on Thursday? What time was that?"

"About the same time. Probably about noon."

"Did anything look different on Thursday?" she asked. "Anything out of place? Door or windows left open? Lights on? Anything weird?"

"Not that I recall," Tyson said. "It looked like it always looks."

"Where was the ladder that was under Mr. Matsuda's body today?"

Tyson thought for a minute. "Yeah, it was where it always is, in that far corner but closer to the plane. I use it to wash the plane after Mr. Reid arrives, and then again when he's leaving."

"Is the plane locked when not in use?" Joe asked, speaking for the first time.

"No, not usually," Tyson answered. "We keep the mobile staircase up to the door in case Lynette wants to go in to clean it."

"In the future," Rohn spoke to Tyson, "we might want to keep it locked. Or, at least, lock the hangar every night."

"Yes, we can do that," Tyson said. "It just never seemed necessary. Until now, I guess."

• • •

Saturday, February 24, 2024 — Port Stirling, Oregon

Tamryn stepped onto her deck from the beach path and turned to look one last time at the glorious, rambunctious surf with the sunshine sparkling on the sapphire blue water before she entered her house. She wanted a hot shower and breakfast, and then planned to head to downtown Port Stirling and have her day's adventure exploring the shops and getting to know some of the residents in her new hometown. She removed her sandy shoes, slapped them together twice to knock off the loose sand, and left them on the deck.

Moving quickly to her bedroom, she shed her jacket in the hall closet on the way. The overhead light was on in her bedroom. *Funny, I don't remember turning that on*, she thought. She dropped her sweatpants, jersey turtleneck, and socks in the laundry hamper inside her closet and turned to go to the bathroom.

The force of the fist to her face knocked her to the floor. Barely conscious and seeing stars, Tamryn was unable to get up. In the swimming haze, she could make out her husband—soon to be ex-husband, Barry—straddling her body on the floor.

"Did you think you could hide from me?" he snarled, leaning over her, and moving his face close to hers. She could feel his spittle on her cheek, and tried to move it away with her hand, but he stepped on her arm, pinning it to the floor. "That you could humiliate me? What kind of man would I be if I let my wife leave me? Answer that, bitch!" He stomped his foot into her stomach, and she curled up in pain.

"I'm sssorry," she stammered.

"What's that? I can't hear you."

She was unable to speak, which seemed to enrage him further. He kicked her in the ribs, and the right side of her body exploded in agony.

"You will NOT divorce me, do you understand?" he yelled. "I will NOT allow it, and I will track you down again. If you think you can run away, you can't."

Tamryn tried again to speak, but the words wouldn't come out. Only a desperate moan escaped her lips. He kicked her in the head, and the lights went out.

CHAPTER 9

Saturday, February 24, 2024 — Cold Rock Island

Fern and Joe wrapped up their interview with Rohn and Tyson. Essentially, they had no idea when Hiroshi Matsuda arrived on the island, how and where he arrived, or why he had come there. No one had heard anything or seen him until yesterday afternoon when they found him hanging. Tyson hadn't met Matsuda previously. Rohn did meet him briefly during the negotiations when he purchased the island, but that was decades ago and the memory had faded. His previous knowledge of Matsuda was primarily because of his friendship with Fred Leufeld, and because of his role in the history of the island.

Fern turned the page in her notebook while she waited for Aaron and Noah, Tyson's security and maintenance employees, to arrive. Tyson had texted them, "your turn", and then with Fern's permission left the room.

Joe Phelps told Rohn it was OK if he left now, too, but Reid elected to stay. Fern would have preferred that Rohn not be present during their next interrogation, but her polite add-on to Joe's comment was met with the same reaction. He was staying.

The two workers came into the room still in their work clothes — jeans, tee-shirts, and flannel shirts over them. Noah, the taller of the two, was also wearing a sleeveless black vest zipped up. Neither man was as good-looking as broad-shouldered, square-jawed Tyson, their boss, and they looked extremely uncomfortable and out of place in this room.

Fern felt sorry for them. She knew one or both could be killers, but they looked so pathetic, her heart went out to them.

"Take a seat, gentlemen," she said in a friendly tone. "This won't take long, and there's nothing to be afraid of."

They visibly relaxed.

"Please tell me your full name, and a little about yourself," she said. "Aaron, why don't you go first."

"Aaron Rogers, and I'm the maintenance man. I fix everything that goes wrong," he said, in a stilted voice. He sat up razor straight, and his hands were rubbing his thighs.

Fern smiled. "Like the football player?"

Aaron returned her smile. "No. Mine is r-o-g-e-r-s, no 'd' in it. But people make that mistake all the time." He looked nothing like Aaron Rodgers, Fern thought. This Aaron was clean-shaven with blond, pointy hair, slight build, and looked about twelve years old.

"How long have you worked on Mr. Reid's island?" she asked.

"Tyson hired me about two years ago. I live here full-time. I love it here," he added. "I'm not that great with people."

"I think you're fine with people," Fern told him. "How old are you and where are you from originally?"

"Twenty-six, and Seattle."

"Can you fill us in on your primary duties here?"

Aaron did, and he became animated talking about his work. He wasn't fooling; he did love it here.

"When was the first time you saw Hiroshi Matsuda, the man hanging from the beam in the hangar?" Fern asked.

"When Tyson told me to come and look at him yesterday," Aaron answered.

"And what time was that?"

Aaron looked at Noah. "I don't know for sure. About noon, I think."

Noah shrugged.

So, Tyson had told his guys before he went to Rohn Reid, Fern thought. She and Joe exchanged glances.

"Was anyone else with Tyson and you when you discovered the body?" asked Fern.

"No, Noah was asleep. He had the night shift on Thursday night. Just me and Ty."

"What was your reaction?"

Aaron ran a hand through his spiked hair. "I'm not afraid to admit it. I was scared. I've never seen a dead body before. Well, except for my grandma, and she was laid out to look normal. This one was spooky. Just hanging there."

"I can imagine you were afraid, Aaron. Anyone would've been. What did you do?"

"Ty asked me to go wake up Noah, so that's what I did."

"What did Tyson do then?"

"I don't know for sure. Just waited for me and Noah, I guess. He said he was going to talk to Mr. Reid, but he wanted to talk to Noah first to see if he knew anything."

"And did you know anything, Noah?" Fern asked. Noah had been sitting quietly, his hands clasped on his lap. He looked older than Aaron, but not by much. Noah was stockier, with lank brown hair that he now pushed out of his eyes.

"I was out," Noah answered. "I came off my shift at 6:00 a.m. and was sound asleep when Aaron woke me up."

"And what time was that?"

"Like Aaron said, about noon, I think. Maybe a little after."

"Tell me about yourself," Fern said.

"Name's Noah Stricker, and I'm from Seattle, too." Asked and answered, and then he buttoned up, and it was clear to Fern that she would have to drag information out of him.

"How old are you, and how did you end up working here?" she asked.

"I turn twenty-seven tomorrow. Aaron and I both worked with Tyson at Amazon."

"Happy birthday," Fern said. She smiled at Noah. He gave her a slight nod. "Tell me about your Thursday night shift," she said. "Anything strange happen? Unusual?"

"No. I would've reported it," he said defensively. "It was all quiet."

"What was the weather like?" asked Fern.

"Pretty crappy. Stormy around midnight—windy, rainy—and then it got real foggy."

"So, poor visibility?"

"Yeah. I had the windshield wipers running non-stop on my golf cart."

"Did you go down to the dock?"

"Yeah. Several times. That's mainly where I watch on night shift. It's the most likely spot for someone to come ashore."

"And did you see anyone?"

"No. As I said, all quiet. Except for some pretty big, nasty waves hitting the dock."

"Did you go inside the hangar where we found Mr. Matsuda?"

Noah hesitated. Just a nano-second too long, and Fern thought, *he's going to lie to me.*

"I did."

"When and how many times?" Fern asked.

"Only one time. Early in my shift."

"Can you be more specific, please?"

"I'm not sure what time it was."

"Guess," Fern said impatiently.

"Probably before midnight."

"And you didn't return to the hangar until Aaron woke you on Friday? Is that correct?"

"Well, I drove by it again later, but I didn't go inside."

"What time was that?"

"Maybe 2:00 a.m. Ish."

"Did you see or hear anything on that visit?" *Like pulling teeth*, Fern thought.

"No. It was quiet."

"Was it too foggy to see?" she asked.

"Yeah. Maybe."

"Was it too foggy to see if any boats had moored at the dock from where you looked?"

"No, I drove my cart onto the dock a couple of times. Nothing there. The ocean was too rough for a boat to dock. I'm sure about that."

"Thank you, Noah," Fern said. "It appears, then, that Mr. Matsuda killed himself or was placed in the hangar sometime between midnight Thursday and noon Friday. Does that sound right to the two of you?"

Aaron and Noah nodded in unison.

"Did either one of you have a reason to want Hiroshi Matsuda dead?" she asked, staring each one down in turn.

"We never knew him," Noah said. He was belligerent. "Why would we want him dead?"

"Yeah," Aaron said. "We don't know anything about this. All we know is the guy was dead in our hangar." He looked pleadingly at Fern. "You're not going to try to pin this on me, are you? I didn't have anything to do with it!"

"We follow the evidence, Aaron," Fern said calmly. "If you had nothing to do with it, you shouldn't worry."

"I didn't, I swear. I love my job here. Please don't screw it up for me."

For a horrible moment, Fern thought he was going to cry. But he pulled himself together. She stood up. "OK, guys, that's all for now," she said. They both nearly leaped out of their chairs and started for the door. "We'll see if the medical examiner can pinpoint the time of death in her post-mortem exam to what you've established here, and then our investigation will proceed from there. Thanks for your time."

"How close can the medical examiner come to the actual time of death?" Rohn Reid asked.

Joe Phelps looked at Reid and spoke before Fern could answer. "It depends. It's not an exact science, but Bernice has been close on previous homicides. Isn't that right, Fern?"

Fern got the hint. *Be vague but give them all something to worry about.* "Yes, that's correct, Joe. Bernice has nailed it on several deaths we've worked on together. But each case is, of course, different." She smiled pleasantly at Rohn. He looked uneasy.

* * *

Up next were Reid's two sons, the twins Rick and Randy. Again, Rohn Reid did not make a move to leave the room during their interrogation, and Fern knew it was useless to suggest. They took the two chairs closest to their father.

"OK, I'm lost," Fern laughed. "Who is Rick and who is Randy?"

The young man on the left wearing the navy sweater said, "I'm Rick. The oldest by twenty minutes."

"That must make you Randy," she said looking to the other twin.

"Correct," he said.

"Are Rick and Randy your full names?" she asked.

Rick answered first again. "No, my name is Richard Reid, and my brother is Randolph Reid. But we've gone by Rick and Randy for as long as I can remember."

They really were identical, Fern thought. But as Rick continued to speak, she noticed a slight difference in the way their mouths looked; Randy's turned up just a smidge more at the corners than Rick's did. And their dress set them apart somewhat, with Rick looking tidier and more coordinated than the more casual Randy. But both were the same height and build — about six feet three inches and skinny. *Clearly they take after their mother more than dumpling dad*, she thought. Fern knew that Mrs. Reid had been a slim, successful fashion model before she married Rohn, and those genes appeared in her two sons. Each twin had killer-sharp cheekbones in well-defined faces, which made them arrestingly handsome. Couple their looks with choosing their parents well from a financial perspective, Fern suspected that the twins did well with women. And probably in life, as well.

What was freakiest to her was that both men had medium brown hair worn on the long side, and each had one stray lock that slanted the exact same way on his forehead. And, during the course of their interrogation, each had brushed the lock back with their left hand in an identical fashion. It was all Fern could do to keep from laughing.

"What is your age?" she asked.

"Twenty-nine," Rick answered for both of them.

"When did you arrive on the island?" Fern asked.

Rohn started to say, "I already told…," but Fern held her hand up firmly, and said, "These questions are for your sons, Mr. Reid."

He shut up, but he didn't look happy about it.

Randy looked over at his dad, and Rohn nodded, almost imperceptibly.

"We got here the day after the Super Bowl," Randy said.

"Came with dad on the plane," Rick added.

"Do you come here often?" Joe asked, his first question.

"Depends on what you mean by often," Randy said.

"Let me rephrase," Joe said. "How many times have you been on your island in the past twelve months?"

The twins looked at each other. "Probably about five or six times," Randy said. "Does that sound right to you?"

"Yes, that's about right," agreed Rick.

Do they do everything together? Fern thought. *Odd at their age, even for twins.* "That's fairly frequent," she said. "Where do you consider home?"

"Oh, Seattle, definitely," Randy answered quickly. "That's where we were born, and we share an apartment downtown."

"You live together? Please tell me that address," Fern said, pen poised.

"It's 1101 Spring Street," said Randy.

"The penthouse," added Rick. "Plenty of room for both of us."

Of course, thought Fern. *Nothing but the best for Rohn Reid's kids.*

"Sounds nice," she said. "Why come here so often with a great place like that as home?"

The twins looked at each other again.

"It's relaxing," said Rick, finally. "You know, an escape from the daily grind."

"What is your daily grind?" Fern asked. "Do you work?"

"Sure. We both work in dad's company. I work in Marketing and Randy works in IT."

"Pretty liberal paid time off policy?"

The twins laughed, and so did their father.

"We try to not abuse our time off, but he is the boss." Rick pointed at Rohn. "Plus, we do work remotely a lot."

"I noticed my cell phone and Wi-Fi work well here," Joe said, looking at Rohn. "Is the island tricked out technology-wise?"

"It has been my life's work, so, yes," Rohn said flatly.

Fern turned her attention back to the sons. "What were the two of you doing Thursday night? And do you have rooms in this house?"

"Yes," Rick answered. "We each have quarters in the west wing; small apartments really. Dad is on the opposite end, east wing. Thursday night we were all doing what we normally do at night here—watch a movie and drink a couple of beers."

"Where does this happen?" she asked.

Randy pointed over his head behind him. "Other side of the hall. That's our screening room."

"Who is 'all'?"

Randy again. "Dad, Rick, and me."

"Were any of your help here in the house?"

"Nope," said Rick. "At least, not for the whole night. Moira brought us all some pie and ice cream right after we started our movie, and then she left for her room. She reads and doesn't like our taste in movies." That brought a smile to the three Reid men.

"What did you watch?" Fern asked.

"Quantum of Solace," Rick said. Seeing the blank look on Fern's face, he added, "James Bond. Daniel Craig. It's our favorite, but no one else liked it." He laughed.

"We like the name of it," Rohn chipped in.

"Ok, if you say so," smiled Fern. "Is Moira's room in this house? Anyone else sleep here other than the three of you?"

"No, family only in this house," said Rohn. "Leonard, Moira, and Lynette have suites at the opposite end of the guest house where you're staying. Moira's connects to the kitchen with a breezeway, and Lynette and Leonard are just beyond. Tyson, Simon, Aaron, and Noah have private rooms in what used to be military barracks in what we call Building 3."

"Where is that building?" Joe asked.

"It's the two-story one closest to this house...before you get to the airplane hangar."

"Back to Thursday night for a sec," Fern said. "How late did your movie run? What time did you go to bed?"

"I watched the end of the movie," Rohn said first, "and went directly to bed when it was over, about 11:15 p.m."

"Do you read in bed or go right to sleep?" she asked.

"I usually read some light fiction for a short while, but I think I went right to sleep Thursday night."

"What about you guys?" Fern said to the twins.

"We stayed up a little longer than dad," Randy said. "We started watching a WWE event."

"It was hilarious," said Rick.

"That's wrestling, right?" asked Fern.

"Sort of," Rick laughed.

"So, what time did you turn in?"

The twins looked at each other. They did that a lot.

"I'd say it was about midnight," Rick said. "Not later than that, I don't think."

"Yeah, about then," said Randy.

"Did you hear anything outside the house?" Fern asked. "A plane, a boat, any yells?"

"No," they said simultaneously. "But we had the TV on," added Randy.

"What about when you went to bed? And this question is for all three of you."

"I didn't hear a thing except the ocean," said Rohn. "It was very dark, foggy, and quiet except for some crashing waves. Fairly stormy that night as I recall."

"Do you sleep with your window open or closed?"

"Closed. The surf and the wind can get mighty loud some nights."

"Yeah, I didn't hear anything either," Rick said. "But I conk out easily. Especially after a beer."

"My room is closest to the runway," Randy said, "and I would hear a plane land no matter how many beers I'd had." He smiled a dazzling smile.

He really is handsome, thought Fern. "And you didn't hear one Thursday night?"

"Nope. Like dad said, it was a quiet night except for the storm. I'm afraid we can't help you." He made aggressive eye contact with Fern. *Is he daring me to challenge him further?*

CHAPTER 10

Saturday, February 24, 2024 — Cold Rock Island

Just as Fern and Joe were finishing up their questioning of the Reids, Simon, the landscaper, knocked at the open entrance to the living room.

"You must be Simon," Fern said. "Please come in." To Randy and Rick, she said, "Thanks, guys. Obviously, no one can leave the island just yet."

"We weren't planning to," Randy said. "Will we see you at dinner tonight?"

Fern looked at Joe, wondering if Lynette had told him the same thing as she'd told her. "Yes," Joe said, "your father has graciously invited us."

"Great," said Randy. "We promise to not make you watch a James Bond movie," he said to Fern.

"We're not here to watch movies," Fern said coolly.

Simon took a chair and looked expectantly at Fern and Joe. "I understand that you must question everyone on the island because of this unpleasantness," he said. His accent was upper-crust British. "I was hopeful I could go next. I have a phone call with a client at five o'clock I'd really prefer not to cancel."

Fern looked at her watch. Four-fifteen now. "Sure, that works. Have you heard the details of who we are and why we're here?" she said.

"I'm afraid so. Dreadful business."

"Yes, about as bad as it gets," Fern nodded. She eyed Simon. He was about forty-five, with thin, receding blond hair. Average height and build. He wore jeans and a denim shirt with a red handkerchief tied neatly around his neck. He looked like a gardener, but a jaunty one. His face was cheerful, and ruddy from being outdoors.

"Have you been on the island long?" she asked.

"Only since Wednesday. I've been on a new garden installation project in Los Angeles and thought I would pop over here and do some late winter cleanup before I returned home."

"And where is your home?" Joe asked. Fern thought something about Simon had piqued Joe's interest. She sat back in her chair.

"London. I know, I'm a long way from home," Simon said with a friendly smile. "I have clients all over the world, and I try to plan my travel accordingly." He looked at Rohn, still sitting in his chair as if his butt was glued to it. "Mr. Reid is flexible with my schedule, which I really appreciate."

"I need you more than you need me," Rohn said. "In this world, you have to know when to give people leeway. You get the job done — that's all that matters to me."

"Please tell us your full name, Simon, and your home address and cell phone number," Fern said.

"Certainly. Simon Marsons, and my home address is #30 Carlyle Square, London. That's in Chelsea." Fern thought he sounded smug, as if no one else in the room had a worthy address. "To reach me on my mobile phone, you must first dial the international code, which is 44. Then, I'm at 07-377-918-335."

"Thank you," Fern said, jotting notes. "When did you arrive here?"

Simon looked at Rohn. "It was Wednesday afternoon, wasn't it?"

"Yes," Rohn said. To Fern and Joe, "I lease a second plane that I keep in Palm Springs, and I sent it to L.A. to pick him up. I think they arrived back here about 3:00 p.m."

"That sounds correct," Simon nodded.

"What have you been doing since you arrived?" Joe asked.

"The usual. Pruning, especially the roses. Weeding, always," he giggled. "It never ends, of course. I'm also putting down some early spring lawn fertilizer and killing the crabgrass. I brought three new varieties of David

Austin roses with me from Los Angeles, and I planted those yesterday. And, in general, just tidying up."

"That seems more like regular maintenance than an in-demand garden designer would do," Fern noted.

"Mr. Reid compensates me well," he smiled. "And I started out as a landscape maintenance worker, and I still enjoy making sure my designs remain artful."

Fern gazed out the window. "It looks beautiful. Give me one secret for my garden in Port Stirling."

"The only consideration here is the wind," Simon answered. "It's probably your only issue on the coast of Oregon as well, I would imagine. The moisture and the sun here will grow anything, even some tropicals. But the wind is the enemy. I added the low walls at intervals to provide some protection, and I plant more tender things close to the house. We'll lose some plants on occasion due to the wind, but we make as comfy a home for them as we can."

"Where is your room?"

"I'm in the old barracks, building three, when I'm here." His smiley face while talking about plants had acquired a distasteful look. "I'm never here for more than a few days and I'm outside most of the time, so it's fine for me."

It's anything but fine for you, Mr. Fancy Pants, thought Fern. "You arrived on Wednesday. Can you walk me through what you did the next day, on Thursday?"

"I got right to work, shortly after sunrise, and kept going until after sunset," Simon reported. "I only stopped for meals."

"Where do you take your meals?"

"We have a nice, fully stocked kitchen in the barracks that I share with the workers, and Moira is kind to bring us food we can just grab from the fridge."

"What did you do Thursday night after your workday was finished?"

"I'm a reader, and Mr. Reid keeps a nice library on the island. I don't care much for TV, especially American programs. Sorry, Rohn," he smiled at his host.

"No offense taken," Rohn smiled back at his gardener. "Most of it is garbage these days."

"So, you read Thursday night?" Fern said, wanting to clarify for certain.

"Correct. I took a shower, ate my dinner, and had a couple of glasses of wine while I read."

"What are you reading while you're here?"

Simon fidgeted in his chair. "Oh, I have two or three books on my nightstand currently."

Joe scribbled a note.

Fern decided to leave the subject of Simon's reading material behind for now. She could tell that Joe would check his nightstand at his first opportunity.

"What time did you retire for the night?" she asked.

"It was about ten o'clock. I go to bed early and rise early. Always have. I attribute it to growing up on a farm in Sussex."

"Did you hear anything unusual Thursday night? Or see anything?"

"No, not really," Simon replied. "I may have heard Noah leaving our building after I got in bed, but that's not unusual. He works the night shift, you know. Otherwise, it was quiet except for the ocean's power. It's a lovely, calm sound to me, and I always sleep well when I'm here."

"Did you see anything, either inside your building or outside?" Joe asked, leaning in. "Do you have a window?"

"Yes, my room faces south, that's toward the dock. I always look out before I retire to see the moon, but it was foggy Thursday night, and I couldn't see a thing. The fog is beautiful in its own way, if not a little eerie, don't you think?" He stared at Joe.

"Considering what happened here, I guess so," Joe said quietly. And then, "Did you know Hiroshi Matsuda?"

"Actually, I did know him," Simon said. He twisted his hands, rubbing the right one with his left.

"I didn't know that," said Rohn Reid, quickly swiveling toward Simon, one eyebrow raised in surprise.

"Yes, I met him in Honolulu shortly after he retired there. He and his gorgeous wife, Naomi, hired me to design their garden. They bought into a ritzy enclave where I had another client whose garden turned out beautifully. Naomi wanted the same look for their property."

"Did you know him well?" Fern asked, also surprised at this news.

"Not really," Simon answered. "I mostly worked with Naomi. It was her project, and the mister just checked in occasionally to make sure I was on budget." He added, "He was a charming man. It's so awful." He looked down at his hands, seemed to realize that they were moving and silenced them in his lap.

"Did you see him on this island?"

"No."

"Did you see anyone on Thursday who does not belong here?"

"No."

"You didn't see any boats landing at the dock or anywhere else while you were outside working?" Fern persisted.

"No. Nothing. There was nothing but island, sky, and ocean. I wish I could help you, but I have nothing to add to your investigation. I'm sorry," he said. Fern thought he was sincere, but Joe kept staring at Simon. *Can't wait to hear what bug Joe has up his butt about Simon*, she thought.

• • •

Saturday, February 24, 2024 — Port Stirling, Oregon

Tamryn Gesicki awoke on her bathroom floor. She was on her back, eyes looking vacantly at the ceiling. A distinctive metallic smell hung in the air. *Blood. My blood.*

She tried to sit up, but the sharp pain in her abdomen and ribs made that idea not worth the effort. Instead, she brought her hand up to her face and gently probed. *Lip is cut, there's the blood.* She further explored. *Forehead is bleeding, too. Shit.*

Tamryn raised her head just enough to look out through her bedroom sliding doors to the deck. Only one eye seemed to be open. *Still daylight. Wonder how long I've been lying here?*

She knew she should roll over and attempt to get up, but her whole body was shaking, kind of a quivering she'd never experienced before, and she didn't trust it. *Is he still here?*

Too tired to care, she closed her eyes and went back to sleep.

CHAPTER 11

Saturday, February 24, 2024 — Cold Rock Island

Fern and Joe had finished up their initial interrogations of all the men except Leonard on the island by 5:30 p.m. Dusk was approaching, and it was decided that questioning of Leonard, and the two women, Moira the cook and Lynette the housekeeper, could wait until after they completed their work in the kitchen on dinner for all.

They walked back together to their guest quarters and discussed next moves, saving the lengthier talk of their thoughts on the interviews so far until later. Both of them had some phone calls to make now to keep the investigation moving on the mainland. They would compare notes after dinner.

Fern noted the thin orange and pinkish lines forming over the sea to the west. "Looks like it's going to be a nice sunset."

"Do you wish you were home with Matt to watch it?" Joe said.

"Yes," she answered honestly. "But I'm not, and I chose it."

"And I'm glad you did."

They didn't speak again, each going to their room to continue their work.

Joe was anxious to talk to Fred Leufeld, but he knew the Secretary of State would not have arrived in Honolulu yet. In his line of work, Joe had often been the bearer of bad news to the families of his employees, and he didn't envy Fred's job on this journey. Before Fred had left the island, Joe shared with him how he broke the news to Clay Sherwin's wife that the former secret agent had been murdered, his head separated from his body, and found in a marshy area near Port Stirling. But Joe knew that no amount of carefully calibrated wording would lessen the shock for Naomi Matsuda, just like it hadn't for Arlette Sherwin. Dead is dead.

Joe hit the speed dial button for Rod McClellan, his deputy and right-hand man at the State Department. Rod was currently managing operatives in other parts of the country, primarily Florida and the Gulf Coast, but he was familiar with their operations on the west coast.

"What's up, boss?" Rod answered. "Where are you? Big secret at HQ, I understand."

"Have you ever heard of Cold Rock Island?" Joe asked.

"Sure. In the Pacific off Oregon, right? Used to be owned by us and the Japanese."

Joe laughed. "Then you're about one in ten thousand people who know of its existence. Even the Port Stirling cops had never heard of it. I'm on the island currently."

"Why? It's privately owned now, isn't it?"

"Yes. Billionaire Rohn Reid bought it from us several years ago. It's his hideaway from the real world, as he puts it. But it's about to be discovered because a Japanese military hero died here on Thursday night, we think. Found Friday swinging from a beam in an airplane hangar building."

"Suicide?"

"Fern and I don't believe so. It looks like murder."

"Oh, boy. What can I do?"

"I need you to run some searches on the island residents who are here now. They are all suspects at this point. See if any of them have a record or are crime frequent flyers. I'm going to email you with names, addresses, and phone numbers when I hang up. We've interrogated seven of the eight men in residence this afternoon, and those are the names you'll find. There are two women, and one more man, Leonard O'Conner, and our plan is to talk to them after dinner. I'll send their info later tonight. One of these ten people might be a killer, Rod, so be thorough."

"Are you and Fern safe?"

"Who knows?" Joe said and ended the call.

* * *

Fern took a quick shower and changed into a sweater and pants she found in her room's closet. The fit was good, and it was nice to be clean and comfortable. *It feels like I've been away from home for days instead of a few hours.*

She quickly scanned the notes she'd made talking with Joe, reached for her phone, and called Matt.

Matt answered immediately. "Are you OK?"

"I'm fine, honey. We just finished doing our first run-through with seven of the men on the island, and Joe and I will have dinner with Rohn Reid in about forty-five minutes. I wanted to let you know we're alright, and to ask your help on a couple of things. Do you have a minute?"

"Yeah. Jay is at the house with me. Ed went home after we cleaned out the Twisty River of fish, and Jay and I decided we'd grab some food here tonight. He's out on the deck cleaning two of our trout, so he can't hear me talking to you."

Fern laughed. "You boys need to leave some fish in that river for the rest of Chinook County."

"Hell with them," Matt smiled into the phone. "It's every man for himself."

"Also, Jay can be brought up to speed on what's going on out here. Joe wants the department to help us out on this murder investigation."

"I was hoping you'd say that, darlin'. We're twiddling our thumbs around here."

"It's the weekend, cowboy, you're supposed to take some quiet time to relax and reflect on life."

"Yeah, I'm good at that," he joked.

"Why don't you call Tamryn and see if she wants to come over for a fish feed, too? She's just down the road from our house, and she hasn't had time to get to know anybody but us cops so far."

"Jay and I just talked about that, but we decided she might rather have a night in her new home to chill. The retreat yesterday was heavy lifting for her."

"She might," Fern agreed. "But she'll tell you if that's what she wants to do. It wouldn't hurt to extend an invitation. My guess is she'd love to pop over and have a beer with you two. I know I would about now."

"You're probably right. As usual. I did see her on the beach this morning and she was in good spirits." He paused. "So, is your gut telling you that you'll make it through the night in that god-forsaken place?" He tried to sound light.

"Everyone so far seems completely harmless. Of course, no one heard or saw anything Thursday night when we think Hiroshi died. Which reminds me, I suppose it's too early to have heard from Bernice?"

"I talked to her, and she's going to do the PM tomorrow morning. I'll be attending."

"That's great news. Joe and I are ninety-nine percent sure it's murder not suicide, but we need Bernice to tell us before we totally rule it out. In the meantime, Joe and I will have dinner, talk to the two women and one man who weren't available earlier, and then retreat to our guest house to compare today's notes. I'll put a chair against my room's door, and sleep with my Glock under the pillow. Joe is a connecting door away. We'll be fine and can hopefully wrap up our work here tomorrow. Captain Adams is standing by in Buck Bay HQ to bring us home."

"OK. Are you going to give me names to start checking?"

"Yeah. Joe's getting Rod McClellan to run them through State's computers, but I'd like your department to do some research, too. Bring in Sylvia, for sure, and any of our local gang you need. Everyone on the island except the gardener seems to have ties to the Seattle area, so start there while Rod looks further afield, OK? I'll email the details on the remaining three people after we have our chat later."

"What about the victim's family? They'll need a thorough background check," Matt said.

"Yes, but we have to wait for the Secretary of State to give the news to Mrs. Matsuda."

"When is that happening?"

"Tonight." Fern looked at her watch. "He should be in Honolulu in about three hours, and he told Joe he'd call him after he talked to her."

"I will want the names and information on all the immediate family members, and I'll handle that research personally."

"You always think it's the family," she noted.

"And how often have I been right?"

She sighed. "A few times, husband."

"That's correct, wife."

"But not every time."

"Also correct," Matt admitted. "But I like to rule them out first. Send me their info."

"I will, as soon as Fred calls."

"Please tell me that you don't call the Secretary of State 'Fred'."

"He insisted. He's a great guy; you'd love him."

"Do we know where 'Fred' was on Thursday and Friday before he flew out here with Joe? He knew Hiroshi, right?"

Fern was momentarily speechless. "You can't possibly think that the United States Secretary of State had anything to do with the murder of a Japanese hero, can you?"

"I think anyone on the periphery of this strange case is a potential suspect. You should think that, too."

"Well, I'm keeping my eyes and ears open, Chief Horning, but I think you're out of line where Fred is concerned."

"Sorry, I didn't realize he is your new best friend."

"He's not, but he's also not a murderer."

"Until you know that for a fact, don't get too snug with him. You don't get to be Secretary of State for this great nation without stepping on some toes on the way up. Or worse."

"I'm smarter than that, Matt. Let me do my job. Please."

"Always, darlin'. Just trying to help. Send me the names. And pull your curtains and sleep with a light on tonight, will you?"

"Yes, dear. I promise."

• • •

Matt and Jay cleaned up their fish mess on the deck and opened a beer. Although it was starting to get dark, they camped out on deck chairs, zipping up fleece jackets against the chill. Their backs to the house, they stared out to sea and watched the sky put on its light show. Neither man would ever sit with his back to the ocean again.

Matt had put all but three of their fish in freezer bags and stored them in his garage freezer for now. Jay knew he could get his whenever he wanted them.

"Good haul today," Jay said. "I love the days when the fish just seem to want to go home with us."

"River to table, doesn't get any better, huh?" Matt said. "How do you want me to cook 'em?"

"Throw them on the grill, keep it simple. Got any fresh lemon?"

"Yep."

"Got any potatoes?"

"Yep. Big Russets."

"Perfect. Sour cream?"

"You know it."

"An heirloom tomato?"

Matt looked at him. "Getting picky, aren't you?"

"Might as well ask for the moon. Won't get anywhere in this world if you don't."

"Well, you're in luck," said Matt. "I went by the farmers' market, and remember Fergus from the Bushnell case? He's now growing heirloom tomatoes and peppers in one of his old pot greenhouses. And they're first rate. Fern and I always pick up some from him."

"I knew that," Jay snickered. "Saw them on the corner of your counter in a basket."

Matt laughed. "OK, so it's fresh trout on the grill, massive baked potatoes with sour cream…"

"And butter."

"And butter," Matt continued. "Heirloom tomatoes. Anything else, your highness?"

"Ice cream?"

"But of course. Mint chocolate chip or old-fashioned vanilla?"

"Do we have to decide that now?" Jay asked.

"No. But we do need to decide if we're going to call Tamryn to join us.

Fern thinks we should, and I have news from her on her case. Joe Phelps wants us to help them," Matt said.

"Sure, then, let's call her. Yesterday went well, don't you think? I thought we handled it brilliantly."

"*We?* I handled it brilliantly."

"I helped," Jay said, somewhat defensively.

"Yeah, I guess you did," Matt agreed reluctantly. "The crowd loved your bit about the new donut shop."

"Call her." Jay held out his beer. "Tamryn would love this beer."

Matt pulled out his phone and put it up to his ear while it rang. "That's odd, no answer. It's going to voicemail." Into his phone, he said, "Tamryn, howdy, it's Matt. Jay and I are hanging out at my house, and we want you to come over and have some of the beautiful trout we caught today. Gimme a ring."

"She always answers her phone," Jay said. "It's like attached to her hand."

"Maybe she's in the shower. Let's give her fifteen minutes to pick up my message. I'll go put the spuds in the real oven since we have time. Better than nuking them."

Fifteen minutes came and went. No Tamryn.

"Maybe we were right the first time, and she wants some time to chill," Jay said. "Fern's not always right, you know."

"Yes, she is," Matt scowled.

CHAPTER 12

Tuesday, December 12, 2023 — Honolulu

Hiroshi lifted his mango martini and clinked glasses with Naomi. "I love retirement," he said.

She smiled. "I love that you love it. Deep inside me, I was afraid a quieter life with me would not be enough for you. That you'd get bored."

He nodded. "I was a little afraid of that, too," he admitted. "Not that I'd ever get bored with you," he hurriedly added, "just that I might miss the action and all the drama of my work. I do miss the camaraderie of my colleagues, but not the day-to-day slog."

Naomi swept her arm out in a big arc. "Invite them. It's not like we don't have the best terrace in all of Honolulu for entertaining."

"I will. I want to create a little distance first and let them get on with the show without me."

"That's wise."

"What's on for tonight?" he asked her — Naomi, social chairman.

"Not a single thing. We've been out a lot this week, and I want to continue my Zen feeling from the spa. I thought a light supper, followed by popcorn and a movie in our jammies with our feet up. What say you?"

"Sounds good. Does that mean I can have a second drink?"

"You're retired, dude, do what you want." She looked at her drink. "These are really delicious. I'll have another, too, but let's not make a habit of this." She grinned at him.

"My trainer won't allow it," Hiroshi said.

"You don't have a trainer. You don't need anyone." She looked puzzled.

"It's this guy on my Tonal workout. He's a few years younger than me and funny as hell. He's always telling us what we have to accomplish in the workout before we can even think about one drink. Two are not allowed, unless as he says, 'It's your wife's birthday.' It's not your birthday today by any chance, is it?"

"'Fraid not. But we can pretend."

"I'll go make…" His cell phone rang, and he reached into his pocket, looking at the screen. "This is Shuji and I want to talk to him. I'll be just a minute."

"I'll go make the drinks while you talk. Give him my love."

"Hi, son. Thanks for returning my call."

"Sure thing, dad. What's going on?" Shuji said.

"Something at your bank, I fear," Hiroshi said. "Do you have a minute to talk now? Privately?"

"Yes. I'm outside, and there's no one around. Shoot."

"Do you know a vice-president named Scott Thurman?"

"Sure. He's on the management team with me. Why?"

"Has he ever mentioned a cryptocurrency scheme he's involved with?"

"Nooo," Shuji said, dragging out the word.

"Does your bank service any crypto clients that you know of?"

"Yes, we have two, one in New York and one in Seattle."

"Is one of them called Nugget?"

"No. The New York company is RealZ, and Seattle is called Venus," Shuji answered. "What is Nugget?"

"It's too soon to know for sure, but I suspect Scott Thurman of running his own crypto operation and not mentioning it to any of you."

"No way," Shuji said vigorously. Hiroshi could almost feel him shaking his head. "It would have turned up on our email security checks."

"Not if he's running it from a private email on his own server at home."

"Is that what you suspect?"

"Yes. And my big fear is that he's roped in some of your bank's biggest clients."

"And they think the bank is behind it because Scott's the lead guy, and everything is guaranteed?"

"Quite possible."

"Shit!" Silence on the other end while Shuji thought it over. "Here's what we're going to do. You keep digging, dad. Find out how and where he's doing this."

"You don't seem surprised," Hiroshi noted.

"I'm surprised I'm not on to him, but I'm not surprised that Thurman would try something like this. He has a con man streak in him. Plus, he's the kind of guy who thinks he's smarter than everyone else in the room. We need to find his server somehow. Get access to it."

"I might be able to do that, but I wanted to check with you first. I was hoping I was mistaken. And I still might be, but it is suspicious."

"How did you discover this?"

"Almost by accident," Hiroshi said. "I was going through emails from one of your managers who reported one of the threatening notes. She had forwarded it to Thurman. He replied to her on his bank email, but blind-copied another address that seemed like it might be a personal email address. It read 'SJTHURMAN@SPACEN.COM.' Have you ever heard of SPACEN.COM, or seen this email from Thurman?"

"No on both questions. What the hell? Is there a web domain name for SPACEN, and who owns it?" Shuji asked.

"I haven't had the chance to look yet. I'll keep digging until you get back to Honolulu, and I can show you what I've got."

"Coming home Friday night. I'll be in touch. And, dad?"

"Yes?"

"Thanks a ton."

"It's no problem, son." They ended the call.

"What's no problem?" asked Naomi, handing him drink number two.

"Oh, it's nothing. Just some business Shuji wanted to run by me. Let's rustle up some food and find our jammies."

Naomi lovingly clasped her husband's arm, and the two strolled into the house.

• • •

Saturday, February 24, 2024 — Port Stirling

Matt and Jay sat at the kitchen island, chowing down on their dinner. "Nothing beats eating fish I just caught," Matt said. "Nothing."

"Agreed," said Jay, between bites of his gigantic baked potato. He squeezed some more lemon on his trout.

Matt checked his watch. "Eight-fifteen. Why hasn't Tamryn returned our call?"

"It's not like her," Jay said. "Maybe she went to a movie."

"Maybe," Matt said, not sounding convinced.

"Should we be worried?"

"I kinda am," Matt admitted.

"Call her again."

Matt did so. Same result; no answer, straight to voicemail. He held out his phone toward Jay so he could hear the recording.

"Let's have our ice cream, and if she hasn't called me back by then, let's go over to her place and check, OK?"

"Can't hurt," Jay nodded.

• • •

Tamryn Gesicki's rental house was about a mile and a half down Ocean Bend Rd from Matt's home. The house was set well back from the road in a private clearing, with a gravel lane winding through the trees separating it from Ocean Bend.

Matt and Jay were happy for Tamryn to rent this place at a good price, and she was thrilled with it. But the house brought an unpleasant memory to the two cops involving a former case.

"Does it feel like this house is evil to you?" Jay asked from his driver's seat.

"Totally," Matt deadpanned. "Cursed. All who enter will die." He wiggled his fingers and made an eerie 'woo' noise.

"Not funny. You're jaded, but I will never get the image of Clay Sherwin's murder out of my brain. This friggin' house reminds me of him."

"If it's any consolation, I was just thinking about Clay, too. But don't you dare bring it up with Tamryn," Matt pleaded with the younger cop. "She loves this place, and I want her to be happy here. She's a terrific detective and an asset to our department."

"I know, I know. I spend all day with her making sure she's happy at work, and letting her know she belongs here with us," Jay said. "Plus, she's very cool. Laid back, funny, smart—just a great partner. But I can't help that this house gives me the heebie-jeebies."

"How old are you?" Matt laughed. "That's something my dad says."

"Mine, too. But it fits here." Jay pulled up in the circular driveway in front of the small, one-level house. Tamryn's leased Honda Civic in Blazing Orange Pearl was parked in the pullout just in front of him. "Can't miss her car," Jay noted.

The front door of the house was wide open, and there were no lights on anywhere.

"I'm not loving this," Matt said, glancing over at Jay.

"What do you want to do?"

"Her car is here, the door is open, and the house is completely dark. Clearly, something's wrong. We have to go in, don't we?"

"Yeah. We have to go in. Crap. I hate this place."

Jay doused the lights on his car, and the two cops silently got out of the vehicle, pulling on their crime-scene gloves…just in case. Watching where they stepped on the gravel driveway, they tip-toed up the three wide wood steps to the front door. Standing on the porch, Matt whispered, "Follow my lead."

He did not announce their presence, nor call out Tamryn's name. Not knowing what they'd find, Matt was uneasy about the possibility of someone else in the house. If that was the case, the last thing he wanted to do was warn them.

They entered the foyer, and, gratefully, the light from the almost-full moon shone brightly through the living room's sliding glass doors, illuminating this section of the house. Tamryn's purse sat on the dining room table. Matt pointed it out to Jay, still silent, and then gestured to his left, to the kitchen down the short hallway.

Being on the east side of the house, the kitchen was darker, and Matt bumped into the door frame at the entrance. He swore to himself and pulled out his pencil flashlight from his jacket pocket. His sweep of the kitchen showed a spotlessly clean room — no dirty dishes, no clutter, virtually nothing on the countertops.

He pointed his arm back to the hallway and moved it in a forward motion. Jay stayed close to Matt's back as they made their way through the living room and down the hall to the bedrooms. Both cops remembered the layout of the house all too well.

Guest bedroom and bathroom — clear.

Tamryn's bedroom and walk-in closet — clear.

Matt turned to her bathroom and swung his flashlight around. It landed on Tamryn's face on the bathroom floor.

"No! No! Jay!"

Jay reached for the bathroom's light switch and flicked it on.

Matt quickly knelt to her side and checked for a pulse. "She's alive." Gently, he touched her arm, leaned down close to her ear, and said, "Tamryn. Tamryn. It's me, Matt. Can you hear me? You're safe. Everything's alright."

Softly, he stroked her arm, and kept up a quiet dialogue until, after a few moments, she stirred, moving her head ever so slightly.

"That's it, Tamryn. You're safe. Can you open your eyes? Can you do that for me? It's Matt."

He turned to Jay over his shoulder and whispered, "Ambulance."

Jay quickly moved to the front door, turned on the porchlight and dialed 911. "Hi, Milton. It's Jay. We need an ambulance right now at — just a minute." He went outside and looked for the house number. "At 9280 Ocean Bend Rd. There's a gravel road through the trees to the house. It's Tamryn Gesicki from our PD, and we need medics. I'll go out to the road and wave them in."

"Got it," said Milton, and hung up.

Jay ran back to the bathroom. "How is she? Is she coming to?"

"Yes," Matt replied, "she's beginning to stir a little. Is the ambulance coming?"

"Yeah, on the way. They aren't far away. What do you think happened here?"

"She's been beaten." Matt's voice cracked. "Again."

Jay left to direct the ambulance, and six minutes later, he saw its flashing lights. He waved them into Tamryn's driveway.

"Need two of you and a stretcher," Jay said to the first medic to exit the vehicle. "We've got a woman badly beaten. Follow me. And don't touch anything you don't have to."

The paramedics were the same three guys who came when Jay called them last Thanksgiving Day. The lead medic, Mike, who had stabilized Matt on that awful day, quickly examined a slowly-coming-around Tamryn. He stood and told his team to get her on the stretcher and out to the ambulance. They would rush her to Buck Bay Hospital.

"At least, she had the brains to not get a bullet through her neck...like some people I know," Mike said to Matt. Smirk.

"Yep, I guess she's smarter than me," Matt said. "What do you think happened?"

"She was beaten, and badly, I suspect," Mike said, now serious. "I need to see yours and Jay's hands, please." Apologetically, he added, "Protocol."

In a heartbeat, Matt and Jay produced their hands and forearms for the medic to check.

"Is there anyone else in the house?" Mike asked.

"No," said Matt. "We went through the house before we found her, and Jay did a quick search of the grounds while we waited for you. No sign of anyone."

"Well, someone was here. She didn't punch herself in the face."

Matt walked out with the stretcher, gently rubbing Tamryn's arm and talking softly to her. "You will be good as new very soon," he promised her. "Jay's going with you to Buck Bay, and I'll make sure Bernice is standing by to take charge of your care. You're going to be alright."

Tamryn slowly opened her one good eye, and croaked, "Matt."

"Yep, it's me." He leaned over closer to her ear. "How are you feeling? Dumb question, huh?"

"Hurt."

"Can you tell me who did this to you, sweetheart?"

"Him." She closed her eye.

CHAPTER 13

Wh," hen are you coming home?" Joe Phelps' wife, Margo, said into the phone.

"Probably Monday, Tuesday at the latest," he answered. He pictured his wife of forty-one years seated at the desk in their Washington, D.C. town-house library. They'd lived in the house for thirty years, and the library was Margo's favorite room. It was small but perfect, with its wood pan-eled floor-to-ceiling bookshelves, a dainty fireplace with a TV mounted over it, and two easy chairs with matching ottomans facing the TV. Margo had found a coral and navy area rug years ago at an antique shop, and it anchored the room.

"We'll finish up interrogating the island residents tomorrow," Joe con-tinued, "and then the Coast Guard will pick up Fern and me to go back to the mainland. As soon as we get the autopsy results, I'll head home. This is all for your ears only, my dear."

"Of course. You don't need to tell me that after all these years," she bris-tled. Then softer, "Have you met the famous Rohn Reid?"

"Yes."

"So, dish. What's he like?"

"Eccentric. Friendly. Private. Pudgy."

"Next to you, everyone is pudgy, Joe." There was a smile in her tone.

"You aren't. Fern and I have been invited to dinner, and we're guessing there will be plenty of food on Cold Rock Island dinner plates."

"How is Fern? Are you pleased with her work?"

"Sometimes in life you get lucky with the people you hire," Joe mused, "and this time, I got real lucky. She is the consummate pro. Fearless and committed to justice. And, she's a pleasure to work with. No ego, just the right amount of self-confidence to get the job done. It's such a relief."

"I can hear the relief in your voice, honey, and I'm happy for you. It's about time you got the right person for the west coast."

"And the bonus with Fern is that she has access to a darn good local police department, medical examiner, and the ear of the Oregon State Police. It's a win-win. I haven't yet met anyone in the local law enforcement scene who's not smart and effective at their job."

"Maybe you won't have to be out there as much as you have been recently."

"That's my goal, for both Rod and me. Fred wants us to spend more time on our southern border—all kinds of problems down there. Although, the Pacific Northwest is a beautiful part of the country. I want you to come visit with me sometime when it's safe. Safer than now, especially."

"When you retire, I want to see everything with you."

"There's that word again," Joe said.

"And you're going to keep hearing that word," Margo laughed. "You've given enough to your country, Joe. It's our turn."

"I'm happy to discuss it further with you, just as soon as I figure out if we've got an ugly international incident on our hands."

• • •

Fern decided she could get used to having a cook prepare and serve dinner to her every night. Moira served the family and their guests, while Leonard and Lynette took care of the staff's meals. She and Joe had joined Rohn, Rick, and Randy Reid in the dining room at 7:30 p.m. and dinner went on until shortly after 9:00 p.m...literally, soup to nuts.

"Where do you get your fresh vegetables?" Fern asked. The salad of spinach, green onions, and radicchio was delicious. As was the shredded cabbage, perfectly braised, accompanying the pork tenderloin.

Moira smiled at the question. "You should know," she said mysteriously.

"I'm sorry, but I don't," Fern answered.

"Once a week, Aaron and I take the boat over to Port Stirling. Your village has one of the best farmers' markets up and down the coast."

"Ha!" exclaimed Fern. "This is Fergus's radicchio, isn't it? I buy it every week, too!"

"Fergus is an odd duck, but the man can grow veggies," Moira said.

"Now that I think about it, I actually think I've seen you there."

"You never know who you might be standing next to, do you?" Moira said. She left the room, tossing a "Back in a minute with dessert and coffee" over her shoulder.

"Do you have everything in your rooms you need for tonight?" Rohn asked.

"All set," Joe said. "Thank you for your hospitality."

"What's the plan for tomorrow?" Reid asked.

"We'll talk with Moira, Leonard, and Lynette before we leave the house tonight," Fern said briskly. "Joe and I will compare notes, and circle back first thing in the morning. We'll want to take a further look around the island, right, Joe?"

Joe nodded. "Yes."

"What are you looking for?" Rohn asked. He sounded genuinely curious.

"We don't know," Joe said. "But we'll know it when we see it." He cranked his thumb in Fern's direction. "Or, she will, to be more specific."

"Do you want us to escort you?" asked Randy. He and Rick had been mostly quiet throughout dinner. Fern had the feeling they'd been told to button up.

"We don't want to keep you from your work," Fern said. She was trying to not be blatant about not wanting them around. "We'll just wander around, if that's OK with you, Mr. Reid?"

"Do what you have to do," Rohn said. "I'm sure you'll be glad to get home."

"And you'll be happy to get back to normal here," said Fern, stating the obvious. "We'll wrap up our investigation as soon as we can."

"You will keep me posted?" Rohn inquired. "Will you have the autopsy results tomorrow from Dr. Ryder?"

"Probably Monday," Fern told him. "And, of course, we will update you as we work through the case." *You'll be told what we want you to know and nothing more*, she thought.

"In the meantime, you should be vigilant," Joe added. "Until we know exactly what happened here, everyone on this island bears some risk."

"It is somewhat nerve-wracking," Rohn admitted. "I know none of us had anything to do with Matsuda's death, but it's still unsettling."

"Excuse me," Fern said, "but you don't know for sure that there isn't a killer on your island. Please take Joe's words to heart and be extra cautious until we can unravel this. All three of you should lock your bedroom doors and close your windows. Is there a security system on the house? If so, activate it tonight."

"Yes, I had a system installed about five years ago," Rohn said. "But I don't think we've ever turned it on. Not much use for it out here." He looked at his sons.

They both shook their heads. "Don't think so, dad. Guess we should try it out tonight, huh?" But neither twin looked scared. They were smiling.

• • •

After they questioned Moira, Leonard, and Lynette about Thursday night—none of the three employees had seen or heard anything out of the ordinary, blah, blah, blah—Fern and Joe had started back toward the guest house, when he took her arm and said, "Let's make a quick detour over to building 3."

"You want to look on Simon's nightstand and see what books he's reading, don't you?"

He laughed. "Guilty as charged. Am I that easy to read?"

"You were antsy about Simon from the first word he spoke. He kinda bugged me, too. Let's go."

She zipped up the quilted jacket she'd found in the closet, and the two took a left turn once they were out of sight of the main house.

They entered the large building through the small white door the staff entered and left through.

"Not locked," said Joe, shaking his head in disbelief.

"Almost as if the occupants know there is nothing to be afraid of," remarked Fern.

The interior was quiet, but there were lights on throughout the building. The staff private bedrooms wrapped around the far, southwest corner.

"Where do you want to start?" Fern asked.

"We know Simon has a room on the south side, so let's start with the first one." They took off striding across the vast, open space, and knocked on the first door on their left. They could hear classical music playing softly inside the room.

Simon opened the door immediately but blocked the entrance with his body. "Yes?"

"We'd like to come in and talk for a minute," Joe said. "Is that OK with you?"

"Why?"

"We just want to clear up a couple of things. Just routine."

"Don't you need a search warrant or something?" Simon asked. He didn't budge from his stance.

"Yes, unless you don't mind, and let us come in. Also, I could get one in ten minutes with a quick phone call to my counterpart at the FBI."

Fern nodded solemnly. "That's true. I've seen him do it."

"Alright, but it's not very convenient," Simon blustered. But he stepped aside and let them enter.

The room was large, and more like a studio apartment than just a bedroom. There was a small kitchenette against the wall opposite the door with modern stainless-steel appliances and a luxurious bamboo wood floor. A nice window over the sink would fill the room with light during the day, Fern thought. The king-sized bed, a dining table for two, a small desk, and a TV with two recliners made up the room's furniture, and there was a hallway to the right of the kitchen which likely led to a bathroom.

"Comfy," Joe said looking around. He shot a look at Fern. A look she recognized.

"We wanted to follow-up on your relationship with Mr. Matsuda," she said. "Can you describe it a little more fully? Was it friendly? Business-like? Frequent?"

Fern had gotten Simon's attention, which was what Joe wanted. He meandered over to the desk first while Simon had his back to it. It was, unfortunately, very tidy, with only one piece of paper on it, an invoice from a plant nursery in Texas.

"Most definitely, Mr. Matsuda and I had a business-only relationship," Simon answered. "I rarely saw the man — as I told you. I dealt almost exclusively with Naomi." He turned to see what Joe was doing. Not much to see; Joe standing quietly with his hands stuffed in his pants pockets.

"Did you like him?" Fern asked quickly to regain his attention.

Exasperated, Simon said, "I barely knew Hiroshi. He was pleasant enough on the few times I did encounter him. Nice to me, you know? He would ask if I had everything I needed to create his garden — that kind of thing. He wanted to make sure that Naomi got what she wanted."

Joe wandered over to the bed's nightstand and picked up the top book in a pile of four books while Fern kept talking.

"How long were you in Honolulu?"

"About a month," Simon answered. "It was a full design job — hard surface, fencing, and complete planting."

"I'll bet it turned out beautiful," Fern smiled at him.

"It did," he beamed. "I love doing tropical gardens. So different from our English projects. Naomi was thrilled with it."

The book Joe was holding was titled "Japanese Military History." While Simon and Fern nattered on about gardens, Joe opened the book to a page that had a turned-down corner. Staring out at him was a smiling photo of Admiral Hiroshi Matsuda.

• • •

After they left Simon's room, Fern and Joe took a quick look in the other staff rooms but discovered nothing of interest. Tyson and Noah were cooperative; Aaron was out on security duty now. In answer to Fern's questioning, all three owned a gun, for which Tyson and Noah said they had a permit.

Tyson shared that Aaron had his gun with him as was their policy while on duty, and, yes, he also had a permit for it. Fern would check on that.

"Hope Aaron doesn't shoot us," Joe said dryly, as he and Fern walked back to the guest house.

"Everyone's jumpy for sure, but Aaron strikes me as the least possible killer on the island. He's too sensitive."

"Who do you think is capable of murder, then? What do you make of our ten suspects?"

Fern hesitated. "Gut feeling? Based on our interrogations?"

"Yes."

"All of them, with the possible exceptions of Aaron and Lynette. Those two have what I call 'sweet souls', the others do not."

"I thought you liked Rohn Reid?"

"I do," Fern said. "But he's not a sweet soul. I don't believe he is ruthless, either, as you might expect from someone with his kind of money. He could kill under the right — or wrong, I should say — circumstances."

"I notice you didn't include Moira on your least possible list. What's your reasoning there? And I happen to agree with you on her, by the way."

"Right? She's cold. I admire her loyalty to the family, but I think if anyone did anything to hurt them, she could kill without losing sleep."

"Is she strong enough to have killed Hiroshi? He looked fit to me. He and I are about the same age, and I'm pretty sure I couldn't take him."

"That's always the question, of course, when we're considering a female killer of a male victim. But Matt has taught me that women can be crafty killers when pushed to the brink. He was dead right about a recent case, you will recall."

Joe nodded. "We need Bernice's post-mortem report. Need to know how he died."

"Agreed. The 'how' can often point us to the 'who', and usually helps us eliminate potential suspects. Bernice is an ME with a strong curiosity streak. She'll want to know as soon as possible. I'm guessing we'll hear something from her tomorrow night or Monday at the latest," Fern said. "What's your take on the Reid twins?"

"They scare me," Joe said.

Fern laughed. "They are somewhat strange, aren't they? Randy is the ruthless one in the family, I think. Rick seems mellower. Also, Randy strikes me as liking the family money more than either his brother or even his father. Greed can be a powerful motive."

"You think they felt threatened by Matsuda in some way?"

"I don't know yet," Fern said. "But there's a reason why he died here. And Rohn Reid owns this island. Those are the only two facts we know so far."

CHAPTER 14

Saturday, February 24, 2024 — Port Stirling

Jay rode in the ambulance with his partner, Tamryn. After she was loaded into it, she drifted off again, and the medics said to let her sleep. Fifteen minutes into the ride, Jay's phone rang. Bernice.

"How is she, Jay?"

"Asleep and I would say 'stable' for now." He spoke quietly into his phone.

"Did the medics give her anything?"

"I think something for her blood pressure. They said it was high, probably caused by the degree of pain she suffered."

"Does she have any cuts on her?"

"Yeah, a couple of nasty ones on her face. The guys cleaned them up, but said they needed a doc's attention. Stiches, likely. They also said she might have broken ribs and internal injuries."

"Dammit!" Bernice swore. "Is her loser ex-husband in town, do you suppose?"

"We think so. Matt asked her who did this to her, and she only got out one word: 'Him'. The medics want me to let her sleep for now, but when she wakes up, I'll talk to her. We're partners, you know. Why do bad things happen to nice people?" Jay asked forlornly.

"Because there are more mean and selfish people in the world these days. I'm sorry, Jay. I like her, too."

"Are you at the hospital?" he asked.

"I'm here, and I'll wait at the ER door for the ambulance. Matt called and he wants me to send a forensics team down to her house. I'll call my guys next."

"Tell them the front door was left open, and that's obviously how her attacker entered the house. They should pay special attention to the lock. Also, we think the action took place in the primary bathroom off her bedroom. That's where we found her, and nothing else in the house seemed to be disturbed."

"Matt said he would wait at the house for my crew."

"Good. He can fill them in."

"Right," Bernice said. "How did you find her? Why were you there?"

"Matt and I got back from fishing and called her to see if she wanted to come and eat with us at his house. She didn't answer. Like, for over two hours, and that's not like her, so we thought we should check on her."

"Thank God you did."

. . .

Matt, respectful of the crime scene, carefully backed out of Tamryn's bathroom after they left with her. While he waited for the forensic team to arrive, he pulled his gun out of its holster, and went outside to do a more thorough search of the property surrounding the house.

He paused to study the front door more closely after checking the two sets of sliding doors on the west side of the house, and all of the windows, all of which were locked. There was no obvious sign of damage to the door or, specifically, to the lock, which was in the unlocked position. There was no way in hell a former Boston detective would leave her front door unlocked, whether she was out or home. Someone either picked the lock or used a key, and, again, knowing Tamryn, she wouldn't give anyone else a key to her home.

Was it a random event? Maybe a burglary gone bad? Had she surprised the intruder when she returned home from her walk on the beach this morning? He hadn't been in the house since she moved here, and therefore couldn't tell if anything was missing or not. But the usual targets—flat screen TV, woman's purse, artwork, jewelry—were intact as far as he could tell. He didn't dare rifle through things until forensics were finished. Plus, he knew Tamryn didn't bring much with her to Oregon; she'd bailed out of Boston in a hurry. He would ask Fern if she'd noticed anything of value in the house when she helped Tamryn move in.

But deep down, Matt knew who the intruder had been. Tamryn would only have answered 'him' if it was her husband. His temper and violence were the reasons she'd left him, and Boston. And being a cop, he would certainly know how to pick a lock—they all did.

How did he track her down?, Matt wondered. Tamryn had been very cautious in who she told where she was living now. She'd left her parents' address with the Boston PD as a forwarding address, and she'd instructed her mother and father not to give anyone her new address. She hadn't even told her two best girlfriends exactly where she was, only that she'd moved to the west coast and would contact them once things settled down.

Matt thought it was possible that hubby might have searched the police recruiting websites and figured out the timing of Port Stirling's hiring of a new detective. Even if he had been that smart, though, how did he know where to find her once he got to town? City hall would never give out an employee's home address.

Had he been in town a couple of days and somehow followed her from city hall? Possible, but Tamryn was a sharp cookie; she would have noticed a tail in a split second, especially in a small town like Port Stirling. Matt considered that he should call her parents, but that didn't feel comfortable to him. He would wait until she was able to talk clearly with him, and they would take it from there.

Matt circled the house with his flashlight. He knew Jay had taken a quick look around, but Matt was now looking for anything he could use, like a footprint in the soft, damp earth that didn't belong there, or a clothing fragment caught by a jagged shrub—anything. He'd just made a full loop, finding nothing of interest, when he saw the forensic team pulling into the driveway.

He went to meet the two forensic scientists and briefed them on what

he and Jay found. He also shared his belief that the attacker might be a
cop, and for them to keep that in mind. While they worked, Matt drove
Jay's car to his house, packed an overnight bag with a couple of things,
grabbed his laptop, and returned to Tamryn's house. With Jay and Bernice taking care of Tamryn at the hospital, he planned to spend the night
in her house in case anyone decided to try again.

 Fern called as he was driving back down Ocean Bend Rd.

"I'm sorry it's so late," she said. "Joe and I just finished up our day here,
and I'm back in my room now."

"It's OK, we've had some excitement here," he said.

"What kind of excitement?"

"The bad kind. Somebody surprised Tamryn at her house today and
beat her up. She's in the hospital."

"What?!?"

"Yep, and it's only thanks to you that we found her tonight. I tried to
call her several times to invite her to join me and Jay, and she didn't answer
her phone or return my voicemail. We thought that was strange and came
to her place to check."

"Is she going to be OK? This is horrible."

"I think she'll heal, at least physically," Matt said, swallowing hard. "Jay
rode in the ambulance with her to Buck Bay, and Bernice is there to play
doctor. Before you ask, I think it was her husband." He shared with Fern
what Tamryn had said when she regained consciousness.

"That fucking creep! How could he know…"

Matt interrupted her. "You're about to ask me all the same questions
I've just asked myself, darlin'. I won't have any answers until I can get to the
hospital tomorrow and hopefully talk to her. I'm going to spend tonight
in her house and see if there's any more action."

"That's a good idea. Looks like we may both have an interesting night.
Wish you were here with me." She sounded lonely to Matt.

"Do you feel safe?"

"I feel uneasy," Fern said truthfully. "You used the word 'strange' and
that's exactly what this place is. Something evil happened here, and it's
an uncomfortable place. But Joe is next door, and we know what we

need to do tomorrow. We'll get the work done and get home as soon as we can."

"Once I get to talk to Tamryn and get some clarity on her situation, I'll do some research on your island's residents' names."

"Great. And check to see if all the residents have gun permits. Joe and I know that at least three of them have guns on site, and we suspect the Reids probably do, too. I think the Reids and the three workers will be registered in Washington state, but I don't know about the others."

"Will do. Question for you: when you helped Tamryn move in, did you notice anything of value that a thief might grab? I need to remain flexible on who the intruder might have been until I can talk to her."

Fern thought. "Not really. She came with very few things from home. She did show me her wedding ring she kept in a small black case—should be in her closet somewhere. No other important jewelry, I don't think. A small painting that she told me her grandmother painted, and her laptop—that's about it. She joked that her Keurig was her most valuable possession."

Matt had to smile at that. "That sounds like her. I'll look for the ring. Let's talk about you. Did Rohn Reid poison you at dinner?"

Fern laughed. "Don't think so. I feel good and the dinner was delicious. Even finicky eater Joe cleaned his plate."

"Sounds like the billionaire is trying to be a good host to throw you off the track. He doesn't know you're too smart to fall for that ploy."

"To be honest, I don't know what to think—neither does Joe. Reid is convinced it was suicide, but I'm not buying it, at least, not until Bernice tells me so. Is she still planning to do the autopsy tomorrow? What with Tamryn and all?"

"Yeah. I'm going to the hospital around 7:00 a.m. to first see Tamryn, and then Bernice said she'd start the post-mortem at 8:00 a.m. She understands it's crucial to your case to know what killed Matsuda."

"It is, because we're getting nowhere here. Only Rohn Reid's gardener, Simon Marsons, has given us reason to be suspicious."

"How so?"

"We casually searched all the employee rooms tonight, and Simon has a book on his nightstand about Japanese military history. Joe opened it, and there are two pages turned down on Hiroshi Matsuda's brilliant career. Photos and everything."

"Wow. Did you ask him why he had the book?" Matt asked.

"Sure. He said he found it in Rohn's library and was interested because of the Japanese role in the island's history."

"Did you believe him?"

"Not sure. Joe didn't, and he doesn't like him. But I don't think Simon is a murderer; he's kind of wimpy and delicate, even though he looks outdoorsy."

"But he probably has strong hands because of his profession. Strong enough to strangle a man before stringing him up."

"Maybe. The truth is that no one here stands out as having a motive or the personality or the opportunity to commit murder. It just doesn't make any sense. We need to do this one by the book: forensics, autopsy, background checks, all the legwork, because no one is giving us an inch. We're going to have to find it. But I'm too tired right now. This day has felt like a week. I'm going to bed."

"You mean, you're going to bed after you put a chair up against your door, check your window lock, and place your gun on the nightstand, right?"

"Right. But don't worry. Joe and I have discussed our personal safety, and we have a plan. And, it's only one short night. What could possibly happen?"

"Do. Not. Say. That," Matt said.

• • •

Fern slipped off her bra, and put her jewelry on the nightstand, but she'd decided to sleep in the comfy pants, sweater, and socks she'd found in the closet. Just in case. She did as Matt instructed: checked the window lock, and unholstered her gun, placing it on the nightstand as well. On usual nights, she turned her phone off so as not to disturb her sleep, but she left it on tonight, noticing it was still forty-two percent charged from this morning.

Before washing her face and brushing her teeth, she walked off the number of steps between her side of the bed and the front door, and then did the same to the window in case she had to escape the room in the night. She then knocked four times on the connecting door to Joe's room. That was their signal that she was going to bed. Joe returned the four knocks.

Lights out.

Even though she was dead tired, her brain kept re-hashing today's interrogations. After about thirty minutes, she turned her bedside light back on and jotted a few notes for tomorrow, and then tried again to sleep. Counting backward from 100, her best shut-my-brain-off sleep trick, the last thing she remembered was sixty-one. At least, until someone tapped on her window at 3:30 a.m.

CHAPTER 15

Immediately awake, Fern jumped out of bed and grabbed her gun off the nightstand. Remembering her 'Club Fed' training at FLETC in Georgia last year, she instinctively moved not to the window, but to her door. If someone meant her harm, the window noise was likely a diversion. She put her ear to the door and held her breath for thirty seconds while she listened intently.

Nothing. No sounds of breathing, body shuffling, nothing. There was no one there. Soundlessly, she crept to her window, gun held out in front of her with both hands and repeated the listening she'd done at her door. Again, there was no sound except for the ocean's waves hitting the shore.

I know I heard someone knocking on my window. I didn't dream it. She stood perfectly still for about five minutes. *This is bullshit*, she finally told herself, and then moved back toward her room's door. Silently, she opened the door and looked up and down the breezeway. A movement to her right—in the opposite direction of the main house—caught the corner of her eye. She sprinted down the covered sidewalk, gun at the ready.

About fifty feet ahead of her, she saw a figure in all black moving quickly away from the guest house and turning left toward building 3 and the hangar. "Stop!" she yelled loudly, closing ground at a face pace. "Put your hands in the air and stop! I have a gun pointed at you and I will use it!"

Noah stopped and did as she said. "Please don't shoot," he said over his shoulder.

"Turn around," Fern ordered. She kept about ten feet between them, and her gun steadily trained on him.

Slowly, Noah turned to face her. He didn't speak again.

"Did you just knock on my window?" she asked.

"Yes. I wanted to make sure you were alright."

"You didn't consider it might scare the hell out of me?" Fern said angrily, not waiting for his answer. "Why are you out here?"

"I'm on duty. Night shift, remember?"

"I'm going to ask you this again, Noah, and I want a straight answer. Why did you knock on my window?"

"I figured if you or Joe were in any kind of trouble in your rooms, you would yell out if I knocked on your window. Based on what's happened, Mr. Reid told me to make sure you were both safe tonight."

"Are you sure he didn't tell you to frighten me and make sure we leave tomorrow?"

"No. And I wouldn't do that, ma'am. That's not how I roll."

"Well, I don't really know you well enough to know whether that's how you roll. From where I stand, it looks as if you were trying to scare me off," she challenged him.

"Nope."

"I hope not, because I don't scare easily. Usually, it pisses me off more than anything."

"Can I put my hands down?"

Fern knew she had no choice but to let Noah go about securing the island. His story was plausible, and at least he didn't lie about knocking on her window. "Yes," she told him. "Go back to work but stay the hell away from our rooms the rest of the night. Understand?"

"Yes." Noah turned and walked toward the outbuildings without another word.

Fern considered whether or not to wake Joe. *What, exactly, would I tell him? Noah knocked on my window to see if I was OK and scared me, but now he's back on security detail? Or, Noah's acting suspicious, and we should both get up and watch him?*

She went back to bed.

• • •

Sunday, February 25, 2024 — Cold Rock Island

Fern's phone rang and woke her from a restless sleep. "Hello?"

"Are you up?" Joe asked.

"I am now." She threw off the covers and sat on the edge of the bed, getting her bearings. "What time is it?"

"Seven fifteen. Time to rise and shine."

"Easy for you to say," Fern laughed. "You weren't up at 3:30 a.m. like I was."

"Doing what?"

"Chasing Noah down the breezeway with my gun. Long story. Let me get up and get dressed, and I'll be over. What are we doing for food?"

"There's a basket outside both of our doors. Moira to the rescue, I suspect."

Fern knocked on Joe's door at 7:30 a.m. holding her breakfast basket. Joe had retrieved his already and made coffee in his room. The aroma was just what Fern needed. "Fill it up," she said, lifting a coffee cup she found in his little kitchenette area. She quickly drank some of the strong brew, and then said, "Let me tell you about Noah now." She related the story to her boss.

"I can't believe I didn't wake up," he said.

"Neither can I. I yelled pretty loud."

"These rooms must be solidly built," Joe said. "Although, I do always sleep well when I'm near the ocean. I find it soothing compared to the cacophony that is my hometown at night. Did you believe his story?"

"I must have. I went back to bed and slept soundly until you called. Clearly, it wasn't troubling my mind."

They ate the beautiful breakfasts in their baskets: cheese, fruit, and croissants with real butter, washing it down with lots of good, strong coffee.

"Let's go do our job, and then get the hell off this island," Joe said.

• • •

Sunday, February 25, 2024 — Port Stirling, Oregon

Matt awoke in Tamryn's bed, and it took him a few seconds to figure out where he was. It was 6:20 a.m. and he could tell it was just a few minutes before sunrise. It felt bizarre to be sleeping in his new detective's bed, but he'd figured if her attacker came back intending to do more harm, her bedroom would likely be the target. He grabbed his gun from the night-stand and rummaged around for his shoes; he'd slept in sweatpants and tee-shirt in case there was any action during the night. There wasn't, and he'd slept a solid eight hours.

He did a quick check of the house, and everything was as he'd left it last night. Grabbing his jacket, he opened the sliding glass door from her bedroom to the back deck that overlooked the Pacific Ocean and stood quietly for a moment listening for any sounds that shouldn't be there. Nothing but the waves crashing onto the shore, and the occasional loud screech from overhead seagulls.

Matt zipped up his jacket against the breeze and took off down the sandy path from Tamryn's deck to the beach. As he did so, the sun peeped over the hills behind him, and lighted his way. There wasn't another soul on the beach as far as Matt could see, but he knew it wouldn't be long before the local residents would appear, walking their dogs or just out for their morning constitutional.

It was a chilly morning, and he jammed his hands in the pockets of his down jacket. Rolling banks of fog swirled around him as he walked down to the shoreline, where a curtain of mist hung above the restless water. He didn't mind the odd spit in his face because the early fog usually meant a day of some sunshine would follow. The dampness on his face helped bring him fully awake, and a short stroll was his intention. *Get the motor running.*

He walked north parallel to the ocean and toward his home, into the wind with his chin tucked down against the brisk breeze. Something caught the corner of his eye, and he stopped to look out to sea.

A harbor seal. *Roger! Are you following me?,* he said to his pet seal, with a broad grin. Roger bobbed up and down in the affirmative, returning Matt's grin. Or so it appeared.

This is a fine mess, huh?, Matt said to Roger.

"Yes," Roger replied. "It was her husband, you know."

I know. I have to find him.

"You will," said Roger. "You always get the bad guys."

But first, I need to talk to Tamryn, and make sure she's OK this morning. You didn't happen to see anything yesterday, did you?

"Nope. Just me and the fish out here. The occasional bird."

OK, I'm off then. Great to talk with you, Roger.

"Same here, Chief. Have a good one." Roger bobbed down into the surf, disappearing from view.

• • •

Matt gently shook Jay awake. It was 7:15 a.m. and he'd found his detective asleep in a chair in Tamryn's hospital room, snoring lightly.

Jay wiped a drop of drool off his chin, pushed his jacket he'd been using as a blanket off to the side, and sat up. He looked around for a second, not sure where he was. His usually slicked-down cowlick was sticking straight up.

"Hospital. Tamryn," Matt said, helping him out.

"Oh, crap. Now I remember."

"Guys, I'm awake," Tamryn said faintly from her bed.

Matt pulled a folding chair close to the bed and took her hand in his. "How are you feeling?" he asked.

She smiled weakly at him. "Not so hot. Will I live?"

Matt smiled back. "Yep, 'fraid so. You're not getting rid of us that easily. You may never get rid of Jay. Looks like he slept here all night."

Jay came to the other side of her bed. "Hi, partner. Welcome back." He grinned broadly.

"Good to be back," she said. "Bet I look like Miss America, right?"

"Not at the moment," Jay said, ever truthful. "But you will again soon."

Tamryn snorted. "Maybe in my next life."

"You're not done with this life yet, lady," Bernice said, coming into the room like a force of nature. "We will, however, avoid mirrors for a couple of days, and concentrate on your body. Do you want me to tell you about the state of your health with these two clowns in the room, or do you want privacy?"

"These two clowns probably saved my life, so I think they should stay, don't you?"

Bernice smiled and nodded. "Your X-rays show one broken rib and serious bruising, and the CT scan shows a kidney contusion or bruise. I was somewhat worried about a lacerated kidney, but you escaped that horrible trauma. You will be very, very sore for a few days, but you'll heal up just fine. The two cuts on your face required suturing, but again, after the Frankenstein period is over, you'll be good as new.

"Lastly, I suspect you have a concussion. I base that on a couple of symptoms: you appeared to be unconscious for a period of time. I don't know the duration. When you arrived last night, you appeared dazed and complained of a headache. Is your vision blurred and/or are you nauseous?"

"No to both. But I do still have a headache. Not as bad as last night, though."

"My diagnosis is that you have a mild concussion, and that it will go away in a few days, or a week at the most."

"What do I do in the meantime?" Tamryn asked.

"I'm going to keep you here for the next 48 hours at least. We'll apply ice to help the swelling go down, and make sure you do some deep breathing—which will hurt—every hour or so to clear your lungs. We'll keep your bed in a more upright position, make sure you rest, and we'll help you walk around a little to breathe and clear out any mucus. After two days, you can start taking Ibuprofen to help with the pain, and we'll talk about going home."

Tamryn frowned. "Sounds like a blast, doc."

"Don't make me tell you that you were lucky," Bernice scolded. "This could have been much worse."

Dr. Ryder turned to her good buddy, Matt. "You," she said, poking his chest with her index finger, "find whoever did this to your detective, and bring him to me. I have just the treatment for over-testosterone men who like to beat up women. It involves a scalpel."

Matt instinctively shifted his legs together and recoiled back from a visibly angry Bernice.

"May I talk to your patient now?" he said.

"Yes." Bernice turned back to Tamryn. "I'll be back soon with some ice. Tell Matt the truth." She squeezed her hand.

Matt and Jay pulled their chairs as close to Tamryn's bed as they could get.

"Did you see your attacker?" Matt asked her.

"Yes, we chatted amiably for about five seconds," she said.

Even battered and bruised, Tamryn's Boston sense of humor was still intact. Matt was relieved he hadn't stolen her personality.

"Can you identify that person?"

"Yes, it was my soon-to-be ex-husband, Barry Gesicki." She grimaced and placed a hand on her abdomen. "He was waiting in my bedroom when I came in from my morning walk on the beach. He surprised me, and he hit me in the face twice with his fist. It knocked me down to the floor. Then he stomped on me for what felt like hours. He finished me off with a kick to my head. That's the last thing I remember."

Matt and Jay were both trembling by the time she finished telling them what happened.

"We're so sorry, Tamryn," Matt said. "How did he get in? How did he even know where you lived?"

"No idea to either question," she said. "But I sure as hell will find out. I'm done with this shit. This time he's going to jail. Will you help me?"

"You don't need to ask that question," Matt said. "We'll get him. Are his fingerprints on file in Boston?"

"Yes. Every cop in the department is on file before we can start work. Did a forensic team go to my house last night?"

"Yep. Do you know if he wiped down everything before he left?"

"I was out, Matt. Most of the day, I think. I don't know when he left or even if he came back."

"Is there a photo of him on the Boston PD website?"

"I think so," Tamryn said. "Oh, wait a minute. I think I still have a small color photo of him in my wallet. Never cleaned out the scum. Where's my purse?"

"I have it," Matt said. "I took it to city hall this morning and locked it in my safe."

"Good," she said. "Did the asshole take my cash and credit cards?"

Matt shook his head. "I don't think so. After forensics dusted it for prints, I looked through it, and everything looked intact to me. About $120 in cash, driver's license, and credit cards still there."

"That sounds right. Guess he just wanted to make a point. Did you phone my mom?"

"No," Matt said. "It didn't feel like that should be my call. Do you want me to now?"

"No. I need to talk to my mother and figure out how he knew where to find me. My family are the only people on this planet who know exactly where I am."

Matt hesitated before speaking. "Does it really matter how he found out? Maybe it would help you heal faster if you just let that part go."

"It matters to me," she said defiantly. "If I can't trust my family, I need to know that now."

"OK," Matt conceded. "Where is your cell phone? Do you remember?"

"I'm not sure, but it might still be in the jacket I was wearing when you saw me on the beach. Front right zipped pocket."

"I'll go to your house after I do some other business with Bernice. If it's not in your jacket, I'll dial your number and find it."

"What other business with Bernice?" Tamryn asked.

Matt traded smiles with Jay. *Always curious, that's why she's such a great detective.* "It has to do with Fern's case on the island. Bernice and the Coast Guard brought the victim's body back here, and she's going to try to learn the cause of death for the investigation. You need to not worry about that now, OK?"

"Yeah," Jay added. "I need a partner as soon as possible. It's not a good idea for me to be wandering around Chinook County on my own."

"Truth," Tamryn laughed, and then clutched her abdomen in pain.

"Also not a good idea for you to laugh right now," Jay said. He patted her gently on the arm.

"We need to take some photos of your injuries," Matt said. "Do you feel up to that now?"

"Sure. I should have thought of that, huh?"

"We're the cops today, you're the patient," Matt said. He smiled at her. Using his phone, he snapped about ten photos of her face and head wounds, along with her ribs and abdomen.

"Lovely, I'm sure," she wheezed. Her eyelids fluttered, and she gave up and closed her eyes.

"C'mon, Detective Finley," Matt said. "Let's get out of here and let Detective Gesicki get some rest."

Tenderly, Jay leaned close to Tamryn's ear and said, "Take care of yourself."

• • •

Sunday, February 25, 2024—Honolulu, Hawaii

Secretary of State Fred Leufeld presented himself at the door of the Matsuda home, after a brief phone call to Naomi to inform her he was coming by to see her.

She opened the door, and her face immediately collapsed into the greatest of all pain. Naomi had feared when Fred called that he would be delivering bad news to her in person. But the agonized look on his face when she opened the door told her everything she needed to know. Hiroshi would not be coming home.

As gently as possible, Fred explained the circumstances of Hiroshi's death. Naomi held it together as she listened to the horrific news, trying to bring some sense of dignity to his undignified death. Slow tears rolled down her flawless face, and she twisted her wedding ring more and more violently as Fred finished his story, but remained silent until he was at the end.

Then she spoke. "Thank you, Fred, for coming here to see me. It's very thoughtful of you, and Hiroshi would be grateful. Where is my husband now?"

"The U.S. Coast Guard transported his body to the hospital in Buck Bay, Oregon. Local law enforcement and the U.S. State Department would like your permission to conduct a post-mortem exam," Fred said calmly.

"What good would that do?" Naomi asked.

"It would help them determine if his death was caused by murder or suicide." Fred looked down at his shoes when he said the last word in that sentence.

"Then they should proceed. And, of course, it will be found to be murder." Naomi, still crying softly, sounded matter of fact.

"How can you be sure?" Fred asked.

She dabbed her eyes with a Kleenex and looked directly at him. "Because

I always knew that someone would kill him. Because of his job, and because of the man he was. His moral compass. Hiroshi was bound to eventually come across someone who would disagree with his sense of right and wrong."

"Was he working on anything? What did he tell you when he left?"

"Not that I specifically know of," she answered, "but he and our son Shuji had been spending more time together than usual. I had a feeling that Hiroshi was helping him with something. Something they didn't want me or anyone else to get involved in. We will have to ask Shuji. But first, I have the awful duty to tell him and our daughter that their beloved father is dead."

"Do you want me to stay with you while you call them to come here?" Fred asked.

Naomi paused. "Yes, I would like that, Fred. You will give me the strength to do what I need to do. I will call them now."

"You have more inner strength than anyone I know," he said. "But we will handle this together. I owe it to Hiroshi."

The two old friends sat holding hands and crying together.

. . .

Sunday, February 25, 2024 — Buck Bay, Oregon

Matt and Jay joined Dr. Bernice Ryder in the Buck Bay Hospital morgue in the basement.

In a somber tone, Bernice said, "May I introduce you to Admiral Hiroshi Matsuda."

Matt, wearing his favorite 'Hook 'Em Horns' cap, removed it, and stood for a few seconds with it over his heart. Jay clasped his hands behind his back and looked down at the concrete floor.

"Some days, I hate my job," Matt said in a low voice. "Today would be one of those days."

"Yeah, not pleasant," Bernice said, "but we have a job to do, nonetheless. Naomi Matsuda and the Secretary of State have given me the green light to proceed with the post-mortem. Not that we needed their permission since it's a suspicious death. Think of it as us helping the U.S. avoid an international incident."

"That does help, Bernice," Matt said. Jay nodded in agreement.

"Shall I get started then?" she asked.

Equally fascinated and repulsed, Matt and Jay watched Bernice do her job. Working quietly and efficiently, she occasionally jotted something down on the notebook behind the slab.

Just when the two cops thought she was finishing up because she set down her tools and rested her hands on her hips, she suddenly grabbed her small pincers and moved in close to Matsuda's face again.

She plucked what looked like a fiber or hair from his left nostril, and immediately bagged it in one of the small clear bags she kept handy. She'd already studied his hands and fingernails, but she now returned to them with a more powerful microscope. After another minute of close study, and another pincer retrieval from under the fingernail of Hiroshi's right index finger, Bernice set down the microscope, pulled the sheet over what was left of Hiroshi Matsuda's body, and took off her gloves and facemask.

"Homicide. Someone killed him alright," Bernice said.

ɛ

CHAPTER 16

Sunday, February 25, 2024 — Cold Rock Island

Joe and Fern hiked around the perimeter of the island, looking for potential landing sites that Matsuda might have utilized. They also checked trees, shrubs, and flora for any broken branches, or signs of disturbance.

They came up empty, concluding that there were only three possibilities for Hiroshi's landing on the island: the primary boat harbor, the small beach on the north side of the island, or the airplane runway. The rest of the island was much too rocky and wild near the water to make any kind of landing safely. If he arrived surreptitiously, it had to be the north beach. The harbor and the runway were simply too visible and out in the open for anyone to sneak ashore.

Standing on the small beach, Fern could imagine a skiff or other small boat coming ashore here. However, there were no visible signs that had happened in recent days. No upheaval of the beach's sand, no tracks, or ruts. But it had also not been raked or swept clean, nothing to indicate anyone was trying to hide evidence. It looked like a normal Pacific beach would look if no one had landed or walked on it.

"I suppose there's a possibility that he got off a boat anchored somewhere off the island, and swam to shore," Joe said.

Fern looked at him as if her boss had gone stark raving mad. "Are you crazy? The waves would have smashed him to smithereens. Not to mention he would've died of hypothermia without a wetsuit, which we haven't found. And what would his exit plan have been? Swim back out to the boat?" She looked out to the wild Pacific.

"People swim in the ocean," he said defensively. "You swim parallel to the shore and let the waves bring you in when you want to."

She rolled her eyes. "I'm sorry, but that's not on my list of possibilities. This is the northern Pacific, not Hawaii. Look out there." She pointed to the ocean where riled up dark, tall waves were incessantly pounding the rocks of Cold Rock Island. And today was milder than usual.

Joe followed her hand, and said, "Yeah. Not likely he would have survived entry. I guess we have questions we need answers for," Joe said, stating the obvious.

"Like, how did Matsuda arrive here," Fern said, ticking off her thoughts on her fingers. "Why did he come here? Is it possible he was an invited guest? And, if so, why is everyone lying about it?"

"You think he might have been invited?"

"It's a possibility, Joe. I'm having trouble imagining how he got here without being seen. And what possible reason could he have had for wanting to come here without announcing his presence?"

"Maybe he did want to die on this island, or maybe he wanted some sort of souvenir from his time here, and he didn't want the current owner to know."

Fern looked at him. "Like what?"

"I have no idea."

"Or," said Fern, "maybe there is something going on here that Matsuda didn't like."

Now it was Joe's turn to ask, "Like what?"

"I have no idea," Fern repeated, with a laugh. "The only thing I know for sure is that it's very odd that not one of the ten people on this island saw or heard anything unusual. No one knows anything. How could all of them be so out to lunch that a Japanese admiral comes ashore, does whatever he came to do, and hangs himself in one of their buildings, and not a single person knows anything about it? Including one man, Tyson, who has a sterling resumé in security work?"

"Matsuda did have the advantage of knowing this island inside and out," Joe noted. "If he didn't want to be seen, he would know best how to avoid it."

"True. But Matt taught me to go with the odds, and the odds in this case are that someone would have noticed something. I think at least one person here is lying to us. But we've done everything we can do until we know the cause of death. We might as well go home and work it from there."

"Yeah," Joe agreed. "We've searched everywhere, interrogated everyone, and we don't have a single lead. Plus, it feels dangerous for us to be hanging around here, especially with Noah creeping around at night near your room. I'll call Captain Adams and request a pick-up."

"I'm not afraid to stay, but there's nothing more to be done here today. Roger that, let's go," she said.

They hiked back to the guest house in silence, frustrated by their lack of progress on the case. Joe, at least, managed to enjoy the fresh outdoors that he got so little of in D.C. The sun had been shining brilliantly all morning, and for the first time since they arrived, there was only a whisper of a breeze. Even the wild waves crashing on the shore seemed to appreciate the lack of the relentless wind and landed more softly than usual. But as he looked off to the southwest, increasing clouds, charcoal gray and pregnant with trouble, caused him to pick up his pace.

. . .

Back in her room, Fern changed into her own clothes that she'd arrived in yesterday—was it only twenty-four hours ago?!?—and placed the borrowed ones in the closet's laundry hamper. While she awaited word from Joe that the Coast Guard had arrived at the harbor, she sat in the corner of her sofa, and made some notes.

Her cell phone rang. Matt.

"I have good news for you," she told him, skipping pleasantries. "We're headed back. Just waiting on Captain Adams to get here."

"That's better news than you even know," Matt said.

"What do you mean?"

"You and Joe are in danger, and you need to get off that island right now! Bernice just completed the autopsy of Hiroshi Matsuda, and he was murdered. It was most definitely not suicide."

"How does she know?" Fern asked, excited. "What did she say?"

Fern heard a crackling noise, and figured Matt was looking at his police notebook and his scribbled notes from Bernice's autopsy results. "Her official cause of death reads 'Death by suffocation by a person or persons unknown.' In other words, Matsuda was dead before he was strung up."

"Did she give you a time of death?"

"She says the time of death is difficult on this one because we don't know for sure how long he might have been hanging there before they reported it. Her best guess is that he was smothered or somehow deprived of air about twenty-four hours before he was moved."

"But can't that be caused by hanging? Cutting off the air supply?"

"Yes, but that's usually because the neck is broken. It snaps and cuts off the oxygen to the brain. But she says that's not what happened here. There are other telltale signs that doctors and pathologists look for." Matt paused. "And are you alone right now?"

"Yes. Joe and I are in our rooms waiting for Captain Adams and our ship. My door is locked and I'm safe. What other signs did Bernice find that led her to murder?"

"She told me she was suspicious on the island when she got up close to the body. Said his eyes were bloodshot, and she saw some bruising around the nose and mouth. Those indicate he might have been forcefully smothered. Then, she found high levels of carbon dioxide in his blood—another sign of death by suffocation."

"Oh, good Lord," Fern said, distressed. "So, someone on this island is a killer after all?"

"Most likely," Matt said. "Especially if you haven't found any signs of how Matsuda arrived—boat, plane, etc. That tells me that it's unlikely a second person also arrived unnoticed and killed him. I think you have to take another hard look at the residents."

"And after hiking all over this place this morning, Joe and I didn't find any trace of Matsuda's arrival. We're stumped."

"But wait, there's more. We think we know what the murder weapon looks like. She found a fiber in his left nostril, and a possible matching one under a fingernail. We think he was smothered by a pillow and fought back valiantly. A purple pillow."

Silently, Fern looked down at the sofa pillow her left hand was resting on. A purple pillow.

. . .

Joe knocked on Fern's door. "The CG is just pulling into the marina," he said as she opened the door to admit him.

"I saw them approaching," she said urgently, her voice more high-pitched than usual. "You need to help me, Joe. We need to take this pillow with us." She pointed to the purple pillow on the sofa. "And we need to get it on the boat without anyone seeing it. It's probably the murder weapon. I'll explain later."

Joe didn't hesitate, or question Fern. He pulled a pillowcase off her bed pillow, handed it to Fern, and quickly remade the bed to cover the naked pillow while she bagged the purple one.

"What will we say is in here?" she asked him. "It's too big to fit into our suitcases. We'll just have to carry it out."

"It's sand and rock samples for us to take to the lab. No one will question us, and they certainly won't look inside the pillowcase. I'll take it. Follow my lead and downplay it. Are you ready to go?"

"I'm more than ready," she said. She grabbed her wheelie, jammed her phone in her pocket, and left with only a quick backward glance around her room.

Joe held the pillowcase in his right hand and steered his suitcase with his left as they made their way through the breezeway toward the main house. Rohn Reid was waiting for them around the front, sitting at the wheel of a golf cart. Tyson was occupying a second cart parked next to Rohn's.

"We saw Captain Adams coming in, and figured you could use a hand," said Rohn. "Looks like you're leaving us."

"We've finished our investigation here…for now," Joe said. "Fern and I are going back to the mainland now to do some follow-up."

"Are you stealing one of my pillowcases?" Rohn asked Joe, chuckling.

"I prefer the word 'borrowing'," Joe said, with a rare smile. "We'll get it back to you soon, I promise."

Fern felt for her gun handle.

"What's in it?"

"Oh, just some sand and a few rock samples. Nothing you'll miss, I suspect."

Rohn shrugged, not giving the pillowcase a second look. "Whatever floats your boat. Hop in."

Not needing to be told twice, Joe and Fern hopped into their respective carts, and they took off down the hill to the harbor. Captain Adams was standing on the tarmac at the bottom of the Resolve's staircase ramp.

"Thanks for your promptness, Captain," Joe said, and shook Adams' hand.

"I never miss a chance to get out of port," Adams said. He reached for Fern's suitcase, saying, "Ready?"

"Let's go, Captain," she smiled.

Joe turned to Rohn and said, "Thanks for your hospitality, Rohn. This is a difficult situation for all of us, and Fern and I appreciate your grace under fire. She will be in touch as needed as we work through these awful circumstances." And then, holding tight to the pillowcase, Joe followed the Captain and Fern up the ramp.

Rohn and Tyson sat motionless in the golf carts until the ship lost sight of them.

. . .

Fern and Joe stood alone at the ship's aft railing, watching Cold Rock Island slowly disappear from view. Overhead, it was clouding up, and the waves were getting a bit more rowdy. A fine sea spray provided an occasional misting. Joe continually wiped it from his face, but Fern knew it was good for her skin, and let it land.

"Do you want to tell me why I'm holding a stolen pillowcase with a pillow inside?" he said.

"Borrowed, you mean," she said, grinning, but quickly turned serious. "Bernice found tiny fragments of a purple fiber in Matsuda's nostril and under one fingernail. She believes he was suffocated with a purple pillow. And this one" — she pointed to the pillowcase — "just happened to be in my guest room."

"Wow. If she's right, it means Hiroshi was a guest of Rohn's after all."

"And he lied to us," Fern said. "Or, he wasn't a guest, but was being held in my room for some reason. Probably against his will."

"In which case, maybe several of the residents were involved. It would have been difficult for Rohn or one other person to hide the fact of Hiroshi's presence, don't you think?"

Fern nodded. "Exactly what I was thinking. Although, Rohn didn't seem to be bothered by us taking the pillowcase. Maybe this case is like *Murder on the Orient Express* where a bunch of people band together to kill someone."

Joe shuddered. "I hate that story. It creeps me out because, on some level, it made so much sense."

"But in our case, none of this makes any sense. At least, not yet it doesn't. We need to talk with Hiroshi's family. The 'why' in this mess is the most important part. Until we know why he was here, we can't make any progress." Fern stared out to sea, a grim set to her face. "Here's what I'm going to do, Joe. I will write down all my questions for the widow and her children this afternoon, working backwards from what we know now. Then, I'll talk to the Honolulu police chief and ask him to recommend his two best detectives to go talk to the family on our behalf. How does that sound?"

"Like a plan," Joe agreed. "Let me talk to Fred Leufeld first while you work on your questions. Also, we need to consider our personal safety. Rohn Reid or Tyson may know what is really inside this pillowcase, and, if so, they won't be thrilled it's in our possession."

"Yeah," Fern said, "you're right. What are you doing when we land?"

"I need to head home as soon as I can. I'm going to ask my oldest son and his wife to go stay with Margo. She's alone in our home, and suddenly, that doesn't feel right. Besides, this is now a murder investigation, and you will take over. If I know Matt, he's already in overdrive, and you all will do what needs to be done. I assume that your home is pretty safe these days?"

"It is. After Matt's incident, we got more serious about security. You could break into Fort Knox more easily than our house."

"Good to hear. Although I don't suppose that added security would have prevented what happened to him." Joe looked serious. "You need to watch your back, Fern. Somebody had the will to kill a Japanese naval hero. That says to me that this is not someone to trifle with."

Fern turned to look directly at her boss. "I'm not Clay Sherwin. I was kidnapped once because I ignored my gut feeling in a situation I knew to be questionable, and that will never happen to me again. I accept that I may get taken out some day on this job, but I won't ever make it easy for them."

Then the most surprising thing in the world happened. Unemotional, dry, by the book Joe Phelps gave Fern a hug. "Good," he said. "Don't."

"Are we almost there?" she asked him, looking down at the increasingly rough water. "I feel a little queasy."

CHAPTER 17

Friday, December 29, 2023, Honolulu

Hiroshi Matsuda was attempting to display the geographic location of Scott Thurman's device on a Google map. His expected first hurdle became a non-event when he determined that Thurman had—incredibly—allowed location sharing on his user account. Bingo!

Hiroshi had acquired tools over the years in his military service that helped him identify the IP address owner and the approximate latitude and longitude of an IP address location, even if the owner had taken precautions to evade detection through encryption and IP address redirects.

He sat upright in his chair, and carefully set down the cup of jasmine tea he'd been drinking. He stared at his computer screen. The geo-location of Scott Thurman's crypto account server was Cold Rock Island in the north Pacific Ocean.

That's impossible, he said to himself. *Hardly anyone knows that place exists, even after Rohn Reid bought it. There has to be a mistake somewhere. I've obviously screwed up with my tracking tools.*

Hiroshi pushed his chair back from the desk and walked to the kitchen through his darkened house. The hour was late, and Naomi was long asleep. He made another cup of tea, grabbed a couple of chocolates from a box of Christmas candy they'd been gifted, and returned to his office.

He sipped the tea and went back to work.

• • •

Sunday, February 25, 2024 — Buck Bay, Oregon

Matt arrived at the port of Buck Bay just as the Coast Guard cutter was docking. He reached into the back seat and pulled on his cap for protection against the downpouring skies. After the conclusion of Bernice's postmortem, Jay had gone home to Port Stirling to take a nap, while Matt went to pick up his wife and Joe Phelps.

Matt saw her immediately. His beautiful wife looked so colorful contrasted with the Coast Guard uniforms and the head-to-toe grey that was Joe's look. Her red hair and raspberry jacket were the first things he saw as he exited his car. He exhaled. *Huge relief to have her back on the mainland.*

Fern saw him standing at the end of the dock, and gave a big, exaggerated wave. Matt noticed that Captain Adams had ahold of Fern's elbow and was steering her carefully down the ramp. *What's that about?,* thought Matt.

"Everything alright?" he said as he approached Fern and gave her a big squeeze.

"I got a little seasick," she said to Matt. "Sorry," to Captain Adams.

"You do look a little on the green side," noted Matt.

"And I didn't even eat tuna fish sandwiches," Fern said, with a weak wink at Adams.

"She'll be OK in a few minutes once you get her on land that's not moving," Adams said. "It got a little bumpy further out."

"A little?" smiled Joe. "More like a roller coaster at Coney Island."

"Thanks, Bob," Matt said, clapping the Captain on the back. "Appreciate you bringing these two back safely."

"My pleasure," Adams replied. "Unpleasant journey all the way around, I'm afraid."

"I may need to call on you again, Captain," Fern said. "Could I maybe borrow your helicopter instead of the ship next time?"

Laughter all around, and they each headed off the dock, Adams back to his ship to file a report, and Phelps, Matt, and Fern to Matt's car.

Fern reached over to Joe and took possession of the pillowcase, storing it carefully in the car's trunk. Matt looked from it to Fern with a raised eyebrow, and she whispered, "The murder weapon. Be careful with it."

On the short drive to the airport, Joe called Fred Leufeld to tell him Fern's plan involving the Honolulu police. Fred agreed but wanted the fewest people possible to know of Hiroshi's murder, and said he would back up Fern's call to the police chief with one of his own to express the need for discretion.

"Good idea," Joe said. "I will do what the Secretary of State tells me to do."

"That would be the first time," Fred said, hanging up.

They dropped Joe off at the airport for his flight to Portland to catch the D.C. redeye later tonight.

"You kids keep me posted," Joe said.

"OK, gramps," joked Matt. "You stay sharp. There's probably at least one person out there"—he looked west out to sea and motioned with his head—"who's not loving you right now. Cover your butt."

"Elegantly put," Joe said, with a slight smile. "I just told your wife the same thing. This is ugly, Matt. You both need to take every precaution. And if you can spare me an international incident and the wrath of Fred Leufeld, I would be most grateful."

"We'll do our best, Joe," Matt said. He grabbed hold of Fern's hand. "She's the smart one and I'm the brute force and awkwardness."

"I seem to recall that somehow that system works," Joe said and waved good-bye as he walked through the airport's glass doors.

"Where to, lady?" Matt said to his wife.

"I'd like to see Tamryn while we're here, but I'm not sure I won't puke on her," Fern said. Some of her color was coming back, but she still looked pale to Matt.

"How about we come over tomorrow morning first thing?" he said. "Bernice has a plan for her recovery, and the fewer visitors the better for the next forty-eight hours."

Fern nodded. "Works for me. Let's drop off the pillowcase with Bernice, and then I would like to get home."

Matt punched Bernice's button on his phone and when she answered, "Dr. Ryder," he said, "We're bringing in something purple now. Be there in ten."

At the hospital, Fern took charge of the pillowcase, keeping the chain of custody intact, and Matt walked on the other side of it. They took the stairs down to the morgue and Bernice's office.

Pulling on gloves, Bernice carefully opened the pillowcase and gently eased the purple pillow out and onto her exam slab. She looked up at Fern and grinned. "That's it," she said. "This is exactly what I was hoping to see. Nice work, Spy Byrne."

Fern slapped her playfully on the arm. "Don't call me that. Especially in public. When will you know for sure?"

"This afternoon. I was just heading upstairs to do my patient rounds, and then I'll analyze this before I go home to my long-suffering husband for our Sunday night date." She looked back down at the pillow. "But I'm 99 percent sure it's a match."

She and Fern high-fived.

By the time Matt drove into their driveway, Fern was feeling more like herself, and got out of the car before he pulled into their garage. She took some big gulps of the fresh ocean air while he parked, and immediately felt less wobbly.

After taking a quick shower, she dressed in her comfy sweats, and went out to the deck. The rain that had accompanied her and Matt home from Buck Bay had stopped just before they arrived in Port Stirling. The air was so clean and sweet, and the sun was just starting its drop into the Pacific. Streaks of pale pink and grey wove nicely into the few remaining clouds off to the west. The surf was calm, coming ashore politely with its meek bright-white waves.

Fern wiped off two chairs with a towel from the stack they kept in a cabinet under the home's overhang. Matt had a couple of calls to make and would then join her.

She closed her eyes and continued her deep breathing until he arrived with a glass of Chardonnay for her and a dark lager for himself, setting them on the outdoor table. He bent over and planted a meaningful kiss on her lips.

"There," he said. "That's better."

"Yes," was all she said.

"Are you feeling a little spunkier now?"

"I'm fine. That damn boat. I don't really like boats, never have."

"They have been causing us grief lately, haven't they?"

"Yes, and we should vow to steer clear of them whenever possible."

"Deal."

"What shall we do for food tonight?" she asked. "I'm getting hungry."

"All set. I just called Vicky at Whale Rock, and she's holding a table for us tonight. This is not a night we need to cook, plus I need to talk to her anyway."

"Can I go in my sweats? I'm so comfortable right now."

"Why not? Sunday night, not many tourists in town. Should be quiet."

"Perfect." She took a sip of wine. "What do you need to talk to Vicky about?"

"I've got a photo of Tamryn's asshole husband, and I want to show it to her and ask her to keep a lookout. Jay's taking it around to all the restaurants and markets in town. If he's still here, he's gotta eat. Walt and Rudy are covering the rental car agencies, airport and Greyhound, and the hotels and motels, too. But we know he's fond of our Ocean Bend Road area since he found Tamryn, so I figure Vicky is a likely detective for us."

"Is she in really bad shape?" Fern dropped her chin and looked up at Matt with big eyes, like she was almost afraid to hear his answer.

"Pretty bad. You'll be shocked when you see her tomorrow. But Bernice says she'll heal up. It's just a time thing. It pisses me off." His face was dark and stormy, like it only got when he was truly angry.

"Do you think he's still in the area?"

"Who knows? But we'll know more tomorrow after covering all the bases today."

"How did he find her? Does Tamryn know?"

"No, not for sure. She says the only people who knew where she moved to are her parents."

"Surely they wouldn't spill the beans to her husband?" Fern said, incredulously.

"You wouldn't think so, but family can be weird. I'm trying to get her to not dwell on that now. I want her to focus on getting well. I'll find that out when I catch him…and I will catch him."

"I know you will," Fern said. "You're my husband, and you're the best."
They clinked glasses.

$\bullet \ \bullet \ \bullet$

"Casual night out for the Hornings?" Vicky said, archly. She eyed Fern in her sweats. Fern pulled her coat closer around her to hide them.

"I had a tough day, Vicky. Cut me some slack."

"You could come here naked as a jaybird for all I care. It's just not like you. You feeling OK? You look a little peaked."

"I was on a boat ride on the open seas this afternoon, and I got seasick. I'm fine now, and we're hungry."

"Then let's go get you some food," Vicky said. She grabbed two menus from the dining room stand and took off to the far corner by the window. Their table, for her long-time friends.

"I'm a mess, but you're looking good tonight," Fern said to her, sitting down. Vicky, her blond bob hair-sprayed within an inch of its life, was wearing a fawn-colored short leather skirt, topped with a leopard-print ¾ sleeve sweater, and leopard pumps.

"We've got a group of English golfers coming in about an hour from now, so I thought I'd dress better than I usually do on Sunday night."

"Any other tourists around?" Matt asked.

"Just the odd three-day weekend Californians, although the golf trade has been steady all month, kinda unusual for February."

"Any lone men in the past three or four days?" he asked.

"A couple," Vicky said. "Why?"

Matt slipped the photo Tamryn gave him out of his pocket and held it up to her. "Any chance you've seen this guy?"

Vicky pulled the photo in closer and took a hard look. "Maybe," she said, finally. "Might have been here last Friday night. Was that the day you guys had your cop retreat at our event center? I think I saw him that night."

"Yes, that was Friday," Matt said. "How did he act? Why do you remember him?"

"Well, he was a real charmer," Vicky said. "Which doesn't work on me, for the record."

Fern laughed.

"And he had an accent. East-coast like, I think."

"How old was he?" Matt asked.

"About your age — mid-forties, I guess."

Fern and Matt looked at each other. Right age, right accent.

"Did he pay with a credit card?" Fern asked.

Vicky thought. "I'm not sure, but I can look through Friday's receipts. I remember what he had; pork chop, coleslaw, and apple pie."

Matt stared at her. "How do you do that?"

"It's my superpower. Now, what'll you have tonight?"

"Normally, I'd have your oyster stew," Fern said, "but seafood doesn't sound as good to me tonight as usual. How about the meatloaf and scalloped potatoes? And a glass of your house red."

"Excellent choice. And you, husband?"

"The same, please. And bring me whatever beer you think I should drink tonight." There was no point in arguing about beer with Vicky; she always brought what she thought he would like.

They settled into their comfortable chairs and discussed the Hiroshi Matsuda case while they waited for their food. Not for the first time, Fern was so grateful for Matt. They'd met the first day he arrived in Port Stirling, and if it wasn't love at first sight for her — it was for him — she had quickly come to admire his work ethic. He'd unlocked a love for law enforcement in her that she hadn't realized was lurking under the surface in her professional life. Under his guidance, she'd blossomed into a superb detective, and she couldn't imagine being married to anyone who didn't share her love for her work.

"How am I going to figure out which of the island's ten residents murdered Hiroshi?" she asked him now. "They were all cool and calm, and acted like they had nothing to hide. Joe thinks Simon, the visiting gardener is suspicious, but I can't see it."

"Why is Joe suspicious of him?"

"He had a book in his room on Japanese military history, and Hiroshi was in it."

"How did he explain it?"

"He said he'd found it in Rohn's library and thought it would be interesting. He wanted to know more about the history of the island. Said it 'informs his aesthetic outlook' or something like that," Fern said.

"Your next steps are going to depend on what Bernice tells us about your pillow. If it was used to smother Hiroshi, then you start over with the residents because if he was in that guest room, one and probably more of them are lying to you. The knowledge that he was murdered, that it wasn't a suicide, might shake something loose from one of them."

"It is a game-changer, and Rohn and the rest of them can't dance around the possible suicide angle anymore."

"Also," Matt continued, "I checked all of the island residents for registered guns, and everyone but Lynette has a permit to carry."

"Wow. Prepared group, huh? Even Leonard?" Fern asked. "He doesn't seem the type."

"He's been with Rohn a long time, and probably sees his role as protective, even if it's not officially his job title."

"Does anyone have a prior?"

Matt shook his head. "Nope. I ran a Triple I backgrounder, and only Randy has a speeding ticket that he got on I-5 about eight years ago. That's it, no other brushes with the law from any of them. I haven't been able to check on Simon in the U.K. yet, but will follow-up on him, too."

"No need," Fern said. "Rod told Joe that everyone is clean on the feds' records as well, and he checked with the U.K. on Simon. Clean as a whistle."

"Good to know. But we need to keep in mind that they could all have guns in their possession. Therefore, and this is not open for discussion, but if you have to go back to that island, Jay and I are coming with you. Maybe Ed, too."

"You'll get no argument from me," Fern said. "It's a spooky place, and it had a bad vibe. It's hard to explain, but it's a kind of evil feeling. And my boss gave me strict orders to not go back alone because something strange happened last night."

"What kind of strange?" he asked, senses alert.

"There was a knock on my window about 3:00 a.m," she reluctantly shared with him. "I grabbed my gun and went to look. Ended up running down the night security guard, Noah."

"Jesus H. Christ!" yelled Matt, loud enough for folks at a table ten feet away to turn and stare. He held up his hand at them. "Sorry," he said, sheepishly. "What'd he have to say for himself?"

"He was just checking to make sure that Joe and I were alright," she said, knowing how weak that sounded.

"This joker wakes you up in the middle of the night to check on you? Why? Was he expecting you to be dead?"

"He thought if we were in trouble, we'd yell out."

"And you bought that?"

"Not really. I think he was trying to scare us off. Either of his own accord, or on someone's orders. He was surprised when I chased him."

"Could he be a killer, do you think?" Matt asked.

Fern nodded. "We haven't ruled out anyone on that island. They're all a little peculiar, in my view. What we need is a motive. I can't figure out why Hiroshi was on that island in the first place, and it's clearly the key to what happened to him."

"If he was suffocated with the purple pillow from your guest room, you will know that they've all been lying to you," Matt said. He reached across the table and squeezed her hand.

CHAPTER 18

Sunday, February 25, 2024 — Honolulu

Naomi Matsuda gathered her two children: son Shuji and daughter Fumiko close to her on the sofa in the living room. During the previous hour, she had taken them into the elegant, beautiful bedroom she shared with their father, and told them the sad, horrific news. The three had held each tightly and sobbed.

Holding hands and trying valiantly to compose themselves, they now awaited the police to question them about Hiroshi's activities leading up to his death. On Naomi's nod, Fred Leufeld answered the door to admit the two detectives from the Honolulu police department.

"I'm Detective Koa Hale," said the taller of the two men who entered with Leufeld. "This is Detective Jamie Anderson. We're so sorry about your loss, ma'am." The native Hawaiian approached Naomi and gave a slight bow.

"Thank you, Detective," Naomi whispered. "Please take a seat," she motioned to chairs across from them. "Please tell my children and me how we can help you understand what happened to my husband."

Secretary of State Fred Leufeld started off. "The main thing we need to know, Naomi, is why Hiroshi was there. Why had he returned to Cold Rock Island after all these many years? Do you know?"

Naomi shook her head. "I do not. He left here last Wednesday, and only told me that he had a quick business trip. I pressed him, but he didn't want to give me the details. He said I wasn't to worry, and that he would be back home in a couple of days. He never mentioned Cold Rock Island to me. And he rarely talked about his earlier days there." She twisted the large diamond wedding ring on her left hand.

"He mentioned the island to me last week," Shoji said, speaking to Fred. All eyes turned to him. He swiveled to look at his mother and began to cry. "I'm so sorry, mom, I should have stopped him." He bent over, clearly in agony, and buried his face in her lap.

"What is it, Shuji?" Naomi asked. "What do you know?" She patted his back tenderly, but then said more firmly, "Please sit up, son, and talk to us."

Shuji did as she asked, wiping his eyes with his shirt sleeves. "Dad was working on a project for me," he said haltingly at first, but then gathering momentum. "It was to do with my bank."

"Which bank do you work for?" asked Detective Hale.

Shuji told him, and explained the threatening messages, and how his father had uncovered the cryptocurrency scheme being run by Scott Thurman. "Dad and I suspected it was fraud, and he was researching the technology behind it for me."

"What does this have to do with Cold Rock Island?" Detective Hale asked.

"Last week, dad traced the host server's physical location, and it's on that island. He couldn't believe it."

"Why was that?" Hale asked.

"Because Hiroshi Matsuda had been stationed there to run a joint operation with the U.S. a couple of decades after the Second World War," Fred Leufeld said. "It was a top-secret operation at the time, and he and I were both there for several years. It's a strange coincidence."

"Are you telling me that your father went to Cold Rock Island to investigate a fraudulent scheme on your behalf?" Naomi asked her son. There was a chill in her voice.

Shuji looked beyond miserable. Unable to find the words, he nodded, his face crumpled, and his body collapsed in a heap in his mother's lap.

"Why didn't you tell us?" shrieked Fumiko at her brother.

"Would it have made a difference?" Shuji choked out. "You know our father. He would do what he would do. I told him not to go, that I would hire someone to get to the bottom of this. I couldn't stop him. He never listened to me," he said, with more steel in his voice now. "He was always curious. And Cold Rock Island was an important part of his past. He *wanted* to go."

Shuji sat up straight now and said to the detectives, "I will tell you everything I know, but I don't know anything about after he arrived on the island."

"Do you know how he got there?" Detective Hale asked. "I assume he flew. It would have taken too long from Honolulu to go by ship, based on the timeline of his death as we understand it."

"Yes, he flew," Shuji answered. "He told me that a man named Rohn Reid bought the island from the U.S. government, and that he had met him briefly years ago at the sale and handover."

"The west coast billionaire Rohn Reid?" Hale asked.

Fred Leufeld replied, "Yes. The same. He's there now and is the person who called me when they found Hiroshi's body."

Naomi moaned.

Shuji continued. "He reached Mr. Reid and told him he wanted to visit Cold Rock Island 'for old times' sake.' Reid not only invited him to come, he flew his private jet to pick up dad. He left on Wednesday. I took him to the airport." His face crumpled again.

"Did you hear from your father when he got there?" Naomi asked.

"No. I never talked to him again."

"Well, I'll be a son-of-a-bitch," said the Secretary of State, slapping the arm of his chair violently. "Rohn Reid looked me in the eye and flat-out lied to me. He told us that neither he nor any of the island's residents knew Hiroshi was there until they found him dead." He stared at Shuji. "Are you absolutely certain that it was Rohn Reid your father talked to?"

"Yes. I was on the speaker phone with dad here when he talked to him. It was Reid. And he piloted his plane. I met him."

"What does Rohn Reid look like?" Fred quizzed him, needing to be sure.

"Mid 60's, about 5'9" and probably 200 pounds. Gray hair, fat. Sorta rumpled."

Fred turned to the detectives. "That's him, alright," he scowled. "Sounds like my old friend Rohn has some explaining to do."

. . .

Sunday, February 25, 2024 — Port Stirling

Vicky approached Matt and Fern's table, waving a receipt in the air. "I found it!" she exclaimed. "Barry M. Gesicki, Mr. pork chop and coleslaw. Friday night, 8:42 p.m."

Matt took out his phone and snapped a photo of the receipt. "You are worth your weight in gold, Miss Vicky."

"I am. Please tell all your friends. Especially any handsome ones." She retreated to present a bill to another table across the room.

Matt smiled at his wife. "Got him! Are you done eating?"

"Yes." She'd been pushing her remaining meatloaf around the plate for the past ten minutes.

"Let's go then," he said, leaving cash on the table to cover their meal and a generous tip for Vicky. "I want to check some hotels personally tonight. You can either come with me, or I'll drop you off at the house."

"I think I've had enough excitement for one day," she said reluctantly. "Take me home."

"Are you sure you're OK? It's not like you to miss out on all the action," he grinned.

"I've been pretty much awake since three o'clock this morning. I'm feeling the need for my bed and a book. That's all. Some quiet time to regroup for whatever tomorrow brings."

"You're allowed." He kissed her on the cheek, waved to Vicky, and they set off for home.

. . .

Once he saw that Fern was settled, house locked up, and security system enabled, he drove first to one of the beachfront hotels on Ocean Bend Road, the one closest to Tamryn's end of the road. Showing the photo he'd retrieved from Tamryn's wallet to the elderly but sharp gentleman on the front desk, Matt had no luck; the clerk had not seen Barry Gesicki, nor was he registered.

He drove to the next motel, just a few blocks up the road, and also on the beach side of the road. Same story, no joy for Matt.

He dinked around in this beachfront neighborhood until he'd exhausted all the reasonable lodgings, and then drove to Port Stirling Links on the north edge of town. It was pricey accommodation for a cop, but also the best known. He pulled into the swanky looped driveway and stopped in front of the valet stand.

Flashing his badge at the valet, Matt said, "I'll be right back. Just going to check with your reception desk for a minute." He tossed his keys to the kid, just in case he needed to move Matt's car.

"Sure thing, Chief Horning," the kid said, smiling at Matt. Everyone in Port Stirling knew him. *Good thing I'm not the philandering type*, Matt thought. *Fern would know before I even did anything.*

There was someone new at the reception desk, a man Matt didn't know. Again, he showed his badge, and the man asked, "How can I help you?"

"I'm looking for a man we believe is in Port Stirling. A tourist." He pulled out Gesicki's photo and showed it to him. "His name is Barry Gesicki, and I'm wondering if he's staying here. Can you check for me?"

"I don't have to check," the man said, "he's here. He's in the bar over there now." He pointed to the small, snug bar in the corner by the huge fireplace. "He's the guy with the mustache in the blue plaid flannel shirt."

Matt hesitated. *Should I call Jay or Rudy for back-up? I should, but I don't want to.* He spoke quickly to the man at the desk. "Please tell your security guys to man the front door. Now! I'm about to make an arrest, and he may try a runner." The man was on his phone before Matt finished talking.

He strode across the lobby toward the bar.

Gesicki, sitting alone at a small table just inside the entrance, had his back to Matt as he entered the cozy bar. Scanning the room, Matt noted there were only five patrons, plus the bartender. At one square table in the far corner sat four men still in golfing attire, even though the hour was late. Two of them leaned against the forest-green walls with their dark wainscot paneling, while their companions sprawled out into the tiny room, lifting whisky glasses to the newcomer as he entered the intimate space.

That gesture caused the lone male sitting at the bar chatting with the bartender, and Barry Gesicki to turn to see who was joining them. The bartender, Don Swigert, worked Matt and Fern's wedding last year and they were now friends. Matt gave Don his 'police chief at work' nod, and the bartender gave him a subtle thumbs up.

Matt approached his target, who was looking warily over his shoulder at him. "Are you Barry Gesicki?" Matt asked, taking out his badge.

"I'm just a tourist having a drink," Gesicki said, playing to the golfers, who responded with laughter. He turned back around to acknowledge his fellow drinkers' laughter. As he did so, Matt grabbed the back of his shirt and lifted him up out of his chair.

"It's a yes or no question, Mr. Gesicki," Matt said loudly, leaving no doubt in the room that he was here on business.

"OK! OK! No need to get rough. I'm Barry Gesicki. Who are you?" He glared at Matt. Gesicki was a couple of inches taller than Matt, making him about 6'1". He was substantial with broad shoulders and beefy arms, and he also showed the start of a beer belly. He had longish but receding brown hair, a neatly trimmed mustache, and a bulbous nose that ruined his entire face. He wore wire-rimmed glasses. The two men were facing each other now, inches apart. Matt let go of his shirt.

"Barry M. Gesicki, I'm police chief Matt Horning of the Port Stirling PD. I'm arresting you for assault and attempted murder of Tamryn Gesicki. You have the right to remain silent. Anything you say can and will be used against you in a court of law. You have…"

"Yeah, yeah, yeah," Gesicki muttered. "I'm a cop. I know the drill."

"Which is why I intend to fully inform you of your rights in front of these witnesses," Matt said. "I'd hate for you to get off on a technicality." He finished his Miranda warning in full. "Please place your hands together in front of your body." Gesicki did so, and Matt took the handcuffs from his belt loop, and placed them firmly on the suspect.

"I didn't do anything to my wife, you know," said Gesicki. "We just talked."

"Must've been some talk," Matt sneered at him. "Tamryn's in the hospital with broken ribs, a bruised kidney, stitches all over her face, and a concussion. You're lucky she's not dead."

A gasp went up from the bar patrons.

Gesicki seemed to shrink a little. "That wasn't me," he protested.

"Your wife said it was you. Seems like she'd know her own husband." Matt looked down at Gesicki's hands in the cuffs. "And, it looks to me like you were in a fight."

"Nah, just some scrapes from a hike in the woods out back."

One of the inebriated golfers staggered the few steps toward Gesicki and stared at his hands. He got in Gesicki's face. "Dude, you beat up your wife? Thass not cool."

"I did not beat up my wife or anybody," Gesicki argued. "I'm a cop with the Boston PD."

"Why are you here?" Matt asked. He knew the answer, but wanted to hear what his prisoner would say.

"I just wanted to see where my wife was living. And I heard Oregon is nice. Thought I might move here, too."

"Oh, you'll move here alright," Matt said. "Right into our finest correctional facility. Let's go." He nudged Gesicki with a bit more force than was necessary and marched him out through the lobby.

• • •

Fern was wearing a Beyoncé tee shirt that was a size too big for her and sitting up in bed reading. It was raining again, but she liked the tinkling sound of it on the skylight in their bedroom. She was beyond happy to be cozy at home tonight, and out of harm's way.

The book, the latest installment of Robert Galbraith's Cormoran Strike series, was heavy at 970 pages and hard to hold up tonight because Fern was dead tired. But she loved J.K. Rowling's writing in this series, and it was fun for her to read English crime fiction. She also enjoyed a good old American police procedural, too, and always had a stack of books on her nightstand. *Should have read this one on my Kindle*, she thought now, *easier to hold up!*

Her phone lying on the bed next to her vibrated. She kept it close whenever Matt was out working. But this was a call from Bernice. Fern grabbed it and hastily answered, "Hi, Bernice."

"Hi. Glad I caught you. Are you home?"

"Yep. In bed reading. Matt's out looking for Barry Gesicki, and I'm trying to wait up for him. Whatcha got?"

"Does Matt think he's still in town?" Bernice asked.

"Not sure. But he ate dinner at the Whale Rock Inn Friday night. Vicky had the receipt and recognized his photo. Matt thinks there's a chance he's still in the area."

"I hope he gets him. Tamryn's in bad shape, and that guy needs to rot in jail. But that's not why I called. You need to know that your purple pillow is indeed the murder weapon. The fiber I found in Hiroshi's nostril is an exact match to the fibers in this pillow. Also, I went back and looked more closely inside his mouth, and I found another matching fiber there. He was definitely smothered with this pillow, and that's what killed him. You did good, Fern."

"Yes!" Fern pumped her fist in the air. "I'm going to text Joe with this news now so he can call the Secretary of State first thing tomorrow to inform Matsuda's family. Do you have any other forensics info yet? Fingerprints on the beam or the ladder?"

"Not yet. The lab is slammed, and they said it might be Tuesday before they can tell me anything definitive. Sorry."

"It's OK. I've got plenty to do with this confirmation. I'll take a hard, very hard look at each person on that island."

"Will you go back out there?"

Fern shuddered. "Probably at some point. But I'll be taking Matt, Jay, and Ed with me, you can be damn sure. Thanks, Bernice, this gives us a path forward."

The two friends agreed to talk tomorrow and ended the call. Fern went back to Cormoran Strike, happy to be back in a fictional world tonight instead of her real world. Just as she was starting to nod off, her phone pinged with an incoming text.

"Got him!" read the text from Matt. "Taking him to the county jail. Home soon. Don't wait up."

CHAPTER 19

Monday, February 26, 2024 — Buck Bay, Oregon

Matt, Fern, and Jay sat talking with Tamryn in her hospital room. Matt would forever remember the look on her smashed face when he told her that Barry Gesicki was in jail in Twisty River.

She tried to smile but winced in pain. "Come over here, Matt," she said. "Fern, is it alright if I give your brilliant husband a kiss?"

Fern laughed. "Please, be my guest. He deserves a kiss."

Gently, Matt leaned over her and brushed her bruised, swollen lips with his. "Thank you," she whispered.

"You're welcome," he whispered back, and then added, "All you have to do now is get well."

"Piece of cake," Tamryn said. "What happens to him next?"

"I talked to Earl this morning, and he's working on Barry's arraignment. Told me it will be tomorrow afternoon." Earl Johnson was the Chinook County Sheriff.

"Will you go?" Tamryn asked.

"Oh, yeah," replied Matt. "I wouldn't miss this one for anything."

"Can I go with you?"

"I anticipated that question," Matt smiled, "and Dr. Ryder says no. Her exact words were, 'big fat no'. She says you're not going anywhere until tomorrow at the earliest, and probably not until Wednesday morning. But

I will take you to see him at the jail as soon as you're able to. I left the photos of your injuries with the sheriff, and he has shared them with Judge Hedges."

"Did she recognize me?" Tamryn asked.

"Earl said that Cynthia recoiled in horror at the photos and told the sheriff to tell you that she's so sorry this happened to you," Matt said. "She is looking forward to Barry's arraignment."

"Good," Tamryn smiled.

"In other news," Fern said, "your landlord is having the locks on your house changed today, and a keypad is being installed on the front door. You will program it when you leave here."

"Is that necessary?" Tamryn asked. "With Barry locked up..."

"She insisted," Fern interrupted. "She feels awful and says she should have installed better locks on her rental. Let her do this."

"It's not her fault. He's a cop, remember?" Tamryn said. "He would have figured out a way in no matter what. Please tell her that. I don't want her to feel bad."

"I will pass that along," Fern said. "Also, Sylvia is going to move into your guest room for a couple of days to ease your transition from here to home."

Tamryn started to talk, but Fern, smiling, held up her hand. "She volunteered. And none of us are about to tell Sylvia she can't do something she wants to do."

"How on earth are we so lucky to have an admin like Sylvia in the department?" Tamryn chuckled. "Can she cook? I appreciate the care I'm getting here, but it must be told that the food isn't great."

"Not only is Sylvia a terrific cook," Matt answered, "she's already been food shopping and is on her way to stock your kitchen. I gave her the key this morning. If I were you, I'd ask her to make you her prized prime rib and Yorkshire pudding. Tell her you're going to need extra protein."

Matt was happy to note that Tamryn laughed and didn't grimace in pain.

"What's the latest on your island case, Fern?" she asked.

Fern filled her in on the pillow evidence. "We," she waved her hand to include Matt and Jay, "will be working from here today and tomorrow following up on the island's residents' background info. Then, after

Barry's arraignment tomorrow, we'll be returning to the island. Ed's coming with us."

"That's going to leave our department short-handed," Tamryn lamented.

"Don't worry about that," Matt said hastily because he knew what she was thinking. "Walt and Rudy can handle things for a day or two. Plus, Buck Bay PD is on call if we need extra help, and the sheriff and his deputies will spend some time in Port Stirling, too."

"All hands on deck," Tamryn said. "Guess it's nice to have the support when we need it, but this sucks." She slapped her hand on the bed.

"We help each other out," Matt said. "And there's not a cop in this county that doesn't want you back in action as soon as possible. But a lot of them have been right where you are currently, and they know how you feel—including me. Take your time, Detective Gesicki. Heal up properly."

"And that's an order from your chief," added Jay.

• • •

Matt, Fern, and Jay returned to Port Stirling city hall, where they were to meet up with Oregon State Police Lieutenant Ed Sonders to brief him on the murder of Hiroshi Matsuda. PSPD Sergeant Walt Murphy, and Detective Rudy Tomaselli were holding down the fort on a slow Monday afternoon.

"What are you doing here?" Rudy asked Fern, giving her a hug. Before she'd taken the job with the State Department, Fern had been a detective in the PSPD. She now worked from home, although she had a small office down the hall from the police department that she frequented on occasion.

"My boss has asked me to look into the murder of a Japanese man that happened on Cold Rock Island—I was out there yesterday," Fern said. "It's turning out to be an ugly situation, and I need this department's help, along with the Oregon State Police."

"I've never heard of that island," Rudy said. "Where is it?"

"About thirty minutes by ship due west of here. It was the site of a top-secret military operation for several years. I'd never heard of it either until

Saturday. And what I'm going to share with you is also confidential—at least, for now," she said. "Have you seen Ed today?"

"No, but Sylvia told us he was expected. She took off to Tamryn's house," Walt said.

"Yeah, I gave her the key," Matt said. "She's getting the place cleaned up and ready for Tamryn to come home from the hospital. She says 'hi' by the way."

"How she's doing?" asked Rudy.

"She's tough, and she'll be OK, but this isn't a picnic for her," Matt said.

"Did someone say 'picnic'?" said big Ed Sonders, coming in the door. At 6'4" with a barrel chest, and dressed in his state police uniform, including holster, gun, and distinctive bowler-style hat with its broad brim, Sonders was a force to be reckoned with.

"Howdy, Ed," Matt said. "Thanks for coming over." Ed lived about twenty-five miles inland from Port Stirling, on a nice piece of property fronting the Twisty River.

"I was due to come out here anyway, but when I heard Fern is in charge today, I skedaddled."

"Don't you be flirting with my wife, big guy," Matt said to his best man.

"She's not your wife today, Chief, she's the representative of the United States government, and I'm here to do whatever she tells me to do. Ma'am," he saluted Fern.

The room broke down in laughter, as Matt said, "You're so full of shit, Ed."

"I am."

"Well, I think you're charming as always, Lieutenant," Fern grinned. "And I am in charge today, but I desperately need all of your help. Now that Matt has put Tamryn's attacker behind bars, we're all going to focus on the Hiroshi Matsuda murder case, and my boss appreciates our local help." She filled in the guys on all the particulars of her case, including Bernice's findings during the post-mortem, and what Fred Leufeld told Fern in an early-morning phone call about Shuji's bombshell.

"Two possibilities then," Ed said, after listening intently to Fern's summary. "One, and the most likely it seems to me, is that one of your ten residents is the killer."

"But we don't know which one or why," Fern added. "And that needs to be our focus today and tomorrow. Extensive background checks on all of them."

"Right," Ed said. "Or, two, someone else sneaked onto the island, killed him, and then sneaked off."

"Which you will see when we go out there is pretty close to an impossible scenario," Fern said. "It's not that big an island, and Rohn Reid has round-the-clock security."

"There's one more possibility," Matt said. "Hiroshi's family. By his own admission, his son Shuji appears to be the only person who knew where his father was going. I'd like to know more about him and their relationship." He turned to Fern. "Do we have the Secretary of State's permission to deal directly with the Matsuda family, or do we have to go through the Honolulu PD?"

"Secretary Leufeld told me this morning to do whatever we have to do to find out who murdered Hiroshi," Fern said. "Nothing or no one is off limits, is what I understood him to say. But Detective Koa Hale with the HPD seems sharp. I liked him in my phone call to him earlier, and he asked all the questions I told him to ask the family. You should call him first if you have thoughts you'd like him to follow up on. He knows what he's doing."

"Sounds good," Matt said, nodding.

Fern went to the department's white board and wrote Detective Hale's cell phone number. "He told me to not worry about the time difference between here and Honolulu—he's available around the clock on this case. However, I'd like to be respectful of his time as much as we can. Honolulu is two hours behind us this time of year."

Matt looked at his watch. Ten minutes after two. "So, it's 12:10 p.m. there now." He got up from where he'd perched on Sylvia's desk. "I'll go in my office and give him a call. I'll work the family angle today. Fern will give you assignments, and everything else is on hold today and tomorrow, OK guys? As soon as we get past Barry Gesicki's arraignment tomorrow afternoon, Fern, Jay, Ed, and I are going to Cold Rock Island."

To Walt and Rudy, Matt said, "If anything comes up in Port Stirling that the two of you can't handle, call Dan in Buck Bay and his crew will help you."

"Understood," said Walt, and Rudy nodded.

"Thanks, honey," Fern said to Matt, which never failed to get a laugh in this room. "This is a big case with important ramifications at the international level. Let's give it our best effort."

• • •

Monday, February 26, 2024 — Twisty River, Oregon

Barry Gesicki sat on the hard, lumpy twin bed in his cell at the Chinook County jail. Pulled up next to it on an equally uncomfortable folding chair sat his court-appointed attorney, Ryan Lopez. The young lawyer was wearing an ill-fitting blue suit with a frayed-collar white shirt, and red tie. His shoes, which should have been black, were scuffed and dirty brown lace-ups.

"Your arraignment in front of Judge Cynthia Hedges is tomorrow at 3:00 p.m.," Lopez told his client.

"A woman?" Barry said. "Dammit! Can't we ask for another judge?"

"Judge Hedges is the only Circuit Court judge in Chinook County," Lopez replied. "So, no."

"I'm screwed from the get-go then."

"Did you attack your wife, Mr. Gesicki? Whatever you tell me is privileged information, and the truth can help me craft your case."

"Of course I hit her," Barry growled. "A fact which she will no doubt testify to in court. Your job is to convince the judge that I didn't mean to, and it was an accident. And to get me a plea deal which will get me out of this hellhole and on probation so I can go home."

"I've seen the photos of Mrs. Gesicki, and, to be perfectly honest with you, it doesn't look like an accident." He shut up and stared at his client.

"I'm a big guy," he shrugged. "Shit happens."

"Why did you hit her?"

"She made me look like a fool at work. It pissed me off."

"How did she make you look like a fool?"

"She left me, didn't she? No bitch female is ever going to leave me and get away with it. I'm a catch, aren't I?" Barry grinned a sick, manic grin at his attorney.

Lopez shifted in his chair. "Obviously, we can't say that in court," he said nervously. "You'll have to say something like 'you came out to Oregon to talk to her, to win her back, and it didn't go well. You pushed her out of frustration, and she fell', something like that."

"I can do that," Barry said, nodding his head in agreement. "Do you think the judge will believe me?"

"In all honesty, probably not. But we won't worry about that right now. Tomorrow's arraignment is just for you to hear the charges against you, what your rights are, and to enter a plea. I will be formally appointed to represent you, and your next court date will be set. You want to enter 'not guilty', correct?"

"Yeah. Not guilty, that's me alright." He laughed. "What about bail? I want you to get me out of here tomorrow."

To his credit, Ryan Lopez didn't flinch when he imparted the following information to his unpleasant client. "Bail may not be possible," he said. "It's up to the judge and your extenuating circumstances."

"What do you mean?" Barry demanded. "It's assault 4. Simple probation."

"Maybe. Maybe not. You knowingly assaulted a public safety officer. In Oregon, that's a Class C felony. There's also the question of your hands being a dangerous weapon because you're a cop, too, and a big guy. And if the arresting officer thinks you exhibited extreme indifference to human life, you could be charged with Assault 2, which in this state carries a possible sentence of at least five years."

"Ridiculous," Gesicki fumed.

"I also need to know about your criminal background," Lopez continued. "For starters, have you ever been convicted of driving under the influence of intoxicants in another jurisdiction?"

"Yeah, so what?"

"Please tell me about it."

"I was driving a boat in Boston Harbor. Had a couple of beers and got picked up by the harbor police. No big deal."

"Was your blood alcohol level above Massachusetts' permissible blood alcohol limit?"

"Yeah."

"So, it's on your record as a conviction?"

Gesicki shrugged again.

"Is that a yes or a no?" Lopez persisted.

"Yes, it's on my record, although my boss at Boston PD deleted it from my file."

Lopez, appalled, just nodded, and made a note. "Have you ever been convicted of domestic violence?"

"Convicted? No."

"Accused?" asked Lopez.

"Only by Tamryn, and everyone knows she's a crazy bitch."

Lopez sat back in his chair. "In my honest opinion, you're closer to a felony than a misdemeanor here because she's a peace officer. I'll go for bail, obviously, but I think you need to be prepared to stay here until your trial."

"You can't let that happen," Gesicki said leaning forward, threateningly.

"I'll do my best. The good news is that our court log is not as busy as usual. I think you'd come to trial in about two weeks."

"You say that like it's a good thing," Barry smiled at his lawyer. "I'm telling you that's not a possible outcome. And you should listen to me."

CHAPTER 20

Matt had a long, informative talk with Detective Koa Hale from the Honolulu PD. Hale walked him through his interview with Hiroshi Matsuda's wife, son, and daughter until Matt got the drift of their reactions.

"Your view, then, is that the family exhibited the normal level of grief at this sudden news?" Matt asked.

"I would say yes," Hale responded. "Naomi Matsuda is clearly heart-broken and is probably experiencing some level of shock. I called the family's doctor before I left, and he is with her now at her home. Pretty sure she could use a mild sedative."

"And you don't believe that could be an act on her part?"

"I do not. No. She's a gracious, lovely woman, and she tried to remain dignified—I suspect, for her children's sake—but she is devastated. I've been doing this for fifteen years, and I know fake when I see it. Naomi was truly shocked at the news and has a rough road ahead of her."

"What is the family's financial situation?"

"We don't know that yet for sure; we're looking into it now," Hale said. "But I can tell you that the Matsudas paid $4.5 million for their Honolulu home about five years ago and own it free and clear."

"My admin assistant is crackerjack at that kind of internet research, and I'll have her look into this, too," Matt offered. "What about the kids? What was your take on…" Matt consulted his notes, "Shuji and Fumiko?"

"That was more interesting. When it came out that Shuji knew about Cold

Rock Island, Fumiko was furious at her brother for not telling them. Naomi was clearly not pleased with her son either, although she did a better job of hiding it. I felt that Shuji was overwrought with guilt, but…" Hale paused.

"But what?" Matt prompted.

"Parts of his story didn't add up for me. Like he told us that Rohn Reid piloted his jet to Honolulu to pick up Hiroshi. Why would a billionaire like him not have a pilot?"

"I thought it was odd, too, but my wife works for the State Department, and she was with Secretary Leufeld on the island this weekend. She said that there wasn't a pilot in residence, and that Reid told them he almost always flies his jet personally. Loves it, I guess."

"The thing that really bothered me was why didn't Shuji go with, or instead of, his father? It was his project, after all. His bank involved."

"Yeah, that bothers me, too," Matt said. "Did you ask him that question?"

"I did, and he answered that Hiroshi was retired with not enough to keep him busy, and he thought a technical research project like this would be good for him. And, that Shuji's position with the bank is very demanding currently, and it would have been suspicious for him to take some leave right now."

"Sounds logical," Matt said. "But you didn't totally buy it?"

"Just a feeling," Hale said. "Shuji was upset, but I had the feeling he knew more than he was telling us. Or, more than he was telling his mother."

"Then you need to talk to Shuji again. Alone. Let me work up some questions for him, and I'll email it to you."

"Thanks, man. That would be helpful," Kale said. "This is going to be the mother of all shitstorms in Honolulu when word of Hiroshi's death gets out. The man is beloved here, and if we don't solve his murder, well…"

"I get it," Matt said. "My wife, Fern, is relentless and very clever at her work. Trust her to get to the bottom of this case. Plus, I'm good at this, too, Koa, and so is my department. We'll all help you, and we'll get it done."

"Mahalo, Matt. I'll look for your email."

• • •

While Matt was focused on the Matsuda family, Fern and the guys were working together in the squad room, looking into Rohn Reid and his sons, Rick and Randy, specifically on the technology angle, as that was what apparently brought Hiroshi to the island.

"Bit of a coincidence that Hiroshi was working on a technology issue, and, as Rohn told me, that's been his life's work," Fern said. "Do you suppose that Hiroshi told Rohn in a phone call last week that he suspected something related to Shuji's bank was going on at the island? I originally figured he'd somehow snuck onto the island, but now we know that's not the case."

Jay said, "By all accounts, Hiroshi was a smart guy. Why would he tip off Reid if he suspected funny business on his island? That doesn't make sense."

"Maybe he didn't," allowed Fern. "Maybe he gave Rohn another reason for wanting to visit."

"Like, he wanted to see how much it had changed since he was stationed there?" suggested Rudy. "That would make sense for an old, retired guy, wouldn't it?" Rudy was the fittest member of the PSPD, and he couldn't imagine being old and retired.

"I can see that, yes," agreed Fern. "And, considering Hiroshi's storied past relationship to the island, Rohn would almost have to agree that he should come and visit."

"But to the extent that he flies to Honolulu himself and picks him up?" Ed questioned, shaking his head. "I can't see that. That behavior smacks more of wanting to control the situation than it does of welcoming a guest."

"It is a little overzealous, isn't it?" Fern said.

"It would be in my book," Ed said.

"So, Hiroshi makes up some excuse for why he wants to go to the island, Rohn is hiding something and gets immediately suspicious, brings him to the island, and kills him when he discovers what Hiroshi's true reason for being there is," Jay summarized. "Something like that?"

"That makes more sense to me," Ed said.

"I think that's what happened," Fern said quietly. "Or, Rohn had someone else do his dirty work. And I think Hiroshi was killed in the guest room I stayed in."

"There's just one thing," Rudy said, holding up a finger. "Why would Rohn Reid call to report Hiroshi's death? Why not just throw his body in the Pacific Ocean?"

"Because we would have eventually learned about Reid's plane picking him up in Honolulu," Fern explained, with a twinkle. "Like we did learn it."

"Oh, yeah," Rudy said sheepishly. Fern playfully smacked his head.

Walt, who had been working on his computer during this discussion, now said, "Here's something." He swiveled his monitor around on his desk to face the others.

"What are we looking at, Walt?" Fern asked the sergeant.

"This is the Seattle address Rick and Randy Reid gave you." On the screen was an opulent condo with views over the Seattle skyline, and out to Elliott Bay and beyond. Over 15,000 sq. feet, penthouse with a wraparound covered terrace. It was a real estate listing from a little over one year ago. Walt moved his mouse down to the bottom of the screen. "The list price was a whopping $35 million," he said.

"Wowza!" exclaimed Fern.

"How old are these boys?" asked Ed.

"Late twenties," she said. "But they *are* Rohn Reid's sons. Nothing but the best for them, I'm sure."

"Maybe," said Walt, "but it still seems excessive for kids that age. And the title is held by Randolph Reid; no mention of dear old dad…or his twin either, for that matter."

"Well, Rohn must have ponied up the dough," Fern said. "They work in dad's company now, in Marketing and IT, but that surely wouldn't pay enough to buy this place. Unless…"

"Unless," Jay jumped in, "they were also running a cryptocurrency con with Shuji's bank VP from the safety of Cold Rock Island."

"Pocketing the deposits, you mean?" Fern asked.

"Yeah." Jay explained, "Trusting clients send Scott Thurman crypto deposits, Thurman and somebody on Cold Rock Island split the deposits and run a humongous Ponzi scheme. It's been known to happen."

Added Ed, "Like in the billions—not millions, billions—of dollars.

A respected international bank vice-president and a respected billionaire would have contacts. The right contacts."

"Like taking candy from a baby," Jay said.

"That theory could explain how two guys in their twenties have the cash to buy real estate in that price range," Walt said. "Maybe their father doesn't have anything to do with the scam."

"But maybe Hiroshi told Rohn, and he's protecting his sons," Fern said. "The three of them are very tight. If Hiroshi told Rohn about the server's location, Rohn might have feared that Rick and Randy were involved, and he dealt with Hiroshi before he could find any proof on his twins."

"Or," said Matt coming into the squad room, "Maybe Shuji and Scott Thurman are in cahoots on the crypto scam, and Shuji followed his father to Cold Rock Island and killed him before he ruined their goldmine." He pulled up a chair in front of the whiteboard where Fern was jotting down potential suspects and making notes under each name.

"But Shuji asked his father to get involved," she pointed out. "Why would he do that if he was personally involved in the scam?"

"We only have Shuji's statement that he requested Hiroshi's help—no one else knew anything about what would've brought Hiroshi to the island," Matt said. "I've sent Detective Hale some follow-up questions, and he's going to request that Shuji come down to the station alone. He and his partner are also going to talk to Scott Thurman at the bank…see what they can shake loose there. If there truly is an electronic trail here originating from Thurman, they will find it. A lot depends on whether or not Shuji is telling the truth."

"Well," said Fern, "he was telling the truth about Rohn Reid's plane picking up Hiroshi at Honolulu's airport—I checked with the airport officials, and they confirmed it. Do you really think Shuji may have killed his father?" She stared at Matt, and her left eyebrow arched like it did when she didn't believe what she was hearing.

Matt hesitated before answering his wife. "Fathers and sons often have difficult relationships—it's fairly common. And everything I've read and know about Hiroshi is that he would be a tough act to follow for an only son. He's a national hero in Japan, and he and Naomi are elite in Honolulu, too. It's possible Shuji might have gotten himself involved in something like a crypto scam to make a ton of money, therefore — at least, in his eyes — drawing equal with his father."

"I understand the psychology of what you're saying," Fern said. "But to put a pillow over your father's face and hold it down for the time it would take to kill him? That's an act of extreme violence and hatred. I can't see it."

"Or an act of fear," Matt countered. "Fear that his father was about to expose him. Fear and anger can be powerful motives for murder."

"When is Detective Hale going to question Shuji and Scott Thurman?" Fern asked. Her arms were crossed, and one toe was tapping. "We need to keep moving forward."

"This afternoon on both, Honolulu time," Matt said. "Hale will call us tonight." He could tell Fern was anxious, and he understood that this was a big case for her; actually, it was huge for all of them, but especially for his wife. They could not fail.

• • •

Feeling stronger after resting most of the afternoon, Tamryn decided she had the resolve to call her mother and report what had happened to her. She reached for her phone on the hospital swing-out tray. A bouquet of bright yellow daffodils paired with pink tulips had arrived earlier today. She was touched to read the card from Sheriff Earl Johnson.

When she'd first arrived in Port Stirling, she'd all but accused Earl of dropping the ball on Hannah Oakley's case. She wanted to show the local law enforcement team that she knew her stuff, but — as she could clearly see now — she'd gone too far. The sheriff, understandably, was not amused, and he and Tamryn had gotten off on the wrong foot.

But while crusty on the outside, Earl was a cupcake on the inside, and once he'd understood what Tamryn had been through in Boston, he became her biggest fan. After decades of public service in Chinook County, he also really hated wife-beaters. The card read, "We're delighted to have Barry Gesicki as our guest. You heal up." It was signed 'Sheriff Johnson and Chinook County.'

What a sweetheart, she thought, putting the card back in its plastic pitch-fork holder. She punched her mother's phone number.

"Tamryn! Hello, darling," her mother answered. "So nice to hear from you."

"The reason for my call is not so nice," Tamryn started hesitantly. "I want to tell you something in case my news hits Boston."

"What's wrong? Are you alright?"

"I am now, but I've had some trouble. Promise me you'll keep this call to yourself?"

"Of course, if that's what you want. What's happened?"

"Barry is here. In Port Stirling. He broke into my house and surprised me Saturday morning. He beat me badly, ma. I'm in the hospital."

"Oh my God. Are you going to be OK? Will you recover? What are your injuries this time?"

"This time was worse. Broken ribs, concussion, a bunch of stitches on my face and stomach. I was unconscious for a while until my boss and partner found me."

"Oh, honey, this is terrible. What the hell is wrong with that guy?"

"He is mentally unstable, but this time we're going to make sure he goes to jail. Maybe some time inside will get him the help he needs, and some time to think about his actions." She paused. "There's something I need to know, ma. Did you or dad tell him where I am? I can't figure out how he found me."

There was silence on the line. And then, "I didn't talk to Barry, but your father did. He told your dad that he just wanted to talk to you, that he wanted to make things right. Your father hoped that if the two of you talked things through, that maybe everything would be OK again. That your marriage could be saved."

"Jesus Christ, mom! What did I tell you?!?"

"I know. I know. I'm so sorry." Her mother was crying now. Tamryn felt strangely untouched by her tears. "It won't happen again, sweetheart."

"You can be sure of that," she said coolly. "Good-bye, mom."

CHAPTER 21

Fern, Ed, Matt, and Jay were still in the squad room at PSPD at 6:30 p.m. when Detective Koa Hale called Matt with his report on the two interviews he'd done that afternoon. Matt had dismissed Walt and Rudy earlier, telling them to go home and rest up for their heavy duty the next couple of days.

"Putting you on speaker phone, Koa," Matt said. "I'm here with Fern from the State Department, Lieutenant Ed Sonders from the Oregon State Police, and Detective Jay Finley from my department. The four of us are going out to Cold Rock Island tomorrow afternoon to further investigate."

"Aloha," said Koa.

"Howdy," said Matt. "We thought your call might come later tonight, but it's good to talk to you."

"Yeah. I'm calling you now because my interviews were brief." Hale sounded discouraged, Matt thought.

"Let me guess," said Matt. "Shuji doesn't know anything more than what he told you yesterday, and he got huffy at your insinuations."

"You could have been in the room," Koa said. "He had the world's greatest relationship with his father, and he tried to talk him out of going alone, but Hiroshi wanted to go. I probed and tried different avenues of questioning, but it was the same story. The last thing he knows is waving good-bye to his father at Honolulu airport."

"Did you ask him how often he saw his parents?"

"Yeah, and it's more often than I see mine," Koa said. "Shuji and his dad played tennis every weekend, and he usually went to dinner at their home once during the week. He doesn't live that far from them. I will confirm this with the tennis club and Naomi, of course."

"Can you get a subpoena to look at the family's bank records and investment accounts?" Matt asked.

"I've asked my boss that very question, and he's working on it. This is a 'follow the money' case, don't you think?"

Nods around the squad room. "We do think that," Matt answered, "and if Shuji has a lot more money than he should, that will make me suspicious. Do you know the neighborhood he lives in? Does he own his house?"

"Yeah, it's a good neighborhood, but nothing like the gated community his parents live in. His house is relatively modest—I drove by it earlier. About what you'd expect for a young bank vice-president in Honolulu, maybe a little nicer."

"What about Fumiko, the daughter?" asked Fern. "Where does she live?"

"She has a roommate—female—and they share a two-bedroom apartment on Ala Moana Blvd. Fumiko works at the Hawaii State Capitol, and the roommate works at the Honolulu Museum of Art, both fairly close to their apartment building. They were high school friends and moved in together downtown after college. The apartment building is nice, but again, nowhere near her parents' standard of living."

"So, it sounds like by all accounts that both of Hiroshi's children work and earn their own way, is that a fair statement?" Fern asked.

"It is. They aren't poor by any means," Hoa said. "But they haven't been showered with millions either. Or, if they have, they don't live ostentatiously. And I would add that both kids are very upset about their father's death. The family is distraught."

"Why didn't Shuji tell his mother where Hiroshi went when he didn't turn up as expected?" Matt persisted. "That bugs the hell out of me."

"I asked him that, and he got all agitated," Koa said. "Said I didn't know his father, or I wouldn't ask him that question. Told me that his father was

Superman to him, and he'd learned to trust him. That things always went right for Hiroshi."

"Until they didn't," Matt growled.

"But surely, knowing what Shuji knew about his father's trip purpose, he would naturally be worried when he didn't show up," Ed said. "Why wouldn't he tell his mother at that point?"

"He didn't tell her that he knew where Hiroshi was, but he said he did tell her to call the authorities," Koa said. "He told me that he still believed there was a chance that his father was OK, and that something unexpected had come up. He didn't want to interrupt him if that was the case."

"What's your take on that?" Matt asked.

There was a brief hesitation from Koa. "I'm not sure," he said honestly. "Family is everything in both Hawaiian and Japanese culture. Part of me can't believe that Shuji wouldn't have put his father's safety above all else."

"But he didn't do that, did he?" Matt said. He scratched his chin. Changing the subject, he said, "What about Scott Thurman? How did your interrogation of him go?"

"He didn't fess up if that's what you're asking. In fact, he brought his lawyer with him."

"Crap," Matt said.

"My feelings exactly," Koa said. "The lawyer buttoned him up tight, and I only got basic info about him and his work. I asked him point blank if he was running a cryptocurrency operation outside of the bank's parameters and he denied everything. Deny, deny, deny…it got repetitious real quick."

"Did his facial expressions or body language change when you asked him that?" Matt asked.

"Not really, and I watched him closely. He kept his eye contact with me, there was no change in his face color, and he didn't shift in his chair."

"Sounds like he was expecting your question and had prepared."

"Possible," said Koa. "And he kept his answers short on this question. He answered, but his responses on the cryptocurrency issue were more clipped than his replies on other general questions. He didn't give me any openings to pursue this line of questioning."

"Did you get a feel for him?" Fern asked. "What kind of person he is?"

"Well, he's a smart guy, well-educated, slick but personable. Seemed mostly calm under the circumstances of being called in to police headquarters for questioning. Overall, he was polite and well-spoken. Only one thing stood out to me."

"What was that?" Fern again.

"When I went for the jugular with the crypto question, his lawyer wheeled around quickly and looked at his client with a worried expression. Like he thought he might be guilty or something. He visibly relaxed when Thurman denied knowing what I was talking about."

"So, he wouldn't have been surprised if Thurman was running an illegal scheme of some sort," Matt stated.

"That was the impression I got."

"But that reaction from the lawyer suggests Thurman didn't inform him of the crypto scheme ahead of time and get advice on how to handle any questions."

"Correct. He was truly surprised. My take is that Thurman feared that we might be onto his activities, and he developed his own plan on how to answer. His lawyer had not been consulted."

"Does Shuji know if Hiroshi left a paper trail of his suspicions of Scott Thurman?" Matt asked.

"We talked about that, and Shuji thinks not. He says he looked around his dad's home office and found nothing of interest. We haven't found his laptop or cell phone, and Shuji said he's fairly certain that Hiroshi took both with him to Cold Rock Island."

"All we have, then, is Shuji's word on what Hiroshi was working on, and Scott Thurman's role in it. And Thurman has denied any knowledge."

"Right," said Koa. "So, nothing, in other words. I'll scan copies of both interviews and email the PDFs to you. You can weigh in with your thoughts and any additional follow-up ideas," Koa said. "Right now, I've got zip on my end. Sorry, guys."

They ended the call and agreed to talk again tomorrow night once the Port Stirling crew arrived on Cold Rock Island.

Fern took a seat around the group. "I would really like to arrest Scott Thurman on bank fraud charges so we could snoop around in his life,"

Fern said, "but we don't have any physical evidence at all. It's only Shuji's word that Hiroshi found a trail involving him. He seems adamant, but it's not enough—we need proof. I believe the answer lies on Cold Rock Island, not in Honolulu."

"We've got a good starting point with Rohn Reid," Matt pointed out. "Witnesses that put him and his plane with Hiroshi in Honolulu. That's a fact, and he's gonna need answers to our questions."

"And I don't believe he has a good answer, considering he lied to Joe and me about not knowing Hiroshi was on his island or how he arrived. Not to mention that everyone—every single person—backed up Rohn's lie. How should we do this, gentlemen?"

Ed said, "Let's put them all in a locked room like Hercule Poirot and see if anybody cracks. I'm joking…but maybe not."

"I like it," Fern said, "but no one will contradict Rohn. He's the leader of the island cult. I think we have to talk to him first and alone. Let's hear what he has to say for himself and why he lied. Once we know his stance, we'll know better how to approach the others. Right?"

"Agreed," Matt said. "The lie started with him, so he needs to clarify. Will you tell him you're coming back with more questions, or should we just show up with the Coast Guard?"

Fern's eyes sparkled. "Oh, let's surprise him."

* * *

Tuesday, February 27, 2024 — Buck Bay

Tamryn rang the nurse call button from her hospital bed at 6:00 a.m. and waited patiently for her arrival.

"Good morning, Ms. Gesicki," said the cheerful nurse after arriving one minute later. "What can I do for you so early in the day? Your coffee? I'm afraid breakfast doesn't happen for another hour."

"I don't want breakfast. I want to go home," Tamryn barked at the young woman.

The nurse chuckled. "I've been waiting for that. It's up to Dr. Ryder."

"No, actually, it's up to me," Tamryn said calmly. "I'm the patient, it's my body, and my decision. Please ask Dr. Ryder to come and see me as soon as she arrives. Can you do that for me?"

Somewhat chagrined, the nurse said, "Yes. I'll go get you some coffee now." And she turned and left the room quicker than she entered.

Tamryn, feeling momentarily bad for being rude to the nurse, took a deep breath. *I want to go home so badly!* She thought for a minute, then reached for her cell phone, checking the time. *6:15 a.m. I'll bet Sylvia is up.* But to be on the safe side, she sent her a text, speaking into the microphone:

> I'm about ready to spring from this place. Understand you've volunteered for the unpleasant duty of taking care of me for a day or so. Any chance of you driving to Buck Bay this morning and taking me home? Waiting on Bernice's OK.

As she expected, Sylvia replied almost immediately:

> You betcha! Everything all set at your house. Call me when ready.

Tamryn smiled. She made up her mind right then and there that she would not only heal from this beating, but she would also live a long and useful life with a great attitude just like Sylvia. She'd had other mentors throughout her life, particularly one female instructor at the police academy who had taught her how to shoot, along with how to succeed in a man's world as a woman, but Tamryn was beginning to admire Sylvia more than all of them.

Sylvia didn't have to work, but she worked just as hard as everyone else in their department, and infallibly, she showed up with a positive attitude and a get-it-done mentality. She worked smartly and efficiently and maintained her sense of humor no matter how dark the day. *Please God, let me banish my demons, and let me grow up to be like Sylvia.*

While she waited for Bernice, she adjusted her bed to a more upright position, and scrolled through the latest news on her phone. About an hour later, Bernice came bustling into the room, holding a breakfast tray.

"I'm not about to let you leave on an empty stomach, young lady," Bernice said, setting the tray on Tamryn's lap.

"Does that mean you're letting me go home today?"

"How's your pain level on a scale of one to ten?"

"Everything still hurts, if that's what you're asking me, but the ibuprofen helps. I'd say about a four right now. I took ibuprofen about 6:00 a.m."

"Four is acceptable with where you should be. Were you able to get up and use your bathroom this morning?"

"Yes."

"Alone or did you call for help?"

"All by myself, like a big girl."

Bernice grinned. "Excellent. Let me take your blood pressure and check your oxygen level. If you're the same as last night, you're good to go." She wrapped the cuff around her arm, and Tamryn, knowing the drill well by now, stuck her index finger in the pulse oximeter, and tried to make herself calm inside.

"I can live with this," Bernice pronounced, ripping the cuff off her. "You're doing great. Is someone available to drive you home? I don't want you behind the wheel of a car for at least another week — do you understand?"

"Yes, doc. If I had to slam on the brakes, my ribs would not be amused. No worries there. Sylvia has volunteered to help me out. She's coming to get me, and apparently she's going to camp out in my guest room for a day or two."

"That's ideal," Bernice said. "You should still hang out in your bed as much as possible. No heavy lifting, and no long periods on your computer. My daily monitoring of your concussion symptoms is positive, but additional rest will only help you fully recover sooner. Have you had any blurred vision since I saw you yesterday? Headaches better or worse?"

"No vision problems, and my headaches are going away. Thank God for ibuprofen, huh? I don't currently have a headache, and I slept through most of the night."

"OK, that all sounds good. But I'm serious about the computer. You can work some, but your sessions need to be interspersed with an hour or more of bed rest."

"That won't be a problem, Bernice. Matt hasn't given me anything to work on, and he says he won't until you tell him it's OK. Now that my charming husband is behind bars, I want to help out on the Cold Rock Island case. There's research and background checks I can do from home, but I promise I'll go slow. I've never been a person who had many headaches, and I can say I don't really care for them much. Not eager to return to a throbbing head."

"Good. That's smart," Bernice said. She took Tamryn's hand and moved in closer to her side. "I'm so sorry this happened to you. I hope you won't let it color your view of Port Stirling. We need good cops like you. You're going to be fine, and I can't wait until you're up and at 'em again!"

A tear slipped out of Tamryn's eyes, and she squeezed Bernice's hand. "Thanks, doc, for everything. You don't need to worry about me; this was a Boston thing, not a Port Stirling thing."

* * *

Matt woke up at daybreak on Tuesday, and stared at Fern for a while to see if she was awake, too. *But no, my wife can sleep through anything.* He rolled from his side to his back, staying motionless and taking some deep breaths for several minutes to see if sleep would return to him. *Nope, I'm awake. Might as well make some coffee.*

He would dress in his uniform today because he would likely be called on to testify in Barry Gesicki's court arraignment this afternoon as the arresting officer. He and Jay would attend.

But the uniform could wait because he didn't want to shower and shave now while Fern was still sleeping. He went into their closet and found sweatpants and a rust-colored sweatshirt that Fern had gotten him for Christmas. Across the chest, it said 'Hook 'Em Horns,' and she'd enclosed a note that read: "To be worn inside your home when no one else is around." The Ducks and Beavers don't much care for Texas, or any teams in the SEC for that matter, not that that would stop him from rooting for his alma mater. He slipped on fleece-lined slippers that he referred to as his outside slippers—he only wore them on his deck, not really outside outside.

He paused on the staircase landing with the double-height windows and looked out to sea as the sky slowly lightened. It was an overcast morning, low clouds that turned everything gray — sky, water, and sand. The rough slate waves rolled in furiously, but the tide was out and especially low this morning, exposing a wide beach that was empty of people for the moment.

He made coffee and sat at the kitchen island while it brewed, making some notes for both his day and the points he wanted to make in court if called upon. Then he poured himself a large cupful, adding nothing to the strong, hot coffee, and went out to the deck.

A seagull immediately landed on the deck's railing, eyeing Matt but trying to be coy about it. *No food for you buddy. All you do is poop on my deck.* He waved his hand, and the bird took flight, swooping its way down to the water below, noisily calling out to its friends along its route.

The air smelled salty, with its slightly fishy, seaweedy fragrance that accompanied low tides. Matt found it invigorating, and he drank his coffee and enjoyed the moment, leaning on the railing. His work 'to do' list wasn't as lengthy as it had been during the past few weeks; still plenty of loose ends, but manageable. He wondered if that was because he had more trust in his staff now and could give up some control over less-pressing matters. Sylvia, Walt, Rudy, and, especially, Jay, had all nailed it while he was in the hospital, and it was a turning point for his faith in all of them.

He and Fern needed to talk about their philanthropic foundation soon. She'd done all the heavy lifting since they formed it after his 'incident' but with her up to her eyeballs on Hiroshi's case, he figured they'd better go over some details and see if there was anything he should be doing this week to keep the ball rolling. He was proud of their work to establish it, and they were both increasingly eager to see some results in the health care realm they were focusing on. It was a good use of his family oil money.

Matt was also keenly aware that they kept saying, "When this case is over, we should finish our honeymoon." Last year's wedding and honeymoon in Maui had been interrupted, first by Fern's boss requesting her early return for a potential international smuggling operation, and then by Matt's shooting. Maybe he should start planning a trip for the two of them once they solved the Matsuda case, and when Tamryn was back to full strength.

Just to be able to think about a vacation was a treat for Matt. He'd worked so hard for so long, and work was part of his core being. But there was more to life, and maybe it was time to investigate how normal people enjoyed themselves. The thought of surprising his wife made him smile. But on cue, as if he dared to smile at life, his phone vibrated in his sweatpants pocket.

"Tamryn!"

"It's me. Back from the dead. I'm sorry to interrupt you, but I wanted you to know that I'm getting out of here today. Bernice has given the green light, and Sylvia's coming at noon to pick me up and take me home. Yippee!"

"Yippee is right. That's great news. Please do whatever Bernice and Sylvia tell you to do."

"I've made promises," Tamryn said. "I will be an exemplary patient in the comfort of my home. But I'm calling because Bernice also said I could work a little from home, and I want you to email me later with a couple of things you could use my help on. My hours are limited, but I want to help on the Matsuda case."

"This is also good news. I will email you the transcripts from the interviews the Honolulu police did Sunday and yesterday. They're from Detective Koa Hale—he's been our guy on the ground over there. I'd like you to read through them as you can, and then I'll want to hear your thoughts on the case."

"Is there anything new?" she asked.

"Actually, there is. Hiroshi's son, Shuji, told us why and how his father ended up on Cold Rock Island. It's all in the reports. I won't say anything more now because I want you to go into it cold and give me your first impression."

"Wow. Sounds intriguing."

"It is, and we have more questions than answers. Fern, Ed, Jay, and I are going back out to the island after your husband's arraignment today. Jay and I are going to court in case Judge Hedges has any questions about the circumstances of his arrest."

"Give him the finger for me, will you?"

"I will do that," Matt laughed, and then became serious. "Try not to think about him now. This is just the arraignment, and then you and I will get down to the business of building the case against him."

"That will take us five minutes, Matt. It's open and shut."

"I agree. Can I ask you one question?"

"Let me guess. Why did I ever marry this asshole?"

"That's it. Now that I've met him, I can't picture you ever falling for him."

"That's because I never really did. Barry lived with his family in our north Boston neighborhood. Our families were friends, in fact, his dad and my dad worked together, and we saw a lot of the Gesickis. My dad loved Barry, and from the time we were in high school, it was just sort of assumed we'd hook up. He was handsome and a good athlete, and I just went along with it. Then, we both went to cop school, and it seemed like the easy thing to do. To get married. So, we did."

"Wow."

"I can't honestly remember having a real conversation with him about anything important. I was too young to even think about whether I loved him or not. My parents liked him, and that seemed like enough at the time."

"You deserve better, Tamryn. Once you're free of this joker, your life will improve."

"I just hope I'll truly be free of him," Tamryn said wistfully.

CHAPTER 22

By the time Matt came inside, Fern was up. He could hear the shower running, and he made a quick decision to join her. He set down his coffee cup, and ran up the stairs, taking them two at a time.

He dropped his clothes in the closet and strolled into their bathroom. "Mind if I join you?" he said.

In the middle of washing her hair, Fern first jumped at the sound of his voice, then squealed with laughter, and reached over to open the glass shower door.

"No woman in her right mind would turn down that offer," she said, moving to him. "Good morning, husband."

Matt leaned down to kiss her and said, "Good morning, wife."

The shower took longer than Fern expected.

Downstairs in the kitchen, they enjoyed a quick breakfast together, and then left for city hall in separate cars, as their afternoons would take different tracks. As curious as Fern was about Barry Gesicki, her attention was solely focused on Hiroshi's case, and she planned to continue her work in the squad room with the guys while Matt and Jay went to court in Twisty River.

Finishing up his plate of eggs, toast, and an orange, Matt told her about Tamryn.

"Wonderful news," Fern said. "I'm relieved that Sylvia volunteered to help her. It should be me, but I can't get distracted from this case right now."

"Tamryn understands that better than anyone. And the other truth is that I want Sylvia and Tamryn to fully bond. They haven't spent that much time together yet, and this will be a chance for them to get to know each other better. It's a win-win. Also, Tamryn wants to help us with Hiroshi's case. What do you want me to assign to her?"

"Perfect. I need someone to look into the backgrounds of the two women on Cold Rock Island — Moira the cook, and Lynette the housekeeper. I'm so focused on the men, especially Rohn and his sons, but we can't overlook the two women either. Tamryn's work on Hannah Sorenson's case, looking back to her college years, was important, and I'd like her to take the same hard look at these two. Do you want me to email their info to her?"

"Send it to me and I'll forward it to her. I want to keep the PSPD chain of command intact," Matt said. "Our lines are getting a little blurry, and I think we need to pay attention to protocol."

"Of course, you're right," Fern said. "Being the boss's wife is still new to me, and I need to think about reining it in." She extended her lower lip, mocking a pout. "Sorry."

He pushed back his island bar stool and stood to hug her. "I don't want you to rein in anything about you, understand? This is not an ego thing for me. I only want to make sure we don't make our team uncomfortable. The guys will push me on the ground and step on me to work with you again, but Tamryn needs structure, especially right now."

"I totally get it." She put their breakfast dishes in the dishwasher. "I'll send their stuff to you now, and then I really need to get going." She kissed him, smiled, and said, "You smell clean, husband."

• • •

Tuesday, February 27, 2024 — 12:10 p.m. — Buck Bay

Sylvia pulled her red Volvo into a parking spot as close to the hospital's front door as she could get. She remembered breaking a rib in a water-skiing accident when she was nineteen, and she knew how much walking and moving would hurt Tamryn today.

The car smelled good because she'd stopped by her boyfriend Sheldon's café and picked up hot pastrami sandwiches for them to eat on the drive back to Port Stirling. She also knew from experience how quickly patients became tired of the hospital food, and Sylvia guessed this sandwich could cure just about anything.

It was funny to think of Sheldon as her 'boyfriend', but that's exactly what he'd become. Sylvia, in her early seventies, was a few years older than Sheldon, but that didn't matter one whit, as she was the one in the couple with the young spirit and non-stop energy. They'd met in the aftermath of the catastrophic earthquake and tsunami when Sheldon, a recent widower from New York, decided to make a big change in his life and move to the west coast. He picked Oregon because he thought he could make a difference to the badly wounded state, and his business had done just that in torn-apart Port Stirling.

They had become close companions and were discussing the pros and cons of moving in together. Sylvia was opposed to the idea at first, primarily because, like most women her age who'd lived alone a long time, she was set in her ways.

But something had changed inside her on Sunday morning when Matt had phoned to tell her what happened to Tamryn. She realized what a good man Sheldon is, and how lucky she was to find him. He would come by Tamryn's tonight to make sure they were doing OK, and she planned to tell him that she'd changed her mind, and he should move in with her.

But first things first, Sylvia said to herself. *Let's get this woman out of here.* She found Tamryn's room on the fifth floor, and the patient was sitting in a chair with her coat on, holding her dismissal instructions.

"Looks like you're ready to blow this joint," Sylvia said, laughing when she saw her.

Tamryn had a smile on her face, at least, Sylvia thought she was smiling. The swelling on her fat lip was receding, but her face was still a fright. Sylvia tried not to react badly to her appearance, but she was shocked to see the spunky detective looking like this.

"I am, and you, young lady, are a sight for sore eyes," Tamryn said. Sylvia was a colorful, cheerful apparition in a flowing, mostly apple green with cream flowers silk skirt, a crew-neck cream sweater, and a green, red, and cream scarf looped around her neck.

"I thought about wearing a 'hospital blue' outfit, but I figured you were probably sick of that color."

Tamryn laughed. East coast born-and-bred, Tamryn was usually wearing black, which she had on now. "I didn't like blue before, but now I *really* don't like it. I might give your green a try when I'm back on my feet, it's pretty on you. What's the plan today? And, thank you so much for helping me out. It means a lot, Sylvia."

"We all need help at times in our lives," Sylvia said. She took Tamryn's bag out of her hands, and picked up the plastic bag on the chair next to her which she supposed contained the clothes Tamryn came in wearing. "No plan today other than getting you home, washed, and fed. You will need to let go of the idea of plans for a couple of days at least, and I'm the person to ensure you do that. You dig?"

"No plans, got it," Tamryn said, nodding. "I'll let you know when I'm ready to run a marathon, OK?"

Sylvia laughed. "That's the spirit. Let's go. Can you stand up on your own or do you want me to help?"

"I've got this part." She stood up, gingerly, but with spirit, and the two women awaited the departure wheelchair.

* * *

Tuesday, February 27, 2024 — 2:00 p.m. — Twisty River

Barry Gesicki's attorney had picked up some clothes for him to wear to his court appearance. His lawyer had suggested he wear a suit, but Barry poo-pooed that idea, and told him to bring him the black Henley sweater and khaki pants in his suitcase. "Twisty River, Oregon, is the boonies, man, a suit would be out of place," Gesicki said. "I'll look clean and respectable, and I'll fit right in."

His attorney wanted to tell him that he'd never fit in here with his heavy east coast accent and bad attitude, but he kept quiet. He'd soon be rid of this guy.

Sheriff Earl Johnson assigned his top deputy, Victoria Dixon, to escort Gesicki from his cell in the basement to the third-floor courtroom. Earl enjoyed the irony of a man who didn't like competent women being brought to justice by a tough, smart, female cop. And besides, if anything went wrong, Dixon, at an even six feet tall and a muscled 165 pounds, could bench press more than most of the male deputies in the sheriff's department.

The jail guard opened Gesicki's cell door. Dixon introduced herself and instructed Gesicki to face the wall and put his hands behind his back. He did so, and she slapped the silver metal handcuffs on him.

"Let's go," she said to the prisoner and his attorney. "There's a party for you upstairs. Thanks, Jake," she said to the guard, and the three headed for the elevator.

Dixon forced Gesicki into the elevator first and told his attorney to stand in front of him. She entered and pressed the button for the third floor. They got off when the doors opened and started down the long hallway to Courtroom 1 at the end of the hall, Gesicki between his lawyer and Victoria Dixon, who held him firmly by his arm.

About one-third of the way, as they were passing a restroom, Gesicki stopped and said, "I really need a piss. Can I use this restroom?"

"Why didn't you go earlier?" she said, disgusted.

"You were early, and came before I thought you would," he replied. "I'm sorry, but it's urgent."

"OK, but you'll have to go with the cuffs on. You," she pointed at the lawyer, "go in with him, and help him with his zipper."

"I'm not paid enough," the attorney muttered under his breath, but opened the single-user restroom door and ushered Gesicki inside, flipping on the light switch.

Once inside, the attorney adjusted Gesicki's zipper and looked away.

"I can handle it from here," Gesicki said to him. "You can go and guard the door while I do my business."

The attorney didn't hesitate, and quickly left the small room. Gesicki reached over and locked the bathroom door as his lawyer exited.

Taking up a position outside the door, the lawyer avoided looking at the deputy. He and Victoria Dixon looked at the floor, both of them uncomfortable. The deputy rocked back and forth on her heels to kill the time. The attorney stood stock still, his hands at his sides.

Inside the restroom, it was a different story. Barry Gesicki was very busy. He bent forward from the waist, dropping his arms close to the ground behind him, and stepped backward over the handcuffs, bringing them in front of his body. He looked at the side of the cuffs to see if the double-lock mechanism was depressed and therefore engaged. It was not, which didn't surprise him because of the speed with which the deputy had slapped them on him.

All he needed to do was disengage the single-lock bar. *Yes!* Quickly, he removed the padding from the temple end of his glasses, exposing the small metal frame, the end of which he knew would fit in the keylock hole. Pressing against the cuffs, he put a slight bend in the metal of the glasses stem. Then, he pushed the angled stem upward and pried it toward the center of the handcuff first, and then downward, jiggling it until the metal teeth of the single-lock bar disengaged. *Bingo!*

Quietly, he set the handcuffs down on the floor, lowered the lid of the toilet, stood on it, and took another step up onto the tank. He raised his arms up to the ceiling and pushed up on the ceiling tile directly overhead, easily moving it aside.

Then, he pulled himself up through the ceiling opening and into the crawl space. Moving along a beam in the direction he thought would be away from the courtroom, he made steady progress for about thirty seconds, and then lowered himself into a storage closet he'd noted on the way down the hall. He removed his black sweater, revealing a white Hanes tee shirt underneath. It was the only thing he could do to change his appearance. He hid the sweater behind some cleaning products.

He opened the door carefully and could see his lawyer and the bitch deputy about forty yards away, both looking away from him and toward the courtroom door at the end of the hall. Smoothly, he eased the door open, and walked to the stairs next to the elevator they'd ridden up in. Once he rounded the corner onto the stairs, he moved quickly down the two flights to the ground floor, found an exit door at the back of the building, and took off.

* * *

Matt and Jay headed to the Twisty River courthouse in the department's squad car. Rain had started to fall, and a foggy mist drifted over the river and onto the road as they drove. The fog hung over the low hills on the other side of the river as they made their way east. Chilly, damp day.

"I understand the circumstances are grim," Jay said, driving. "But I'm pumped to see this Cold Rock Island."

"I'm curious, too," Matt said. "Did you notify the Coast Guard we want to leave at 4:30 p.m?"

"Yeah, I talked to Bob Adams. He told me that the Secretary of State wants him to be available on this case full-time. Bob said he'd be personally ferrying us back and forth as we need. Said he's prepared for he and his crew to spend a day or two on the ship."

"That's good to hear. Can we sleep on the ship, too, if we need to stay, rather than rely on Reid's hospitality? I don't think my wife is keen on sleeping in that guest room again, knowing what we know."

"Bob said yes, they've prepared accommodations. He said to warn you that it's bunk beds." Jay grinned.

"That's unfortunate," Matt said with a straight face.

"Figured you'd say that. But think how much fun it will be to see Ed try to get into a bunk bed."

"There is that," Matt laughed.

They pulled into a parking space reserved for Chinook County sheriff's deputies and made their way to the courtroom on the third floor.

Sheriff Earl, Deputy Dixon, Judge Hedges, and Barry Gesicki's attorney were the only people in the courtroom, and they were huddled together at the defendant's table. Matt approached them, the hair on the back of his neck standing up — he sensed trouble.

"Where's Gesicki?" Matt called out, still fifteen feet away. He strode purposefully to the table, Jay on his heels.

Earl stood to greet him. The sheriff was pale and drawn. "He's gone, Matt. He escaped."

"What do you mean, he escaped?" Matt bellowed.

Deputy Dixon stood tall next to Earl. "It's my fault, Matt. He had to use the restroom on the way here, and—somehow—he defeated his restraints, climbed up into the ceiling crawl space, and obviously lowered himself into a supply closet. We found the sweater he was wearing in there. He got away. I'm so, so sorry."

"This is unbelievable," Matt said. He smacked himself in the head. "Did you search the building?"

Earl said, "Yeah. My entire department, and every courthouse employee joined. We've looked in every room on every floor, every nook and corner. He's gone," he said dejectedly.

"Did anyone see him leave?"

"He walked away undetected," Earl said. "He can't have done much to alter his appearance, but no one saw him. We've talked to everyone. I believe he walked down the staircase and went out the back door. We're testing for prints now. It's our bad, Matt, and you have every right to be upset."

"Damn right I'm upset. This man nearly killed my detective, and now you're telling me he's loose in the county?" Matt seethed. He turned to the attorney, still seated. "Who are you?"

"Ryan Lopez. I'm Barry Gesicki's appointed attorney." He looked like he might throw up.

Matt walked over to the seated lawyer and leaned over him. "Did you help him escape?" He didn't have to tell Lopez to tell him the truth; his tone indicated he meant business.

"No, I most certainly did not," Lopez said, with both fear and indignation in his voice. "I didn't know he was planning this. It didn't occur to either me or the deputy he would try something like this. I've never seen anything like it."

"What did he say before he entered the restroom?"

"He said he needed to take a piss," Lopez recounted. "That was all."

Deputy Dixon said, "I asked Mr. Lopez to accompany him inside the restroom and he did, but the prisoner asked him to leave so he could have some privacy. He was handcuffed, Matt, and I didn't see a problem."

"He's a cop," Judge Hedges noted. "They all know how to get handcuffs off, and you should never have left him alone." Her tone was severe.

"But what's done is done, and now I need to know what you all are going to do about it."

"I didn't know he was a cop, Cynthia," said Deputy Dixon. All color drained from her face. "All I can do is apologize again. I'm so sorry this happened on my watch."

"We're done with apologies," Matt said. "What we need now is a plan for how we're going to search Twisty River for this guy. I'll have Walt and Rudy come over and join me and your folks, Earl. Jay, I want you to go immediately to Tamryn's house and search the area. If she and Sylvia are there, make sure they're OK, but tell them you're just checking on them. I'll decide when and if we need to tell Tamryn about this. Got it?"

"Yes," Jay said. "I'll search all around her house."

"He can't get far on foot," Matt said, "and it's likely he's still in Twisty River, but I'll feel better if you check out her house and surrounding area."

"Leaving now," Jay said. "I've got the squad car keys."

Matt reached out and grabbed Jay's arm. "Call Walt on your way, and tell him to get here asap with Rudy," Matt instructed. "I'll call Sylvia and tell her what's happened and tell her she should use her judgment whether or not to tell Tamryn. Does that sound like the right way to handle it?"

Jay nodded. "I think so. It will only upset Tamryn on a day she's supposed to be resting. What do I tell Captain Adams?"

"Oh, shit. I forgot we were going to Cold Rock Island," Matt said. "Ed and Fern will have to go without us. Barry Gesicki is a Port Stirling problem; he's our job until he's back in custody. I'll call Fern after I warn Sylvia. Take off."

Jay turned and hurried out of the courtroom.

Matt turned to Earl. "I expect the sheriff's department to be all hands on deck. This is a real dangerous guy."

"Everyone I've got will be on the manhunt," Earl promised. "We'll find him." The sheriff rubbed his cheek and frowned. "We have a plan in our manual for how to search Twisty River in an emergency. Never used it before. Guess now's the time."

"Dust it off, Earl," said Matt. "Tamryn is headed home today, and I need to be able to tell her that Barry is back in the slammer."

CHAPTER 23

Fern paced the pier at the Coast Guard headquarters. She and Ed were waiting for Matt and Jay, as the four had planned. The cutter was ready to depart as soon as they arrived. Her phone buzzed.

"Hi. Where are you?" she asked her husband.

"Change of plans, darlin'. Barry Gesicki escaped while headed to court, and we have an all-out manhunt underway. Jay and I can't go with you today."

"What?"

"I'll give you the details later. Just know that he is on the loose in the county, probably still in Twisty River."

"But Tamryn is going home from the hospital today."

"Tell me something I don't know," he barked. "That's why I'm staying here to help with the search. We can't let that low life get out of Twisty River. Jay is on his way back to Port Stirling to check Tamryn's house and the area."

"Can't Earl and his department handle this? I really want you two to go with me."

"I know and I'm sorry, but this is my case, and he's a local threat. It's my job, honey. Jay and me. Think how we'd feel if he hurts Tamryn again. I have to track him down and put him away."

"Of course, you're right," Fern said resignedly. "Ed and I can handle this. We're going to interrogate Rohn Reid and the others, if necessary, with our new info and see if anything shakes loose. Whatever we learn will focus our efforts going forward."

"Promise me you will stay on the CG boat tonight."

"You know it. There's no way in hell I'm sleeping in that guest room again."

"Jay said to tell you that Captain Adams said your accommodations are bunk beds, and he wants you to take a picture of Ed in his."

Fern chuckled in spite of her nervous feelings. "Tell Jay, 'it's done'. Please don't worry about us. I'm a trained killer, you know."

"I hope it won't come to that," Matt said quietly.

• • •

"We're going without them," Fern said to Ed. "You OK with that?"

"I guess," Ed answered. "But why? What's up?"

Fern filled him in on the Barry Gesicki escape.

"Oh, Lord, I bet that made your husband happy. All the trouble he went to in order to locate him in the first place, make the arrest, and transport him to Twisty River. Gotta sting a little."

"He's frustrated for sure. Plus, the timing sucks. Sylvia is taking Tamryn home from the hospital today. She's staying at Tamryn's house for a couple of days until Tamryn is back on her feet. But Matt thinks he's still in Twisty River and won't get far."

"They'll get him," Ed agreed. "The sheriff's got some vicious dogs, not to mention a bunch of deputies that know every inch of Twisty River. I'll go tell Bob we're ready to sail."

The trip out to Cold Rock Island was, blissfully for Fern, a smooth one. It was raining, but the ocean wasn't as riled up as her last trip. She and Ed dropped their bags in the crew quarters. They would share a small space that included two bunk beds, and a head and washroom. A work area plus one armchair took up the open space. The two tall adults looked at each other and laughed as they stood in the middle of the space.

"One night, right?" Ed said.

"There's a killer on this island. We're going to figure out who it is, and then return to our regularly scheduled lives. Not to mention our spacious homes."

By the time they, along with Captain Adams, stepped on the ramp leading down to the dock, there was a welcome party awaiting them. *Actually, not sure I'd call it a party,* Fern thought. Rohn Reid, both of his sons, and Noah Stricker stood side-by-side, and not one of them had a smile on his face. *I suppose I wouldn't be smiling either if someone barged onto my property uninvited. But then, I didn't murder anyone. At least, no one who didn't deserve it.*

"Mr. Reid, hello," Fern said. She moved toward him, briskly and with confidence. "Sorry to intrude on you further, but we've got some additional questions for you. You know Captain Adams, of course, and this gentleman is Lieutenant Ed Sonders with the Oregon State Police. They will both be assisting me today in our investigation."

"I didn't know you were coming," Rohn said. "We aren't prepared for guests, I'm afraid." His doughy face had a slightly grayish tinge, but his voice was pure steel.

"Not a problem," she said. "We're not guests. We'll be staying on the ship tonight, and we'll take care of ourselves. Hopefully, we'll be out of your hair early tomorrow. Can we adjourn to the house? We'd like to talk with you alone in the time we have left this afternoon."

"I really wished you'd called and made an appointment," Rohn said. "I'm rather busy today." He stood stubbornly with his hands on his hips.

Fern reached into her pocket and took out her State Department ID, holding it up in front of his face. "This means I don't need an appointment, sir. Can we please go now? It's chilly out here."

Reid turned without another word, got in the waiting golf cart, and drove up the hill to his house. Rick, Randy, and Noah followed in the second cart, leaving the newcomers to walk up the steep grade.

"Love him so far," Ed said.

They settled in the living room, where they'd first interviewed Rohn. Leonard discreetly brought in coffee, setting it down on the coffee table between them. Fern smiled at him and said, "Thank you, Leonard. It's much appreciated."

Leonard smiled back and wordlessly left the room.

"So, you have questions?" Rohn said, making it sound like a question.

"Yes," Fern said. "Did you fly your plane to Honolulu and pick up Hiroshi Matsuda?"

Rohn blinked fast twice and drummed his fingers on the end of his club chair before answering. "If you're asking me that question, you must already know the answer. Yes, I did, and brought him here to my island."

"Why did you lie to me?"

He shrugged and made a face, doing a winky thing with his mouth. "I'm not sure why I lied. I suppose it was because I truly believed he'd killed himself, and we weren't involved. I thought perhaps all this would be over faster the less you believed we knew about it."

"Surely you can now see how that changes everything for our investigation?" Fern told him, not waiting for him to answer. "Now we don't believe anything not only you, but everyone on this island told us. If you were hiding that fact from us, and your family and employees went along with the lie, we naturally think there's a reason for your subterfuge."

"We aren't hiding anything, Fern. It was simply a case of wanting things to be easier."

"I don't believe you," Fern said, ice in her voice. "We have more questions, and it would be in your best interest to tell the truth this time." She paused and stared at him. Reid yawned, nodded, and clasped his hands over his prodigious belly.

"Please tell us how this all started," she said.

"Hiroshi called me," Reid said. "He wanted to come to my island."

"Why?"

"He said he was feeling nostalgic and wanted to revisit his years here. Wanted to know if it was alright with me if he came just for a day."

"How did you feel about that?" Fern asked.

"I wasn't crazy about the idea, but what could I say? It would have been viewed as ungracious, considering his history on my island."

"It seems a big step from being a reluctant host to happily flying your plane to Honolulu to get him," noted Ed. "Why did you do that?"

"Well, I talked his visit over with my sons, and they thought it would be a nice gesture to the military hero. So, I called Hiroshi back, and we arranged his transport."

"Who from here went with you?" Fern asked.

"Rick is my co-pilot. Noah accompanied us."

"Why Noah?"

"He's my personal bodyguard when I'm on the plane," Reid explained.

"Randy didn't go?" asked Fern.

"No, he was busy on a project."

"What's he working on?" Ed asked.

"I don't know."

"You don't know what your son, who works for your company, is working on?" Ed asked. "That seems odd."

Rohn glared at him. "I'm not his supervisor, Lieutenant. I'm CEO emeritus and Chairman of the Board; there are many, many layers between me and my boys."

"Aren't you curious?" Ed persisted.

"Do you have children?" Reid asked Ed.

"Yes. Why?"

"There are, of course, many different styles of parenting, but I prefer to stay in the background of my sons' lives. Let them come to me, if you will. I suspect you are more hands on, Lieutenant."

"I know what my kids are doing, even now that they have flown the coop," Ed said, staring him down.

Moving on, Fern asked, "Did you meet Hiroshi's family at the airport in Honolulu?"

"Yes. His son was there with him. I forget his name."

"Shuji Matsuda," Fern said. "Does that ring a bell?"

"Yes, that's it. Nice young man." He hesitated. "How did he take the news? I'm sure he's devastated."

"The entire family is taking it very hard," Fern said. "As I'm sure you can imagine. Did you talk with Shuji?"

"Just small talk," Reid said. "We were somewhat rushed to take off again in the window that air traffic control gave us."

"Did you talk about Shuji's business at all?" she asked.

"I don't believe so. No."

"So, you don't know what he does for a living?"

Reid looked blankly at Fern. "I just said 'no'. Why would I care about what Shuji does?"

Fern ignored his question. "Did Hiroshi talk about Shuji on the way here?"

"We didn't talk. I flew the plane, and he was in the back cabin. I think he took a snooze."

"What happened when you returned here?" she asked. "This was Wednesday afternoon by then, right?"

"That's correct. We took Hiroshi to a guest room to settle in. He put on hiking boots and said he wanted to hike around for a while."

"Which guest room?"

Reid thought. "I believe he was in the one you stayed in Saturday night."

Fern shivered involuntarily. "When did you next see him?"

"We all had dinner Wednesday night."

"What time was that?"

"About seven-thirty. Hiroshi came to the main house about six, I think, and we had drinks in the library first. He got to telling us interesting old stories about his time here, and we didn't move into the dining room until almost seven-thirty."

"Who else was present?"

"Just Rick and Randy and me."

"What did you talk about while you were eating?" Ed asked.

"More of the same," Reid answered. "He was a charming man, very social."

"Did he ask about you, your sons, anything about the island and what you do here?" Ed again.

Reid looked off into space, considering Ed's question. "Not really. No."

"You'd think he would have been interested in why you bought this island and how you use it," Fern said, following up on Ed's direction.

"No. It was mostly about his past, the history of this place. He didn't seem interested in what we're doing here now."

I'll bet, thought Fern. But seeing no wiggle room on this topic, she asked, "What did your sons think of Hiroshi?"

Reid shrugged. "They liked him, I guess. Thought his old stories were fun."

"Why did they lie to me about not knowing Hiroshi was here?" Fern asked. Her jaw was clenched, and she had two bright red spots on her cheeks.

"That's my fault," said Reid. "I told everyone to pretend we hadn't seen him until, you know. I'm to blame. I'm sorry now, but at the time I thought it would be best to not get involved. Rick and Randy had nothing to do with it, and I just wanted them to stay out of the mess. You'll understand when you have your own children, Fern."

"I would hope that my children will be honest. That they will respect authority and tell the truth."

"I did what I thought was right. I'm sorry."

That hung in the air for a moment, and then Ed asked, "What happened after dinner?"

"We all went to our separate quarters and lights out," Rohn said. "I read until about eleven o'clock."

"What was the last thing Hiroshi said before leaving your dining room?" asked Ed.

"I don't remember exactly. Something like 'Don't worry about me in the morning—I'm just going to look around and reminisce.' Something like that."

"Did you discuss the flight back to Honolulu?" Fern asked.

"Oh, yeah, sorry, we did talk about that, too," Rohn said. "He said he'd be ready to go anytime Thursday evening. And to do what was best for my schedule."

"So, he was flexible, and you didn't set a definite time for his departure?"

"Correct."

"Did anything happen Wednesday during the night?" Fern asked. "Any noises or anyone out and about?"

"Not that I heard. I sleep soundly here, one of the things I love about this place. As I'm sure you discovered, the only sounds are the ocean's waves."

"That, and Noah's tapping on my window in the middle of the night," she said flatly.

A flush crept up Reid's face. "What do you mean?"

"I mean that he tapped on my window in the middle of the night. Scared the heck out of me."

"I didn't know about that."

"Are you sure?" She looked directly into his eyes.

"I don't know why Noah would have done such a thing," he said, not flinching. "I will talk to him."

"I think he was trying to scare me so Joe and I would get the message and leave."

"Noah had no reason to want to scare you, Fern. I'm sure it was harmless."

"It didn't feel harmless. It felt purposeful." She paused and looked down at her notes before continuing. "Did you see Hiroshi on Thursday morning? Did you eat breakfast with him?"

"No, I didn't see him all day. Moira took breakfast to his room, I understand."

"Did he eat it?" Ed asked.

"I have no idea. She would know."

"So, you have an important visitor, and you don't see him all day?" asked Ed.

"He wanted to do his own thing. And I'm busy."

"So you keep telling us," remarked Ed. "Busy, busy, busy."

Reid glowered at him. "You don't get to be one of the world's richest men if you sit around all day doing nothing."

Ed waved his hand dismissively at Reid, and Fern knew he was trying to rile him.

"What do you think he did all day?" Fern jumped in. "Did anyone else see or talk to him?"

"I believe that no one saw him until he was found swinging from the rafters in my airplane hangar." Reid grabbed the arms of his chair and pushed himself up. "I have nothing further to say to you."

CHAPTER 24

Tuesday, February 27, 2024 — Somewhere between Twisty River and Port Stirling

Barry Gesicki, cold and hungry, jogged along what he hoped was the back road from Twisty River to Port Stirling. An occasional car went by, but nobody seemed to pay any attention to the stranger in a white tee shirt and khaki pants.

He figured he was about six miles from the courthouse, which left him about fourteen to go if he was to make it to his Port Stirling hideout where he could change his clothes and alter his appearance. He had two choices: keep jogging or try to flag down a car going in his direction. For that, he would need a story.

An older-model blue Ford pickup truck materialized out of the misty fog, having just come around a sharp corner in the road. Gesicki was walking in the same direction, next to the river, and noticed the pickup was traveling slowly. *Probably an old grandpa driver*, he thought.

He turned, waved at the driver, and stuck out his thumb. The pickup slowed, and Gesicki smiled gently at the driver, an older male alone in the cab.

The driver reached over and rolled down the passenger side window. "Where you headed?"

"Port Stirling," replied Gesicki. "Name's Doug Davis. My car broke down and I need to get to my place."

"Hop in." The driver, about seventy, with a full head of silver hair and wearing a red and black flannel shirt and baggy jeans, unlocked the door.

"Thanks, man," said Gesicki. "I can pay you if I'm out of your way." His attorney had given him his cash, ID, and credit card from his wallet before they went to the courtroom.

"I'm Harry McNulty. No need for money, I'm headed to Port Stirling, too. Where do you want to go?"

"Just a little south of downtown. I've got a motel room. My car needs fixing, but I left my phone at the motel."

"I don't carry one — hate the dang things," Harry said.

Gesicki laughed. "Yeah, they're not my favorite either, but at times like this, I guess they're useful."

"Interesting accent, Doug. You from the east coast?"

"Yeah, New York." He figured the old geezer couldn't distinguish between Boston and New York. "Just visiting out here. Pretty country."

"We think so. Wouldn't live anywhere else."

The remainder of the drive to Port Stirling was uneventful. Gesicki tried to not engage Harry, and Harry didn't seem to mind the cordial silence. He dropped him off at the southern intersection of highway 101 and Ocean Bend Rd, and Gesicki walked the mile or so to his cheap motel, letting himself in his room at the back through a window he'd left cracked open an inch.

He figured that ol' Harry would be the type to watch the local evening news on TV, and he also figured that 'Doug Davis' would be all over it tonight. Quickly, he shaved off his mustache, cut his hair, and rooted around in his bag for his spare pair of glasses, which were a weighty charcoal gray frame instead of the wire rims. White tee shirt and khaki pants were replaced with a brown sweater, dark jeans, and his Columbia waterproof jacket.

He pulled the sheets and blanket off the bed and stuffed them in his suitcase with a change of socks and underwear, leaving his other clothes behind. Grabbing his backpack filled with some protein bars and other snacks, a water bottle, binoculars, gloves, and a wool beanie, he left the dumpy motel without checking out. Hurriedly, but trying not to attract attention, Gesicki walked the two miles down Ocean Bend Rd, and took off in the woods near Tamryn's house.

She started it. Time to finish the job.

• • •

Jay drove the squad car straight to Tamryn's house. He parked just off Ocean Bend Rd and walked slowly down the gravel road to her house in the clearing, checking out the wooded areas off both sides of the driveway. It was silent, and his eyes could see nothing stirring. Tamryn's car was in the same spot they'd left it when the ambulance took her to the hospital, and there was no sign of Sylvia's car. He circled the house, stopping periodically to listen, and only hearing the rowdy surf hitting the soft sand below, and the occasional seagull's cry.

Coming back around to the front, he rang the doorbell just in case, peering through the glass side panels. The house was dark, and they weren't here yet.

He called Matt. "No sign of him," Jay reported. "And it's obvious that they aren't home from the hospital yet."

"OK, good," said Matt. "Stay there until they get home and are safely inside the house."

"Will do. Any luck there?"

"Not yet," Matt said.

• • •

Later, deep in the woods between Ocean Bend Rd and Tamryn's house, Barry set up a lean-to with the sheets, just big enough to provide him with some relief from the elements. He climbed up a medium-sized Douglas fir tree to a healthy branch about six feet off the ground, just within reach, and straddled the limb. From his perch, he could see the final part of Tamryn's driveway and her front porch. He trained his binoculars on the front door—*shit, a new keypad!* He swung the binocs to the kitchen window at the front of the house, but the inside was dark. *Still in the hospital, I guess. She'll show up soon.*

He ate a protein bar and waited.

• • •

By Tuesday at dusk, the sheriff's department search had turned up no sign of Barry Gesicki in Twisty River. Even though the prisoner was tending toward middle age spread, he was still a relatively young man in reasonably good shape and had obviously made a hasty departure from the town, as Matt feared. The question was: in which direction?

Logic told Matt that Gesicki had headed toward Buck Bay, the county's largest city and the most obvious place to hide. However, his gut was telling him that he might not be through with Tamryn.

He called Jay. "Hi. Did you find him?" Jay asked hopefully.

"Nope," said a dejected Matt. "He obviously got out of Twisty River fast. Probably hitchhiked out of town. No way to know where he is now. Are you still at Tamryn's?"

"Yeah. She and Sylvia got here a couple of hours ago, and I went in with them to make sure the coast was clear. He's not here, Matt."

"Did you tell them about Barry?"

"No. I just said that I was there to welcome her home, and make sure they had everything they needed."

"Good. Thanks, Jay," Matt said. "Walt and Rudy and I are coming home now, and I'll have Rudy sneak around the house for a while after it gets dark tonight. I don't want to upset Tamryn if there's no need, but she should be warned to stay alert. I'll call Sylvia now and talk to you later. Appreciate you, man."

He called Sylvia's cell phone.

"Hello, Chief," she answered. "What can we do for you?"

"By 'we', does that mean you're with Tamryn?"

"Not as this precise moment. She is taking a bath, and I'm in the kitchen working on dinner."

"Good," Matt said. "I've got some unpleasant news, and I need your judgment on how best to handle it."

"Hold on while I set the cheese grater down. OK, shoot."

"Barry Gesicki escaped on the way to the courtroom this afternoon, and he's still at large. The sheriff's department and I have been out looking for several hours, and we think he's high-tailed it out of Twisty River."

"And you think he might be headed here?"

"It's a possibility we need to consider. He might go to Buck Bay and get out of the area that way, but..."

"But, he might return here and torment that poor woman even further," Sylvia finished his sentence.

"Yep, he might. Do we tell her the news?"

"Of course. I'm obviously no match for a forty-something male cop, but Tamryn is."

"Even though she's still bruised and battered?"

"She's much better today. Moving around without much pain. Still taking ibuprofen, but she's even weaning off that some. I had to force her to rest in bed after we got here from the hospital, and she worked some on her computer after that. She didn't need my help getting in the tub and told me she's relishing her privacy again."

"Ok, then, please tell her to call me when she can, and I'll explain what happened. In the meantime, I'll have Rudy come over and keep an eye outside."

"I'm not sure that's necessary, Chief. The owner installed a new keypad on the doors, and Tamryn programed it when we arrived home from the hospital. She's the only one that knows the new code, and we are safely inside the house. Jay came by to make sure all was well."

"That's good news, but I still think it's prudent to have Rudy come over later and look around. He'll be discreet. Call me if anything changes, OK?"

"Sure thing. I'm making chicken and cheese enchiladas, and then we're going to watch a movie."

"Thanks for doing this, Sylvia. It's real nice."

"It's my pleasure, Chief. Gotta run. I want to get her fireplace going before it gets dark outside. Cozy it up."

• • •

I need to know more about this jerk, Matt thought. Walt and Rudy had dropped him off as darkness had enveloped Port Stirling, and he was now ensconced in his home office, a cold beer in his hand.

By the time he'd had the thought that he should call the Boston PD and talk to Barry's captain, it had been too late in the day. He would check with him first thing tomorrow morning, but, for now, he'd try good old Google and see if he could learn anything about the man behind the badge.

Matt typed 'Barry Gesicki' into the search engine. The first thing that popped up was a front-page article in yesterday's Boston Herald. The headline read: **"Fugitive Cop Barry Gesicki Thought To Be In Oregon."** *What in the actual hell?,* thought Matt. He quickly scanned the article:

> 'Boston PD cop on the beat Barry Gesicki, who is wanted for the alleged homicide of his long-time partner Leo Pistorio, has turned up in a small town near the coast of Oregon in the Pacific Northwest. Pistorio was found critically injured from a beating on Thursday, February 22, and died on Sunday. Gesicki has not reported for work or been seen anywhere in the Boston area since Pistorio was found near Gesicki's apartment in the north end.
>
> Gesicki's estranged wife, former Boston PD Detective Tamryn Gesicki, relocated to Oregon recently, according to her father. Her boss, Lieutenant Frank Camron, thought there was reason to believe that Barry may have followed her. A police search Camron did late yesterday uncovered an arrest for assault for Barry Gesicki in Twisty River, Oregon, a county seat. Camron said he intends to follow up with the Oregon authorities. Camron also cautioned that Gesicki is armed and dangerous and should not be approached if seen. Boston PD is asking for the public's help in locating him by calling Lieutenant Camron at (857)-724-6687.'

Matt set down his beer and leaned back in his rocking desk chair, thinking. *Well, this changes everything. He's clearly a psycho with nothing to lose.* Matt wondered what Barry's beef was with his partner. He needed to talk to Camron…now. He picked up his phone and checked the number again in the article. It was after 10:00 p.m. in Boston and he was prepared to leave a message if Camron didn't pick up.

But he did, saying, "Lieutenant Frank Camron."

"Lieutenant, this is Chief of Police Matt Horning calling from Port Stirling, Oregon. I arrested Barry Gesicki. Can you talk for a minute?"

"Hello, Chief. I was planning to find you tomorrow," Camron said. "Looks like we might have an asshole in common. Thanks for calling."

"Yep. I figured Gesicki was just a DV and we'd teach him a lesson about beating up his wife, but now I see that you have an even bigger issue with him. Did he kill his partner?" Matt asked. He hoped what he'd just read was not the whole ugly story.

"We think he did, Chief. And I've had a real bad evening here feeling guilty for how I handled things with Tamryn. I didn't believe her, and I should have done more."

"The way she told me, you should have done something…anything, rather than the nothing-burger you served up to her," Matt said, not hiding his irritation.

"I deserved that. But you need to understand that Barry was convincing in his denial, and it did seem out of character for him. He's always been hot-tempered, but harmless. He lets off steam on the job, and then it's over with. His colleagues and I couldn't see him actually doing what Tamryn said he did. Obviously, I'm sorry now."

"You're going to be even sorrier when I tell you what happened out here today. Barry escaped from our county jail on the way to his arraignment for putting Tamryn in the hospital." Matt filled him in on the details.

"That doesn't surprise me, unfortunately. There's not a cop on the planet who doesn't know how to escape handcuffs. How could your deputy not know that?"

"Now it's my time to say I'm sorry," Matt said. "We didn't communicate as well as we should have. His deputy escort hadn't been told that Barry was a cop. She didn't know it. Just that the prisoner was a man who beat up his wife. She never would have let him go in the restroom alone if she'd known. That's our bad."

"None of us is perfect, huh, Chief?" Camron said. "So, we move forward. Where do you think he might be now?"

"Have you been to Oregon, Captain?"

"Haven't had the pleasure, I'm sorry to say."

Matt snickered. "Well, it's big. Lots of forests. Lots of miles and acres with nobody or nothing. He could be anywhere. His lawyer told us he has his ID, a credit card, and some cash with him. I believe he got out of Twisty River, our county seat. It's real small, only about 4,000 people. We did a hard search this afternoon until it got dark, dogs and lots of sheriff's deputies who know the town well, and we didn't turn up anything. We'll knock on every door in town tomorrow, but we're also going to spread out to the county's biggest town, Buck Bay, in case he's trying to blend in. But me? I'm scared to hell he's come back to my town, Port Stirling, to have another go at Tamryn. What do you think?"

"Exactly what I think you're thinking: Barry has nothing to lose at this point. He knows I'll be looking for him if I think he killed Leo, his partner. He snapped, Matt. I don't know why or the details, but Barry Gesicki went off the rails."

"And you're sure he killed him?"

"Leo Pistorio crawled to the apartment next to Gesicki's, and when the resident found him, Leo said one word before collapsing: 'Barry'. It was him, make no mistake. And, keep in mind, Barry liked his partner. He hates Tamryn."

CHAPTER 25

Tuesday, February 27, 2024 — Cold Rock Island

After Rohn Reid left his living room, Fern and Ed remained there for a few minutes.

"Now what?" Ed asked her. "He's lying, by the way."

"I know that," Fern said impatiently. "I also think that Hiroshi said something to Rohn and his sons while they were drinking or during dinner that got him killed. Is it time to let him know that we have the fibers from the guest room pillow?"

Ed hesitated. "We're outnumbered, Fern," he said seriously. "I think, at a minimum, we have to assume that Rohn, Rick, and Randy are in this up to their necks."

"I would add Noah to that, too," she said. "He's been hiding something. And, I agree with you. This could turn bad for us in a heartbeat." She deliberately placed a wayward handful of hair behind her ear as she thought. "How many CG crew members are with us? Do you think Captain Adams and one or more of them are armed?"

"I'm certain they have weapons on board, and since they migrated to the Department of Homeland Security, they are law enforcement officers as well as military."

"Let's talk to Bob and find out how many officers are with us," Fern suggested. "I only saw two guys plus the captain. And what if we have to arrest ten people?"

"I think there's probably several more crew we didn't see," Ed said.

"OK, then, let's go talk to Rick, Randy, and Noah separately, and see if we can detect any common thread with what Rohn told us about how this came down. If we don't get anything concrete from those three, we'll talk to Bob and get a head count. If we don't have enough bodies on our side, we'll have to go home and return with full back-up tomorrow."

"Agreed," Ed nodded. He stood up and said, "Where do we find these chaps?"

"I'll lead the way," Fern said.

• • •

They found Randy in the office section of his quarters at the other end of his father's house.

Fern rapped on the open door. "Can we come in?" she said, striding into the room.

Randy calmly closed the lid of his laptop and turned to face them. His eyes got big when he saw Ed's size up close as the state cop stood beside Fern. His cheekbones looked sharper than ever.

"Detective, it's nice to see you again," he said politely, and smiled his dazzling smile at Fern, making eye contact with her.

"She's taken," Ed said drolly. He stepped forward and thrust out his hand. "Lieutenant Ed Sonders with the Oregon State Police. Got a minute to talk?"

Randy was taken aback, but Fern smiled. "Lieutenant Sonders is helping me with the investigation of Hiroshi Matsuda's death. We have some follow-up questions for you, Randy."

"How can you be sure I'm Randy, not Rick?" he grinned back at her.

"I have my ways," she said. On the way here, Fern had shared with Ed how to tell them apart. Randy's mouth turned up at the corners slightly more than Rick's. Once she'd noticed it, it was the obvious difference between the brothers. That, and the way they dressed, with Randy always more casual than Rick.

"How can I help you?" Randy asked. "Have a seat." He gestured to a sofa opposite his desk.

"For starters, we know you lied about not seeing Hiroshi until he was found on Friday," Fern said, all traces of her smile gone. "You had dinner with him Wednesday night after your father picked him up in Honolulu and flew him here. Let's start with you telling me why you lied to me. How about that?"

Randy stared at her for a moment. "Dad said we'd get rid of law enforcement faster if we didn't know anything about him being here."

"Apparently, that plan didn't work," Ed said. "Why don't you tell us what you do know about how Mr. Matsuda got here, and let's start over."

Randy considered and said, "I'm sorry, Fern. I don't like to lie, but dad made a certain sense. We value our privacy here. That's all it was." To Ed, he said, "Yes, dad and Rick went to Honolulu to pick him up. When I heard that Mr. Matsuda wanted to come for a visit, I thought it would be a nice thing to do because of his service here."

"Did you see Hiroshi any time after dinner with him on Wednesday night?" Fern asked.

"No. On Thursday, I was either in my room, or in the gym. Didn't run into him."

"Where's the gym?" Ed asked.

"In building 3. Close to Simon's room."

"Do you know if any of the other island residents saw him on Thursday?" she asked.

"I can't say. We haven't really talked about that day, only about finding him on Thursday night."

"Why do I get the feeling you still aren't being completely truthful?" Fern asked.

"I'm telling you the truth! I didn't see him, and I don't know if anybody else did or not. I was doing my thing on Thursday, and I can't help you."

"What, precisely, is your thing?" Ed asked.

"I work for dad's company in the IT department. We're working on a project."

"That would be information technology, correct?" asked Ed.

Randy looked at him like he was an alien, but he replied politely. "Yes, information technology."

"So, you know your way around computers, programming, servers, and so forth?" Ed asked.

"Yes, it's my field. I take after dad, I guess." He smiled again.

"What's the project about that you're currently working on?"

"We're updating our global accounting software. It's a couple of years old, and things change."

"Like banks? Cryptocurrencies? That sort of thing?" Ed again.

"All financial platforms," Randy answered. "Dad wants to stay ahead of the world. Cutting edge stuff."

"And you help him do that."

"Me and about 2,000 other employees."

"Do they all live in 30-million-dollar penthouse condos?" Fern asked sweetly.

Randy hesitated, but then laughed.

"Probably not," he said. "You're referring to Rick's and my Seattle home, I guess."

"I am," she said. "It seems like a pricey starter home for two kids in their twenties. Is your salary that high?"

"Not quite," Randy said. "Dad loaned us the down payment. Rick and I split the monthly mortgage."

"Why is it in your name only?" Fern asked.

"Um, yeah, I think Rick was out of town at the closing. I handled it."

"I see," said Fern. "Mind me asking how much your monthly payment is?"

"Actually, I do mind," he said pleasantly. "We were raised to not discuss family financials. I suppose you could find out if it's critical to your investigation, but I'd rather not say."

"Fair enough. Have you ever heard the name Scott Thurman?" she asked, changing the subject.

"No, I don't think so," Randy said. "Who's he?"

"So, a man named Scott Thurman has never been to this island when you were here?" she asked, ignoring his question.

"Not that I know of."

"Have you ever been to Honolulu?"

"Of course," Randy responded. "Everyone in Seattle goes to Hawaii regularly. I've been there lots of times, starting when I was a kid. But I never met Mr. Matsuda or this Thurman guy."

"How do you know Scott Thurman is related to Honolulu?" Fern asked in a sharp tone. "I never mentioned that."

"Well, I just assumed he was somehow connected to Matsuda and, therefore, Honolulu."

Fern studied his face. *He's a cool customer, but he knows more about what happened. How can I get it out of him?* She said, "Did you see your brother on Thursday?"

"Again, of course," Randy said. "He's my twin. We see each other every day."

"You're pretty close, then?" she asked.

"Yes."

"Look out for one another—that kind of thing?"

"I suppose so. Yes. I love him. He's my brother and my best friend."

"Does he feel the same about you?"

"Sure."

Ed jumped in. "Do you always know what the other brother is working on? What you're up to? Do you talk about it?" he asked.

"I don't know that we're 'up to' anything," Randy answered somewhat belligerently, "but, yeah, we talk about what we're doing. Mostly about the company."

"Do you have a girlfriend?" Ed asked.

Randy smiled. "Not at the moment. Had one, but it didn't work out."

"Why not? What happened?"

"She wanted me to move to L.A. with her. But now is not a good time for me to move. The business is in Seattle, you know?"

"But you're here," Ed said, and there was a question in there.

"Yes, but only temporarily. We'll fly home when this mess is over."

"What's her name?" Fern asked. "Where can I find her?" *Time to start making these guys uncomfortable.*

"Is that really necessary?" Randy asked. "Honestly, I don't want anything more to do with her."

"It's necessary," she said.

Randy looked at her. "I don't have anything to do with this. I didn't kill him."

"Someone did," Fern said.

. . .

It didn't go any better with Rick Reid. He got flustered when confronted with what they'd learned about the flight to Honolulu to pick up Matsuda, but confirmed his presence on board as his father's co-pilot.

"Why did you lie about it?" Fern asked.

"Dad told me it would make it easier on all of us if you thought we didn't know Matsuda was here until we found him in the hangar. I apologize for lying to you. It's not my nature."

Exact same story, thought Fern. "So you say. Let's hope you tell me the truth from now on." She paused. "Did you talk to Matsuda on the plane?"

"A little bit. Mostly he read and slept."

"What was the 'little bit' of conversation about?"

"He talked about his kids, and about being on our island."

Fern's ears pricked up at the mention of Hiroshi's kids. "Did you meet his son at the Honolulu airport?" she asked.

"Yes."

"Had you met him previously?"

Rick stared blankly at her. "No. We didn't know either of them before this. I think dad had met Mr. Matsuda when he bought the island, but that was very brief."

"You're sure you'd never met Shuji Matsuda before last week?" Ed doubled down. "Or talked to him on the phone, or emailed?"

"No. Why would you ask that?"

"Because it might be relevant to our investigation," Fern put it out there.

"How is that possible? Did his family have anything to do with his death?" Rick asked. His complexion was a titch paler.

"We can't say anything more yet," she said, now that the seed was planted.

The only bit of new info they got was that Rick, unlike his twin, did have a current girlfriend. Fern took down her name and contact information from a now-cooperative Rick. His only departure from his brother's answers were that he thought he 'might have seen' Hiroshi on Thursday morning. However, he couldn't recall where he was at the time, or any further details.

The rest of his story was practically identical to Randy's; almost like they had practiced it.

• • •

Essentially, everyone was sticking to the story that Rohn wanted them to tell, and that it had been a harmless lie to speed up their investigation.

Getting anything out of Noah was like pulling teeth. Ed tried to intimidate him, but not even that worked. As he and Fern prepared to leave the island, Ed told her, "Noah is more afraid of Rohn Reid than he is of me. I don't get that often."

Fern chuckled at the big man. "No, I suppose it is a new experience for you. What does that tell us about this case?"

"That whatever happened on this island, Rohn wants it clamped down tight. He may not be guilty of murder, but he's definitely in charge of the coverup."

"Yeah," Fern said. "You didn't see Hiroshi's body, but there is no way in hell that Rohn could have smothered him single-handedly. He and the victim are close to the same age, but Hiroshi was very fit. The complete opposite of dough boy. If he was involved with the murder, he had to have had help."

Fern's phone buzzed in her pocket. "Bernice," she told Ed.

"Hi."

"Hi, girlfriend," Bernice said. "I have news for you. There are two sets of fingerprints on Hiroshi's rafter. One set is clear, the other smudged."

"As in 'gloves' smudged?" Fern asked.

"Exactly."

"Do you have a match for the clear set?"

"That's why I'm calling," Bernice said. "The good set of prints do not—I repeat, not—match any of the seven people on your island who cooperated with me. This will be the point where you say 'shit'."

"Shit," said Fern. "So, we now need to force the hand of the three Reid men. And I mean that literally."

"Yep. Your killer, or at least the person who helped string up Hiroshi, is either one of the Reids or an unknown person. How will you handle it?"

"Only Ed and I are here currently from local law enforcement. Matt and Jay had to deal with Barry Gesicki's escape from the courthouse. We're going to talk to Captain Adams next and find out how many officers are on the ship and can help us in case we confront Rohn and it goes bad. If we don't have enough good guys with weapons, we'll have to come back tomorrow with additional backup."

"What do you mean 'Barry Gesicki's escape'?"

"Just like it sounds. He escaped while they were taking him from the jail to the courtroom. Matt's beside himself. There is a county-wide manhunt underway."

"Damn," Bernice said. "I've been in my lab all morning and missed the news. Is Tamryn alright?"

"Yes, as far as I know. Sylvia is there with her, and they installed a new lock on her front door."

"This guy. If he goes near her, I will need to be deputized," Bernice said.

"Matt will get him—I guarantee it. In the meantime, I'll talk to Joe about how to go about getting the Reids' cooperation on fingerprinting. I fear I'm going to have to get a probable cause court order; I don't think Rohn will voluntarily submit. He has his heels dug in."

"And now, I think I know why," Bernice said.

CHAPTER 26

Fern and Ed boarded the Resolve and met with Captain Adams.

"We need help, Bob," Fern said.

"I take it your interrogations didn't go as well as you expected?" Captain Adams said.

"'Fraid not. Ed and I think there's a good chance there's more than one island resident involved—we don't know how yet—and we might be outnumbered. We're wondering how many crew are on board who could provide us with backup if things turn nasty?"

"Our standard crew on this ship is ten, but considering today's mandate, I only brought six. We may be tiny in numbers, but we're mighty," the captain smiled.

Ed said, "In addition to those cannons," he pointed at the mounted machine guns on the prow, "does your crew have handguns?"

"Yes. We're trained in law enforcement, and, these days, it's just as much a part of our duty as homeland security."

"That's great, Bob," said Fern. "We're going to grab our fingerprinting kits and go back to the house. Bernice wants all three of the Reid men printed, and I expect them to decline, which is their right because nobody's getting arrested…yet. But if we show force while I explain to Rohn that we will return with a court order based on probable cause, he may relent."

"I understand," said the captain. "Give me ten minutes to assemble and update my crew. Protocol requires me to stay on my ship, but my first lieutenant can fill in and lead."

"OK, we'll meet you back here in ten," Fern said. She and Ed went below decks to their quarters and retrieved the kits. Ed banged his head on the end of the top bunk, drawing blood, while reaching for his bag.

"Ow." He straightened up and said, "I would prefer to not stay here tonight."

Fern giggled. "I hear you. And I think it's probably going that way. If we can't get prints off the Reids, and everyone keeps sticking to the story, I think our only option is to get a court order tomorrow and return in force."

Ed dabbed at his wound with a Kleenex, and said, "Let's go up on the deck and get some fresh air."

They waited for Captain Adams to reappear, and studied in silence what they could see of the island from the ship's deck.

"So, they fly Hiroshi from Honolulu to here," Fern said, thinking through what they knew for certain. "On the flight or during dinner Wednesday night, Hiroshi either tells the Reids his true reason for being here — to learn about Scott Thurman's crypto scam — or he slips and mentions that Shuji works for the same bank they know Thurman works for, and they put two and two together."

"The Reids figure out Hiroshi's real reason for coming here is to snoop around, with the goal of ratting out Thurman," Ed continued. "They don't want that to happen because someone on this island is working the fraud with the banker."

"That's what I think," Fern said, nodding. "Randy Reid works in IT, so he's a prime suspect in my book. These cryptocurrency operations require a lot of technical expertise. It's all about servers and mining with crypto algorithms. I understand it also requires a lot of electrical power, and I suspect the military set up ample power here when they established the base. Scott Thurman is the respected banking face of the operation, but he needs back-end support, and it looks like that help is right here in front of us."

"I don't know if you're right about Randy, but I agree that's what happened. They got on to Hiroshi's real purpose in coming, and he had to be stopped. But, man, I can't understand why Randy would need this gig.

Why don't you just live the good life in that Seattle penthouse, and be the handsome, blessed son of a billionaire? Why does he—or any of the Reids, for that matter—need this risky business?"

"Remember Zhang Chen?" Fern asked. "It was all about greed and ego. He didn't need more money. Maybe that's what's going on here. Thurman may need the cash to live the Honolulu lifestyle he craves, but maybe it's just a game for Randy Reid. To prove he can do it and he's as smart as his old man."

Ed nodded. "Possible, for sure." He hesitated before speaking. "Do we know Rohn Reid's current net worth? Between this island, all of his homes and properties, airplanes, employees, jet-setting lifestyle, he's got to have a heavy burn rate, wouldn't you say?"

Fern's eyes widened. "You think he's running out of money? I never considered that for a moment. He's a freakin' billionaire."

"All we know for certain is that he WAS a freakin' billionaire ten years ago. I don't know that for sure now. Just asking the question," Ed said.

"It's a darn good question," she agreed. "But don't billionaires just keep getting richer?"

"Most do. But there have been some spectacular falls from grace. They invest in some bigtime cash burner like space or underwater sea exploration and it crashes, or they buy businesses they don't know anything about, and run it into the ground. It's been known to happen, even to really smart guys like Rohn Reid."

"We should look into it. Thanks, Edward. I never would have thought of that as a motive for Rohn."

"You sound like Millie—she calls me Edward when she wants to make a point."

"How is your fabulous wife? I haven't seen her since Christmas."

"She is as fabulous as always," Ed smiled. "Don't you stop and think every once in a while how you and I won the lottery when it comes to spouses?"

"Every single day of my life. Especially since Matt got shot. I had some bad moments that week, and if it hadn't been for you and Jay and my parents, I would have gone off the rails. He's everything to me."

"Same here with Millie. You would think she and I would be bored silly with each other after all these years, but we're still best friends. She might prefer the dog to me, but I'm a close second."

Fern laughed. "I think it's the other way around; you're first and your dog is a close second. And he's only close because he warned you about the tsunami in time to avoid a catastrophe."

"True that. He's a keeper, and I hope I get to see both of them again."

"Why on earth wouldn't you?" Fern asked, incredulous.

Ed frowned. "There's something about this island that weirds me out. I'll be happy when you and I are back on terra firma in Port Stirling."

"And you didn't even see Hiroshi Matsuda strung up in that monstrous hangar. It was awful, Ed. One of the worst things I've ever seen. I don't understand how human beings can do that to one another. I'm going to get justice for that poor man if it's the last thing on earth I do." She looked at Ed who'd blanched when she said that. "But it won't be the last thing I do, don't worry," she added hurriedly.

Ed, Fern, and the now armed and ready Coast Guard crew—five men and one woman—stood talking on the Cold Rock Island dock. Fern spoke.

"First, thank you for the backup. Ed and I really appreciate you guys, and we hope we can accomplish our goals here today with your support. Here's what we're going to do. First, we talk briefly to the other island residents. I say 'briefly' because we think they will stick to the same story as Rohn Reid—everyone seems to do as he says. If we get any new info, great, but it's really just a step we have to take to cover all the bases. We want you to hang with us during these meetings. And look ferocious," she grinned.

"When we're done with the others, we'll go back to the main house, and this is where it might get gnarly. Dr. Ryder wants us to get fingerprints from the three Reids—father Rohn, and his twin sons, Rick and Randy. Rohn has already refused to cooperate, and we believe he likely will again. I'm prepared to seek a court order when we get back to the mainland, but Ed and I are hopeful that your presence will encourage him to participate. If nothing else, you guys will help him to understand that we mean business here. Any questions?"

One crew member raised his hand. "Do you know if Mr. Reid is armed?"

Fern shook her head. "We don't think so, no, but he does have a license to carry. He travels with security, but when he's on his island, it feels slack. Frankly, I can't see Rohn Reid ever shooting a gun—he's not the type. But I want to emphasize that we don't know for sure."

Ed added, "I can't see him flying a plane either, but he does, so, bottom line, you never know, and it pays to be alert at all times."

Fern pointed at Ed. "What he said. Any other questions?"

Another hand. "How far do you want us to go? What if the suspects produce weapons?"

Fern and Ed looked at each other. She said, "The U.S. State Department would prefer that we not shoot a well-known, global businessman. However, if we are physically threatened, you should respond as your training demands. Clear?"

All heads nodded.

"Good. Let's go," Fern said.

• • •

First, they tracked down Tyson and Aaron. They were both stationed at the top of the roadway up the hill, watching the cops carefully on the harbor's dock. The sky was a gunmetal gray, and it looked antsy off to the southwest, but was dry for now. The temperature had dropped a few degrees, and Fern and Ed both zipped up their bomber jackets. Fern turned the collar up on hers to snuggle against her neck.

The two employees, thirty seconds into the interrogation, admitted lying about how Hiroshi arrived and pinned it on Rohn.

"Mr. Reid told all of us that you all would leave us in peace sooner if we played dumb," Tyson said, "so that's what we did. I felt bad for lying to you." And, indeed, Tyson did look sorry, Fern thought.

"You can redeem yourself by telling us the truth now, OK? You're head of security, Tyson, why weren't you on the plane with Mr. Reid?" Fern asked.

"Because I'm head of security on Cold Rock Island," he said. "My job is to safeguard this island no matter what. I stay here almost all the time. Noah occasionally goes with Mr. Reid on the plane if it's a trip where he might be at risk."

She jumped at that statement. "Why would he have been at risk on a flight to Honolulu just to pick up one man? Especially a man with a pristine reputation, and a long history with your island? Where's the risk factor? I don't see it," she said.

Tyson scratched the stubble on his chin. "I didn't mean 'at risk', I meant he would be mostly alone. That's all."

"But his son Rick was with him. Couldn't he protect his dad in the event of any trouble?"

"I guess. But Noah's kinda the muscle around here. Mr. Reid likes having him nearby. Same with Moira. Not the muscle, I mean, but just that he likes having her near him."

Ed and Fern looked at each other. Fern spoke. "Moira was on the plane to Honolulu, too?"

"Yeah," Tyson said. "Mr. Reid and Rick flew the plane, Noah was along for protection, and Moira brings the food and drinks."

"We were told only Rohn, Rick, and Noah were aboard," said Fern.

"Nope. Moira went, too. We were all on our own for meals that day."

Fern jotted notes in her book. "Thank you, Tyson," she said, and then turned to Aaron.

"What about you, Aaron, why did you lie to me?"

"Same reason. I didn't want to get fired."

"But you swore to me," she persisted.

"I know." His lower lip quivered. "It won't happen again, detective."

"Can you add anything to what Tyson said?"

"No, I only saw Mr. Matsuda briefly on Wednesday night, and didn't see him at all on Thursday, not until Friday when…"

"Where and what time on Wednesday night did you see him?" Fern interrupted.

"I was doing my rounds about 10:45 p.m. and I saw him going into the guest house."

"Was he alone?" Ed asked.

"Yes."

"How did he appear to you?" asked Ed. "Was he moving fast or slow? Was he wobbly at all?"

"He looked normal," Aaron said. "Just a man walking from the main house to his room."

"Which room did he go in?" asked Fern.

Aaron thought. "It was the same room you stayed in. We call it the purple room."

"I really wish you'd told me that the first time we talked, Aaron."

He looked down at his interesting feet.

"It's not his fault," Tyson said. "We love our jobs, but they come with a price tag—loyalty to Mr. Reid."

• • •

Moira, Rohn Reid's longtime cook, was not apologetic about lying to Fern. In fact, she was downright belligerent. With her blonde wavy hair, apple cheeks that were now quite red, and tall, stocky body, the fifty-four-year-old was ready for a fight.

"You come here, all uppity and official, upsetting Mr. Reid, and expect us to treat you like a queen," she thundered at Fern. "We are a family here, and we value our privacy and our serenity. What did you expect?"

If she was taken aback by Moira's outburst, Fern was committed to not showing it. Calmly, she said, "I'm sorry that my job requires me to ask what you may perceive to be difficult questions. But I'm a representative of your government, Moira, a government that is sworn to protect all Americans. We didn't come here looking to disrupt your lives; one of you did that yourself. A man was murdered, and we can't let that stand."

"He was a Jap. Why do we care what happened to him?"

"That's enough," Ed jumped in. "The victim was an ally, living in the United States. The same country you live in, I might point out. We're not letting this become an international incident because of people like you."

"Ed's right," said Fern, no longer calm. "And you're darn lucky your fingerprints aren't on that rafter because, after that remark, you'd be suspect #1. Now sit down and answer my questions. Sit down!"

Moira frowned and muttered something under her breath, but she sat down and looked at Fern.

"Did you talk to Hiroshi Matsuda on the flight here from Honolulu?"

"Only to inquire whether he wanted any drinks or food, and if he was comfortable," Moira answered. "It was my job to make sure he got what he needed during the trip."

"And did you serve him anything to eat or drink?"

"Of course. We were in the air several hours."

"What, exactly, did you serve him?" Fern asked.

"He only drank water — Pellegrino mineral. He did eat some of my lasagna and a small salad. No dressing." She turned up her nose at that affront.

"Did anyone else on board eat and drink the same things as Mr. Matsuda?"

"Yes. Everyone did. Except for the mineral water; my boys all drink Coke."

"OK, let's jump to Thursday morning," Fern said. "Did you see Mr. Matsuda at any time? Did he come to the main house for breakfast, or did you take his to him at the guest house?"

"I did not see him, but, yes, I delivered a tray to his room. I left it at his door and rapped lightly. As you probably remember, we have baskets outside the door."

Fern nodded.

"What did you do then?" Ed asked.

"I went back to the kitchen and started prepping lunch for everyone. Since I'd left the other employees on their own Wednesday, I wanted to make something nice for everyone on Thursday."

"Did Matsuda bring the tray back to the main house Thursday?" asked Ed.

"Someone did," Moira said. "I didn't see who. It was left on the counter just inside my outside door."

"Was the food eaten?" asked Fern.

"Yes."

"What time did the tray appear?"

"I don't know. Like I said, I didn't see who brought it back, so I must have been in another room. I assumed Lynette picked it up when she went to clean."

"You're one hundred percent sure you didn't see him on Thursday?" Fern asked, taking one last stab.

"I am."

In turn, they had brief conversations with Leonard, Lynette, and Simon, the gardener. Only Simon, like Rick Reid, thought he might have seen Hiroshi Thursday morning. And like him also, he couldn't remember what time or where he was when that happened. Lynette reported that she had picked up the tray, and 'assumed' the food had been eaten.

They were all very sorry to have lied to Fern previously, but Mr. Reid had said it was necessary, blah, blah, blah.

CHAPTER 27

At five o'clock, the sky finally started spitting at them, and twilight was moving on from the day. Ed, Fern, and the CG crew were gathered in the central courtyard adjacent to the main house.

"OK, peeps, it's fingerprint time," Fern said to the group gathered round. "We're going to the house, and we're going to get this done." Her voice held more conviction than she felt internally. "Everyone with me?"

"Yes," they all answered in unison. Ed added, "I want to go home, so let's just do this." He rang the doorbell, and they stood waiting at the ready.

Leonard answered. "Oh, hello again, Fern. Would you like to come in?" He stood aside and held open the large door.

"Thanks, Leonard. We have one more question for Mr. Reid, and then we'll get out of your hair for today," she said. "Can you get him for us, please?"

"Sure. Come in and wait here. I'll be right back," Leonard said.

They waited quietly in the foyer while Leonard went down the hall in the east wing. After a couple of minutes, the double doors to the living room were flung open inward, Rohn Reid holding a doorknob in each hand. "Yes?" he said.

"May we come in?" Fern asked. "We have one additional question for you." Her heart was in her throat, but she stood firm and held her ground.

Reid sighed loudly, let go of the doors, and turned to walk to his favorite chair. The cops followed into the room. He plopped down, clasped his hands over his belly, and waited for Fern to speak.

"We got a call from Dr. Bernice Ryder, our medical examiner, about the fingerprints she took off the rafter holding Mr. Matsuda." Rohn didn't say anything, so Fern continued. "She was able to gather two sets of prints, and they did not match any of your employees."

Rohn smiled slightly.

"Unfortunately, they did not match Mr. Matsuda's fingerprints either, which adds to the evidence that he was murdered."

"Are you telling me we have an unknown assailant?" Reid asked her. "Potentially loose on my island?"

"It remains a possibility," Fern answered. She swallowed. "However, the ME is requesting that you and your sons submit to fingerprinting now so we can rule out any involvement on your part."

Rohn's face clouded over, and he made a move to stand. Ed and the CG crew moved in a step closer to Fern, looking ready for whatever Reid had in mind. He glanced at them but returned his focus to Fern.

"I told you before, detective, and I'll tell you again — we will not be fingerprinted," he grunted. "You're quite the firecracker, aren't you?"

"No, sir," Fern said. "I'm just a woman doing my job. And, as long as the fingerprints on that rafter are unaccounted for, I'll keep working."

"Are you planning to arrest me?"

"No. You may not believe me, but this step is my best effort to eliminate you and your children as suspects. However, I will request a court order based on probable cause. Probable cause because, to my knowledge so far, there were ten people on this island when Hiroshi Matsuda was murdered, and seven of them are unlikely suspects. That leaves three of you that my colleagues and I would like to move into the 'unlikely' column. It would be nice if you would cooperate now, but if not, we'll go home and talk to the judge."

He was silent for a moment, and Fern was hopeful he might capitulate. But no.

"I think you should go home, and I think it's time I made a phone call to Secretary Leufeld. We're old friends, you know."

"Whatever you prefer, Mr. Reid. We'll let ourselves out, and we'll be taking off shortly."

They filed out of Reid's living room, Fern bringing up the rear. She turned at the last moment and said, "See you tomorrow. Don't leave this island."

• • •

They pulled the Coast Guard cutter into Buck Bay port a few minutes after 7:00 p.m.

"I'll miss Millie's dinner, but at least I'll sleep in my own bed tonight," Ed said, grabbing both his and Fern's bag as he started down the ship's ramp to the dock.

"Yeah, it's nice to be almost home," Fern said. They walked to their respective cars. "I'll go see Judge Hedges first thing in the morning, and I'll call you from Twisty River once I see which way the wind is blowing. I need to call my boss tonight just to make sure that State is going to back us."

"They will. Do you want me to meet you at Cynthia's office? I'm happy to," he said.

"No. Let me make sure we're on before you leave home."

"Your wish is my command. Watch your back tonight, Fern. I didn't like the look on ol' Rohn's face when we left."

"Me neither. Same goes for you, although no one would ever find your house in the boonies."

"Which is precisely why I live there," Ed laughed. "You and Matt might as well have a flashing red beacon over your place."

"That's the truth," she said, shaking her head. "Which became very clear to us last year. But we love our house. It's now tricked out with every security feature known to mankind."

"Yes, Matt told me what steps he'd taken in the aftermath of his shooting, and I approve. You should feel safe there. But still…drapes closed, dinner in, and everything locked up tight tonight."

"Don't worry, Ed. Say hi to Millie for me."

He waved and got in his car.

Fern called Matt and told him she was on the way home. With her windshield wipers on intermittent to clear off the light rain, the spits of which were causing smearing, she headed out to Highway 101 and, on this dark Tuesday night, turned south on the familiar road.

What the heck am I going to do if the Secretary of State tells me to back off Rohn Reid? If he does and I'm forced to do so, my career is in the tank before it barely gets started. Should I call Joe now, or should I go straight to Fred Leufeld and make my case?

A private person herself, Fern understood why Rohn Reid, a very famous man, objected to having his fingerprints on file. But was there another reason for his reluctance? Could he actually be involved in Hiroshi's murder? She thought it more likely that Rohn was protecting his sons and was using the ruse of privacy for his family as an excuse to not cooperate. Whatever the reason, Fern and the eleventh richest man in the world were in a standoff, a fight she desperately needed to win.

A few miles south of Buck Bay, where 101 splits—one road going inland to Twisty River, and 101 continuing south to Port Stirling—Fern noticed a car following too close behind her. She hoped it would take the other road, but it continued south with her. On the first straight stretch with a passing lane, she slowed, hoping the car would pass her. It didn't. It slowed to match her speed.

Probably just a driver not paying attention, she thought. *But I'd better test him.* She sped up considerably, trying to lose the car. It sped up, too.

I've got a tail. Why is he being so obvious? Trying to scare me?

She decided to go the speed limit, continue on to Port Stirling, and see what the tail would do. He settled in close behind her again. She kept her eyes on the rear-view mirror as much as she dared to on this rainy night.

And then the bullet whizzed past her right ear, making a hole in the front windshield. The plastic membrane layer in the laminated rear windshield held it intact, but she couldn't see out of it clearly.

"Shit!" she screamed, and hit 9-1-1 on her phone, which was mounted to the right of the steering wheel, while she simultaneously tried to speed up.

Buck Bay emergency answered immediately.

"This is Fern Byrne and I'm on 101 headed south just south of the split with Highway 42," she said, speaking loudly and quickly. "The car behind me just shot at me. I need assistance immediately!"

"I'm contacting our police right now, ma'am," said the operator. "What kind of vehicle are you in?"

"A blue VW beetle, Oregon license plate NVJ229." Fern felt the air beside her head move, and she screamed again. "Shit! A second shot! Please hurry. They're trying to kill me!"

"Stay calm and keep driving, ma'am. A team is on its way to you. Do you know what kind of car is behind you?"

Fern risked a glance at her left mirror. "It's white, and it might be a Mercedes. Big, though. Like maybe an SUV."

"OK, that's good. Two of our units are close to you. Should be just a couple of minutes. Keep driving, head down, and keep this line open!"

Fern did as she was instructed. She ducked down so her eyes were barely over the steering wheel and pressed down hard on the pedal. She couldn't see out the back, but she felt the car was keeping up with her. She'd never driven her VW over 85 mph and was scared to do so now. Although every fiber in her body wanted to drive as fast as she could go, it occurred to her that the slower she drove, the faster the cops might catch up to them, so she slowed back down.

As promised, she soon saw flashing blue lights coming up behind them. Two police cars! *Thank you, thank you!* Simultaneously, the car behind her slowed, flipped a U-turn in the highway and headed north. One of the police cars did the same and took off in a high-speed chase.

The other police car pulled alongside Fern and motioned for her to pull over on the shoulder. She did and slowed to a stop. Shaking, she put her arms on the steering wheel and rested her head on them as one of the officers approached the VW.

"Oh, my God," he yelled back to his partner, "it *is* Fern!" She rolled down her window and recognized the Buck Bay officer. "Dave," she said, "am I ever glad to see you."

"We thought it looked like your car," he said. "Are you alright? Did you get hit? Can you step out?"

Fern opened the door and stood up, a little shaky, but clearly unharmed. "I'm OK. Scared, but OK. Thanks for getting here so fast."

"Who's in the car that shot at you? Any idea?"

Fern shook her head. "Not a name, no, but I'm working on an issue for the State Department, and it's taking an unpleasant turn. I suspect this is related." She waved her arm toward her shot up car. "I'm not at liberty to discuss the details yet. I need to call my boss."

"Shall we leave your car here tonight, and we'll take you home?" Dave said.

"Maybe," Fern said. She looked up the road northward. "What's happening with the chase? Can you find out?"

"Jim, any news yet?" Dave said to his partner, leaning down to his vehicle's open window.

"Dispatch says they got away on the bridge. Bad guys drove on the southbound lane, dodging traffic, and Greg and Jessica were afraid someone would get killed, so they were forced to stop the chase. Said to tell Fern they were sorry."

"They did the right thing," Fern said to Dave. "Can you imagine going off that bridge in your car into the bay?" She shivered. "Can they request a roadblock up north where the road to Eugene takes off from 101?"

Dave's partner heard Fern's request, and said, "They've already done it. Blocking both 101 and the Umpqua Highway. They'll get them."

"Thank you. Please keep me posted. Here's my cell number." She gave them her number and then turned to Dave, "I'm taking you up on your offer. I'd love a ride home."

She retrieved her bag from the passenger side and grabbed her phone from its mount, then she patted the VW's roof. *I'll be back for you in the morning, baby. Thanks for saving my life.*

. . .

Matt, of course, was horrified when Fern called him from the patrol car. "I don't want you to be startled when a Buck Bay patrol car pulls up in our driveway. They're bringing me home. I had some excitement on the highway."

"An accident?!? Are you alright?"

"I'm fine. No accident. I'll fill you in when I get home. Should be about twenty minutes. I'm hungry."

"Well, that sounds like my wife. I'll throw something together."

"Love you," she said.

"Love you back."

• • •

Matt clung to Fern for a long time. She told him what happened, and he didn't want to let go of her.

"Jesus, you were lucky," he said, stroking her hair. "So, Rohn Reid has nasty connections on the west coast."

"It sure appears that way, doesn't it?" Fern agreed.

"Can you think of anyone else who would want to do you harm?"

"Zhang Chen, of course, but he's rotting in prison. And besides, the timing is the key, don't you think? I've just had a disagreeable conversation with Reid, and both Ed and I got a bad vibe from him. Oh, no!" she shouted, "Ed! I have to warn him."

Fern dialed her phone and smiled when Ed answered. "You OK?" she asked.

"I'm OK. You? Why are you calling me?" Ed asked.

"I was shot at after I left Buck Bay. Two shots, to be exact."

"Someone shot at your car? Is that what you're telling me?"

"Yes. Followed me onto 101 and started shooting at me just after the 42 split in the road. You were ahead of me a ways. Did anyone tail you when you got on 42?"

"Oh, good God," Ed said, exasperated. "No one bothered me, although I did think I spotted a white Mercedes behind me for a while when I first left the Coast Guard parking lot. But it turned off just as I was through downtown Buck Bay."

"Was it an SUV Mercedes?"

"Yes, I would say so. Dark out and raining, so I can't be positive, but that's what I'd guess. Are you alright? Any injuries?"

"I'm good. Shaken, not stirred," she said. She poked Matt in his stomach, and he smiled, hugely relieved that his wife could joke after what just happened to her.

"I'm going to personally turn Rohn Reid inside out tomorrow," Ed fumed. "Tell Cynthia what happened to you tonight, get this warrant, and let's go get him."

"Yeah, it certainly adds to my probable cause case," she said. "Get some food in your big body, get a good night's sleep, and be ready for action tomorrow. 'Night, Ed."

Matt said, "OK, Ed's taken care of. Now we take care of you." He took her by the hand and moved into their kitchen. "I realize it's a Tuesday, not Friday night, but I'm making us martinis anyway."

"Wonderful idea. I'm calmer now, but I'm not calm," she said.

"It's not for you, it's for me. I'm a wreck." He grinned to try to get her to relax a little. It worked; she laughed. "And, I'm getting fucking tired of people shooting at you and me. From now on, it's no more Mr. Nice Guy. I'm going to be a pain in the butt to everyone who's in our way."

"No, you're not," Fern said. "It's not in your nature. But I do need to wrap up this Hiroshi Matsuda case. I'm afraid of that island. Ed is, too. We need you, Matt. Seriously. What's the status of Barry Gesicki and Tamryn?"

"Unfortunately, he's still at large. But Tamryn and Sylvia say they're safe at her house. A new keypad was installed, and Tamryn programmed it when they got to the house this afternoon. I talked to them an hour ago, and they were watching a movie. However, Milton called me earlier, and said he'd had a 9-1-1 call from a local farmer who said he'd given a ride this afternoon to a man matching Barry's description. Picked him up on the old road about six miles out of Twisty River and dropped him on the south end of Port Stirling."

"So, he's in the area," she said.

"Yep. And there's more. He killed his partner in Boston last week and is on the run."

"Yikes."

CHAPTER 28

Barry Gesicki balanced himself on the tree limb while he took the pen out of his jacket pocket and raised his binoculars to focus on the keypad. As he'd expected, there was a Port Stirling cop with Tamryn and some old woman. The cop and the woman stood off to Tamryn's side and chatted while she approached the door.

The stupid bitch. She should know to stand in front of it while she reprograms the code.

He wrote 1-7-4-9 on the palm of his hand.

• • •

After drawing their living room draperies closed, blocking out the night, Matt and Fern enjoyed their martinis curled up on their sofa while Fern filled him in on Cold Rock Island. They rarely closed the heavy gray velvet drapes because even at night, they liked to look at the ocean's white-tipped waves as they connected with the beautiful Oregon shore. But mindful of Ed's reminder and what happened on the highway, it seemed the prudent thing to do tonight.

"A part of my brain understands why Rohn Reid would lie about Hiroshi's arrival on the island; he just wanted us to go away quickly," Fern said.

"And if he'd gotten an ME less efficient than Bernice, it might have been simply resolved as a suicide in a place that was meaningful to him,"

Matt commented. "I get it, too. But he's not an ignorant man, and he should have realized that you would somehow learn about his plane going to Honolulu to pick him up. That tells me that it was worth it to him to take that chance."

"Right," she said. "And that logic tells me that if he's willing to take such a big chance, the payoff for him must be more important than just his privacy. Like making sure his sons didn't get caught up in a major fraud scheme."

"Or, that he himself didn't get caught up in it. You only know that someone on that island is working with Scott Thurman; you don't know for sure that it's one of his sons."

"I'm convinced it's Randy," Fern said. "He's an IT genius just like his dad, and he's trying to find his way in the world. Rohn doesn't need to — he has already built one of the world's most successful companies. Plus, Randy is closer in age to Scott Thurman, and, therefore, more likely to be acquainted."

"Have you found the servers yet?" Matt asked.

"No. We've tried to snoop around, but there's always someone with us. There's only so much I can do without a warrant. But first, I need to make sure that Joe and Fred Leufeld are going to back me, then I'll talk to Cynthia in the morning."

"They have to. Especially now that you've been shot at. It's too much of a coincidence. We should know soon if the roadblock was successful — you haven't gotten a text yet, have you?"

She looked at her phone. "Nothing yet. It would be nice if they catch them, wouldn't it? Can I take your car to Twisty River in the morning to meet with the judge? I'll try to not get it shot up."

"I'll be driving you," Matt said firmly. "Jay and the guys can start the hunt for Gesicki as soon as it gets light, and I'll catch up with them once I know you're safe."

"But…"

"No buts, it's settled." He took a drink of his martini.

"Will you check in with Tamryn tonight?"

"Yep. Sylvia's been great about texting me while Tamryn's resting, and I asked her to let me know when they're retiring for the night."

"Great. What are we eating?"

"Penne pasta with spicy Italian sausage, and a big ol' salad," Matt said. "How does that sound."

Fern jumped up and headed to the kitchen.

• • •

Joe Phelps was brushing his teeth in preparation for bed in his Washington, D.C. townhouse when his cell phone buzzed. *Fern.*

"Hello, Fern."

"Sorry to bother you so late, Joe."

"It's fine. I'm not in bed yet, and you wouldn't call me unless it's important."

"Yeah, it's important," she said. She shared the details of the fingerprint situation on Cold Rock Island, and finished by saying, "Rohn Reid is probably going to call the Secretary of State if he hasn't already. He's not fond of me, I'm afraid."

"No, he's not," Joe said. "And he's already talked to Fred."

"Why didn't you phone me and tell me that nugget of info?" Fern asked. "I'm on pins and needles here, Joe."

"Because it's a non-issue for me and for Fred. We have to find out who killed Hiroshi Matsuda, and, guess what, the laws apply to billionaires just like they apply to the rest of us. Get your probable cause warrant and hold him down if you have to in order to get his prints. Same goes for his kids."

"And Fred feels the same?"

"Even stronger than me. He and Reid are old friends, and the last thing your Secretary of State needs is the perception of favoritism in an international murder investigation with a key strategic partner country like Japan."

"Whew," Fern said. "That's a huge relief."

"Rohn and all of those people on that island have lied to you. It may be for the reason Rohn told you, but maybe they lied for another reason. You've got to either rule them in or rule them out. And make sure Judge Hedges includes a search warrant. You've got to find that server room, Fern. It's a crucial piece of your evidence."

"I don't think I'll have any problems with the judge. There's a new piece

I haven't told you yet — just happened tonight, a couple of hours ago. My car was chased and shot at while I was driving back to Port Stirling from the CG station."

"You're obviously OK, or we wouldn't be having this conversation, right?" Joe asked.

"I'm fine. Didn't get hit but they tried twice."

"So, whoever it was, they were serious about getting rid of you. Did we catch them?"

"Not yet. The local cops showed up to rescue me, and the shooters took off north. We've set up a roadblock further up the highway, though, and they should get them. I'm waiting for a call."

"And this was only a few hours after you and Rohn had your tiff over fingerprinting."

"Correct," she said. "Not a good look for him, is it?"

"What in God's name is so important to Rohn Reid that he would murder a Japanese hero, and take shots at an agent of the U.S. government? You're going to need a full contingent of backup when you step foot on that damnable island, Fern. Who've you got lined up to go with you?"

"Your question should be 'who's NOT going with me?'" she laughed. "Captain Bob Adams has ten law enforcement-ready sailors, plus Ed Sonders, who was with me today. My husband has also just informed me that he will accompany me to both Judge Hedges' chambers and to Cold Rock Island in the morning. And I suspect that when Jay Finley hears what's going on, he'll want to come, too. The sheriff and Patty Perkins are busy on the Barry Gesicki manhunt, or they'd want to string along as well. I am not hurting for backup."

"I like your close-knit group, Fern. You're lucky, and I wish more of my agents had this kind of local support. Please tell Matt I'm very sorry you are at risk in this deal. But also tell him that there's no one more capable than you and he shouldn't worry when you're in the field."

"I tell him that every day. I want you to please tell Fred I said, 'thank you' for not letting me down, and that I'm very happy I voted for his boss."

Joe wasn't much of a grinner, but he did so now.

• • •

Sylvia texted Matt:

> We're going to bed now. All quiet on the western front.

He texted back:

> Great. I'm going to Twisty River in the morning but will check in with you girls.

Sylvia:

> Did we catch him yet?

Matt:

> No. Make sure Tamryn has her gun handy.

Sylvia:

> She does. Goodnight, Chief.

"They're OK," Matt told Fern.

"What a nightmare this guy is for Tamryn," Fern said. "I feel so badly for her."

"Yep. It stinks alright. She's such a great person. I can't believe he escaped, what a disaster. A disaster that didn't have to happen."

"Speaking of escaping, could you call Dan in Buck Bay and ask him if they stopped my shooters yet? I should have heard by now, don't you think?"

Matt looked at his watch. "Depends on how it went down…if it did. They might want to wait until they've got everything wrapped up before they call you. But, yeah, let's call Dan and find out what's going on."

He pressed the button on his phone for Buck Bay police chief Dan McCoy, and Dan picked up immediately.

"Matt. Just going to phone you. They got away. Never showed up at the roadblock, and we've doubled back all the way to the bridge." Dan said.

"Are you fucking kidding me?" Matt bellowed. "What's going on in this county? Are we a bunch of amateurs?!?"

"Calm down. Your attitude isn't helping the situation."

"Oh? It's not? You mean the situation where my wife was shot at just outside your town? That situation?"

"Look, I'm sorry, OK? But it was too dangerous for my guys to keep a high-speed chase going over that bridge. People could have been killed."

"My wife could have been killed!"

"But she wasn't, and I understand she's OK, for which I'm very grateful, Matt. We know her assailants are somewhere between the bridge and the cutoff to Eugene, and we will find them. They're in a white Mercedes SUV, and there aren't many of those around here. Clearly, they took a side road. My guess is the one that goes alongside Jensen Lake. It runs for a long ways, but it doesn't really go anywhere. We'll start there as soon as it's light in the morning. In the meantime, you'll want to arm your security system and stay in your house tonight."

"I don't need you to tell me how to protect my wife," Matt stormed. He didn't get angry very often, but there was no consoling him now.

"Just trying to be helpful," Dan said. "Let's talk again in the morning."

"Damn straight we'll talk again in the morning," Matt said, and hung up. To Fern, who was watching him with wide eyes, he said, "I never did like that guy."

So, Matt and Fern both had their guns handy as well. Lights out in Port Stirling.

• • •

Lights had been out for Barry Gesicki for over an hour. He watched Tamryn's house through his binoculars, but he couldn't see into her bedroom from his perch. The only lights visible on this east side were the kitchen, the glass panels on either side of the front door, and the guest bedroom, where that old lady was clearly preparing to spend the night.

Damn! Surely she'll leave tomorrow. I'll have to wait to make sure I can do the job with no slip ups or collateral damage.

Soundlessly, he climbed down from the tree, crawled into his makeshift tent deep in the forest, ate a protein bar, and went to sleep.

CHAPTER 29

Wednesday, February 28, 2024 — Twisty River

Circuit Court Judge Cynthia Hedges welcomed Fern and Matt into her chambers.

"Good morning. It's nice to see you both," Hedges said. "Especially you, Fern. I heard you had some excitement last night. Is that the reason you're here?"

"Word travels fast…as always," Fern said. "It was a scary drive home, but I'm fine. And, yes, I believe that whoever shot at my car last night is connected to a case I'm working on for the State Department. A case we desperately need your help on."

"Tell me about it," said Cynthia.

Fern informed the judge of the facts of Cold Rock Island, and where her investigation stood as of this morning.

"So, Bernice has identified the murder weapon as the purple pillow that you found in a room on the island…do I have that right?" Cynthia asked.

"That's correct," Fern said. "There is no doubt that Matsuda was smothered with that pillow."

"Did she find the same prints on the pillow as she extracted from the rafter?"

"There were more identifiable prints on the pillow — including mine — than on the rafter, but, yes, the rafter and the pillow have a shared set of clear prints. I believe that Matsuda was killed in the same guest room I stayed in Saturday night when my boss and I were on the island."

"Creepy," the judge said.

"The whole island is creepy," Fern said, "but, yeah, I'm not staying in that room again. Bob Adams has been assigned to ferry us back and forth and provide accommodation on his ship in case we have to overnight again. But after what happened to me last night, we'll be coming home every day rather than sleep on the island."

"I'm happy to hear that," the judge said, and she sat up straighter in her leather chair. "I'm prepared to give you a probable cause warrant to force Rohn, Rick, and Randy Reid to submit to fingerprinting." She looked directly at Fern. "You're prepared to take a backup crew with you, correct?"

"Yes, ma'am."

"Are you going along for the ride, Matt?" Cynthia asked him.

"I am. Shooting at my wife is not allowed," he smiled.

"I wish you could be in two places at once," Cynthia said. "I want Barry Gesicki found today and put back in jail where he belongs. But I understand why you need to help with Fern's case."

"Yep, it's a tough one," said Matt. "But Earl and his crew have help from all the local cops, including my officers. My money is on them, and Gesicki will be lucky to get out alive."

The judge nodded and said, "I'm also prepared to allow a general search warrant for Cold Rock Island. It sounds to me as if that island is hiding secrets, and I want you to uncover them."

Fern beamed. "Thank you, Cynthia! I really appreciate this, and I won't let you down. Just between us, the Secretary of State is anxiously awaiting a resolution of this case. He was close friends with Hiroshi Matsuda, and he's upset on both a personal and professional level. It's important that we don't mess it up."

"You won't. You'll get your prints, and they'll either match Bernice's evidence or not. And if they don't, you'll start over," Cynthia said. "Get to work and good luck."

The three friends shook hands, but that wasn't enough for Fern. She moved in and gave the judge a hug. Cynthia returned the hug with a peck on Fern's cheek, and whispered, "Go get 'em."

• • •

"Let's stop in Earl's office for a minute while Cynthia executes the warrants," Matt said. He grabbed Fern's hand, and they took the stairs to the sheriff's floor.

"Mr. and Mrs. Horning," the sheriff said when they walked into his office. Earl was eating a maple bar and drinking a large coffee. He looked Matt in the eye. "Be advised that I don't allow any yelling at me while I'm eating. It's bad for my stomach, doc says."

"I'm not here to yell at you, Earl," Matt said. "We're here to see Judge Hedges, and I just want to update you on everything I know this morning, which isn't much." He and Fern plopped down in the chairs facing the sheriff's desk.

"I'm sure you saw the report about the farmer who gave Barry Gesicki a ride yesterday afternoon to Port Stirling," Matt said.

"Yes, I saw it, and we took a statement from him last night. It was Gesicki alright. We know exactly where he dropped him, and my guys, your guys, Patty, and all of Buck Bay's force are headed there now."

"Excellent," said Matt. "Tell them to cover the ground between the drop off point and Tamryn's house."

"Already did that. Have you talked to Tamryn?"

"No, but I'm in regular contact with Sylvia, who is staying at Tamryn's house and making sure she follows Bernice's orders. I decided that it would be better for her recovery if she and I aren't talking about work. Sylvia texted me this morning that nothing happened during the night, and they both got a good night's sleep. Tamryn is urging Sylvia to go to work and hold down the fort while we're all out today and promised her that she would stay put at home and keep on the program."

"Is it a good idea for Tamryn to be home alone with this maniac on the loose?" Earl asked.

"I don't like it either," Matt agreed, shaking his head, "and we're keeping a close watch. We've offered her the guest room in our home, but she politely declined." He smiled. "She's got a new lock on the door and only she can unlock it."

"Sounds like she's feeling better," Earl said.

"She is, according to Sylvia," Matt said.

"As a matter of fact," Fern said, "Tamryn emailed me yesterday to let me know that she'd tracked down the girlfriend of Rick Reid, one of my suspects, who I would like to talk to."

"Should we have Rudy posted somewhere near her house, Earl?" Matt asked the sheriff. "To keep watch at a distance…do you think?" He was uneasy.

"I'll talk to him when I get over there," Earl said. "I think we'd both feel better if young Rudy was close to her house. Now, what about you Miss Fern?" Earl said. "Had a close call, I understand. Are you OK?"

"Doing well this morning. Much better than last night." She jerked her thumb at Matt. "This man took good care of me."

"That's what we all have to do; take care of each other," Earl said pointedly, looking at Matt. "Even when one of us screws up."

"I was frustrated, Earl. It was no reflection on you," Matt said. "I'm sorry."

Earl shook his head. "It's not me you owe an apology to. It's Victoria Dixon. My deputy is in agony over something that isn't her fault, and you piling on didn't help. She was never made aware that Gesicki is a cop. It's a system failure."

"I'll catch up with Deputy Dixon when I get back from Cold Rock Island," Matt said. "You have my word. Where is she today?"

"Exactly where she should be; helping Jay lead the charge to find that asswipe."

● ● ●

Fern called Ed from the car. "We're on," she said. "Captain Adams will have the ship and his full crew ready to sail at 10:00 a.m."

"You have the warrant?" Ed asked.

"Plural. I have two warrants in my grubby little hands. Fingerprints and general search of the entire island," Fern said.

"Hot diggity dog. I'll be there. Did you have any further action during the night?"

"Nope. Slept like a baby. You?"

"Same. I'm ready to rock 'n roll, but I'd like to make it clear that I hope this is my last visit to that island."

"I feel the same," Fern said. "Maybe we'll get lucky today. See you soon, big guy."

While he drove, Matt arranged for a tow truck to pick up Fern's VW and take it to the shop in Buck Bay for repairs on the windshields. "This might be a good time to buy you a new car," he suggested when they stopped to look at it.

"I don't want a new car."

"Why did I know you were going to say that?"

"Why did I know you were going to suggest a new car?" she countered.

"Because it's the logical move. This car has served you well, but it's getting old. And now, every time you get in it, you will remember last night and get upset all over again. Do you really need that?"

"Let's get her fixed, and see how I do," she said. "How does that sound? If it bothers me to drive her again, then we'll talk. A compromise, OK?"

"Better than a flat-out 'no'," he reasoned.

She turned to the VW and rubbed the driver's side door. "You have to go to the doctor to get repaired, but I'll be back soon. You'll look pretty again."

"You're talking to your car," Matt observed.

"Said the man who talks to a seal."

• • •

Once everyone was on board the Resolve, Fern led a team meeting before they pulled up anchor.

"We hope that Rohn Reid behaves like a law-abiding citizen of the United States when presented with these warrants from Judge Hedges, but, if not, here's the plan," she said. "Lieutenant Sonders and Chief Horning will hold him down while I get his fingerprints. There are two entrances to the room we'll likely be in: one off the entrance foyer, and one in the east wing hallway. One of you will stay in the room with the three of us and Reid, standing guard, and the rest of you will split up and guard the two entrances so we aren't disturbed until his prints are safely stored. Then we'll repeat the procedure with Rick and Randy Reid. Questions?"

"What if he's not there?" a crewman asked.

"If he's left the island—and his plane is gone—we will immediately issue an arrest warrant for him," said Fern, her voice steely. "I don't think he'd be that stupid. Although, I didn't think he'd be stupid enough to hire someone to try to kill me last night either." She filled in the crew. "I don't know for sure that Rohn Reid was involved, but it's a mighty big coincidence."

Ed spoke, "Her point is that we need to be ready for anything because we don't know what the hell is going on."

"Right," Fern said. "Once we get the three sets of prints off the family members, then I'll serve Rohn with the search warrant. We'll fan out and search the buildings first. I'd like you to divide yourselves into three groups; the three of us will form the fourth group. When we get to the island, I can better explain the buildings' layout. Now, I have a question for all of you: Does anyone know what a network server looks like? Will it be in a separate room? That's the primary target of our search."

Matt and four of the CG crew raised their hands. Fern laughed. "Of course, my husband knows. Why didn't you tell me when we talked about it last night?"

Matt grinned. "You didn't ask me."

"OK, you're with me then, since I have no idea what we're looking for." To the crew, she said, "Make sure there's one of you guys who will know it when you see it in each group. I think we're ready, Captain."

"Off we go," said Captain Adams.

It was an easy, pleasant trip to the island. Last night's rain had stopped, and while there were some high, thin clouds overhead, the sky was bright with promise. The bar crossing was rough, as always, but once on the open seas, the ship was steady.

Fern, however, was not steady. She was nervous as hell. Matt was at her side at the ship's railing, but he could tell she didn't want to talk. He left her alone to process whatever was going on inside her head.

There are so many things that could go wrong today, she thought. *What if I'm not up to a case of this magnitude? What if I let Joe down while his boss is watching our every move? And even worse, what if we're walking into a trap, and our side gets hurt? Maybe this is a case that won't ever get solved. If the Reids' prints don't match, and/or we don't find the crypto server, I've got nothing but purple pillow fibers, and that tells me 'how', but not 'who'.* She went over every detail in her head, and then told herself to suck it up.

Finally, Matt said, "OK?"

She nodded and looked directly ahead at the hulking island.

CHAPTER 30

Only Tyson, with his curly hair sticking out from under a Seahawks cap and wearing the same red hoodie he'd worn the first day Fern met him, greeted them on the dock. He was unsmiling, but polite.

"Hello, Tyson," she said calmly. She waved her arm at the contingent behind her. "These law enforcement officers will accompany me this morning. We have warrants to serve on Mr. Reid. Can you direct me to him?"

"He's been expecting you," Tyson said. "He told me to bring you to the main house. He will meet you in the living room. Can I offer you a ride up the hill?"

"We'll walk," she said briskly. "You can go tell him we're on our way."

He turned without saying anything else, got in his golf cart and took off.

Fern, Matt, and Ed walked abreast of each other, followed closely by the CG crew, heading for the house. Matt carried the fingerprinting kit, and Fern clutched the warrants in her hand. Always calm and cool, Ed uncharacteristically drew his weapon and kept it in front of him as they trudged up the hill. Fern gave him a sideways glance, and he said, "Insurance."

Once inside the house's wide foyer, the CG officers efficiently disbursed into two groups, one of which headed down the east wing hallway, as Fern indicated the direction for them. The double doors opened suddenly, and Rohn Reid said, "Please come in, Fern. The Secretary of State told me you'd be coming this morning. How can I help you?"

Matt stepped forward and stuck out his hand. "I'm Chief of Police Matt Horning from Port Stirling. I'm also Fern's husband, and I'm here on both fronts today."

"Ah, the cavalry to the rescue," Rohn said with a slight smirk.

"No, she doesn't need to be rescued, but I do have one question for you, Mr. Reid. Did you, or did you hire someone to shoot at my wife last night as she drove home on Highway 101?"

The smirk stayed in place as Reid said, "No."

"Do you know who did?"

"That's two questions, Mr. Horning."

"That was a Chief Horning question," Matt said.

"The answer is still 'no'."

"You don't seem surprised at the question," Matt noted. "Why is that?"

"I would imagine your wife, or actually, in this case, your colleague, makes enemies along the way. Comes with the territory, I suppose." He shrugged. "But I find her to be a very nice person, and probably fun under different circumstances." He smiled a genuine smile at Fern. "I hope they find whoever scared you last night."

"Thank you," Fern said, somewhat ruffled. "I'd like to get started with today's business." She held out the probable cause warrant for him to inspect. He took it, adjusted his glasses, and read.

"You are not under arrest," she clarified for him. "However, Judge Hedges believes, as I do, that your fingerprints and those of your sons, may be germane to the murder of Hiroshi Matsuda and she has therefore signed this warrant to force you to submit." And then she shut up allowing him time to read the document.

He finished reading and handed it back to her. "Everything looks in order. Let's proceed." He turned and walked to the sofa by the room's immense coffee table. "May I sit while we do this?" he asked Fern.

Fern eyed the coffee table for height purposes. It was lower than the preferred height of having his forearm parallel to the floor, but she could make it work. "Yes, of course," she replied, following him to that side of the room. Ed and Matt hung back, but both cops rested their hands on the butt of their guns.

Moving quickly and efficiently, she retrieved the kit from her bag. "Please look away from my materials, and try to relax," she said to him. Grasping his right hand at the base of his thumb, she guided his index finger on the inking pad, covering the print area with ink, and repeated the procedure on all fingers. His two thumbs were the last to be printed. She carefully labeled and stored the results, handed him a clean-up wipe, and said, "Thank you for your cooperation, Rohn. I'll note it."

"Take good care of those," Reid said to Fern, looking her in the eye.

She returned his stare and said, "I always do. One more piece of business and then we'll leave you alone for today." She produced the search warrant and handed it to him. "This gives us permission to search the entire island, including this house, which we will do as soon as we take fingerprints of your sons. We will not be taking electronic equipment, such as your personal computers and cell phones at this time. If the fingerprint results rule you out as a suspect, that step will not be necessary. But you need to know that everything else is on the table, and our search will be thorough."

"What, specifically, are you looking for?" Rohn asked, the rage slowly building on his face.

"It is a general search warrant, and we are following several avenues of investigation," Fern said, completely avoiding answering his direct question.

"How long do you anticipate this taking?"

"Several hours," she replied, "but we will be departing your island before dark. It would go easier for us and faster for you if you inform your employees and ask them to fully cooperate with us."

"Alright. I will let everyone know." He turned abruptly and left the living room. The law enforcement entourage followed him out and headed to the other wing of the house where Fern hoped to find the Reid twins. Matt reached for Fern's hand and held it tightly. It was shaking.

• • •

The Coast Guard officers split themselves into three groups and fanned out to the hangar and other outbuildings. Fern explained to them where

Matsuda was found, and where each of the employees had rooms. One group went to the guest building area that housed Leonard, Moira, and Lynette.

Matt, Fern, and Ed stayed in the main house, and went to Randy Reid's quarters first. He was there working in the office section of his wing. As he did the last time Fern visited his space, he quickly closed the laptop he was working on.

"Fern. Ed. And you are?" Randy questioned, looking at Matt.

"Port Stirling Chief of Police Matt Horning. I'm assisting this investigation."

Randy ignored the men and turned to Fern. "Dad told me why you're here. I am formally objecting to submitting to fingerprinting," he blustered.

"That's fine," said Fern. "But it doesn't matter because we have this." She waved the warrant in his direction. "Your father has already read this and urges you to cooperate as he did. Will you, or shall I instruct these two policemen to hold you down? Your choice, Randy."

Ed unholstered his gun for emphasis, one of his favorite intimidation moves. It was all Fern could do to keep from laughing.

Randy swallowed hard. "Go ahead," he muttered. "But I don't like it."

"News flash. I don't like it either," Fern said. She moved through the process as fast as she could, while proceeding thoroughly.

"Now what?" Randy asked her as he wiped the ink from his hands.

"Now we ask you to go wait in another part of the house or outside while the three of us search your premises."

"I'm not doing that!"

"Yes, I'm afraid you are," Fern responded. "You are allowed to turn off your laptop, cell phone, and any other electronic devices, but you are not allowed to follow us around while we conduct our search."

"This is bullshit," he raged.

"It's only bullshit if we don't find anything," she said, smiling sweetly at the attractive young man.

Angrily, he pounded some keys on the two computers and the monitor on his desk, and the screens went black. He stood, ramming his cell phone in a pants pocket, and stormed out of the room.

"He liked me better before you guys showed up," Fern said dryly.

"I'll bet he did," Matt grinned. "C'mon, let's see what pretty boy is hiding behind these doors, and then we'll search this room." He headed toward one of the two doors that opened off the room they were standing in. Fern went with him. Ed took the other door.

Ed's room was similar to a small studio apartment. It contained a kitchenette that was sparkling clean and looked like it hadn't been used much. He opened the full-sized refrigerator, and it was mostly empty, save for a big round carton of Nancy's Yogurt, and four bottles of Widmer Hefeweizen. A fancy coffee maker that Ed wouldn't know how to work took up one corner of the countertop and held used coffee grounds. A couple of lonely bananas and a bar of extreme dark chocolate — 88 percent cacao — were the only other food items in sight.

A modern, round dining room table that could seat four at most, and a living area with sofa, two chairs, coffee table, and a huge wall-mounted big screen TV filled up the rest of the space.

Ed opened every cupboard, looked under all the seat cushions, checked behind a painting hung haphazardly on the wall, and pulled out the drawer in the coffee table. The space had one window that looked out to the southeast, but blue and white drapes that reminded Ed of the sky with puffy white clouds were closed across it now. There were no papers, no books, no movies, or CDs — nothing personal at all. Absolutely nothing of interest in this room.

"I got nothing," Ed reported, joining Matt and Fern in their room, which was a large bedroom. Its dominant feature was a huge California King bed, flanked by two hefty nightstands, and footed by a five-foot long white leather bench. An adjoining door led to an also-large bathroom with a long stretch of porcelain countertop abutting a big mirror that ran the length of it. There was no tub; only a substantial walk-in shower that could hold five people and was beautifully tiled in turquoise and white gleaming tiles. At one end of the bathroom was a double-door closet that held built-ins as well as two long hanging racks. The closet was about one-third full.

The long countertop held a desert-looking spiky plant in a small, silver urn, and two turquoise hand towels on stainless racks that stood beside the sunken two sinks. The overall effect was dramatic and luxurious.

There were more personal items in both the bedroom and bathroom, which was logical, but still sparse. No personal photos, and still no books — Matt was afraid that his generation was the last real generation of steady readers — but there were a few magazines on one nightstand, mostly tech-related or pop culture. They went through all the pockets of his clothing, rummaged through every drawer, and found nothing they wouldn't expect to find in the living quarters of a wealthy young man.

While Fern and Ed worked in Randy's closet, Matt walked the perimeter of his entire space, knocking on walls, checking for any secret rooms. He found nothing suspicious, and his search for room cameras or bugs turned up empty, too.

They met back in the office space where they'd found Randy and took it apart thoroughly. Again, nothing. "If this kid is hiding a network server on this island, he was smart enough to not hide it in his rooms," Matt said.

"I was sure it would be in here," Fern said dejectedly. "Are we ready to move on to Rick?"

"Sure," said Matt. "It's our two-for-the-price-of-one day. Does this guy like you as much as Randy does…or did before you made him submit to fingerprinting?"

"Rick is polite and cooperative but has been a bit more standoffish than his twin," Fern said. "He won't like the fingerprinting either, but I don't think he'll raise a ruckus. Plus, he has a girlfriend, so no worries on that front," she smiled at her husband.

"Whew, that's a relief," Matt said sarcastically.

Ed poked him in the stomach. "Women don't appreciate sarcasm," he said sarcastically. "I know this for a fact."

Fern rolled her eyes at the two of them. "Follow me," she said.

Rick was expecting them, and his door was open. On first glance, it appeared his quarters, across the west hallway, were identical to Randy's. The hallway door opened into an office, with two doors opening off.

"Come in," he said to Fern. "I think I can save you some time and trouble." He was dressed in nice jeans and a white half-zip pullover sweater. His footwear looked like high-end, expensive Nikes.

"Oh? How so?" asked Fern.

"I saw you going into Randy's office, and I assume you got his finger-prints, right?"

"Yes, that's correct," she said.

"Well, we are identical twins. That means we came from our mother's one egg."

"I know what it means," said Fern.

"We are genetically identical," Rick said. "So, my point is there is no need to take my prints, too, as they're the same as Randy's."

Matt stepped forward. "Nice try, Rick," he said, with a neutral expression. "We haven't met. I'm Matt Horning, the Chief of Police in Port Stirling."

Rick blanched at this new information, but quickly composed himself. "Hi."

Matt continued speaking. "While you identical twins have a slightly—and I do mean slightly—higher percentage of close genetic traits, today's fingerprinting verification systems can easily distinguish between identical twins. Maybe you're thinking of Sherlock Holmes times."

"That's not what I've heard," Rick said. "I don't believe a small-town cop is up on the latest technology." It came out one half belligerent, and the other half whiny.

"Is that what you were counting on?" Matt confronted him. "Stupid as posts small-town cops? If so, I'm afraid we have to call your bluff. Lieu-tenant Sonders here is with the Oregon State Police, and they have one of the more sophisticated labs in the country. And I worked homicide in Dallas, Texas, for over a decade. We have more knowledge of fingerprint-ing in our little finger than you have in your big brain. Now, let the lady do her work, so we can all get on with our day, OK?"

"I'd really rather not participate in this charade," Rick said. Slowly, as if he was expecting to be stopped, Rick turned away from Matt and started to leave the room.

Matt didn't particularly care for that move, and he grabbed Rick's arm and spun him around. "If you're not careful, son, I might think you're hiding something."

"I've got nothing to hide," Rick said quickly. "I just don't want my fin-gerprints out there in the world." He shook off Matt's grip.

Fern stepped between the two, and in an attempt to defuse the situation said in a gentle tone, "I know how you feel, Rick, and it's unfortunate that Mr. Matsuda died on your island, but we can only deal with the reality of our situation. As I promised your father, I will personally safeguard your prints. This is purely a process to eliminate you as a suspect." She looked over at Matt. "It's alright, Chief. Rick will cooperate."

Matt backed off, although he stepped in front of the door, blocking it with his body.

"Over here, Rick." Fern motioned to a high table across the office. The very picture of disgust, Rick moved to where Fern was positioning her ink pad. She cleaned his hands, wiping them with alcohol, and then dried them off. Repeating the process she'd done with his father and brother, Fern inwardly jumped for joy when she'd safely labeled and stored Rick's prints with the others. A sigh of relief escaped her lips.

"Thank you," she said to Rick. She informed him of the executed search warrant and repeated the instructions she'd given Randy. Rick didn't like it any better than his twin had, but he groused and did as she told him. Once he'd left, the three cops went over his rooms from floor to ceiling. Not only did they not find the server, but Rick's area of the main house was also just as devoid of any personal items as Randy's.

"Almost like they knew this step was coming," Ed noted.

"Is there a chance that the Secretary of State warned Rohn about the search warrant when they talked?" Matt asked Fern.

Fern shook her head. "I really don't think he'd do that. And, Rohn's not dumb. He would have to figure that it might come to this. He's had plenty of opportunity to tidy up prior to today. There's also the possibility that the twins don't have much in the way of personal things here because it's not their primary residence. Plus, they are men."

"What's that supposed to mean?" Matt asked. "I have lots of personal stuff!"

"You're a freak," said Ed.

"I've been to your house," Matt huffed. "You have plenty of books and shit around."

"True. But if I had a second home like these kids, I wouldn't put much in it either. Knowing you, you'd have duplicates of all your stuff."

Fern laughed because there was some truth in Ed's observation. "Moving on," she said, waving at the boys, "all we know for sure is that neither twin is hiding the servers in their wing of the house. So, they're somewhere else, right? Time to search the rest of the house. I'm going to call the CG teams first and see if they want to meet up quickly in the courtyard. Does that suit you two?"

Matt and Ed stood at attention and saluted their commanding officer, and then laughed and jostled each other like a couple of teenagers.

CHAPTER 31

The afternoon wore on, and it was late in the day when Matt discovered the secret room located behind the kitchen pantry.

Earlier, they'd been momentarily excited when they found another secret room behind a panel in Rohn's closet. But it only contained important papers: passports, stock certificates, marriage license, birth certificates for the boys, and approximately $400 million in cash. The cash was in various international currencies—about $200 million in U.S. dollars, and the rest was split primarily between euros, British pounds, Chinese yuan, and Indian rupees, along with a scattering of other currencies. Tall stack after tall stack after tall stack.

"So much for my theory that Reid might be running out of money," Matt said to Fern.

"Yeah," she said. "When this is all over, should we talk to him about investing in our foundation?"

"If we don't arrest him for murder, sure," he said.

Fern snapped photos, and then they closed Rohn's secret room as they'd found it and moved on.

With only the kitchen, Simon the gardener's room, and one of the buildings beyond the hangar remaining to be searched, Fern was beginning to give up hope they'd find what they came for.

Matt was looking through the extensive food stores in the 10' X 20' pantry off the large working kitchen when he noticed a wood panel at the far end not blocked by shelving. The panel caught his eye because it was painted a slightly different shade of cream—a little lighter than the rest of the pantry walls.

What have we here? He pushed on the right side of the panel at waist height and, behold, it swung open inwards. This secret room was enormous. He had noticed it from outside during their walkaround, but it was disguised as a triple garage, and he hadn't questioned it. The room was entirely filled with network server racks.

Two eight-foot-tall rows of server racks marched at least thirty feet out from the door. Between them was an open aisle about six feet wide with a glossy white tile floor. The ceiling was twelve-inch white square tiles with gray borders, and one in every five tiles had lighting that softly lit the enclosed room. The tower racks had black framing, but identical blue lighting emanated from behind clear doors. The room was a cooler temperature than the house.

Matt strolled down the center aisle until he was sure what he was looking at. He didn't detect any surveillance cameras or any access control systems. Clearly, Reid was confident in the security the island provided. Matt turned and hurried back to the open entrance.

"Ed. Fern. In here," he shouted out to the kitchen.

They came to the secret door and peered inside.

"Looks like a fancy wine cellar to me," Fern said.

"It's not," said Ed seriously. "This is a network server room that could power a cryptocurrency mining operation." He gave Matt a high-five slap. "Well done, comrade."

"How do we know the crypto fraud is for sure being run from here?" Fern asked.

"We don't know," Matt said. "But Hideki can tell us." Hideki Ikeda was Port Stirling's IT manager. A young manager, not yet thirty, Hideki had been a key cog in Matt's other cases since he took over as police chief.

"Obviously, there's too much equipment here to take it all with us," Ed said. "Will Hideki need to come to the island?"

Matt shook his head. "No, I don't think so. With Shuji's help, I believe

Hideki can track it from his office. I'll give him a call when we get back on the ship. But the real trick is going to be pretending that we didn't discover this room. Let's back out now, and quietly close it up like I found it."

Quickly, Fern took more photos to send to Joe, and the three cops moved back into the kitchen. Matt wiped off the nearby shelving and the secret door where he touched it.

They rounded up the CG crew, and the search party headed for the ship after Fern told them, "Our work here is finished for today. Let's hightail it home."

• • •

It was what Captain Bob Adams called 'nautical twilight' — that time of day when the horizon was still visible and sailors could read the stars — when the ship pulled away from Cold Rock Island harbor and headed northeast for Buck Bay. The three cops had taken Bob into their confidence and told him they'd discovered the server room.

"Does that mean we're done with this hellish island?" the captain asked.

"Not quite yet," Fern replied, "but we believe we're getting closer to knowing the truth about what happened here. If Matt's IT guy can connect the dots to Honolulu, and if Dr. Ryder gets a match on any one of these three new sets of prints, we're in business."

"How soon will you know anything definitive?" Adams asked.

"My guy is fast," Matt said. "He'll have some info for me by end of the workday tomorrow."

"And, Bernice has been chomping at the bit to take a look at these fingerprints, so it will be a priority for her as well," Fern said. "Please don't go anywhere, Bob, we'll likely need you again fairly soon."

"It's no problem. Business has been slow on our end, which is a good thing," he smiled. "I remain at your disposal until the head of Homeland Security tells me otherwise. Are you ready to go home now?"

"More than ready," Fern said.

The sail to Buck Bay was a beautiful one. A full moon was rising, the sky had cleared, and the Pacific Ocean was glinting, silvery below them.

Fern, still not thrilled with boat rides, took in gulps of fresh sea air, and steadied herself at what had become her favorite spot on the aft railing. Matt and Ed had gone below to have a beer, but Fern couldn't stomach the stale air down there. Matt wanted to check on the status of the search for the white Mercedes SUV and the shooters who had targeted Fern last night. He hadn't heard from Buck Bay PD, and Ed hadn't heard from the state police, so both men worried that likely meant bad news—they hadn't caught them.

A million thoughts were going through Fern's head as the wind whipped her auburn hair around her face. If the network server on the island was connected to the crypto fraud, and if one of the three Reid men's fingerprints matched the rafter and the purple pillow, she would have to make an arrest. But would it be enough evidence to satisfy a grand jury and get an indictment?

She knew she had means, motive, and opportunity locked up, with a caveat. *Rick and Randy are young and strong*, she thought, *and they have the ability to smother Matsuda…but does Rohn, their father? He's not in shape, and not as athletic as his sons.*

And, she still didn't know who had the motive to commit the crime. Who was involved with Scott Thurman? Who had something that was so important to hide they had to kill for it? It was still possible that someone else close to the family had the true motive for wanting Matsuda dead, and the three Reids were simply 'helping out' with the dirty work. *If the network server is connected to Thurman, I need to break him.*

All three Reids had the opportunity to perform the murder, especially Rohn and Rick who were on the plane with Matsuda for several hours. None of them has an alibi; by their own admission, all ten people were present and accounted for on Cold Rock Island at the same time Matsuda died there. Opportunity was the most useful for this case, and she could introduce that evidence first to set the stage.

She had to keep plugging away, and hoped that Bernice and Hideki could shed further light on her investigation.

● ● ●

Sylvia cooked a pot roast and threw in small red potatoes and chunks of cabbage. Earlier in the afternoon she'd made a coconut cake because that made everyone feel better. Her patient was doing very well and getting antsy about Sylvia staying with her.

And, the truth was, Sylvia missed her bed, not to mention her cat, Horatio. Her neighbor was feeding him, but Sylvia knew Horatio would be worried about her if she stayed away much longer.

So, they agreed that Sylvia would make dinner for Tamryn, and do a few other things for her and then head home. Over lunch, she had told Tamryn about Barry's escape. Matt asked her to tell her last night, but Sylvia disobeyed his request because she wanted Tamryn to get another good night's sleep before she went home.

"Is he still at large in the area today?" Tamryn asked, going a little pale.

"He is," Sylvia told her the truth. "And, he's believed to be in Port Stirling or nearby. A farmer from Twisty River picked him up on the old road late yesterday and brought him here. He was on the news last night. I'm so sorry to tell you this, but Matt said you need to know he's out there somewhere."

Tamryn nodded. "Right. Matt's right. I need to be on the alert until they track him down. They *are* looking for him?"

"Oh, yes. All of the sheriff's department, Patty Perkins, almost all of the Buck Bay department, and Jay, Rudy, and Walt. Everyone's involved, and Earl is particularly ticked off. He told me that if they don't find him by tonight, they'll bring in more reinforcements from the state police tomorrow."

"Where are Matt and Ed?"

"They've gone out to Cold Rock Island. Fern was able to get warrants from Judge Hedges this morning, and she needed backup to confront Rohn Reid. You need to know that Matt hated to leave Port Stirling while your husband is free, but he needed to go to the island. The other news is that Fern's car got shot at last night, and the shooters got away."

"What the hell?" Tamryn said. Sylvia gave her the details, as much as she knew.

"It sounds like Fern is getting close to the truth," Tamryn said.

"She's ruffled some feathers, for sure." Sylvia paused. "All of this is why I'm reluctant to leave you alone tonight. There's some bad karma in the Port Stirling universe currently, and I would never forgive myself if something awful happened to you, Tamryn." She reached across the table and squeezed her hand.

"I have a gun and I know how to use it," she smiled. "Remember?"

"I know that, but I also know that you were in the hospital for three days, and you may not be at peak performance." Sylvia nervously played with one of her dangling earrings. "Matt and Fern had a fancy security system installed at their house after Matt's incident, and he wants to know if you would come and stay with them until they find Barry."

Tamryn shook her head stubbornly. "No. That's nice of them, but it's better for me to be in my own home. I just want to read, rest, and eat your wonderful food until my face heals. Is that so hard to understand?"

"I told him you'd say that," Sylvia smiled.

"Listen, Syl, that rat turd is not going to surprise me again. I know he's out there, but he can't get in so easily now, can he?"

"I hope not."

"He can't, and I don't think he'll even try me again. He could've killed me the first time, but he didn't. He just wanted to scare me."

"Terrorize you, is more like it," Sylvia said. "What if his attack was intended to be the first?"

"Again, I'll be ready for him. I'll stay in my house, do a little more research for Fern's case, curl up with a good book, eat your healthy food, and wait for Earl to lock him up for good this time."

"Make sure your phone is charged before you go to bed."

"Will do," Tamryn promised. "What's your schedule?"

"I'm going to cook this afternoon and put some things in the fridge for you, so you won't have to go out for several days. I also planned to make a quick visit to the bookstore down in Old Town and get a couple of new books for you. You can pay me back later."

"I would appreciate that — thanks. Lunch was delish, and now I think I'll take a nap. That meet with your approval, Sarge?"

Sylvia laughed and waved her off.

. . .

Matt switched on the gas fireplace while Fern fussed about in the kitchen, clanging pans around. She was a good cook, but a noisy one. He had invited Ed to spend the night at their place rather than drive the forty minutes to his inland home, but the big guy declined. "I need to see my wife, my dog, and my own bed, not necessarily in that order," he told Matt. "I'll be back here tomorrow as soon as Hideki gives you the scoop on the network server."

The three cops had delivered the Reid fingerprints to Bernice's lab after they'd come ashore, and she had stayed in the building until they arrived about 8:00 p.m. She'd kissed Fern on the cheek, wrapped her arms around the kit box, and told her she would protect them until they'd been analyzed. "I'll call you tomorrow the minute I have an analysis to share."

"Thanks, Bernice," Fern replied. "We think we made some big progress today, and, hopefully, this is a significant part. Otherwise, I have doo-doo for evidence."

"Go home. Practice some self-care tonight, and we'll talk tomorrow. You, too, gentlemen. And try to not get shot at on your way home." Matt had reported that Dan McCoy said they were still searching for the white Mercedes.

But there had been, gratefully, no action on the drive home for either Ed or the Hornings. Fern couldn't decide if she wanted a shower or food more, but hunger won out. Because it was late, she wanted something quick. They had a half-gallon of Sheldon's chicken noodle soup, and she put that on the burner to heat. She found a loaf of French batard bread in the freezer and warmed it in the oven. Some carrots were quickly cut into sticks. Voila! Dinner.

"Let's eat!" she called out to Matt who had gone into his home office for a minute. "I'll be right there," he yelled back.

He strolled into the kitchen just as Fern was scooping up big ladles of the soup into bowls. "Yum," he said, "that smells damn good."

Not for the first time, they said in unison, "Thank you, Sheldon."

Fern added, "What's that paper in your hand?"

"Something you'll want to read. Tamryn emailed the log of her phone call with Tracy Vergara, Rick Reid's Seattle girlfriend."

"Unless it says, 'Rick Reid murdered Hiroshi Matsuda', I'd like to eat this soup first," she said.

"It does not say that, but there's some insight to Rick's personality and some family dynamics that will interest you." Matt took his usual bar stool seat at the kitchen island, cut off a pat of butter, and plopped it onto a piece of batard, where it proceeded to melt luxuriously. "Can I pour you a glass of wine?"

She shook her head. "No, I don't think so tonight. I want to be as clear-headed tomorrow as I can be. And I don't really want any alcohol."

"Is the apocalypse coming and no one told me?" he joked. "Are you sick?"

"Smart ass. It's been interfering with my sleep lately, I think. Don't need that this week."

"You're going to solve this case, probably tomorrow," Matt said. "Once we know that server is hosting Thurman's crypto scam, Koa will rip Scott Thurman to shreds and you'll know who's helping on the island. And, Bernice will fill in the blanks. Practically a slam dunk from my point of view."

"Will it be enough?" she said and shot him a worried look. "Rohn Reid is not going to roll over and play dead. He'll have the best lawyers that money can buy, and I'll be lucky if I'm not the one ripped to shreds if I make a mistake."

"Your evidence, backed up by expert witness testimony from Bernice and Hideki, will be solid, Fern. You won't make a mistake. But I am going to hire round-the-clock security for you until this thing is in the can. Private. Not our guys in case whoever shot at you knows our drill."

"Normally, I would say 'no way', but last night was terrifying," she admitted. "I'd prefer to still be alive when I put away Matsuda's killer. Not that I can't take care of myself," she quickly added.

"Insurance," Matt said. "Just like we take out a little extra on things we really love. Like I love you."

She put down her soup spoon and wrapped her arms around his neck. "I love you more."

"Don't think so," Matt said. "Impossible to do." He took a bite of bread, and said, "Eat up, and let's go to bed."

Mr. and Mrs. Horning retired a few minutes before 10:00 p.m.

• • •

At 10:55 p.m., about ninety minutes after Tamryn had turned out her bedroom light, Barry Gesicki, from his perch in his fav tree and through his night binoculars, saw the young, muscled cop turn the corner around Tamryn's house from the beach side, and walk down her driveway to Ocean Bend Rd. *Was he not planning to stay the night?*, Barry wondered.

Of course, he'd seen him the moment he arrived, skulking around in the trees on the other side of Tamryn's driveway. It was clear to Barry that the cop did not want Tamryn to know he was there. He never approached the house; just kept an eagle eye out for bad guys. *Like me,* Barry smiled to himself. The young buck cop had moved to the far edge of the driveway when the old lady left at 6 o'clock and waved to her. She'd waved back; it was obvious the PSPD knew he was there.

Patiently, Barry waited in his tree. Watching and waiting. At 3:00 a.m., when the cop had not returned, Barry knew he'd gotten lucky. They weren't prepared to watch her house round-the-clock.

Silently, he lowered himself from the tree, and stealthily — keeping to the forested edges of her driveway — made his way to the front porch. One step, two steps, three steps up, and he approached the front door in the pitch-dark night. He shined a tiny beam of light from his pocket flashlight onto the spanking new keypad.

Barry didn't need to look at his palm. He entered 1-7-4-9. The keypad lock made a soft whirring sound and gently opened.

CHAPTER 32

Thursday, February 29, 2024 — Port Stirling

Matt and Fern rose at 6:30 a.m. "Eight and a half hours of sleep!" Fern exclaimed. She stretched and swung her long legs out of bed. "Did you sleep straight through?"

"I think I got up once to pee, but I've figured out how to do it without waking up."

She laughed. "You need to teach me that trick because the only way I sleep straight through is if I don't have any alcohol, and that's not a long-term solution for me."

The couple dressed and headed to the kitchen. As they passed the floor-to-ceiling windows that looked out to the Pacific, Fern paused. "Can you make the coffee and bring me a cup?" she asked. "I want to get some fresh air." She went out to the deck just as the sun made its appearance over the hills east of Port Stirling. The only sound was the ocean rumbling against the rocks below her.

What had caught her eye was Roger the seal, bobbing in the surf straight out from their deck. She leaned on the railing, and said out loud with a little wave, "Hi, Roger. You always seem to help Matt when he has a problem. Do you think you might help me this morning?"

The seal ducked under the water, and resurfaced in exactly the same spot, grinning broadly, as if to say, "Sure. Whadda you got, lady?"

Fern answered. "I might have to arrest one of the world's richest men today, and I'm scared. Do you think I can handle it, Roger?"

Roger asked, "Is he guilty?"

"He very well might be."

"Well, Matt has shared with me that you have a strong moral sense of what's right and what's wrong, so he's probably guilty. And you have to do the right thing."

"I was afraid you'd say that. What if I can't prove he did it beyond a shadow of a doubt?"

"Collect your evidence, tie up any loose ends, and know that justice is on your side. No man is above the law," Roger said, nodding at her.

"You're pretty smart for a seal."

"I am." And with that, Roger dived into the surf and was gone.

"Are you talking to my seal?" Matt asked, handing her a cup of coffee.

"He helped me," Fern admitted. "Just like he helps you. He's highly intelligent, don't you think?" She looked into her husband's twinkling eyes.

• • •

They poured the remaining strong black coffee into their insulated travel mugs, ate some yogurt and blueberries, and took off for city hall. Fern would check in with Joe first, but she wanted to meet with Hideki, too. This network server business was not her strong suit, and she wanted to make sure she understood exactly what it meant and how it impacted her case.

She went first to her cubby-hole office off to the right of city hall's central hallway. As Matt broke off to the left to the police department, Fern said, "I'll be about fifteen minutes."

"That's fine," Matt said. "I will give Hideki a call and let him know we need some of his time. And, I'll catch up with Dan McCoy and the sheriff while I wait for you."

Fern sat in her metal rolling chair with its padded burgundy and white patterned seat and armrests. The chair was hideous, but she didn't spend enough time in this office to really care.

Into her phone, she said, "Hi, Joe. It's me. Is this a good time for you to talk?"

"Yes," Joe said. "How did it go with Rohn Reid?"

"Surprisingly well. He wasn't cheerful about the process, but he was mostly cooperative. We got his prints, as well as those of Rick and Randy Reid. Rick was the feistiest, but Matt shared the facts of life with him, and he calmed down enough for me to get the job done. Dr. Ryder has the prints now and will prioritize their analysis today."

"I should have insisted they submit the first day we were there," Joe lamented. "I'm sorry, Fern, it would have made life easier."

"We both made that decision. It seemed so unlikely at the time that the Reids could be involved."

"Maybe. But it was still chicken-shit on my part. That's the problem living in D.C. — one gets too caught up in the politics."

"It's OK, Joe. The day turned out highly productive for us — we also found the network server. You wouldn't believe this room. It's behind the kitchen pantry and a secret door disguised to look like just another wall. My brilliant husband found it. He also found a second secret room in Rohn's closet, but that one was boring. Only $400 million in hard cash hidden in that one."

"What?"

Fern laughed. "Yeah, it's what my dad used to call — and pardon my language — 'fuck you money'." But my father doesn't have a bunch of foreign currencies in his stash, and he certainly doesn't have anywhere near the amount of Reid's. It was impressive. I've emailed photos of both secret rooms to you. Don't worry, we counted one tall stack and multiplied it by the total number of stacks, checked his personal documents stored there, and quickly closed it up and left the area."

"I would have sat on the floor and fondled it for a while," Joe said.

"No, you wouldn't have," she laughed out loud at the mental picture. "Tell me about the server."

Fern described the room to Joe, and told him the plan for today, both with Hideki and Bernice. "I'm semi-confident we're going to have some answers by tonight," she said. "Once I know the results, you and I will need to discuss how we proceed."

"It's easy," Joe said," now that I have found my cojones. I will make your case for a federal arrest warrant for murder in the first degree, or multiple warrants if more than one person is involved. There is also the possibility of a hate crime in this mess, considering Matsuda's race. Obviously, I'll update Fred Leufeld, but it won't matter how he feels. He and I both hope Rohn Reid didn't kill Matsuda, but if he did, that's all she wrote."

• • •

Hideki was thrilled to be pulled out of a city budget meeting to help his favorite department manager, Chief Horning. His skills with technology had helped Matt crack a couple of previous cases, and the two worked well together. Matt had begged City Manager Bill Abbott to give Hideki the biggest raise he could in the current fiscal year because he was crucial to the police department's success.

Always fashionable in the attire of his generation, today Hideki was wearing acid-washed, cuffed jeans, a black sweatshirt bearing the words 'Dunder Mifflin' in large white letters, and red retro high-top Air Jordans. His shiny black hair was swept across his forehead. Abbott would have liked him to get more frequent haircuts, but he loved his IT manager's constant smiles and optimistic attitude.

"Please tell me you have a project that will keep me out of the budget meeting all morning," Hideki said to Matt. They were meeting in Hideki's office, which was really a double-wide cubicle. Matt and Fern were scrunched into two folding chairs and sat shoulder-to-shoulder.

"Well, it would probably take me all week to ace this project, but you'll be much faster at getting us the result we need, I suspect," smiled Matt. "It's Fern's case, and she'll tell you what she needs. Our department has been appointed by the State Department to proceed on our local level."

Hideki's eyes got big. "Wow. That sounds important."

"It is," Fern said. "On two fronts. One, the victim is a Japanese citizen, and two, the murder occurred on an island in the Pacific Ocean that is now owned by Rohn Reid."

"The billionaire?" Hideki asked. "And one of my professional heroes, I might add."

"One and the same," said Fern. "It's touchy all the way around, and your involvement today is highly confidential, at least for now. Depending on what you discover, you may be called to testify at some point down the road. Do you understand?"

"Cool," he nodded.

Fern continued. "I need to know if the network servers we found on Cold Rock Island are hosting a cryptocurrency operation that originated at a regional bank in Honolulu."

"You think it lives on a centralized server rather than on the devices of users who run the software?" Hideki asked her.

Fern looked puzzlingly at Matt. "Help me," she said.

"We think so," Matt said. "But we're not absolutely positive. We don't know how big the operation is."

"So, you think that someone is providing a crypto hosting service on this island that includes the infrastructure and environment required for mining operations? That would include hardware, software, electricity, cooling, and security? Is that what you're trying to find out?"

"Yes!" Fern said. "That's it. Can you help us?"

"Is the Pope Catholic?" Hideki smiled. "It depends in part on how robust their encryption and firewall protections are, and if they have any intrusion detection systems. But I know my way around."

Matt smiled at Fern. "I told you."

She asked Hideki, "My pitiful understanding of this topic is that crypto takes a lot of power. Will you be able to see if the usage on Cold Rock Island increased at some point that might be related to this case?"

"Yes," Hideki said. "But if Rohn Reid owns the island, a spike in usage could mean various things. Still, it will probably be obvious if you're correct about these servers."

"Will you need to physically see the servers we suspect?"

"No. I can do everything from right here." He waved his arms around his cubicle. "I just need some information about the players involved."

The three huddled for about an hour, and then they left Hideki alone to work his magic.

. . .

Back in his office, Matt got bad news from both Buck Bay's chief, Dan McCoy, and from Chinook County Sheriff Earl Johnson. He'd talked to Dan first.

"We found the white Mercedes SUV," Dan told him. "But it was ditched, and there was no sign of Fern's shooters."

"Where was it?" Matt asked. He tried to control his distaste and anger at this news. His blowing up wouldn't resolve things any faster.

"About five miles north of the Buck Bay Bridge. They took a side road that goes east of 101 up into a watershed, forested area. We found the vehicle about eight miles in with one of our helicopters. And, before you ask, yes, I've sent a team in on the ground to inspect. There was nothing in the car, and I mean nothing."

"So, no car title, rental agreement, used coffee cups, bullet casings?" Matt asked. "Nothing, nothing?"

"Nothing, nothing," Dan replied. "We've towed it here, and forensics is going over it now. I'm not optimistic, Matt. This looks like a pro job. I'm sorry."

"Are your guys checking with the rental agencies? Car dealerships?"

"Yes. It's a fairly distinctive vehicle for our area, so you never know who might remember it, but nothing so far. I've got three teams working on it this morning."

"Thanks, Dan. I'll want to take a look at the vehicle as soon as I can break away from here. OK with you?"

"Sure thing. It's not going anywhere for a while."

"I appreciate that, Dan, and I really mean it," Matt said. He and McCoy had had some differences over past cases, but the two police chiefs needed to work together, a fact they both understood.

"Just doing my job," Dan said.

The call with Earl hadn't been any better.

"We haven't found him yet," Earl said when he picked up before he even said 'hello'. "It's like looking for a needle in a haystack."

"Maybe he just hitched the ride to Port Stirling to pick up his gear, and then he took off again. He could be in California by now."

"One could hope," said Earl. "But I think this guy's a psycho, and I don't trust him to do the logical thing, which would be to bail out of my county as fast as he could."

"Have you had your dogs out?"

"Yeah. We had his sweater that he jettisoned in the courthouse john, but they couldn't find a trail. Jay is borrowing a drone from the Coast Guard as we speak. We should have done that yesterday, I guess. I was so sure we'd find him on the ground."

"Dammit," Matt said. "This is frickin' frustrating. Now I'm worried about Tamryn again."

"Rudy patrolled her place until about 11 o'clock last night. She went to bed about 9:30 p.m. and he waited around to make sure there was no action. He said there was no sign of Barry."

"Get the drone, Earl. Let's make sure he's not still in the area."

"On it. Where are you today?"

"In my office right now. Fern's here, too, and we're waiting on some test results from Bernice, and for my IT guy to track down some stuff. Once we hear from them, the Coast Guard is standing by to take us back to Cold Rock Island. We think Fern will be making an arrest today in the murder of Hiroshi Matsuda."

"I'll think good thoughts for her," Earl said. "Fingers crossed we make two arrests today. I'd like to go fishing."

●　●　●

Matt hated waiting. Some people handled it better than others, but he wasn't good at it. He wanted to ping Bernice and ask how it was going, but that would only take her away from her work. He wanted to call Tamryn, but was afraid he would wake her, and he knew she needed her sleep. He wanted to call Jay and go join the search for Barry Gesicki, but he knew it was important that Jay work to get the drone in the air. He wanted to go to Buck Bay right now and inspect the white Mercedes that shot at his wife, but he knew he needed to let Dan McCoy's team do their work first.

So, he waited.

About 9:30 a.m. Bernice called Fern. "Good news and bad news," she started. "Rohn Reid's prints are not a match with either the rafter, the ladder, or the pillow prints. He is not your killer. He could have been the one wearing gloves that helped the killer string up Matsuda, but he didn't smother him."

Fern breathed a sigh of relief. "That is good news. What's the bad news, Bernice?"

"I haven't been able to distinguish between Rick and Randy's prints yet. They are very similar. And both sets could be a match with the pillow prints. I need more time. I'd like to send them to the state police lab, but I know you won't appreciate that delay."

"Oh, man," Fern exhaled. "You know I don't have any choice but to get this right. We have to be absolutely positive."

"And currently, I'm not."

"What's your best guess? Which twin killed him?"

"It's too close to call, Fern. I'm sorry. What do you want me to do?"

"Send them to the lab. I'll ask Ed to have them expedite their analysis. That's all I can do, I guess."

"It's the right thing to do," Bernice said. "They have some additional equipment that can make a positive ID. I'll have one of my guys drive them to Salem now."

"OK. But make copies so I can look at both sets."

"I already have and they're in a file with your name on it. We'll get our answer, Fern. It's just going to take a little longer."

Fern walked from her office to Matt's and told him about Bernice's call. They were discussing their options when Hideki knocked on the door. They could tell from the look on his face and his giddy demeanor that he had good news for them.

"Come in," Matt said and motioned to the empty chair in front of his desk. Hideki slouched down, positioning himself with one leg at an angle, his foot resting on the opposite knee.

"I will be short," Hideki said. "And sweet," he added with his ever-present smile. "Cold Rock Island is hosting a cryptocurrency mining operation connected to Scott Thurman, and his Honolulu bank. It is also connected to the bank's HQ in Japan. And, here's a juicy bit. There's also a lot of action coming from India."

Matt and Fern looked at each other. "There was a lot of Indian currency in that room of Rohn's," Matt noted.

"There's a lot of cryptocurrency changing hands," Hideki continued. "Like in the high billions. I'm talking big money. Enough to kill for, for sure." He sounded almost gleeful.

"Anything else we should know?" Fern asked.

"Plenty. The Cold Rock Island contact is Randy Reid. He and Scott Thurman have been exchanging emails for almost two years. Randy and Scott are essentially the Chairman of the Board and the CEO. Lots and lots of interaction. Plus, the two of them knew that Shuji's father had uncovered some of their operation, and they had a lengthy exchange when Thurman got pulled into Honolulu PD."

"Could you tell who sent the initial threatening emails to the other bank managers?" Fern asked.

"Oh, yeah. Forgot that part," Hideki said. "Ironically, Scott Thurman sent them. It looked to me like it was an attempt to deflect their attention from his crypto scheme." He chuckled.

"Well, that certainly backfired on him, didn't it?" Fern smiled.

"Anyone else on those email threads between Scott and Randy?" asked Matt.

"None of the other nine names you gave me," Hideki said.

"You're sure that Rohn Reid or Rick Reid don't appear?" Matt asked. "Lots of 'Rs', might be easy to miss."

"Nope, I'm positive. Randy's the bomb. He's your guy," Hideki said confidently.

Matt stood up. "OK, Hideki, this is great work. Can you write up a summary report of your findings and get it to me by the end of the day?"

Hideki nodded, "You bet, Chief."

Fern stood, too, and said, "And can you give me some printouts of messages when it started, and in the aftermath of Thurman's visit with the Honolulu cops. Was there any communication specifically around Hiroshi?"

"Some, but they were both careful in their choice of words. It may mean more to you than it did to me. No problem getting printouts to you right away. There's a couple that might really help your case," he said proudly. "I'll get back to work now." He looked at Matt. "Please tell Mr. Abbott that I am unable to return to the budget meeting today," he said with a straight face, and left Matt's office.

Fern sat thinking and staring at her husband. "It's Randy Reid, isn't it? He's the brains behind the crypto fraud, and he's pocketing millions of their clients' money. He discovered Hiroshi's poking around online, and when Hiroshi called Rohn wanting to visit, Randy knew precisely why. He was the one who suggested to Rohn that they personally fly him to the island."

"So they could keep his visit a secret. And Randy was prepared to do whatever he had to do to make sure Matsuda didn't muck up his sweet gig. I agree, Fern. I think Randy's your killer."

"Bernice hasn't ruled out his prints on the pillow, ladder, or the rafter in the hangar," she noted.

"I think you've got enough to arrest him," Matt said. "It's risky until we get confirmation from the state police lab, but I like your odds. Hideki's trail of evidence on the fraud may be enough by itself to indict him."

"Randy had access to the murder weapon—means. He sure as heck had motive if Hiroshi was on to him. And his own testimony puts him on the island at the time of the murder—opportunity. What am I missing?"

"Nothing," Matt said. "Call Captain Adams and let's go."

CHAPTER 33

Barry Gesicki tiptoed through the front porch door of Tamryn's house and stood silently for several minutes. He took a few steps down the hall toward her bedroom, listening for any sounds of life. Recognizing the light snoring of his wife, he continued stealthily toward her, a demented smile on his face.

He opened the door of the guest bedroom and stuck his head in, making sure that the old broad hadn't returned. Empty.

She's alone. He continued down the hallway, and stood at the end of her bed, watching her sleep for a while. *When did you turn so bad, Tam?,* he thought. *When did you forget how to be a good wife? Decide not to be a good wife? The wife I want. If you just hadn't turned so rotten, so selfish. It wasn't supposed to be about you. It's about me! You're just a pathetic female trying to outshine me in a man's world. But you can't beat me. Not now. Not ever.*

Her face was pale, and her breathing seemed shallow, her chest rising and falling. He raised his gun and moved in closer to her, bending over her body now.

But Tamryn was ready for him. Forcefully, she grabbed Barry around the neck, the shock of her attack causing his gun to fly across the room toward the sliding glass doors that were letting the moon's light shine in the room.

With her right hand, she reached for her gun on the nightstand, while wrestling him off her with the other hand, giving him a violent stiff-arm.

But he saw her move toward the nightstand, and he was able to slap her gun away. It fell to the floor. He was like an animal, hissing and grunting. She almost gagged at his foul body odor.

He wrangled away from her and lunged at his gun on the carpet. Tamryn leapt out of bed and twisted one foot around Barry's leg causing both of them to tumble to the floor. With all of her might and main, she held on to his right arm to keep him from grasping his gun.

Scuffling with him, Tamryn tried to crawl to his gun, but he grabbed her foot and pulled her away from it, sliding her across the carpet as if she was a sack of rice. Barry seized his gun, turned, and drove the butt of it down hard on Tamryn's face, drawing blood from her nose.

But his movement caused him to wobble, and Tamryn, somehow finding a higher power with the growing rage within her, used her entire upper body to flip him over. Quickly, she straddled him, blood streaming from her face, and tried to get control of the gun, forcing it toward his face while he struggled to sit up.

The gun went off.

• • •

Fern called Judge Cynthia Hedges on her personal cell phone to tell her they were going to arrest Randy Reid for the murder of Hiroshi Matsuda. The judge was still at her home in Twisty River, preparing for the day.

"Do you want a warrant from me?" the judge asked.

"Yes, but we're going to Cold Rock Island now," Fern answered. "I believe we have more than enough probable cause. We've uncovered a fraudulent online operation linked to Randy, and evidence that he knew he was about to be exposed by Matsuda. There are millions of dollars at stake, which we can also prove. We know he was here at the time of the murder, and Dr. Ryder has not been able to eliminate his fingerprints as a suspect. I also think he convinced his father to personally fly Matsuda to the island so there would be no way to track his travel. It's enough, Cynthia."

"It is. I'll prepare your warrant. Are you bringing him to Twisty River?"

"Yes, that's the plan. We should be there by early afternoon."

"I'll be ready, and in my chambers. I suppose I'd better dress well today."

Fern laughed. Cynthia Rogers was *always* dressed well, with her sleek black bob always perfect, and her makeup carefully applied. "Yeah," Fern told her, "this might attract some outside attention."

"Good luck, Fern. Please be careful."

By the time Fern, Matt, and Ed got to Buck Bay, Captain Adams and his crew were ready to set sail. The three cops were wearing bullet-proof vests, and suggested to the ship's crew that they don theirs. Matt had brought along extras in case the CG was short some.

The cutter slipped its last mooring line and cast off. It was a remarkable morning for the last day of February. Not a cloud in the sky, and everything Matt could see was either brilliant blue or sparkling white. Fern immediately took off for her corner at the aft railing, and Matt and Ed gave her some space.

"Is there any chance we could make this quick this morning, and get out to the fishing hole this afternoon?" Ed asked Matt, only partly joking.

Matt grinned. "You sound like Earl. This darn work stuff is getting in our way. Maybe we should retire."

"You can afford to. I can't. And besides, Millie doesn't want me around all day."

"What would you do if you were retired?"

"Oh, I have lots of hobbies. I fish, I work on the property, I read, and I watch football."

"Is that enough to make up for this excitement?"

"I've had enough excitement to last most men a lifetime," Ed said. "Before you arrived in Port Stirling, local law enforcement didn't always run smoothly. There were plenty of times when it was pretty much Earl and me handling things, and everything took longer. Although it was all domestic stuff in the old days. Chinook County wasn't on the international radar as a great place to do crime then like it is now."

"Yep, we've been 'discovered' for sure," Matt lamented. "And Fern's damnable case isn't going to lower our profile. We need to make this arrest and try to keep it as quiet as we…" Matt's phone buzzed, and he picked up.

"Hello. Tamryn! I was just goi…" He stopped talking to listen to her. "Please calm down and repeat what you just said—I'm on a ship."

"Matt. Help me," she said. "I shot Barry."

Matt looked at Ed, his eyes wide. "Is he dead?" he said into his phone.

"Yes. His brains are all over my bedroom carpet," she sobbed.

"Oh, God. Are you alright?" Matt put his hand over his phone, and whispered to Ed, "She shot Barry. He's dead."

"I've been better," she said. "I think I passed out when the gun went off, but now I need some help, and soon."

"Shit. I can't get there, Tamryn. I'm out on the Pacific Ocean with the Coast Guard, and even if we turned around now, my car's in Buck Bay. Here's what I'm going to do. I'll call Jay and our department and get them over to help you right now. Here's what I want you to do. Put the gun down by his body. Was it his gun or yours?" he added.

"His. He tried to kill me, Matt."

"I know, honey, I know. It's going to be OK. Leave his gun by his body, pull a blanket off your bed, wrap it around you, and go sit on your front porch. Wait for Jay. Do you understand?"

"Yes. Wait for Jay."

"That's right. Don't try to do anything else, OK? You're in shock. I would be, too. Stay on the line and talk to me. Ed is with me and he's calling Jay now. It won't be long, and he'll be there to help you. Have you put the gun down?"

"Yes."

"Are you standing up?"

"No, I'm on the floor by my nightstand. That's where my phone was."

"OK, good. Stand up, Tamryn. Can you do that for me?"

"I'm shaky."

"I know. But try to stand up. Hold onto the side of your bed and push up."

Silence while she did what Matt told her to do.

"I'm up. I'm putting down my phone while I wrap a blanket around me."

"That's good," he said to silence. He waited for her to rejoin him.

"Oh, no," she said.

"What?"

"My front door is open. He got past my new lock. How did he…"

"Let's don't worry about that now. Don't touch your door. Just keep walking out to the porch, OK?"

"I'm here. Can I sit down on a step now?"

"Yes. Do you see any car or any sign of anything suspicious?"

"It's a beautiful morning, Matt."

"Yes, it is. Here, too. Do you see anything unusual?"

"No."

"No car or clothes or any of Barry's gear?"

"No. Everything looks normal," she said. "But it's not normal, is it?"

"Things will be normal soon," he reassured her. "Take some deep breaths."

Tamryn did as he told her. "Beautiful fresh air," she said.

"It will help clear your head. Can I ask you a question now?"

"What?"

"How did you get his gun away from him?"

"I was awake, Matt. I heard him come down the hallway and into my bedroom. At first, I thought I was dreaming, but then I heard him open the door to Sylvia's room, and I knew it was him."

Matt choked on a swallow. "Is Sylvia there?" he said in a panic.

"No. No, she left last night after we ate dinner. Wanted her own bed and to see Horatio."

Matt let out his breath. "Thank the good lord."

"He would have killed her. He was like an animal, Matt, not a person. It was so horrible," she gasped, and started crying again.

"It's over, Tamryn. It's over for good, and you're going to be fine."

"He hit me in the face with the gun, and we wrestled on the floor. Somehow, I got it pointed at him and I must have pulled the trigger."

"How on earth did you have the strength?" Matt was incredulous.

"Don't know. It came from somewhere deep inside me. I wasn't ready to die. But I don't feel so good now."

She stopped talking, and Matt heard her vomit violently. The next thing he heard was Jay's voice. "I'm here, Matt. Putting down her phone for a minute so I can hold her hair back."

Matt waited, and while he did so, Cold Rock Island came into view on the horizon.

"OK," Jay said. "She's alright now. Rudy's got her in the car and she's lying down in the back seat. Ed told me she shot Barry. Is that correct?"

"Yeah, and you need to prepare yourself for a nasty scene, I'm afraid," Matt told him. "He tried to kill her, Jay. She got his gun away from him, and it went off while they were wrestling. He's on the floor in her bedroom, and from what I gathered, most of his face is probably blown to smithereens."

"Good," Jay said, surprising Matt. "The planet needs this guy to be blown off it. I can't fucking believe he's been hiding around here since yesterday, and we couldn't find him. We looked everywhere, Matt."

"He was cagey. It's my fault, too, I really believed he'd taken off for California and we'd seen the last of him."

"Well, I'm going inside now, and I can't wait to see the last of him. Rudy, too. He's very upset."

"Protect the crime scene as best you can," Matt instructed him. "You go in alone and have Rudy stay with Tamryn—it would be understandable if he doesn't have as cool a head as you right now. And, don't call Bernice just yet. I need to talk to her and make sure she's taken care of two sets of fingerprints for Fern's case first. Then, I'll ask her to send her forensics team to Port Stirling."

"Busy Thursday," Jay said dryly.

CHAPTER 34

The ship docked in the Cold Rock Island harbor, lonely except for Reid's yacht docked on the far eastern end. There was no sign of life on the wharf.

Once again, Fern had gathered everyone together and explained what was going to happen. Matt, Fern, and Ed would go to the main house and ask to see Randy. Three of the armed Coast Guard officers would go directly to the hangar and make sure the plane didn't take off, while another two would monitor Reid's yacht. The rest of the crew would back up Fern's group, ensuring their safety. Once they had Randy cuffed, they would move down the hill to the dock in flanks, with the airplane guards bringing up the rear.

If his father wanted to accompany his son to Twisty River, Rohn would be searched for weapons and then allowed on the ship with them. Everyone else would be ordered to stay on the island until they heard otherwise.

Up the hill from the dock they went.

While they walked to the house, Matt told Fern about Tamryn.

"She's OK now, and Jay and Rudy are with her," he finished.

"And, Barry is definitely dead?" Fern asked.

"Definitely. Most of his head is blown off."

Fern shuddered. "Poor Tamryn. I'm surprised she was able to fend him off, ribs and all. I guess it proves what we're capable of when our lives are truly threatened."

"Yeah," Matt said. "But let's try to not put that to the test today. We get in, we arrest him, we get out. Capiche?"

"I'm with you. This should be a piece of cake compared to what Tamryn went through."

Arriving at the house with a newfound sense of power and determination, Fern knocked loudly on the front door of the house, and yelled, "Police! Open up!"

Moira opened the door and stood looking at them, hands on hips, scowling. She said, "What the hell is your problem now? And quit banging on my door."

Uncowed, Fern said, "We need to see Randy. Is he in his quarters?" Without waiting for an answer, she stepped into the foyer and headed down the west wing hallway.

Moira followed after them, saying loudly, "He is, but he's busy. Can't this wait?"

"No," said Ed, dropping back behind Fern and cutting off the scrappy cook's forward progress. He heard her mutter something under her breath, and it sounded a lot like "fucker."

Randy, as was his morning routine it seemed, was at work at his computer in the front office. Matt entered the room first, flashing his badge in Randy's direction, with his gun drawn. He quickly cleared all the rooms in Randy's wing, and then turned and nodded at his wife and Ed. They came in, with the CG detail pulling up the rear and blocking the door.

Randy stood and stared at Fern. "What is this, Fern?" He looked and sounded scared. Probably something to do with Matt's gun.

Fern showed her badge as well, and said, "Randy Reid, I'm arresting you on suspicion of the murder of Hiroshi Matsuda. We have probable cause to believe that you committed one or more felonies, and we are taking you to Chinook County to be booked." She read him his Miranda Rights, which she now knew word-for-word by heart, not needing the small slip of paper that she always carried with her, just in case.

"Do you understand?" she asked him.

He was speechless for a moment. "I understand what you're telling me, but this is crazy. I didn't do this, Fern. You can't possibly believe what you just said."

"We have evidence, Randy, and I believe we can prove you did. Please do the right thing and come with us now. Don't make this any harder than it needs to be."

"I didn't kill him. I didn't! You have to believe me!" he pleaded with her.

"I don't believe you," Fern said icily. "Please put your hands behind your back and turn around. Lieutenant Sonders will place you in handcuffs that will remain on you until we reach the Chinook County courthouse."

"I need to talk to my father!"

"We will talk to your father. But first, you need to submit to the Lieutenant. Do as I say, Randy. Now!"

Apparently, hearing something in her voice that frightened him, he quickly turned around and stuck his arms out toward Ed, who had produced his badge to Randy in accordance with protocol. Recalling how Barry Gesicki had slipped out of his single-locked cuffs, Ed carefully enlisted the double locks.

By the time Randy was secured and everything explained to him, a small crowd had appeared at his door—Rohn and Rick Reid, along with stubborn Moira, and likely a hastily-called Tyson. The Coast Guard officers stood their ground, and the four island residents were verbally hostile, but didn't physically challenge them.

Fern went out first and addressed Rohn. "We have arrested Randy for the homicide of Hiroshi Matsuda, and we're taking him to the mainland for processing. He has a right to an attorney. If he can't afford one, one will be appointed for him." There were no snickers at this last direction, at least none that Fern heard.

"That won't be necessary," Rohn said, ashen faced. "I have lawyers at the ready, and my son will be out of your ridiculous jail in no time. There is no way on this great earth that Randy killed Matsuda. You're wrong, Fern."

"We have compelling evidence against him, Rohn. I'm sorry," she said.

"I've grown to like and respect you, but this will be the end of your nascent career," he threatened, staring at her. To his son, he said, "I will call the attorneys now, and I'll go with you. Please don't worry, Randy, this is a bad joke, and I will sort it out." To Fern, he said coldly, "I assume I can go with my son?"

"Yes, of course. Captain Adams will insist on searching you for any weapons before you're allowed on his ship, but I'm sure that won't be a problem, will it?"

Rohn ignored her.

"Can I go, too, dad?" Rick Reid said from behind his father.

Matt answered for Rohn. "No. Because we're nice police, we're letting your father go with Randy, but the rest of you are ordered to stay here until we release this place as a crime scene. The U.S. Coast Guard will be watching the island on our behalf, so please follow our directions."

"But this is so stupid!" yelled Rick. "My brother is not a killer. You can't do this. And I don't like my twin being out of my sight." His face had taken on a purplish hue.

Randy spoke quietly, "It's OK, Rick. Dad will handle this, and I'll be back in no time. Please do as they say and let's not make things worse."

"No! It's not right," Rick, still yelling.

Moira grabbed Rick by the arm and pulled him backward into the hallway. She said, "Let your father deal with this. They will soon see the error of their ways, and everything will be alright."

Rick looked at Moira and appeared to calm down slightly. She patted his arm.

"What should I do, boss?" Tyson asked Rohn.

"Stay here, as the police have directed," Rohn said. "Make sure no one leaves my island, and that includes Simon, who will whine up a storm at this delay in his departure. Also make sure that no one else comes ashore unless it's law enforcement and they have a warrant."

Tyson nodded.

Moira pulled at Rick and said, "Come on. Help me make lunch. Lynette isn't feeling well, and I need some help in the kitchen."

Rick, subdued, did as she said, and the two took off down the hallway. Tyson, useless now in his security role, shuffled along behind them.

Fern and Matt glanced at each other, and Matt raised one eyebrow. It reinforced what Fern was thinking: *The cook is telling the owner's son what to do?*

• • •

After a thorough search of Rohn and Randy Reid, and getting them settled below decks, the Resolve took off for Buck Bay. In order, Fern called her boss, and then Judge Hedges to tell her the arrest had been successfully executed. The judge told her the arrest warrant was in place with the sheriff's office in the courthouse. Relieved, Fern then called Bernice, got her voicemail, and left the message, "We need the state lab's fingerprints analysis as soon as possible, Bernice. Call me for an update as soon as you can."

Matt called the sheriff to alert him they were on the way with the prisoner. Earl had left Port Stirling earlier—where he'd been participating in the ongoing hunt for Barry Gesicki—when Matt had called him to tell him what happened at Tamryn's. Now, he said to him, "We need your most secure cell, Earl. Word will get out quickly who we've arrested, and nobody likes billionaires."

"I hear you," the sheriff said. "I'll call PR, too. They got tested in the Hannah Oakley murder, and they'll be ready for this one."

"Fern has alerted her bosses, too, and somebody from the State Department will be in touch with your department soon. This is an all hands-on-deck deal, Earl. No time off for anyone for a few days, OK?"

"I get it. How is Tamryn doing?"

"Jay and Rudy are with her, and she's in shock, but doing better. They took her to the Port Stirling Clinic to have someone look her over and clean her up. Barry hit her in the face with the butt of his gun, and apparently there was a lot of blood."

"Did they give her something for the shock? To get her system back in whack?"

"Yep. And they've taken her to my house for now and are staying with her until I get there. Jay said she refused to go back to the hospital."

Earl chuckled. "That tells me all I need to know about her current state. She's a fighter, for sure. I'm never happy when someone dies, Matt, but I'm happy this asshole is dead."

"I think it's safe to say that not very many people will be upset at this news. Which reminds me, I need to call the Boston PD next. See you soon, pardner."

On the journey to Buck Bay, Rohn and Randy Reid huddled in the cabin where Randy had been secured to a metal pole. Two armed CG guards were stationed outside his door.

"Tell me what evidence they could possibly have on you," Rohn demanded angrily of his son. "And don't insult me by telling me there is none. These are decent cops doing their best job under the auspices of the United States government. They wouldn't arrest you unless they have a reason to believe you might have actually killed Hiroshi. What is it, Randy? Tell me the truth."

Randy looked woefully at his father for a few moments before speaking. "It's not what you think, dad. I didn't kill him, and I don't know who did."

"Then what?"

"They may have some other evidence on me, and believe it connects me to Matsuda's murder. But I swear I didn't kill him. I was as shocked as you when we found him like that."

"What other evidence? What?!?"

"I started an online cryptocurrency operation with a banker in Honolulu."

"Nothing illegal about that," Rohn said, staring at his son.

"There is if you take all their money and lie to them about profits."

"A Ponzi scheme? You're paying the old investors with money from the new ones?"

"Yeah. And keeping millions for myself and my banker friend. Sorry, dad, but it was just too easy." Randy shifted uncomfortably on the bunk bed he was seated on.

"Easy?" Rohn exploded, standing up in the small space and spinning away from his son. "When did I ever teach you to take the easy way out? What the fuck were you thinking?"

Randy shrugged. "Don't know. I met this guy at a party in Honolulu two years ago and we just got to talking. We started it on a lark, but his bank's big clients started handing over buckets of money. It would have been almost crazy to not take it."

"What's your partner's name?" Rohn asked, pulling a pen out of his pocket.

"Scott Thurman. The cops know him and pulled him in for questioning. Fern asked me about him."

"Did he rat on you?"

"No. He played dumb and so did I," Randy said.

"What does this have to do with Matsuda? How does he come into this sordid picture?"

"Scott thinks that Shuji Matsuda asked his father to look into a recent string of bank manager emails, and that Hiroshi discovered the crypto op. That's why he called you to come here. He wanted to find our server and see if it was linked to Scott's work."

"Our server is hosting this fraud?" Rohn asked, his eyes widening. "On my fucking island?"

"I'm sorry to say yes, it is, dad. I'm so, so sorry."

"You're only sorry because you got caught," Rohn said coldly, shaking his head sadly. "So, you had me go fetch Matsuda to Cold Rock, and then you killed him so he couldn't expose your crime, right?"

"You only have part of it right. When I learned that he wanted to visit, I figured that Scott was right about Hiroshi, and I thought it would be better if we could control his coming to the island. More secrecy. But I didn't kill him."

"Did he discover our server room?"

"Yes, we think so," Randy answered.

"Who is 'we'?"

"Moira found Matsuda in the pantry late Wednesday night. He told her he woke up and was hungry, but she didn't believe him. She thought he'd been in the server room, and she told me and Rick."

"Does your brother know what you're up to?"

"He does now. But he's not involved with me and Scott. He didn't know anything about it until Hiroshi showed up."

"Is there any possibility that your fingerprints are on Hiroshi or the rafter or anywhere in his guest room?"

"Absolutely not. I didn't kill him, dad. I'm telling you the truth."

Rohn thought for a minute. "Do you know if Fern brought back the purple pillow from the guest room? Is it back in that room?"

"I didn't know she took it," Randy said. "Why did she do that?"

"Hell if I know. But if she wanted it, it must have something to do with his murder."

CHAPTER 35

Wednesday, February 21, 2024, 8:04 p.m. — Cold Rock Island

Hiroshi Matsuda had just told a funny story about Fred Leufeld, the U.S. Secretary of State, around the dining room table in the main house, and Rohn Reid and his two sons, Rick and Randy Reid laughed loudly. That it happened on their island made it even funnier for the three current residents.

"It's much quieter here now than in my day," Hiroshi told them. "You've built a wonderful environment here. I love my life in Honolulu now, but I can understand why you choose to be here on Cold Rock Island."

"Do you have a family?" Rohn asked pleasantly. He liked this man, this visitor to his island who knew it even better than he did.

"Yes, I'm blessed," Hiroshi answered. "My wife Naomi is my life's partner, and we have two children, Shuji, my son, and Fumiko, my daughter. We all live in Honolulu now, but, of course, my children are grown and have their own homes and lives. Naomi and I are lucky that they seem to want to stick close to their old parents."

"It is nice when that happens," smiled Rohn, looking at his twin sons. "What does your wife do?"

"She was a nurse when we were first married, but stopped working to raise our kids when the Japanese Navy sent me all over the world. By the time they were grown enough, Naomi opted out of going back to a regular job. She volunteers two days a week now at a local hospital. She also cooks, gardens, and takes care of me now. Oh, and she shops. A lot."

The Reids laughed again.

"What about your kids?" Randy asked. "What do they do to keep busy?"

"Fumiko works in our state capitol, and Shuji is a VP at a regional bank. Both gainfully employed, I'm happy to say," Hiroshi said with obvious pride.

"Which bank does Shuji work for?" Randy asked. He shifted in his chair and took a sip from his wine glass.

Hiroshi told him. He paid close attention to Randy's reaction.

• • •

Thursday, February 22, 2024 — 9:22 a.m.

Rick Reid went to his twin's room and closed the door behind him.

"What's wrong with you?" Rick asked Randy.

"Nothing. What do you mean?"

"You were upset at dinner last night with our guest. Why?"

"No, I wasn't," Randy hedged. "I don't know why you think that."

"Are you or are you not the twin of me? You are, and that means I can tell when something is bothering you. Now spill." Rick sat down in the small armchair in Randy's office, preparing to stay until he knew what was going on with his brother.

Much to Rick's dismay, Randy started crying. Not big sobs or anything, just quiet tears rolling down his face. He swatted them off his chin. Finally, he spoke. "I'll tell you, Rick, but you have to promise me you won't tell dad or anyone else. Especially dad."

"If it's important to you, you know I won't say anything. What's going on?"

"I'm running a cryptocurrency op from here, and I… well, I may not have been perfectly upfront with all of our investors," Randy said. "It's possible that Hiroshi's son knows, told his father, and that's why he's here — to spy on me."

Rick, stunned, looked at his twin. He thought for a minute, and then asked, "Why would Hiroshi be involved? I don't understand."

"Do you remember last night at dinner when he said his son works for a Honolulu bank? It's the same bank that I'm working with. One of Shuji's colleagues is my inside guy, directing big-money clients to me."

"What are you doing with the investors' money?" Rick asked. "Where's it going?"

"Most of it is going in the secret room in dad's closet. Please don't tell," Randy pleaded. "I can't let him know what I'm doing—he'll be furious."

"You're stealing your investor money? I can't believe this. Why? We don't need money." Rick was incredulous.

"I want my own money, not dad's. Don't you ever feel that way?"

"I make my own money," Rick said. "It's enough."

"Not for me. But don't worry. Hiroshi won't find anything, and we'll take him home, and everything will be just as it was," Randy said confidently.

"I sure hope so," said Rick. "But we'd better keep our eyes on him today."

• • •

And they did. Hiroshi took off right after breakfast for what looked to Rick and Randy like a harmless hike around the island. Sightseeing, for old times' sake. The brothers were eating their breakfast in the kitchen this morning, at the round oak table that Rohn had imported from France. Moira had a nice fire going in the floor-to-ceiling, red-brick corner fireplace. She served them their favorite Eggs Benedict.

"Here's some fresh melon to go with," she said, setting down their plates in front of each twin. "Eat it all, you need your fruit."

"Yes, mom," Randy said playfully, and Moira smiled.

"Are you taking our guest back to Honolulu this afternoon?" she inquired.

"Probably," said Randy. "He told us last night he just wants to look around a little today to remember the good old days."

"He looked around last night," she said.

"What do you mean?" asked Randy.

"I got up at 3:00 a.m. and came in here to make myself some hot milk, and Mr. Matsuda was in the pantry. He told me he was hungry and looking for a snack."

Randy's face darkened perceptibly, and Rick lost a little color.

"What did you say, Moira?" Randy demanded.

"You heard me. What was he really doing in my pantry?"

"How would I know," stammered Randy. "I barely know the man."

The twins hurriedly ate their breakfast and went back to their wing of the house.

"He can't know about the server room!" Randy said. "There's no way."

"What if your guy in Honolulu talked?" Rick said. "What if he told Shuji? And he told his dad."

Randy shook his head. "That's not possible. Scott wouldn't tell Shuji anything; he hates him. Says he's a suck-up to the board of directors, and in his way for promotion."

"Then why in hell was he in our pantry in the middle of the night?"

Randy rubbed his face with his large, well-formed hand. "I don't know how, but he found the server room, didn't he? He was probably in there and heard Moira in the kitchen. He must know what Scott and I are doing… somehow." He looked forlornly at Rick. "I have to talk to him, don't I? Confront him."

Rick thought for a moment. "No. I'll talk to him and tell him Moira alluded to seeing him last night. See if I can get him to mention the server room. I can play dumb about your operation if he brings it up. You couldn't carry that off. I'll talk to him, and get it sorted. He won't bother you, Randy. It's better this way." He stood to go.

CHAPTER 36

Thursday, February 22, 2024 — 2:40 p.m.

Rick knocked on the door of Hiroshi's guest room about fifteen minutes after he'd watched him return from his wanderings about the island.

Unbeknownst to their guest, Rick had watched him from a small crow's nest at the top of the hangar building, from which he could see about three-fourths of the island. Hiroshi hiked to the north shore, meandering slowly as if he was just sightseeing. But then, he suddenly turned, running into the wooded section as if he was trying to evade any prying eyes. Rick waited, watching, but didn't see Hiroshi again until, finally, he went to his room.

Now, after a brief interval, Hiroshi opened the door to his room. "Rick," he said. "How can I help you?"

Rick smiled. "How can you tell it's me, not Randy? Most people can't tell us apart."

"I guess that makes me not most people," Hiroshi replied. He didn't return the smile.

"Can I come in?"

"Of course. It's your house, after all." Hiroshi opened the door wide to allow Rick to enter.

"Dad is wondering if you want to be flown back to Honolulu tonight?" Rick asked, taking a seat in the armchair without asking if he could sit. Hiroshi sat on the loveseat at an angle to it.

"Yes, I would," Hiroshi responded. "If that fits into Rohn's schedule. And yours. I've seen what I came to see." Now, he smiled.

"OK, great, I'll tell dad. I'm glad you got to see our island after all this time. It must be fun to look back and reminisce."

"It was. Thanks for allowing me this time. It's a special place."

Rick drummed his fingers nervously on the armchair. He didn't like what he needed to say next.

"Moira told me that she ran into you in the kitchen last night. That must have been weird," he laughed. A forced laugh.

"Yes," Hiroshi grinned. "I get hungry in the night, and I'm used to raiding the kitchen. I didn't think anyone would mind or be up at that hour."

"Did you find something to eat?"

"Yes. Thank you."

A pause. "Did you find our secret room?"

Hiroshi looked directly at Rick. "As a matter of fact, I did. I leaned against the panel while I picked up a jar of peanut butter, and to my surprise the door swung open. That's quite a server room your dad has!"

"Yeah, technology is his gig," Rick said, standing up.

Hiroshi stood, too. "Was there anything else?" he asked. "If not, I'll pack up now and be ready to go whenever you and your father are."

"Sounds good. I'll come back here and get you when we're ready," Rick said, reaching for the door.

Hiroshi locked the door behind Rick.

• • •

He's going back to Honolulu and will tell the police everything!, Rick thought, in a panic. *This man—this foreigner!—is going to ruin my brother's life. How could you have been so stupid, Randy? How?? I can't even look at you right now, you're so stupid. I need help. I need mom's help.*

Hurriedly, Rick went to the kitchen, where Moira was working alone, washing and cutting vegetables.

She turned to him. "Hi, what's up?"

"Mom, Randy is in deep shit," Rick said. "I have to bail him out, and I need your help."

Moira dropped her colander in the sink, dried her hands on her apron, and sat down at the table. "It's that damn Matsuda, isn't it? I knew he was up to no good. Tell me, Rick. What is it?"

"Randy is involved in an illegal scam, and Hiroshi knows. He's here on our island to see if he can confirm what he suspects. When you saw him last night, he was looking for our server room—which he found, and which is likely the proof of Randy's operation he was searching for. He's going to take Randy down, mom. And probably all of us along with him."

Moira sat stunned and speechless, until finally, "No. He's not going to take my baby down. Neither one of you. We're not going to let that happen, Rick. Are you absolutely sure that Randy is guilty of this? That he's breaking the law?"

Rick nodded. "Yes, he confessed to me. He's not only breaking the law, he's about to ruin the lives of thousands of his investors. It's a pure Ponzi scheme, and it's only a matter of time until he gets caught."

"Well, I'll deal with Randy later," she frowned. "But if Matsuda spills the beans now, it will destroy our reputation, and our family—all of our lives." She looked around her kitchen. "All of this, our peace, will be shredded into a thousand little pieces." Her face hardened. "We have to act, Rick. You and I have to save our family. Where is Matsuda now?"

"In his guest room. He's packing to fly home."

"He's not going to fly home," she said, taking a drink of her coffee, and then pushing her chair back. She walked to the countertop, opened a drawer, and took out a pair of orange gardening gloves, pulling them on. "C'mon," she said to Rick.

● ● ●

Thirty minutes later, Rick, for the second time, knocked on Hiroshi's guest room door.

"Ready to go?" Hiroshi said when he opened the door.

Rick pushed inside, his mother behind him. "We have a couple of questions for you first," Rick said. "Please sit down."

As Rick hoped would happen, Hiroshi sat on the same loveseat he had previously. The one with the large purple pillow.

Moira took the armchair, and Rick elected to stand. She asked Hiroshi, "What are you planning to do when you get home?"

Hiroshi, now scared, tried to play it lightly. "Oh, you know, the usual—nap, play tennis, nap again." He chuckled…as best he could manage.

Moira eyed him with a steely gaze. "No, I meant, what are you planning to say about Randy?"

"I don't have anything to say about Randy," he lied.

"Rick thinks you do," she said. "Rick thinks you intend to tell the world that his brother is bad. That he's doing something wrong."

"You mean that Randy is running an illegal scheme, and cheating thousands of good people all over the world out of their money?" Hiroshi said, now irritated. "Is that what I'm going to tell? Is that what you think?"

"Is it?" she asked.

"Yes, I suppose it is," Hiroshi said resignedly.

"We can't let that happen," Moira said. "Let you hurt Randy's brother and my baby. Can't let you. You never should have come here. Not to hurt my Randy."

Moira looked up at Rick and nodded. Out of the corner of his eye, Hiroshi saw Rick pick up the purple pillow. Quickly, he tried to stand, but it was too late. Moira was out of her chair pushing him down and sitting on him, at the same time Rick put the pillow over his face.

Hiroshi struggled, but it was a brief period before the world went black.

• • •

Thursday, February 29, 2024 — Twisty River

Randy Reid was processed into the Chinook County jail and taken to his cell. The single room was painted green three feet up from the tile floor, and then stark white to the ceiling. One overhead fluorescent light lit the space. A shiny silver toilet with a small sink above it stood against the left wall, and two bunk beds were attached to the opposite wall. Thankfully, there was no one else in the cell.

"Home sweet home," Randy said with a wan smile, trying to keep a stiff upper lip for his father's sake.

"I'll have you out of this hole in no time," fumed Rohn. "They cannot treat my son like this. Try to get some rest, Randy, while I get with our lawyers." He hugged his beloved son, and whispered, "It's going to be OK. Trust me."

"I've always trusted you, dad," Randy whispered back.

The cell door clanked behind Rohn, and Randy sat down on the lower bunk.

• • •

The director of the Oregon State Police laboratory in Salem called Dr. Bernice Ryder.

"We have a conclusive match for you, Bernice. Your crime scene prints from the rafter, the ladder, and the pillow match those of Richard Reid. The only other documented prints we got are off the pillow and are matched with prints on record for Fern Byrne. Hope this helps you."

"Thank God," Bernice said. "Did you find any matches with Randy Reid in any I sent to you?"

"No, we did not. His prints are indeed close to those of his twin brother, but there is enough differentiation between the two sets for us to be confident in our results. We can't tell you if Richard Reid is your murderer, but we can state unequivocally that he touched both that rafter and that pillow recently."

"That's what I need. I thank you, and Chinook County thanks you. We needed to be sure on this one!"

Elated, Bernice immediately punched in Fern's cell phone number.

• • •

Rohn Reid, holed up in Twisty River's one lone motel, conducted a ZOOM call with his Seattle team of attorneys, laying out what he thought was the likely case against Randy. He read the arrest warrant to them, and with complete honesty, he told them everything Randy had told him.

Howard Schumacher, his lead attorney, listened carefully, asking a few questions along the way. When Rohn had finished summarizing, Schumacher said, "They've got a circumstantial case against Randy, but no definitive evidence that ties him to the murder of Matsuda unless they withheld evidence from the arrest warrant. If they have his fingerprints or DNA on the victim, it should be in the warrant."

"I read you the whole warrant," Rohn says. "It doesn't mention any of that forensic stuff."

"So, it seems their case is focused on motive and opportunity," Schumacher said. "But it won't take them long to link your server to the cryptocurrency fraud, I'm afraid. If Randy's colleague in Honolulu talks, they'll have him dead to rights on that."

"Can't we say that Randy was just doing a favor for a friend and didn't know anything about the scheme?" Rohn suggested.

"We can," Schumacher agreed. "You — and it needs to be you personally, you can't bring in anyone else — need to have a chat with Scott Thurman. Pay him off, Rohn, and make it big, or Randy's going to prison just like Madoff. And do it today. You don't have much time."

"Why can't you do it? Isn't that what I pay you for?" Rohn demanded.

"No. You pay me to represent your legal interests, not to be your fixer," Schumacher replied firmly. "I'm too old and too rich to go that route now in the twilight of my career. But my advice to you is that it is the only way to save Randy from discovery. Whoever did kill Matsuda did you a big favor, but Thurman can sink Randy if the cops break him."

• • •

Matt, Fern, and Ed had gone directly to the Hornings' home after delivering their prisoner and completing their work at the courthouse. All three were anxious about Tamryn and eager to see her.

On their way back to Port Stirling, Ed and Matt discussed the ramifications of Tamryn killing her husband.

"I officially put her on administrative leave," Matt told him. "Standard operating procedure when an officer is responsible for a death. I'll tell her as soon as we get home. There will have to be an investigation."

Ed nodded. "Earl's office would be the logical jurisdiction."

"Yep. I talked briefly to him while we were in Twisty River, and he will take the lead. He also suggested that Barry's Boston PD supervisor might want to be involved, and I think that's a good idea. What do you think?"

"I like it. It takes some of the pressure off the county and your department. And, if I'm Boston, I would want to be involved, or at least, asked."

"Good. I'll call him back. He seems like a good guy and was relieved that Barry's dead and Tamryn is safe. It's an ugly stain on their department, and he's eager to put the whole story to bed."

"I can't imagine that it will take long to investigate," Ed noted. "The only question is how did Barry get into her house a second time."

"We need to figure that out," Matt agreed, "because Tamryn surely didn't let him in."

* * *

Jay had taken photos of Tamryn's bruised and battered body for the record. Her face alone would say to investigators that she shot in self-defense — she was a mess.

Fern gasped when she saw her. "Oh my god, you are a fright, girlfriend."

"Thanks," Tamryn said wryly. "You look good."

"I meant that in the nicest way," Fern smiled. "Are you comfortable? Is there anything I can do for you?" She looked around her guest room as if seeing it with new eyes. It was pretty cozy.

"I'm fine," Tamryn said. "Just don't run out of Advil." She patted the bed next to her. "Sit and tell me about your case."

Matt, standing in the doorway, said, "She can't, Tamryn. I've put you on official leave until the sheriff determines that Barry's death was justified. You know the drill."

"Oh, shit, man," Tamryn wailed. "I know it's just administrative, but don't keep me in the dark on the fun stuff."

"I'm sorry, but I'm doing this by the book," Matt said. "I knew you wouldn't like it, but it's for your own good. And I'm planning to wait for Earl to do his thing, and not ask you all the questions that are burning inside me. This will be tough on both of us, but we'll have to find other topics of conversation."

Tamryn glared ferociously at Matt, but then said, "How 'bout those Chiefs? Some game, huh?"

• • •

Fern took Bernice's call upstairs while she was changing into sweats.

"I have good news for you," Bernice started. "The best possible news."

"The state lab matched Randy Reid's fingerprints to your forensic evidence?"

Momentarily taken aback, Bernice gathered herself and continued. "No, hon. *Rick* Reid's prints are the match. On everything: rafter, pillow, ladder, Matsuda's jacket. Rick is your killer."

"Oh, no."

CHAPTER 37

Once Matt and Fern arrived home to stay with Tamryn, Jay and Rudy went back to her house. They had taken it personally when, it was obvious now, Barry Gesicki had somehow escaped their notice.

They didn't go inside. A forensics team was still working in there, and they didn't want to get in their way. Jay stood on the front porch looking out, while Rudy did a step-by-step search around the perimeter of the house, starting on the ocean side where the path came up from the beach.

After a few quiet minutes of solitude trying his best to imagine the scenario, Jay was disturbed by a large crow squawking in a tree about fifty yards out in the forest to his right. He yelled, "Calm down!" at it, but the black bird kept at it. Jay could only occasionally glimpse the bird through the dense copse of trees, but he sure could hear it.

Another minute, and there were now two birds having a loud, spirited conversation of some sort. Jay decided to see what the fuss was all about, and he headed off the porch and into the trees. As he approached the crows, who were high up in a fir tree, still thirty yards away, something white caught Jay's eye. A sheet.

He ran toward it, dodging tree limbs, shrubs, and brush until he was upon it. A lean-to under a sprawling tree, and a filthy make-shift bed. Jay looked up just as one crow took flight, a paper wrapper in its beak. There in the crook of the tree hung a pair of binoculars and the remains of a protein bar.

Enough to defend and clear his partner in the shooting death of Barry Gesicki.

• • •

Fern trudged downstairs. She interrupted Matt and Tamryn who were arguing over the relative merits of the Dallas Cowboys and the New England Patriots. Matt saw his wife's distressed expression, and said to Tamryn, "I'll be right back."

"What?" Matt asked Fern.

"We blew it. In only my second big case for the government, I've made an unacceptable mistake. It was Rick who killed Hiroshi, not Randy." She put her face in her hands, not able to look at him.

"Rick's fingerprints matched?" he surmised.

"Yes. Matched everything. Bernice just heard from the state lab." She looked up at him. "I was so eager to make an arrest. I'm a fool."

"Put me in that cake and bake it, too," he said, taking her hands in his. "We know Randy is committing fraud and grand theft. It all seemed to fit. He knew why Hiroshi had come to their island, and he must have shared his fears with Rick. Twin brother took it on himself to protect Randy. Damn."

Getting her senses back, Fern said, "Rick couldn't have done this all by himself, certainly not hanging him. Maybe Randy was wearing the gloves in the smudged prints Bernice found. Am I grasping at straws?"

"Maybe. I have to say that Randy was convincing in his innocence when we arrested him. He seemed sincere."

"Well, someone had to help Rick. According to Bernice, he definitely held the pillow to Hiroshi's face, but what happened after that?"

"He carried Hiroshi to his waiting golf cart and drove him to the hangar," Matt hypothesized. "He got the ladder and rope, and…"

"And what?" Fern interrupted. "Single-handedly moving him up a twenty-five-foot ladder with one hand, while maintaining his balance and tying a rope around his neck with the other hand?" She shook her head. "No, not possible."

Matt scratched his head. "Yeah, you're right. But I have doubts it was Randy that helped him."

"So, are we back to Rohn? Or, did Rick enlist the help of Tyson, or Noah? He's their boss's son, putting either of them in a bad position."

"Don't know," Matt admitted. "We need to talk to Rick again."

"What do I do with Randy? I have to let him go, right?"

Matt shook his head. "No. You've charged him with murder, and you can hold him up to 96 hours. With the threat of the fraud hanging over his head, Randy would likely take off, probably with the help of his dad. Let him spend a night in jail. Call Captain Adams and tell him we're going back. I'll get Jay and Rudy here to take care of Tamryn tonight."

"OK," Fern said. She hesitated. "You know, there's one thing niggling at me from today."

"How close Rick and the cook, Moira, seem to be, and how she ordered him around?"

"You noticed it, too. I thought so. I know Moira's been with the Reids for years and she's a fixture on the island, so it's probably natural."

"I thought the relationship seemed a little odd," Matt said. "More like family almost, than owner and employee. Maybe we need to take a second look at Moira."

"She is a strong-looking woman," Fern noted. "Taller than me."

"So, maybe she helped Rick? To protect Randy?"

"Maybe, although Noah and Tyson are more likely. We can fix this, can't we?" Fern said, energized. "If Rick is still on that island!"

CHAPTER 38

Rick, paralyzed with fear, was still on Cold Rock Island. At Moira's urging, he had returned to his wing of the house, and pretended to go to bed like normal. She did the same. Business as usual, so no one would get suspicious.

She told Leonard she had a bad headache, and the rest of them would be on their own for dinner tonight. He made her a pot of her favorite tea, took it to her room, and wished her a good evening.

It was shortly after 11:00 p.m. when Rick heard the ship approaching. He also heard Noah in the golf cart headed for the dock. He jumped out of bed and looked out his south-facing window. *The Coast Guard ship! They know. They know it was me! Randy must have told them I said I would handle things!*

He quickly dressed in the dark and snuck out the back door of the house through the kitchen, down the breezeway between the main house and the guest house, and to the long stairway that led to the north side of the island. His mother's light was off, and he was grateful she was sleeping.

The truth was that he had wanted to run since Thursday afternoon when he killed Matsuda, but his mother convinced him that would be foolish, that they would then suspect him. Besides, it was a friggin island; he couldn't leave without calling attention to himself. But he could hide. He knew just where to go, and he took off running through the night with the sound of the mighty Pacific Ocean all around him.

What Rick didn't know was that Captain Adams had lowered a tender boat prior to docking. Adams' senior officer, one other crew member, and Matt set off to go around Cold Rock Island and land on the north side. Matt and Fern thought there was a good chance Rick would make a run for it when he saw the CG cutter, so the three of them would cover the north side while Fern and a pissed off Ed would go through the front door of the house. Fern had called Ed to alert him to the new evidence, and he'd insisted on meeting them at the Coast Guard HQ.

"I never liked twins to begin with," Ed said now. "They weird me out."

"It's clear that the Reid twins share a couple of bad genes," Fern said. "Randy is a thief, and Rick is a murderer. Nice boys, huh? I wonder where they got it? Their father is a brilliant businessman and a global philanthropist, and their mother is a social do-gooder in Seattle. Where do these criminal tendencies come from? These boys should be living the good life without a worry in the world."

"And, instead, we're going to put both of them in jail, and break their parents' hearts," Ed said, shaking his head.

They banged on the front door of the house, and lights came on almost immediately. Leonard answered the door.

"I heard the ship arriving," he said, and opened the door, allowing entry for Fern, Ed, and six of the CG crew.

"Thank you, Leonard," said Fern. "Who is in the house currently?"

"Mr. Reid and Randy are in your town, but you know that," he said. "That only leaves Rick in the house. Moira and Lynette are in the guest house, and our employees are in their rooms, save Noah who I believe is on security duty tonight. I was just tidying up before turning in myself."

Fern noted that Rick did not appear after her loud knocking. To Leonard, she said, "We are here to see Rick. Please wait here, and we'll find our own way to his rooms."

Leonard nodded, looking sad and tired.

They moved quickly down the west wing hallway to Rick's quarters. Fern went in first, gun drawn, and moved through each of his rooms. Empty. No lights on.

"He's gone," she said, joining Ed and the crew.

"Unless he's planning to swim to Port Stirling, he can't be far," Ed said. There were a few snickers from the CG guys. "He didn't come out the front toward us, so he's probably gone north or west."

Fern pulled out her walkie-talkie, and said, "Matt, he's not in the house. We think he's coming your way."

"Roger that," Matt said.

"We're coming to you," she said.

"No, you're not," said Moira from the doorway. She was holding an AR-15 rifle.

Fern spun around at the sound of her voice. "You!" she squeaked out.

Steady and calm, Moira said, "You are not going to take Rick. I forbid it."

"So, what, you're going to shoot all of us?" Fern said. "You do know that your rifle only fires one round when you pull the trigger, right?

"You may get one of us," Ed added. "But whoever is left standing will put a bullet in your head before you can get off a second round. Is this how you want to die, Moira? Are these boys worth it? Worth your life?"

"They are my boys." Her eyes were dark, and her jaw was firmly set under her sharp cheekbones. "My life is worth nothing without them."

The reality slowly dawned on Fern and Ed.

"Ahh, now I get it," said Fern. "The twins were born illegitimately to you and Rohn. That's why his wife filed for divorce."

"Rohn has always loved me, and we are a family," Moira said. "And I'm getting tired of you interfering in our lives." She pointed the gun at Fern's head.

"You know what?" Fern said, disgusted. "I'm getting tired of you, too, and this fucking island." Suddenly, Fern lunged toward Moira, raising her left arm upward under the rifle and knocking it away in one smooth move before Moira could react. As Moira bent to retrieve her rifle, Fern coolly placed her pistol against Moira's temple, and said, "Leave it. You're done here."

In ten seconds, Ed had angrily pulled Moira's arms behind her back and put his handcuffs on her.

"I second what Fern said," he said, "I'm tired of this island, too." He met Fern's eyes, and they nodded at each other. Job well done.

"Two of you escort Moira to the ship, please," Fern said to the crew, as Moira began to sob and shake uncontrollably. "Make sure she's comfortable. The rest of you come with Ed and me while we find Rick."

Moira let out a howl that a wolf would be proud of.

"And we will find him," Fern said to her. And, to the crew, "Get her out of here."

Outside in the courtyard, Noah drove up in the golf cart, and watched the Coast Guard march Moira down the hill to the dock.

"What's going on?" he asked Fern.

"Rick killed Hiroshi Matsuda, and we suspect Moira helped him," Fern said, looking into his eyes as best she could in the dark. "You know anything about that?"

"No, I don't," he said firmly. "What I've told you is the truth. I just work here, Fern."

"You didn't tell me the truth about why you knocked on my window Saturday night when Joe and I stayed here. This would be a good time for you to tell me the real reason you did that."

Noah held her gaze for a moment and then said, "Rick asked me to make sure that you were in your rooms and not snooping around. Like I said, I just work here and do what I'm told. I'm sorry if I scared you."

She believed him. "We need your help, Noah. Please round up the other employees—Leonard's in the main house, and Lynette is in her room—and bring everyone to the hangar. Lock the door and keep them inside. Understand?"

"Yes, ma'am," he replied.

"Do you have any idea where Rick might be hiding?" she asked.

He thought for a minute. "I really don't. You could look inside the plane, maybe. But he knows every inch of this island, so he could be anywhere."

Ed took off running toward the hangar, a crewman hurriedly following him.

"Gather everyone now, Noah, and come to the hangar." She patted him on the arm, and then ran to the hangar.

Ed's big head stuck out the plane's door and he climbed down the portable staircase. "Nothing. He's not in the plane."

"I guess that would've been too easy," Fern said.

Because of the enveloping darkness, it was slow going as they made their way to the northwest side of the island where Matt's group had landed. The moon was obliterated by a deep cloud cover. One CG crew member stepped in a big hole and turned his ankle. They had to leave him there for the moment, and one of his colleagues stayed with him. Their posse was down to two crewmen as backup.

As they hiked, Ed said, "Doesn't it occur to you that they must have a smaller boat somewhere? If it were me, I wouldn't just rely on the plane and that gigantic yacht to get me off this island in case of emergency, would you?"

"I would have two planes, but that's because I don't like boats. But you're probably right. They must have a smaller, fast boat of some sort."

"A fishing boat with a motor would be my guess."

"We'll find it if there is one," she said.

They kept hiking, occasionally stopping to listen. But all they heard was the ocean's waves and small animals in the brush.

• • •

Rick heard them go by, and he lay very still. When he and Randy were teenagers, and played pirates, they had found an old log from a decades-old fallen tree near the western tip of their island. During one fun summer, they'd hollowed out the inside of the log, making a good-sized cave. Both twins went to the log whenever they wanted to be alone.

Rick would stay there as long as it took.

CHAPTER 39

At about 2:00 a.m., Fern and Ed met up with Matt's party at the little beach on the north side where the CG officer had landed their dinghy.

They related the story of Moira to Matt, who said, "Mom, huh? Makes more sense now."

Fern said, "Rick killed him, and mom helped…and I put the wrong man in jail."

"But you redeemed yourself by taking out mom," Ed said. "You should have seen her moves, Matt. It was a thing of beauty. I was still thinking about what to do, when—BOOM!—it was over, and the rifle was on the floor. I never saw it coming." He grinned.

"That's my girl," Matt said, enveloping her in a hug. "Now, if we only knew where twin number one is."

"He's here somewhere," Ed said. "Obviously, he heard our ship coming and knew it meant curtains for him. But he can't hide forever."

"This is dumb," Matt said flatly. "It's too dark and we're wasting our time tonight. I vote we leave one crew here in case he's got a boat hidden around this beach. We've searched this area thoroughly and haven't found one, however. The rest of us go back to the house, and take turns getting some shuteye, then at dawn we start the search again."

"There's a reason why you're the chief," said Ed, agreeing with Matt's plan.

"OK," said Fern. "Back to the house for us. I'll make some coffee and stay up first because I'm too wired to sleep anyway."

Ed hooked his thumb at Fern. "Young-un."

Two crewmen stayed with their tender, and the rest tramped back to the house.

• • •

Daylight broke a little after 7:00 a.m. It was still cloudy, and there was still no sign of Rick. Leonard and Lynette were in the kitchen, trying to make breakfast for all. Leonard poured the cops mugs of coffee.

"We're not guests, Leonard," Fern told him. "You don't have to feed us. We'll get some food on our ship."

"Not acceptable," Leonard said, shaking his head. "Mr. Reid would be horrified if he learned we didn't make an effort to be good hosts. Even in spite of this unfortunate situation. Please go to the dining room. Lynette and I will be in soon with some eggs, etcetera."

"That's very kind of you, Leonard," Matt said. He took Fern by the elbow, and their party moved to the dining room. True to his word, Leonard and Lynette arrived within a few minutes loaded with trays of eggs, toast, apple slices, and more coffee. Lynette was pale as a ghost, and she silently went about her business, afraid to look anyone in the eye.

"Would anyone prefer tea?" Leonard asked.

"Stop, Leonard," Matt said firmly. "We appreciate some breakfast fuel, but you are now officially off duty. Get your favorite morning beverage and come sit with us. You, too, Lynette."

The two household employees did as Matt instructed, and quietly pulled up chairs around the table.

"We're looking for Rick," Fern said. "Do either of you have any idea where he might be hiding? Or if there's another way off the island that we're not aware of?"

Leonard shook his head. "I haven't the foggiest. I'm not that close to the twins. My job has revolved around Mr. Reid and, to some extent, Moira, for all these years. Yes, I watched the boys grow up, but I never paid that much attention to them. Children aren't my thing," he smiled wanly.

"What about you, Lynette?" Fern asked. "Any ideas?"

Lynette hesitated, and it was clear to the cops that she was weighing what and how much to say.

"Please tell us, Lynette," Matt said gently. "We won't let anyone hurt you."

She looked gratefully at the handsome police chief. "Rick likes the western side of the island. Near the tip. He goes there a lot in the summer to watch the sunset," she said hesitantly. "He and Randy both like it over there."

"Did you ever go with them?" Matt asked.

She lowered her eyes and blinked rapidly. "A few times," she whispered, without looking up.

"Tell us about that," Matt said.

"They made sort of a sitting area. Cleared out some brush around a big old log. In the summer, they left some folding chairs out there, and they wanted me to go out now and then and drink a beer with them while we watched the sun go down. It was nice," she smiled shyly.

"Could you find that spot now?" Fern asked. "Take us to it?"

"Yeah."

Everyone gulped down their food, and headed out en masse, following Lynette.

• • •

Rick was asleep inside the hollowed-out log when they found him. He went without a fight when he saw the three Oregon cops with their guns drawn, and the four armed CG crewmen backing them up.

He looked at Lynette as Matt handcuffed him, and said, "You're fired."

CHAPTER 40

Friday, March 1, 2024 — Noon

Rohn Reid was brought to the Chinook County sheriff's office, where Earl, Fern, Matt, and Ed awaited him.

"Please sit down, Rohn," Fern said politely. "We need to give you an update."

"What is it? What's wrong?" Rohn looked older and more fragile than he had before his exposure to the jail where his son was imprisoned.

"We have terrible news to tell you," she said. "Although, it's not as terrible as the news Naomi Matsuda received last week. I hope you can keep that perspective."

Rohn continued to stare at Fern, not saying anything.

"Your son, Rick, has been arrested. He killed Hiroshi Matsuda in cold blood because he wanted to protect his brother's illegal operation from being found out. He confessed to us on the journey from your island to Buck Bay. He loves his brother."

Rohn gasped for air, and began to cry, his shoulders shaking. Still, he did not speak.

Fern continued. "Moira has also been arrested."

He jerked his head up. "What?"

"Moira, your longtime lover and the mother of your sons assisted Rick in the murder of Matsuda. According to Rick, she held him down while he smothered Hiroshi with a pillow. The two of them dressed him in the uniform he'd worn to return to Cold Rock Island, hung his body from the rafter, and tried to make it look like suicide."

"The purple pillow," Rohn said, now still and emotionless.

"Yes, Dr. Ryder found fibers from it inside Hiroshi's nose and mouth," Fern explained. "And, further, Moira threatened to kill me this morning, and held several of us at gunpoint. She is facing a multitude of charges, as is Rick. I have dropped the murder charge against Randy; he knew nothing of Matsuda's murder and was not involved. However, we intend to press several felony charges against him, including securities and mail fraud, and money laundering. Once we dig further into his operation, there will likely be more counts."

Rohn looked at her through red, wet eyes. "You've destroyed my entire family."

"No, Randy did that," Fern corrected him. "Or perhaps Moira, for living a lie and coddling them all these years."

"I did that," Rohn said. "I couldn't disgrace my first wife with the truth about the twins. That's why I bought Cold Rock Island. So we could all live in peace. Be ourselves and acknowledge the love the four of us shared."

"I'm sorry for you, Rohn," Fern said. "I truly am. But I'm sorrier for Naomi Matsuda and her children who are forever deprived of their father's love and companionship because of your family's ruthless greed."

* * *

Over the next few weeks, indictments were handed down, grand juries convened, and trial dates set. Rick Reid and Moira Simpson were convicted of murder in a lengthy trial, and sentenced to life in prison, with a possibility of parole in no less than twenty-five years. Rick Reid was also convicted of attempted murder of a federal agent. Fern's two shooters had been apprehended at a tavern in Newport, and sang like birds about their 'boss', Rick Reid.

Scott Thurman and Randy Reid were tried on several counts in the cryptocurrency fraud, but the jury believed Randy's testimony that he was only doing a favor for a friend and knew nothing about the scam. He was exceptionally compelling on the witness stand — emotional and very handsome.

Fern tried valiantly to link the cash found on Cold Rock Island to Randy, and Sylvia provided evidence that he had lied about his father giving the down payment on his luxurious Seattle penthouse; Randy had paid for it in cold, hard cash - $30 million. The spike in power usage on the island was proven to coincide with the beginning of the crypto scam, but Randy acknowledged his role while claiming to be an innocent participant in what he thought was a legitimate business.

Scott Thurman's testimony backing up every statement in Randy's testimony put a nail in the coffin for Fern's case. Thurman took the fall, got fifteen years, and was looking forward to restarting his life then with the $25 million hidden in the garden of his Honolulu home.

In Port Stirling, life was gradually getting back to normal, or, at least, their version of normal. Even Tamryn Gesicki, now healed of her physical injuries, if not her mental ones, got in on the Matsuda case action. Her phone interview with Rick Reid's Seattle girlfriend had produced one of the most damning pieces of testimony against him. Her signed statement had included a sentence quoting Rick a few months ago that 'he would do anything to protect his twin brother, even killing another person if he had to.'

He had to, and he did.

. . .

U.S. Secretary of State, Fred Leufeld, in concert with Naomi Matsuda and her children, planned an elaborate celebration of Hiroshi's life in his home prefecture of Okinawa, Japan. Thousands of people from both Japan and the United States came to honor his life, including the Port Stirling police department, representatives from the U.S. Coast Guard's 13th District, the Oregon State Police, and State Department employees Fern Byrne and Joe Phelps.

A touching moment in the ceremony came when Naomi Matsuda rose from her chair on the stage, walked down the steps to the front row of the audience, and placed a small wreath of orchids and plumeria around Fern's

Kay Jennings

neck. She kissed her on the cheek and whispered in Fern's ear, "Thank you for bringing Hiroshi home to us and for giving us justice."

Fern, unable to speak through her tears, just smiled at Naomi and nodded.

CHAPTER 41

Spring had sprung in western Oregon, and with it came Spring Break on the Oregon coast. Two weeks of dread and overtime for every police force in every town up and down the four-hundred-mile coastline of the state.

The Port Stirling PD had their customary 'back-to-school party' on the Monday night following the last day of Spring Break. There was lots to celebrate this year. No serious incidents during the tourist invasion. No drownings, no unsuspecting kids swept off the jetty by a rogue wave, no drunken car wrecks, no wildfires torched by illegal fires on the beach. The hotels and restaurants did record-breaking business, and happily waved good-bye to their visitors, even the ones who slightly misbehaved.

The cops were looking forward to their overtime paychecks and relishing their first day off in two weeks.

"Well, that was something," Tamryn said with a broad smile, after experiencing her first Spring Break on the Oregon coast. "Is it always like this?"

Jay snorted. "This was nothing. We only made two arrests. How many was it last year, Matt?"

"Twenty at least, don't you think?" Matt answered.

"At least. I personally arrested at least five guys peeing on the side of Sheldon's café."

"Maybe it's because we had a female officer in plain sight," Tamryn said, winking at Jay. The death of Barry Gesicki had been ruled a justifiable homicide in defense of herself, and she was back at work on March 11, just in time for the hordes to descend.

"Yeah, I'm sure that's it," said her partner.

"Or maybe it was because word got out about my badass wife disarming a killer with a rifle," Matt said. "No one wants to mess with Fern."

"Damn straight," said Fern, using one of her husband's favorite phrases, her eyes twinkling. "But now, this badass is tired and I'm hoping the police chief will take me home soon."

Matt got the hint, and he retrieved their coats from his office closet. "Last person here, turn out the lights. Nice work, everyone," he said, waving as they exited.

Back home, Fern disappeared into the bathroom upstairs. Matt, exhausted himself, undressed and climbed into bed. He picked up his book from the nightstand while he waited for Fern to come to bed.

Finally, she came out. She looked at him seriously and said, "I have something to tell you."

"You're pregnant?"

She laughed. "You always say that when I have something I want to tell you."

"Always hopeful, I guess," he said sheepishly.

"Well, this time you're right." She waved the pregnancy test, with its obvious light blue line, in the air in front of him.

Stark naked, Matt whooped and hollered, dancing around their bedroom.

For the latest news on my life and my writing—and, who knows, perhaps a freebie or two—please consider signing up for my occasional newsletter at my author website:

www.kayjenningsauthor.com

ACKNOWLEDGEMENTS

I'm a person who probably knows less than anyone on the planet about cryptocurrency, and so, a big thanks to D-Central, a Canadian crypto mining company, for their explanation of crypto mining hosting.

Thank you to John Plock in the Public Information Office at the Multnomah County Sheriff's Office in Portland, Oregon, for pointing me to some online information that was helpful with an important scene in my story.

Thank you to Claire Brown, who continues to design gorgeous, effective covers, along with tweaking the front matter map on my whims. She's also invaluable on graphics for marketing materials, and I would be sunk without her.

Thank you to Sue Trowbridge, who manages my author website, and got me through the MailerLite transition on my newsletter when I was pulling my hair out.

Thank you to Peter Senftleben, my editor, who remains responsive and flexible, comes up with the greatest book titles, and is terrific fun to work with. His thoughts and ideas always make my book better.

Thank you to Steve Kuhn at Kuhn Design Group in Eugene, Oregon, who is the fastest, most efficient formatter anywhere.

My excellent team of BETA readers continues to get the job done via their diverse takes on my manuscripts. It was pure luck that I assembled a group that comes from several different perspectives, all of which are valuable in creating the final product. I'm constantly amazed at their catches — how did I not see that?!? — and I hope they stick with me.

I'm also grateful for the worldwide society of libraries, bookstores, museums, hotels, online groups, and my fellow authors, all who connect readers with those of us who strive to get our stories out there. You are all rock stars and appreciated by me.

Steve Jennings continues to be my biggest fan. Having someone in your court on a daily basis who not only believes in your work, but loves being married to a writer, is pure gold. I know that not every author has this kind of support from family, and I'm eternally grateful. Thank you, Steve.